Hell *in a* Handbasket

Books by Denise Grover Swank

Rose Gardner Investigations

Family Jewels
For the Birds
Hell in a Handbasket
Up Shute Creek (November 6, 2018)

Neely Kate Mystery

Trailer Trash
In High Cotton (July 31, 2018)

Rose Gardner Mysteries

Twenty-Eight and a Half Wishes
Twenty-Nine and a Half Reasons
Thirty and a Half Excuses
Thirty-One and a Half Regrets
Thirty-Two and a Half Complications
Thirty-Three and a Half Shenanigans
Rose and Helena Save Christmas (novella)
Thirty-Four and a Half Predicaments
Thirty-Five and a Half Conspiracies
Thirty-Six and a Half Motives

Magnolia Steele Mystery

Center Stage
Act Two
Call Back
Curtain Call

The Wedding Pact Series

The Substitute
The Player
The Gambler
The Valentine (short story)

Discover Denise's other books at
denisegroverswank.com

Hell *in a* Handbasket

Rose Gardner Investigations #3

Denise Grover Swank

This book is a work of fiction. References to real people, events, establishments, organizations, or locations are intended only to provide a sense of authenticity, and are used fictitiously. All other characters, and all incidents and dialogue, are drawn from the author's imagination and are not to be construed as real.

Cover art and design: Bookfly Cover Design
Developmental Editor: Angela Polidoro
Copy Editor: Shannon Page
Proofreader: Carolina Valdez-Schneider

Chapter One

It was funny how dying put things in a whole new perspective.

Which was why I found myself at the Henryetta First Baptist Church on a hot Sunday afternoon in late July, going to a church picnic with my older sister, Violet, and her family.

The Henryetta First Baptist Church was practically the last place on earth I wanted to be.

I'll admit that I'd tried my darnedest to get my best friend, Neely Kate, to come for moral support. Turned out there wasn't enough money in the world to convince her to come.

"No. Way," she'd said, shaking her head to make sure her answer was clear. "I suspect if I went anywhere near that church, the women's group would try me for being a witch. They know Granny claims to see the future."

"They'd convict me before they'd get to you." Neely Kate's granny couldn't see the future if it stood two feet in front of her. I, on the other hand, had spent most of my life seeing flashes of other people's futures and blurting out what I'd seen (an unavoidable, and mortifying, side effect). Plenty of those visions had been *in* the Baptist church. Fortunately—or not—

most people had presumed I was simply a weird child. It helped that I was usually spouting unimportant nonsense about Laura Gurney's French toast burning or Tim Hinkle getting a ticket for running a red light.

When Momma died a little over a year ago, I'd stopped attending the First Baptist Church, and no one had been sorry to see me go. I'd told my sister that I never wanted to step inside the church again, something I'd reminded her of when she'd begged me to come to this picnic.

But Violet was dying, and I'd do nearly anything to make her happy—even go to a place that reminded me of my visions at a time when I would rather not think about them.

I'd nearly died in the middle of a vision a week and a half ago, and I hadn't experienced a single one since. Surprisingly, no one had noticed. Over the past year, I'd learned that if I forced visions, I had much fewer spontaneous ones. But after a few days of no spontaneous ones, I was enjoying being normal, so I hadn't forced any either. Maybe if I didn't try it, they'd be gone for good. Sure, over the last year I'd learned to see the visions as a gift rather than as the curse I'd always believed them to be, but now I wondered if the cost was too high.

"See?" Violet said, beaming from ear to ear as we got out of the car. "The picnic's outside. You don't have to go anywhere near the church doors."

I resisted the urge to make a face at her, mostly because my niece and nephew were watching.

"What if Aunt Rose has to go to the bathroom?" my niece Ashley asked with a worried look. "What's she gonna do then?"

"She'll just have to hold it," Violet said with an ornery grin.

"Don't you worry," I said to Ashley. "I've got a bladder made of steel."

Her eyes narrowed. "Somebody steals your pee?"

Violet started to laugh, but her husband Mike remained silent as he unbuckled my nearly two-year-old nephew, Mikey, out of his car seat.

Mike had been acting odd the last few months. He and Violet had married young, and he and I had always been close. Living with my mother up until her death hadn't been easy, and Violet and Mike's house had always been my refuge. Mike could have resented my intrusion into their family, but he'd always welcomed me, often taking my side when Violet pulled out her bossy tendencies. He and I had even kept in touch after the two of them split, briefly, last fall. So nothing could have prepared me for how distant he'd become after Violet's cancer diagnosis in February. She'd departed nearly immediately for MD Anderson in Houston, Texas.

Mike read the papers, which meant he knew I had something to do with the fall from grace of one J.R. Simmons.

J.R. Simmons had been the most powerful man in southern Arkansas—a successful, influential businessman who'd used his success to interfere with people's lives in evil and ugly ways that included corruption, extortion, and murder. I'd ended up on his radar as the undesirable girlfriend of his son, Joe Simmons. He'd resorted to bribery to force Joe and me apart, but it hadn't ended there. The more I'd learned about J.R., the less I'd believed he should be allowed to continue ruining people for his own benefit. The notorious James "Skeeter" Malcolm, king of the Fenton County underworld, and I had teamed up to bring him down, something that had become public knowledge. Tongues were still wagging about it.

Mike had tarred and feathered me in his mind, and he'd recently admitted his change in attitude was due to his concerns about the company I kept. Little did he know how involved I'd become in the criminal world. If he ever found out I'd slept with James Malcolm, I suspected I'd never see my sister or her children again.

While I understood Mike's concerns, part of the reason I'd gone after J.R. was to save him. In the early days of his construction business, he'd bribed an inspector and J.R. had threatened to disclose it. Which made me wonder … if Mike had offered bribes in the past, was he still doing it today?

I shoved thoughts of Mike away, only to find myself thinking of James. James, who'd given me two weeks to weigh his suggestion that we start a relationship. Time was running out, and I was no closer to an answer than I'd been ten days ago.

Don't think about that now. You're with Violet.

I needed to focus on spending as much time with my sister as possible—and on making her as happy as possible.

"Aunt Rose," Ashley said, slipping her hand in mine. "Will you do the three-legged race with me?"

"Hey," Mike said as he stood with Mikey in his arms. "I thought we were doing the three-legged race."

"But I get to see you all the time," she whined, squeezing my hand tighter. "And I hardly *ever* see Aunt Rose."

Violet stared down at her daughter with a confused look, then glanced back up to me and Mike. "What's she talking about?"

This wasn't the time or place to let Violet know Mike had kept me from the kids while she was in Texas.

"Nothing," I said, hoping my smile didn't look forced. "We better get going if we want a good spot. It looks like the hill is pretty full."

"That's because everyone else went to the church service," Violet said. "We're getting all the leftover spots."

"There's no need to push it, Vi," Mike said. "You're just now feeling better after your bout with pneumonia. Going to the service would have been too much."

That was something Mike and I actually agreed on.

Mike had popped the trunk open, so I grabbed a quilt and the picnic basket I'd spent the morning preparing. Ashley led the way to a fairly flat spot on the hill that gave us a good view of the grounds where they held the races—not that I knew from firsthand experience. Momma may have been an active member of the First Baptist Church, but the Gardners had never attended the church picnics, which Momma had called "a frivolous waste of time." This year would mark my first—and hopefully last—attendance.

"This looks like a good place," I said. "Your momma can watch us win the three-legged race." I knew I should back down and let Mike run the race with his daughter, but I also wanted to stand my ground and let him know I wasn't going anywhere. Not anymore.

Ashley jumped up and down with excitement. "Yeah!"

She helped me spread out the quilt, and by the time I set the basket on the corner, Violet, Mike, and the baby had reached us. Mike set his son on the ground and helped Violet sit next to me.

"Something sure smells good," she said, peering over at the basket.

"Did you bring fried chicken, Aunt Rose?" Ashley asked, trying to peek inside.

"I sure did. It's one of your mommy's favorites." I glanced up at Mike and offered him a conciliatory smile. "And your daddy's too."

His gaze held mine for barely a second before he looked away, but I saw a flash of guilt.

Why did he feel guilty? Because of the way he'd treated me, or was this something more?

I realized I was still staring at him, so I looked back into the basket and pulled out a plastic storage container. "And here's some potato salad."

"What about cookies, Aunt Rose?" Ashley asked.

I chuckled. "No cookies, but there's a lemon pound cake. Another one of your mommy's favorites."

"How come you made so many of Mommy's favorites?"

A lump formed in my throat, but I pushed out the words. "Because I'm so happy your mommy's back home."

The joy in Ashley's eyes faded, but she didn't say anything. Did she know? Violet had told me that she and Mike had decided to keep it from the kids, but my niece was a smart girl.

"You shouldn't have gone to so much trouble, Rose," Violet said. "You must have been in the kitchen for hours."

"It was no trouble," I said, pulling out the container of chicken. "Besides, I made the cake last night." I could have added that Neely Kate had gone on a date and it had given me something to do, but then she'd ask who Neely Kate was dating, and I didn't want to get into it. Somehow I thought Mike was as unlikely to approve of Jed, James' best friend and longtime enforcer, as he was to invite James himself into the family with open arms.

I filled plastic plates full of chicken, potato salad, baked beans, and still-warm homemade biscuits and passed them out to everyone. Violet focused on helping Mikey get situated instead of eating her own food. I almost insisted on taking over so she could eat—she was skin and bones—but the joy on her face stopped me. I knew that she'd hated missing so much of his life while she was in Texas. She wasn't about to waste any time now.

I couldn't keep the tears from my eyes. I could barely handle the thought of losing my sister, but when I thought about Ashley and Mikey losing their mother, a deep well of sadness opened in my chest.

I didn't want to cry in front of the kids or Violet, so I put my plate on the blanket next to me. "I've got to go to the bathroom."

"Is somebody trying to steal your pee, Aunt Rose?" Ashley asked with wide eyes.

"She's just tryin' to make sure they don't," Violet teased, then gave me a knowing look. "You go ahead. We'll be here waitin' for you."

But for how long? A fresh batch of tears flooded my eyes, and I hurried off before I broke down in front of the kids. I didn't really want to go inside, so I headed toward what looked like a collection of potluck tables, only one was covered with pies and the other with plates of fried chicken. How could I have forgotten the annual pie and fried chicken contest? I may have never attended a picnic before, but the congregants loved to talk about them, so I knew a thing or two about how they were run. I had always wondered if Momma's aversion to the church picnic was due to the fact that she couldn't win the pie contest. Not with Anita Raeburn entering every year.

The chicken contest had a perennial winner too—Patsy Sue Clydehopper—and she was currently standing in front of the chicken display with a woman who looked an awful lot like her. Though both contests were supposed to be blind taste tests, Barbara, the church secretary, always made sure the pastors knew which plate of chicken was Patsy Sue's. She was used to winning, and if she ever lost, she'd likely up and move her membership to the First Baptist Church in Pickle Junction.

The church bank account needed the support of one of its richest and most influential members—hence the cheating.

Only it looked like something had gone wrong this year. Both pastors stood behind the chicken table, staring dumbfounded at Patsy and her bleached-blond look-alike. Barbara, who stood tugging at Reverend Baker's arm, looked like she was either going to cry or start throwing the plates of chicken.

"That's my recipe, Carol Ann, and you doggone know it."

Now I knew who she was. Carol Ann Nelson was Patsy's cousin, although rumor had it that she'd run off to LA to get famous acting. Looked like she was back.

Carol Ann put a hand on her trim hip. "You sure as Pete don't own it, Patsy Sue. It's Grandma Nelson's recipe, and she gave it to *both* of us."

"She may have given it to both of us, but we all know I'm the cook in this family. You can barely make it through the drive-thru of McDonald's up in Magnolia, let alone figure out how to navigate a kitchen."

"If that's true," Carol Ann said as she curled up her bright red top lip, "then how come I just won the grand prize?"

"Uh …" the reverend said, holding up his hands, "there's no grand prize."

Carol Ann turned her attention to him. "Well, did I win or didn't I?"

"Well … you did …" But he didn't seem so certain as he shot an apologetic look at Patsy Sue.

Carol Ann's chin lifted in a gloat. "That's grand prize enough."

"If that's prize enough, why were you darkenin' my doorstep last Thursday askin' me for thousands of dollars?" Patsy asked.

"I needed the money to buy the ingredients to make the fried chicken that beat yours!"

"You're just mad that I refused to give you one more dime," Patsy said. "So instead, you decide to get even and use *my* recipe in *my* church to try to look better than me!"

"I don't have to prove that I look better than you!" Carol Ann shouted back. "All anyone has to do is take one look at your dumpy self then take one look at me to know I look ten times better."

While I was no fan of Patsy Sue Clydehopper, her cousin had just told a bald-faced lie. Patsy may have been in her mid-forties, but she used her resources well in her quest to look thirty-one, the age she'd been claiming for the past decade. Rumor had it she'd started saying she was thirty-two. She had too many crow's-feet to get away with her preferred age anymore. While she wasn't as thin as her cousin, Patsy also looked ten times classier. But then, I guess she had to be since her face was posted all over town on her Clydehopper Realty real estate signs.

"Why, I never!" Patsy said in outrage and slapped Carol across the face.

I wasn't the only onlooker. At the first sign of the trouble, a crowd had gathered, and milliseconds after Patsy's hand connected with Carol Ann's cheek, the crowd collectively released a loud gasp.

Carol Ann pointed a red-painted fingernail at the other woman. "You're gonna pay for that!"

"I've already paid, Carol Ann. I've paid and paid and paid, and I'm not payin' any more. And neither is Aunty Lucille. You've bled her dry. Everyone knows you're here to weasel more money out of all of us. Why do you think nobody's excited that you're home? Go back where you came from, Carol Ann. There's *nothin'* for you here."

"Ladies," Reverend Baker said, finally coming out of his stupor and walking around the edge of the table. "Let's all take a breath, and maybe take this inside."

"No," Patsy said with a firm shake of her head. "I'm not going anywhere with this fool. Now, if you'll hand me my blue ribbon, I'll head back to my blanket."

Reverend Baker looked sheepish. "I can't do that, Patsy. Carol Ann won."

"She cheated! She stole my recipe! She broke one of the Ten Commandments to win."

"And you broke a commandment in your temper tantrum when you lost," Carol Ann said with a satisfied grin, despite the red handprint on her cheek.

"You stole my recipe!" Patsy shot back.

"Like I said, it's *Grandma Nelson's* recipe." She gave her cousin a smirk. "I can't help it if I make it better than you do."

"Why you—" Patsy lunged for her cousin, clipping Reverend Baker's arm. It threw both of them off balance, giving Carol Ann an opportunity to shove him to get to Patsy.

The pastor fell into the pie table, his face landing in the middle of a chocolate meringue while one of his hands slapped into a cherry pie.

The crowd gasped again, but there was no time to react—the two cousins had broken into an all-out skirmish. Patsy tugged a handful of Carol Ann's hair, while Carol Ann pulled Patsy's shirt up halfway over her head and exposed her hot pink bra.

Screams broke out, and Barbara tried to help the pastor up, but Patsy—unable to see where she was going—slammed into him. He fell again, this time face-first into a strawberry rhubarb pie.

Patsy flopped up faster than I would have expected for a woman of her age, then slammed her cousin into the fried chicken table, sending drumsticks, thighs, and breasts flying in all directions.

"It's raining fried chicken," Ashley said in amazement next to me.

I sucked in a breath as I turned to look down at her. When had she gotten here? "Ashley, go back to your momma."

"And miss this? No way!" She squinted at the two women who were rolling from the chicken table into the pies. "Why'd Miss Patsy take off her shirt?"

Sure enough, Patsy's shirt was gone and her top half was slicked up from the oily chicken like she was ready for a wrestling contest.

I covered Ashley's eyes with my hand, but she pushed it away. "I'm not a baby, Aunt Rose. I'm gonna be a first grader."

I didn't have time to respond because the cousins had rolled on top of Reverend Baker. The table gave a loud groan before the legs on the left side gave out, sending all three bodies to the ground. They landed on top of one another in a heap, but even that did little to stop the fight. While Patsy Sue and Carol Ann carried on shrieking and hollering, everyone stood around watching them like this was the most exciting thing they'd seen since Officer Ernie chased a flock of wild turkeys around the town square. While I had to admit that it probably was, poor Reverend Baker was taking the brunt of the fight. He'd never been kind to me, but someone needed to help him.

I was just about to intervene when Officer Ernie himself ran up and puffed out his skinny chest, trying his best to look authoritative. "Stop in the name of the law!"

There was no chance of the crowd intervening now. They took a step back in eager anticipation.

The women ignored his command, so he shouted again, "Don't make me arrest the lot of you!"

Patsy grabbed a pie tin, attempting to shove it in her cousin's face, but Carol Ann bobbed out of the way just as Reverend Baker sat up, getting another face full of pie.

Ernie's confidence wavered, and he slowly reached for the mic on his shoulder, turning to the side a bit as he muttered, "I've got a situation and I'm gonna need backup."

"What's the problem?" a woman's voice called back.

"I've got two women havin' a food fight outside of the First Baptist Church."

The woman started laughing. "Officer Sprout's out on another call. You're gonna have to handle that one yourself."

Exasperated, Ernie turned to the crowd. "Can someone help me out here?"

Everyone watched him with interest, no one volunteering, not that I could blame them. The cousins and the pastor were covered in various pies and pieces of fried chicken. Ernie leaned over to pull Carol Ann away from her cousin, but he got pulled down into the mess.

Calvin Clydehopper, Patsy's husband, slunk to the front, wearing pressed trousers paired with a short-sleeved button-down shirt and tie. Calvin and Patsy were normally considered elite members of Henryetta society, and the look on Calvin's face suggested he wasn't pleased his wife had ruined their carefully constructed façade.

He reached toward the women, then withdrew his hands and said, "Patsy Sue! Stop this right now! You're making a fool of yourself."

Patsy Sue took a moment to glance up at her husband, a piece of chocolate mousse dripping from her hair onto her cheek. "*I'm* making a fool of myself?" she shrieked. "This is all your fault!" She grabbed a half-full pie tin, wound back her arm like a star pitcher, then threw it up at him.

The tin landed on his head and peaches dripped down his nose. His face reddened and he looked like he was about to enter the melee when Joe's voice boomed out from the other side of the crowd. "Everybody freeze!"

Carol Ann paused with her knees digging into Reverend Baker's back and her hand on Patsy's waistband. Officer Ernie's leg was trapped underneath Patsy's lower body, and a smear of blueberries concealed one side of his face. The poor minister moaned underneath all of them.

"Uncle Joe!" Ashley shouted and took off running to greet him.

Joe's face lifted in surprise, and when he caught a glimpse of me, his eyebrows rose into a smirk. He didn't need to express himself in words. I could see what he wanted to say written across his face: "Why am I not surprised to see you with this mess?"

At least I could plead total innocence this time.

Chapter Two

It took Joe thirty minutes to get everything sorted out, including reassuring Officer Ernie, who was livid that his case had been "stolen from him" even though he'd been desperate for backup. Of course, Joe was the only one not covered in food.

Reverend Baker was hauled off in an ambulance because his bad back had been thrown out of whack, and the two cousins said they weren't sure whether they wanted to press charges against each other.

Ernie made noises about arresting them for disturbing the peace, but then he cast a glance at Calvin and quickly backtracked. Calvin Clydehopper was on the city council and could have Officer Ernie fired, an idea that didn't upset me at all, but Ernie decided not to risk it.

When the whole police mess was cleared up, Joe and Officer Ernie left the clucking church women to clean up the mess. Joe walked over to me and Ashley. I hadn't managed to convince her to return to the blanket, but Mike had come down to join us midway through the hubbub.

Joe nodded to my brother-in-law. "Mike."

"Didn't expect to see you here," he said in a cold tone.

My gaze flicked up in surprise. While I knew Mike was upset with me, this was the first indication that he was also pissed at Joe.

"Violet invited me, although I was obviously running late."

"Violet invited you?" Mike and I asked at the same time.

I didn't mind sitting with Joe. We'd long since gotten over our breakup, and last I'd heard, he was dating Dena Breene, who owned the cupcake shop in the town square. The question was why didn't Violet tell me or Mike? Was she up to her matchmaking mischievousness again? Heaven knew she'd tried it before, and she knew my dating situation wasn't exactly stable. I'd recently told her about my short-lived involvement with Levi Romano—I'd gone on a few dates with Henryetta's attractive new veterinarian, but I didn't have feelings for him. (I'd broken it off with him the night Violet admitted she was dying, and typical Levi, he'd been nothing but understanding.) She'd proceeded to guess that there was someone else, someone I cared about despite myself, and I'd admitted it was true, though of course I hadn't mentioned James by name. It would be just like her to try to distract me with another man. A man she thought would make sure I was all right after she was gone.

Joe gave me a stunned look.

"Wait!" I said, "I'm happy you're here. I just know how much you eat," I teased. "I hope I brought enough food."

"Oh, that's okay," he said. "Dena and I brought our own food."

"Dena?" And then I felt like an idiot. Why *wouldn't* he bring Dena? They'd been dating for several weeks, and according to Neely Kate, they were seeing each other three or four nights a week. "That's great!" I glanced around the thinning crowd. "I didn't see her."

He laughed. "She went up to sit with Vi. She said something similar happened last week with her half-priced cupcake day and left me to it." He thumbed toward the hill. "I'm starving. Let's go eat. Dena made some sandwiches I'm dying to try." Then he swung Ashley onto his shoulders and forced Mike into a conversation about the Little Rock Travelers baseball team.

I watched them walk toward Violet and Dena, and my heart filled with gratitude that we'd been given one more day with my sister. And hopefully one more day after that.

SINCE THE PICNIC had ended up in a disaster, there was only enough time left for half the games. Joe ended up doing the three-legged race with Ashley and winning.

It was a good thing that the picnic was cut short because Violet tired out soon after we ate.

"I hate that everyone is leavin' on account of me," Vi said with tears in her eyes. "I wanted to spend more time with Rose."

"We only have a couple of clients tomorrow," I said with a gentle smile. "How about I bring you lunch and hang out with you and the kids for a while? Isn't Mike goin' back to work tomorrow?"

"Only half days," he said defensively, as though I were challenging his place in Violet's world. "I'll be home by lunchtime."

Violet glanced up at him with a patient look I wasn't used to seeing on her face. "Mike, you've been gone from the job sites for weeks. Let Rose come spend some time with me and the kids. We'll all be fine."

He shot me a look that suggested he had his doubts but remained silent.

I packed up the food while Mike corralled the kids. Joe and Dena offered to take me home to save Violet and her family the trip, but I told him he only needed to drop me off at the landscaping office. Mike had picked me up there, so my truck was still parked nearby.

"That works out perfectly," Dena said, "since Joe offered to help me pull out some exhaust vents that are stuck in the hood in my kitchen."

"That sounds like a fun afternoon," I said with a grin. "Not as fun as breaking up an epic food fight, but still ..."

Joe laughed. "Could you believe those two? They were acting like two teenage girls fighting over a guy."

Dena's eyes lit up. "Well ..."

I shot her a look of surprise. "Wait. They *were*?"

"Let's just say rumor has it money wasn't the only thing Carol Ann was looking for when she showed up on Patsy Sue's front porch."

"Calvin?" Joe asked. Then he shook his head. "No way. He's as straightlaced as they come."

"My aunt went to school with the both of them and says they've always fought over him, even all those years ago."

"Still," I said, not wanting to give credence to a rumor. Plenty of false ones had floated around about me. "That was a good twenty to twenty-five years ago. Surely they've gotten over it by now."

"Aunt Theresa and her friend Valerie were in the cupcake shop last week talkin' about it."

Joe pulled up in front of my office a few minutes later, and I decided to make a quick escape. "Thanks for the ride, Joe."

I got out, hauling the picnic basket with me as he rolled down his window. "If you see Neely Kate, tell her I'm looking forward to our painting party tomorrow night."

Dena leaned forward, a frown wrinkling her forehead. "I thought we were going to Magnolia to see a movie with Henry and Tiffany tomorrow."

Joe cringed. "Neely Kate and I made plans a while back. I completely forgot."

"But Monday's the only time they can go. Can't you get together with Neely Kate another night?" She laughed. "I mean, come on. Who likes to paint?"

I was downright pissed. I squatted next to Joe's door and held her gaze. "Joe does. And so does Neely Kate." Before I could say something I'd regret even more, I stood and walked over to my truck and got inside.

I couldn't bear to look at Joe as he drove away. I knew how I'd come across—the spiteful, jealous ex-girlfriend. But that wasn't it at all … was it?

No. She had been gossiping about Patsy Sue Clydehopper. And then she'd made fun of Joe and Neely Kate's bonding time. Still, once my anger had a few seconds to die down, I could acknowledge I'd probably overreacted. Most people actually *didn't* like to paint, and she probably thought Neely Kate was doing Joe a favor, not spending quality time with him.

Which just proved how little she knew about both of them.

Neely Kate and Joe were so new to this brother and sister thing, but it was painfully clear how much they needed each other. I hated to see anything get in the way of their budding relationship. Shoot, even Jed respected those boundaries.

Halfway home, I started to feel a heaviness descend on my shoulders. I didn't feel like being alone, but I knew Jed had taken Neely Kate to Little Rock, which meant she'd probably be gone the entire day. It made sense that they'd go somewhere else to be together. Little Rock was only two hours away, and no one knew them there. That meant no one could go after Neely Kate to get to Jed, who was trying to leave the criminal world after years of working with James. Still, I couldn't help but wonder if it had something to do with Joe and Neely Kate's sister, Kate, who was currently residing in a psychiatric hospital in that city.

Muffy was happy to see me when I walked in the house. After I put the food away, I tried to read a book, but I found myself reading the same paragraph five times.

Lately, I hated being alone. When I had too much time to think, my mind always drifted to the two people who'd changed my relationship with my visions—Jeanne Putnam, Scooter Malcolm's now-deceased girlfriend, who was dead due to my negligence, and Merv Chapman, James Malcolm's traitorous friend. Jeanne had been the sole witness in Scooter's kidnapping but had kept what she'd seen to herself out of fear for her life. Neely Kate and I had convinced her to talk to us anyway, more than once, despite knowing the danger she was in. I'd believed my visions could save her—only they hadn't. She'd been killed on account of us. Merv had died while I was forcing a vision of him, and the experience had very near killed me.

It hurt to think of either of them, but they had free rein in my dreams.

I'd had plenty of nightmares about Merv crushing me to the warehouse floor, his blood drenching my clothes, making me feel like I was drowning in it, while he growled, "I'm takin' you with me."

But the dreams about Jeanne haunted me the most.

I'd find myself standing over her dead body in the woods at the edge of Highway 82. She'd look up at me with vacant eyes, a bullet hole in her forehead, and say, "I trusted you, Rose Gardner, and you got me killed."

She wasn't wrong.

"Muffy, let's go for a walk."

I changed out of my shorts and into a pair of jeans; then we headed out the back door. We spent the next couple hours wandering the north end of my property—purposely staying away from the southern edge that bordered the land where Joe lived. Muffy had fun running loose, but by the end of it, she was dirty and I was a sweaty mess. I couldn't avoid the empty house forever. I went back inside reluctantly, and after giving us both a shower, headed downstairs to look for something to eat.

I started to get out the leftover meatloaf and mashed potatoes from a couple of nights ago, but tears welled in my eyes again.

Violet was dying and soon I was going to be alone.

A wave of loneliness washed through me, and I ached with the need to call James. I'd been fighting the urge all afternoon … who was I kidding? I'd missed him for the past week. James had told me to call if I needed him, but I didn't have an answer for him yet, and I had a feeling seeing him would only confuse things.

There was more to consider than just my feelings for him. He was a known criminal, and while he had a moral code most criminals didn't possess, there was no denying he operated on the wrong side of the law. I would ruin my reputation as a business owner if I openly dated him, and I had multiple employees scattered over two businesses to think about. Not to mention it would be dangerous. People would be able to use me to get to him … heck, they already had. And then, of course, there was the issue with Mike.

In my heart, I knew what my answer should be, so why couldn't I just say no?

James had already told me he wasn't a white-picket-fence kind of guy. Marriage and babies would never be in the cards for him, and while I didn't want either of those things yet, I did want them eventually, which meant whatever relationship we established would be short term. Could I live with that?

Could I live without it?

Neely Kate's worried voice interrupted my thoughts. "Rose?"

I turned to face her, realizing I was standing at the kitchen counter with an empty plate, staring out the windows with tears streaming down my face. I wiped my cheeks with the back of my hand. "Hey," I said in a cheery tone. "How was your day? Did Jed come in with you?"

She studied me with a frown. "No. He had something he needed to do. What's wrong? How did the picnic go?"

My eyebrows shot up in mock excitement. "Well, you really should have gone. You could have seen Patsy Sue Clydehopper and her cousin Carol Ann take out Reverend Baker."

"*What?*"

I fixed us each a plate of the meatloaf leftovers while I told her about the cousins' showdown over the chicken and how Joe had finally put a stop to it.

"Joe was there?" she asked in surprise. "He didn't mention he was going, but I haven't talked to him since Friday."

I carried both plates to the table. "He brought Dena."

"Oh." She grabbed some silverware for us and sat down.

Something about the way she said it reminded me of the awkward moment before I parted from Joe and Dena that afternoon.

"What do you think about Dena?" I asked carefully as I took the seat across from her.

She watched me for a moment. "She's nice. And she makes great cupcakes."

"But what do you think about her with Joe?"

She scooped a forkful of mashed potatoes. "He seems happier."

"But what about *her*?"

Her mouth twisted to the side. "I'm trying not to meddle."

"Because you don't like her?" I asked, trying to contain my excitement, then feeling guilty.

She purposely avoided eye contact. "I didn't say that."

"But you didn't say you did, either."

She glanced up, frustration in her eyes. "She's just so …"

"Pushy."

Her eyes flew wide. "Yes! She's pushy! And bossy! And she's trying to control him already! They've only been sleepin' together for two weeks!"

"You mean seein' each other."

She made a face. Sex had been a touchy issue with Neely Kate over the last few weeks.

"Have you and Jed …?"

"No," she said in a curt tone that let me know the subject of her and Jed sleeping together or, in their case, not sleeping together was still off the table. Then she added, "And this isn't about me and Jed. He doesn't try to control my life, just like I can't control his."

Jed had quit working for James, but that was before Merv, who'd been next in line, had kidnapped me and James' brother in an attempted coup. James had been left with no one. I'd heard that Jed was still helping him, but he'd sworn to Neely Kate that he still intended to get out.

"Has Jed decided what he's going to do yet?"

"He says he has several irons in the fire, but he won't tell me what they are." Her scowl confirmed that she was hurt by it.

"Maybe he doesn't want to get your hopes up."

She shrugged, pretending not to care. "We've only been seeing each other a few weeks. It's too early for me to be so involved in his life." Her gaze jerked up and she jabbed her fork in my direction. "Which is exactly why Dena has no right bein' all up in Joe's business. Who does she think she is, changing his plans like they've been married for twenty years?"

I let out a breath. "Joe called you about canceling tomorrow night."

"*What?*" She got up and walked into the other room and came back about thirty seconds later, holding out her phone so I could see the screen.

Sure enough, there was a text that said, HEY, NK. I NEED TO RESCHEDULE TOMORROW NIGHT. It was time stamped about ten minutes earlier.

Neely Kate practically slammed her phone on the table. "When and how did *you* find out?"

I cringed, sorry to have brought up what was so obviously a sore subject. How many times had Joe changed his plans with Neely Kate on Dena's account? "The two of them drove me back to my truck on the square. When I was gettin' out, Joe said to tell you he was lookin' forward to your paintin' party, but then Dena told him he'd already agreed to go to the movies in

Magnolia with their friends. Tomorrow night was the only night they could go. I was hoping he'd tell her no."

Fire danced in her eyes, but thankfully she'd set down the fork. "That chickenshit didn't even have the guts to call this time. He texted. And hours after he'd told you!"

I offered her a sympathetic glance. "I'm sorry, Neely Kate. He really does care about you. He seemed excited about painting."

"Not excited enough to tell her no. *Again.*"

"If it's any consolation, I stood up for you."

Her face froze. "What's that mean?"

Oh crap. I'd stirred up a hornet's nest. "Nothin' … it's just that when Dena realized Joe was double-booked, she argued she was doin' you a favor, sayin' no one liked to paint. I told her that you and Joe did and it was your bonding time."

Her jaw hardened. "And he still canceled on me?"

I stared at her, speechless. I'd made things worse.

She picked up her phone. "I'm gonna call him and give him a piece of my mind!"

I reached for her hand, trying to stop her before she did something she would regret, but my own cell phone started to ring. I would have let it go, but I was worried it might be Violet. So I snatched up both phones and ran out into the living room.

Neely Kate ran after me. "Give that back!"

I waved her off, terrified when I didn't recognize the number on my screen. "Hello?"

"Is this Rose Gardner?" a woman asked.

Was it someone from the hospital calling to tell me Violet had relapsed? That she'd be taken from us even sooner than we thought? Heart in my throat, I nodded, only to realize the woman on the other end of the line couldn't see me. "Yes."

Seeing the fear on my face, Neely Kate froze. She understood. She'd been with me when I'd gotten the call over a week ago telling me that Violet had collapsed.

"I need to hire you and your friend," the woman said. Her voice sounded familiar, but I couldn't quite place it.

The rush of relief made me light-headed. My knees gave out and I sat on the sofa, nodding to Neely Kate with a soft smile, letting her know that everything was okay. "Neely Kate and I would love to help you with your landscaping needs. What do you have in mind?"

Neely Kate pushed out a loud sigh and sat next to me.

"Not your landscaping business," the woman said. "I need you to clear me of murder."

I sat up straighter. "Murder?"

"Are you deaf? Murder. My cousin Carol Ann's been *murdered*."

Suddenly, I realized how I knew the voice. I was talking to Patsy Sue Clydehopper. "Carol Ann's been murdered?"

"Oh my God, girl. Are you deaf? Maybe I should hire someone else."

Patsy was talking loud enough for Neely Kate to hear our conversation. She snagged the phone from my hand and put it on speaker. "This is Neely Kate, and we'll be happy to help you."

"Then I need you to meet me at the Broken Branch Motel. Room twenty-five. Like five minutes ago." Then the call cut off.

Neely Kate's face beamed. "Looks like we got our first official murder investigation."

Chapter Three

"We need to call Kermit," I said. We'd made it out of the house in record time and were already driving my truck to Henryetta.

Neely Kate waved her hand in dismissal. "We'll call him after we know more about what's goin' on."

I frowned, but in the end, I decided she was right. Kermit Cooper was a private investigator who lived and worked out of a ramshackle trailer on the west end of town. Neely Kate was bound and determined for us to become real private investigators, but the only way to become legit was to shadow a licensed PI for two years or get a criminology degree. So a few weeks ago, Jed had set us up with Kermit the Hermit to get our training … only training wasn't an accurate term. More like we did all of his work and he got paid. We'd already worked two cases for him—a lost parrot and, just last week, a cheating husband. He was essentially useless, but we'd have to bring him in at some point. The only way we could legally investigate an active police case was if we were licensed PIs—or interning for one. Still, I couldn't imagine someone as lazy as Kermit being upset that we'd skipped a step.

"What do you think Patsy's doin' at the Broken Branch Motel?" I asked. "That place is so seedy it could grow a garden."

"Hidin' out?"

I shot her a worried look. "So the police are lookin' for her? She's a fugitive?"

"We really should get a police scanner," Neely Kate said. "Then we'd know for certain. I think I can find out another way." She held out her hand. "But I'm gonna need my phone."

I'd kept her phone in my pocket, but before I reached for it, I said, "No callin' Joe."

Her upper lip curled. "I'm sure as Pete not tellin' him what we're doin'."

"I'm talkin' about Dena. You need to cool off first."

Her brow furrowed. "That's a discussion for another time. We're on a case."

I gave her the phone, and she made a few calls—one to an ER nurse she knew, one to her cousin who knew a sheriff dispatcher, and a last-ditch call to her friend who worked at the courthouse, none of whom knew anything about a murder. I could have sworn she sent a few texts too, but the not-so-innocent looks she shot me meant they were probably unrelated to the case. Something told me Joe was about to get an eyeful.

"Maybe Carol Ann wasn't murdered in Henryetta," I said. "I know she wasn't stayin' with Patsy. Maybe she was stayin' up in Magnolia or over in El Dorado."

"Maybe, but something stinks about this whole mess."

"I agree, and I guess we're about to find out," I said as the motel came into view.

I pulled into the Broken Branch Motel's pea gravel parking lot. Most of the gravel was gone, leaving hard-packed ground. There were only a few cars parked in the lot, one of them a shiny bright red Lincoln with the words "Baby Spice" in the back window.

"That's Patsy's car," Neely Kate said. "She just got it about six months ago and couldn't stop braggin' about how Calvin had bought it for her as an appreciation gift."

"I'm scared to ask why it says Baby Spice."

"That's a story you're probably better off not knowing, but I *will* tell you that it involves some kinky stuff Patsy tried to spice up her sex life with Calvin."

I gawked at her. "*What?*"

Her mouth twisted to the side. "Like I said, you're better off not knowing, but after that, Calvin started calling her Baby Spice."

I frowned. "Dena said she'd heard through the grapevine that Calvin was sleepin' with Carol Ann. That's why the two cousins really got into a fight. Not over the fried chicken recipe."

Neely Kate looked livid at the mention of Dena's name. "Well, *Dena's* slow on the uptake, because Patsy got her shiny new car after she caught her husband cheating with his secretary."

"So Calvin's a serial cheater?"

"The list is a mile long."

The Lincoln was parked next to a beat-up pickup truck several doors down from room twenty-five, so I parked in front of the room and got out, meeting Neely Kate on the sidewalk that ran alongside the building. "If Patsy's hidin' from the police, she's doin' a poor job of it."

Neely Kate shot me a grin. "Patsy may be known as a real-estate shark, but she got there through intimidation, not smarts. She probably figures she's safe since this place is about ten feet outside the city limits. It's the Fenton County Sheriff's Department's jurisdiction."

She really thought that would save her? And why would it matter if Carol Ann had been murdered somewhere else?

I knocked on room twenty-five's door. It opened a few inches, and Patsy Sue's face appeared in the crack.

"Do you promise to help me?" she asked.

"How do you know Carol Ann's been murdered?" Neely Kate asked. "I made a few calls, and no one knows about a murder."

"Oh my God!" Patsy screeched, opening the door a few inches wider. "You told people!"

Neely Kate gave her a look of disgust. "Please. I'm not an amateur. I was discreet and no names were used. What I want to know is how you know she was murdered."

I was starting to get a very bad feeling. "Patsy. What's behind that door?"

Guilt filled her eyes.

"Oh my God!" Neely Kate exclaimed. "Did you call us to the *murder scene*?"

Patsy Sue threw the door open and grabbed my wrist, dragging me into the room before I had a chance to pull away. Relief made me light-headed when I saw there was no one on the disheveled bed.

Neely Kate, who'd followed us in, sighed the moment her eyes met the empty bed. She looked as relieved as I felt.

We'd let our guards down too soon. It wasn't until Patsy shut the door that I saw Carol Ann lying on the floor on the other side of the bed.

Neely Kate came to an abrupt halt as her gaze landed on the body. "Patsy Sue! What the Sam Hill do you think you're doin'?"

"Now you're part of it," Patsy said in a rush, waving her hands around. "Your DNA's all over the place."

Neely Kate gave her the evil eye, not that I blamed her. "That's not how it works, Patsy," she snapped, "and thank you very much for trying to implicate us. We need to call the police!"

"No! They'll think I did it!"

"*Did* you do it?" Neely Kate demanded with both hands on her hips.

"No! I just found her here!"

I held up my hands, my head swimming. Poor Carol Ann was lying on the floor, but I didn't see any sign of blood. What if she was just passed out? "Did you check to see if she's alive?"

"No way!" Patsy Sue said, shaking her head. "I'm not goin' anywhere near her!"

I shot Neely Kate a look, and she tilted her head toward the bed. I was the one closest to the body, so I got the task of checking for a pulse.

I tiptoed around the foot of the bed, then squatted next to Carol Ann. She'd showered and changed since the picnic, but her hot pink capris and white shirt didn't seem to go with the thin blue scarf with giant white whales around her neck. It confused me until I realized it was a men's tie.

Oh crap.

The tie was wrapped around her neck twice, the ends intertwined. Carol Ann's face was pale, and I was sure she was dead, but I apprehensively pressed my hand against her neck and searched for a pulse. Her skin was abnormally cold, so I jerked my hand back and quickly stood. "Yep. She's dead."

Neely Kate swiped the screen of her phone. "I'm calling Joe."

Patsy Sue lunged for Neely Kate, reaching for her phone. "No! I'll pay you a thousand dollars to help me get rid of her body!"

Neely Kate's face paled and she paused long enough for Patsy to snatch her phone and stuff it down the front of her shirt.

"You give that back right now!" Neely Kate shouted, holding out her hand. "Don't you think I won't go after it!"

This was going from bad to worse, so I called Joe myself.

"Rose," he groaned when he answered. "If this is about me canceling on Neely Kate—"

"That's not it," I said in a rush as Neely Kate reached for the front of Patsy's pink button-down shirt.

"I've already had my shirt ripped off once today," Patsy Sue snarled. "What's one more!"

"What's goin' on over there?" Joe asked, sounding more alert.

I could tell him straightaway or break it to him in person. In person seemed like the best approach. Carol Ann couldn't get any deader. "I need you to come to the Broken Branch Motel."

"Why?" His hesitation was evident. "What on earth are you doin' *there*?"

"Let's just say there's a situation we need your help with right away. Room twenty-five."

"And don't you dare bring Dena!" Neely Kate shouted while holding Patsy in a headlock.

"Neely Kate said—"

"I heard what Neely Kate said," he grumbled, then hung up.

"You called the sheriff?" Patsy Sue demanded, trying to twist out of Neely Kate's hold. She reached into her shirt, then threw Neely Kate's phone across the room. It hit the old TV with a hard thud, causing the screen to crack into multiple pieces as the phone fell to the floor.

Neely Kate let Patsy go and ran for her phone, but Patsy took advantage of her momentary freedom and bolted for the door. When she threw it open, it slammed into Neely Kate, knocking her off balance as Patsy ran toward her car.

"Come back here, Patsy Sue Clydehopper!" Neely Kate shouted as she got to her feet. "You're paying for my new cell phone!"

But Patsy had already gotten into her car. She backed out of the lot, sending gravel everywhere when she hit the brakes and shot onto the county road.

"You know Joe's gonna blame us for this," I said, watching her speed away.

"Yep," she said, staring at the car too. "How much trouble do you think we're in?"

"I think we need to make a preemptive call to Carter Hale."

"My divorce attorney?"

"My defense attorney."

She held out her hand. "Give me your phone."

I clutched it tighter. "Why?"

"Because Patsy cracked mine, and I know who we really need to call."

"James?"

She snorted. "How's Skeeter Malcolm gonna help us out of this? I'm calling Kermit."

I shook my head. Of all the people who could potentially help us, the crotchety old detective would probably be last on my list. "What?"

"Just give me your phone."

I did as she asked and she entered my password, tapped around, and then pressed the phone to her ear. A few seconds later, she said, "Kermit, this is Neely Kate." She rolled her eyes. "Neely Kate Rivers. How many Neely Kates do you know?" She paused again and groaned. "Okay. I don't actually need a list, but I *do* need you to listen. Joe Simmons is gonna be calling you, asking if Rose and I are workin' on a case for you, and you're gonna tell him yes." She paused and irritation washed over her face. "*Rose Gardner*. The other woman who's working with you. *Listen!* I need you to tell him we're helping you prove Patsy Sue Clydehopper is innocent of her cousin's murder. Can you do that?"

I gasped in surprise. How could she possibly think Patsy was innocent? We'd found her in here with Carol Ann's dead body, and she'd offered to pay us to dispose of the evidence.

"No, I didn't negotiate a fee," she said. "I was too busy wrestling her for my phone, but whatever she's payin' is more money than you had five minutes ago, and you won't even have to lift a finger." She grinned. "Fine." Then she hung up.

I gaped at her in shock.

Her brow lowered. "If we say we're actually workin' a case, we're less likely to get hauled to the county jail."

"Joe wouldn't dare haul you off," I said. "He already knows you're ticked at him."

"Good. I was worried the insults in my texts might have gone over his head. But you know just last week he threatened to haul us in after he found us takin' surveillance photos of Edgar coming out of his girlfriend's house."

"That's because someone called us in for prowlin'," I said.

"And now he's gonna find us standing in a motel room with a dead body, and we let the suspect run off. He's gonna be pissed."

That was an understatement.

Ten minutes later, we heard a knock on the partially closed door and Joe pushed it open. "What the hell is goin' on, Rose?"

"What's wrong?" Neely Kate asked in a bitter tone. "Was Dena pissed that you had to leave her to come help us?"

The scowl on his face suggested she was onto something.

I held up my hands. "Y'all can continue that conversation later. We need to focus on this first." I held Joe's gaze. "I need you to keep in mind that this wasn't our fault."

Joe groaned. "Oh, God. Did you break into this room?"

"We'll have you know that we were *invited* in," Neely Kate said.

Joe's gaze landed on the busted television screen. "Why's the TV broken?"

"Because Patsy Sue Clydehopper threw my phone at it," she said matter-of-factly.

His gaze jerked back to his sister. "What was Patsy Sue Clydehopper doin' here?"

"She's the one who invited us," Neely Kate said.

Joe turned to me with a look that suggested he was done with nonsense. "What in the hell's goin' on here, Rose?"

I grimaced and moved around the end of the bed. "I think you're gonna want to see this."

With a look of trepidation, he followed—and then abruptly stopped in his tracks. "Is that what I think it is?"

"Are you thinkin' it's Carol Ann Nelson's dead body?" I asked.

Joe's face was beet red as he glanced up at me. "It's like you're a damn mind reader."

"Nope," I said, forcing a light tone to ease the tension. "I just see the future."

"Well, it's not gonna take a vision to see that you've got some explaining to do."

Boy, did I know it.

Chapter Four

How did this happen?" Joe shouted as he pointed to Carol Ann's body. "Please tell me that neither one of you had anything to do with this."

"I already told you we didn't," I said. "I got a phone call from Patsy Sue sayin' she wanted to hire us to clear her name in her cousin's murder, but I swear, I had no idea she was standin' over Carol Ann's body when she made the call."

"Why on earth did you agree to meet her here?" he demanded.

Neely Kate put her hand on her hip. "We thought she was hidin' out from the law."

"This would be the absolute *worst* place to hide out," Joe said, now flinging his hand toward the open door. "The parking lot is right off the highway, and everyone knows the look of Patsy's brand-new Lincoln. How many red Lincolns do you see driving around sportin' Baby Spice on the back window?"

He had a point.

"Not only that, but Bill Peterson owns the place and is as gossipy as they come. If Patsy had rented a room here, half the town would be whispering about it by now."

Neely Kate shook her head. "And how would our client know that? She's a fine, upstanding, church-going citizen."

Joe gave her a blank look. "Her back window says Baby Spice, Neely Kate, and we both know that's not referring to a member of a nineties girl band."

"How do you both know this and I don't?" I asked.

Joe shot me a dark look. "We're getting off track here. Patsy Sue called and asked you to meet her here to help clear her name in her cousin's murder. What happened when you got here?"

"I'll admit she was acting suspicious," I said. "She only opened the door a crack. We asked her if she'd called us to a murder scene, then she jerked me inside. I found Carol Ann lyin' there with the tie wrapped around her neck. Dead. Patsy hadn't even checked for a pulse. Neely Kate was about to call you, but Patsy managed to wrestle her phone away. She threw it at the TV and ran off."

He stared at us both for several long seconds. "Have either of you touched anything in this room?"

I shook my head. "Other than Carol Ann's neck, no."

"And you have no idea where Patsy went?"

"No," Neely Kate said. "But even if we knew, we wouldn't be at liberty to tell you the location of our client."

"It doesn't work like that, Neely Kate," Joe said in exasperation. "You fancy yourself to be a PI, not an attorney, and the truth is you're neither!"

"Not true!" she protested. "We're working this case with Kermit Cooper. Just call him and ask."

He started to say something, then shook his head and made a call. For a second, I thought he had Kermit Cooper on speed dial until I heard him say, "Jennifer? This is Joe. I've got a dead body at the Broken Branch Motel. Send a homicide team out." When he hung up, he pointed toward the door again. "Both of you *out,* but don't you dare leave."

MORE SHERIFF'S DEPUTIES showed up, followed by the coroner and the forensics team. Neely Kate and I sat on the tailgate of my truck, which made me think about all of the times James and I had sat together on my tailgate behind the Sinclair station.

I missed him more than I cared to admit, and it took every bit of willpower not to text him and ask him to meet me at the station later.

Neely Kate was lost in thought too. I'd made several attempts to ask about her day with Jed, but she'd brushed them off. From what I could tell, they'd been up to Little Rock three times now. I still had no idea what they'd been doing there, but her reluctance to talk about it still made me think it was related to Kate.

After an hour, Joe finally came back to talk to us, and I was pretty sure he'd made us stay about fifty minutes longer than necessary just to punish us. He delivered a scathing lecture about how we could have contaminated a crime scene or—worse—been killed or framed by Patsy Sue (thankfully, he had no way of knowing she'd suggested our DNA now linked us to the crime), and that we weren't private detectives, no matter how deluded we were. That was the tipping point for Neely Kate, who had been surprisingly quiet throughout his lecture.

She hopped off the tailgate and poked him in the chest. "You might not like that we're working with Kermit Cooper, but we're not doing anything illegal."

"I'd call tampering with a crime scene illegal."

"We weren't tampering with the crime scene, and you doggone know it," Neely Kate said.

"Why do you like to flirt with danger?" Joe demanded, his face turning red.

"What are you talkin' about?" she said. "We were meetin' Patsy Sue Clydehopper! Who would have thought it was dangerous?"

"What about Little Rock?"

The anger fell off her face. "What about Little Rock?"

Oh, crappy doodles. Did Joe know that Neely Kate had been seeing Jed? Surely not or he likely would have led with that, dead body or no.

"Don't play dumb with me, Neely Kate," he said. "I know you went to see Kate this afternoon."

For once Neely Kate looked speechless.

"What were you doin' up there?"

"What does it matter to you, Joe?"

"Because I care about you!"

"Care about me?" She released a bitter laugh. "If you cared about me, you wouldn't have canceled our plans *again* through a *text* so you could go see a movie with *your girlfriend of two weeks*!"

He groaned and rubbed his eyes before dropping his hand. "I screwed up."

"You're doggone right you did!" She looked madder than I'd ever seen her. "Either you want to spend time with me or you don't, Joe Simmons, and you've made it clear as a bell multiple times that you don't."

His expression softened. "Neely Kate, it's not like that . . ."

"We're *leaving*. Come on, Rose." She stomped toward the passenger door of the truck and climbed inside.

I gave Joe a questioning look.

Looking exasperated, he nodded and gave a short wave toward the truck. "Go. I know where to find you."

I started to walk toward the driver's door but turned around and said in a low voice, "She's more fragile than she looks, Joe."

He ran a hand through his hair. "Yeah, I know."

I LET NEELY KATE have five minutes to mull things over before I asked, "Why were you seein' Kate this afternoon?"

"You wouldn't understand."

"Try me." When she didn't answer, I asked softly, "Are you at least gettin' the answers you're looking for?"

She gave me a look of surprise. "No."

"Then why do you keep goin'?" I prodded gently. "I know she's goin' out of her way to hurt you."

"Just call me a fool," she said in a bitter tone.

"You're one of the last people I'd call a fool, Neely Kate."

She didn't answer.

"Jed's been takin' you?"

"Yeah."

"After she drags your heart through the muck, does he clean it off and make you feel better?"

A soft smile lit up her eyes. "Yeah. He does."

"*Good.* You deserve someone who supports you through the good and the bad."

Her smile fell. "Where does that leave Joe?"

The look on her face made me want to wring Joe's neck. "Joe cares about you, Neely Kate. I know he does, but he's feelin' his way through this new relationship just like you are. Besides, this is his first girlfriend after what happened with Hilary. He seems happy."

Tears filled her eyes. "Yeah."

"He's caught up in the whirlwind of a new romance. He'll realize what he's doing and come to his senses."

"Funny … I'm caught up in the whirlwind of a new romance, and yet I still have time for him."

There was no arguing with that.

"It's like I told you. This isn't the first time he's canceled on me because of her." Her chin trembled, but she kept her eyes on the road. "I'm done with lettin' people treat me like I'm disposable."

I sucked in a breath. Of course she saw herself that way. I reached out a hand and touched her arm. "Oh, Neely Kate …"

She flinched and pulled away. "I don't want your pity, Rose," she said in a tight voice. "I just thought you should know."

"Pity? I don't pity you. I'm so stinkin' *proud* of you." Tears stung my eyes. I wished I wasn't driving so I could get a good look at her, but knowing Neely Kate, we wouldn't be having this conversation if we'd been sitting face-to-face.

"I'm done waitin' for people's leftover scraps of attention, and Joe's made his priorities clear."

I wasn't sure Joe saw it like that at all, but now didn't seem like the time to bring it up.

She lifted her chin, clearly putting her issues with Joe behind her. "We both know that Joe's gonna go after Patsy as the murderer, so we need to come up with a plan of attack to clear her name."

"What?" I asked. "Are you crazy? We found her in the motel room with Carol Ann's body lyin' on the floor. She offered us money to help hide the body, for criminy's sake! She's lookin' pretty guilty."

"Which is why she needs our help."

I shot her a look of disbelief. "You're tellin' me you think she's innocent?"

"Why would she call us if she was guilty?"

"For this very reason. To make us doubt what our own eyes saw."

Neely Kate was quiet for a moment, then said, "It would take someone really brilliant or really stupid to come up with that plan, and Patsy Sue Clydehopper is neither. Which means she's innocent."

She had a point.

I pushed out a sigh. "Okay. So what do you want to do? You seem like you already have a plan."

"Well, first we need to find out who rented the room. I can call Bill Peterson and ask him."

"You think he'll tell you?"

"Please …," she scoffed. "He'll be dying to tell me. He plays bingo with Granny, and I know he loves a good story."

"Okay," I said. "Sounds like a good place to start. That was a men's tie, so we need to find out who it belongs to."

"Yeah," she said. "Bill might be able to help us with that too. I'll see if he noticed any guys comin' and goin'."

"Good idea."

"I'll call him when we get to the farm," she said. "I need to get a notebook. I let Jed borrow mine."

I grinned. "Jed's carryin' around your pink sparkly notebook?"

She laughed. "He looked pretty cute holdin' it."

"I really like him for you, Neely Kate. He's a great guy and I can see he makes you happy. I know you're frustrated that he's takin' things slow, but I think that means you're special to him, you know?" I couldn't help thinking that Jed's care and attention had helped her find this new sense of self-worth … even if it was at Joe's expense.

"Yeah." A soft smile lit up her eyes.

"And he seems to be tryin' to go the straight and narrow. That's a plus."

"Yeah, even if I have no idea what he's up to."

"He'll tell you when he has it figured out."

She nodded, not looking so certain.

So many people had hurt Neely Kate in her twenty-five years. I couldn't bear the thought of someone else letting her down. But Jed was a good man, and from the way he watched her with a mixture of hope, awe, and devotion, it was easy to see he'd never purposely hurt her.

"If we'd been thinkin'," Neely Kate said, "we should have had you force a vision of Patsy to see if she murdered her cousin."

We both knew it didn't exactly work like that. We'd need to find Patsy first, since I couldn't force a vision without touching the person. Still, I couldn't deny she had a point. She didn't know about the change in my visions.

"Things were happening so fast," Neely Kate continued. "It's no wonder we didn't consider it." Then she sat up straighter, excitement washing over her face. "Hey! When we get home, you can force a vision of me, of what you and I will find out about the murder."

I gave her a pained look.

"What? You think it's a bad idea?"

"No …," I hedged. "It might work."

Her eyes narrowed. "When was the last time you had a vision?"

I shot her a long glance. "The night I was kidnapped."

"The night you almost died having a vision?"

"Yeah," I said softly.

"Have you tried to force one since then?"

"No." I kept seeing Jeanne's face in my head, the trusting look in her eyes.

Her death was on my hands. The few times I'd brought it up to Neely Kate, she'd refused to discuss the matter, insisting Merv's crew was responsible, not us. She would also remind me that we'd tried to get Jeanne to go to the sheriff or even James for protection. And while that was all technically true, there was no denying I'd started the wheels in motion. No denying I'd carelessly put her life in danger by talking to her in a public place where anyone could have seen us. I hadn't tried hard enough to ensure my vision of her death didn't come to pass. I hadn't followed up.

Maybe I would have been more willing to accept Neely Kate's account of it if I hadn't seen the guilt in her eyes too.

She watched me for a moment. "Okay," she finally said in a comforting tone. "We won't force a vision." Then she grinned. "We'll do it the old-fashioned way."

"Really?" I asked in surprise.

"I know how much you hate them. What if you force one and it kick-starts them into high gear? You've got a lot to consider."

"Thanks for understanding."

My phone started to ring. Neely Kate snatched it off the seat next to me and looked at the screen.

"Well, I'll be..." She answered it and put it on speakerphone. "You've got a lot of nerve, Patsy Sue!"

"I'm sorry!" Patsy said. "I panicked."

"You left us with one heck of a mess," Neely Kate said.

"I know. I know. I'm sorry, but I knew I'd get arrested if I stayed."

"Because you're guilty as sin?" Neely Kate asked. She was obviously taking the bad cop role.

"No! Because I was set up."

"Who on earth would have set you up?" I asked in disbelief.

"Trust me, I've got a lot of people who would love to see me gone. You have to figure out who did it."

"Let me get this straight," I said. "You think someone killed your cousin, then invited you to come to her motel room?"

"Carol Ann texted me. So I went to see her."

"You two had just had one doozy of a fight at the First Baptist Church. Why would you go see her?" Neely Kate asked.

"I had my reasons," Patsy Sue said with plenty of attitude.

"So if someone set you up, how did they know about Carol Ann's text? Did they take her phone and pretend to be her?"

"No. I'm sure the text was from her."

"How do you know that?"

She hesitated. "I just do. And I didn't kill her. I found her like that when I got there."

"Look," I said. "You have to know running off just makes you look guiltier."

"I'm not comin' back," she said. "Not until you clear my name. I can't afford riskin' even one night of my skin care regime if they toss me into county lockup."

I groaned. "If you want us to help you, you need to tell us more than that. We need to know everything that's happened between you two since she came back to town. And what she sent in that text."

"We need your alibi too," Neely Kate said as though Patsy was a simpleton.

"If you two are such ace detectives, you can figure it out," she said in a condescending tone.

I opened my mouth to tell her thanks but no thanks, but Neely Kate cut me off.

"How much are you payin' us?" she asked. "We do good work, so we don't come cheap."

"I'll pay you two thousand dollars," Patsy said, sounding desperate.

"Most PIs get paid by the hour," Neely Kate pressed.

"I'll make it three thousand," Patsy said. "Let me know when you find out something." Then she hung up.

"You still believe her?" I asked.

"Yeah. I still do. Besides, whether she did it or not, we're each gettin' a thousand dollars."

I considered telling her that I doubted Patsy Sue would pay up if we found her guilty, but Neely Kate seemed dead set on working this case. Nothing was going to change her mind at this point. Given my guilt over Jeanne, I was surprised that I was open to it, but maybe this was exactly what I needed to get over it. "That's Kermit's money."

"And he'll get a thousand of it. We're doin' the work, so it stands to reason we should get paid."

"Huh." I took the turnoff to my farm. When I pulled to a stop in front of the house, I was surprised Muffy wasn't in the front window, waiting for us. I found her in the kitchen, barking out the back window. A family of squirrels had been tormenting her over the past week, and she was obviously eager to make yet another futile attempt to catch them. I opened the back door, and she made a beeline for the barn.

"What's got Muffy so excited?" Neely Kate asked as she walked into the kitchen with a new notebook. This one was covered in gold sparkles.

"The squirrels, I guess." But something didn't seem right. She'd gotten pretty upset a month or so ago when Raddy Dyer had been hiding in the barn. I ignored the flutter in my chest when I remembered that James had been out there too. What if he was waiting for me out there now? "I'm gonna go watch her. She's awfully close to the woods and it's starting to get dark. I don't want her to get lost."

"Okay. My phone still works even with the cracked screen. I'll call Bill and let you know what he says."

"Sounds good." I headed for the door to the living room.

She looked up in surprise. "Why are you goin' that way?"

"I need to pee first," I lied, then let the swinging door close behind me. I grabbed my Taser from my bag before heading out the front door.

The sun was about to set, but a crescent moon was out, lighting my path across the open field to the barn. As I got close, I heard Muffy snarling. I'd been down this path before, but it wasn't any less scary this time.

One of the large double barn doors was slightly ajar, and I almost called Joe, but he was already busy with Carol Ann's death. Besides, as crazy as it was, I wanted to see who was in the barn before bringing anyone else into the situation.

I moved away from the doors and called out, "Who's in there?" When there was no answer, I said, "I'm gonna call the sheriff if you don't announce yourself."

"Wait!" I heard a guy call out. "Don't call 'em!"

My heartbeat picked up. I didn't recognize the voice. "Who are you and what do you want?"

"My name's Marshall Billings, ma'am. I only wanted to talk to you."

"Then what are you doin' skulkin' around in my barn, Marshall Billings, instead of waiting on my front door?"

"I didn't know when you were gonna be home, and I didn't want to bleed all over your porch."

That stole my breath. Why had a bleeding stranger showed up in my barn? But in my gut, I already knew. He wasn't here to talk to Rose Gardner. He was here to talk to the Lady in Black. "Do you have a gun?"

"Yes, ma'am, but I swear to God I won't use it on you. I've only got it to protect myself."

Call me foolish, but I believed him. "Okay, I'm alone, and I'm coming in. Fair warning, if you've hurt my dog, you're gonna regret stepping foot on my land." When he didn't respond, I walked over to the double doors and pushed the unlocked side open enough to slip through the crack.

The barn was pitch dark, so I said, "I'm gonna turn on a light so we can see each other."

"Okay," he said in a shaky voice.

I walked over to the cabinets on the right and flipped on a light over the work station, keeping my eye on the center of the room. Muffy, who'd followed me in, let out a quick growl.

My little dog had the guy cornered, although it didn't look like he was going anywhere based on the bloody towel wrapped around the right thigh of his dirty jeans. He was sitting on the floor with his legs outstretched. He looked young—late teens or early twenties—and terrified.

Seeing the blood-soaked towel made the hair on my arms stand up, and anxiety washed through me like a rolling tide. *Get a grip, Rose.* I'd seen so much worse than this. I could handle it.

"What happened?" I asked as I slowly moved closer. His gun lay on the dirt floor next to him, but it was close enough to reach. I'd been around enough scared animals to know they lashed out when they felt cornered. He might not be a threat, but he could become one.

"I got shot."

"By who?"

He pressed his lips together and gave a slight shake of his head.

"Why'd you come to me?" I asked.

He looked surprised. "You're the Lady in Black, ain't ya?" Then he looked uncertain and even more scared.

I saw no reason to deny it. "Yeah," I said softly. "That's me." Or rather, my alter ego—the woman who'd started working with James last November out of desperation. I'd needed help to protect my then-boyfriend, assistant DA Mason Deveraux, and James had needed my visions to help him ferret out turncoats. Win-win. Then the whole J.R. business had gone down, and I'd retired the Lady in Black … until last month. I'd resurrected her to help make peace in the underworld.

"Can you help me?" he asked.

"I take it you don't want to go to the hospital?"

"No. I can't. They'll tell the sheriff."

It was obvious he needed medical attention. The question was who to call for help. "Who do you work for?" I asked. "And why didn't you go to them?"

"I don't work for no one," he spat out angrily. "Not anymore."

"Okay," I said. "Then who did you *used* to work for, because that'll make a difference in who I call."

"You can't call Skeeter Malcolm," he said, his eyes wide in panic. "I heard that you're neutral. Is that true?"

"Yeah. I'm neutral," I said, and my heart sank. If he was hiding from James, this was bound to stir up trouble between us. "It's a little late to be asking that now, isn't it?"

He stared at me wide-eyed. Now that I was closer, I could see that he looked even younger than I'd first thought.

"How old are you, Marshall?"

"Eighteen."

I had serious doubts about that. "I'm gonna call Tim Dermot. Are you good with him?"

"He works for Buck Reynolds. Buck don't like me neither."

How had this kid made the bad list of the two top criminals in Fenton County? I knew I should be more worried about being alone with him, but he didn't look dangerous at the moment. He only looked scared. "There was a change of guard. Dermot's in charge now and he's a nurse." The kid didn't try to stop me, so I pulled up Dermot's number and he answered quickly.

"Lady. I'm surprised to hear from you."

"I have a medical situation I need your help with."

"Are you hurt?" he asked, sounding concerned.

"Not me. Someone else, but I can't take him to the hospital."

"Malcolm?" he asked in surprise.

"No. Someone else." I considered telling him Marshall's name, but decided to wait until he got here. For all I knew, Buck and James weren't the only people the kid had pissed off. "I found him hiding in my barn looking for the Lady in Black. He has a gunshot wound in his leg and refuses to go to the hospital."

He was silent for a moment, then said, "Have you stopped the blood flow?"

I glanced down at the kid's leg. "He has a towel wrapped around it. I haven't checked."

"It's not bleeding through the towel?"

"It's bloody, but I don't think it's bleeding through."

"Try to get him into your house without taking the bandage off. I'll be there in about fifteen minutes."

"Don't you need my address?"

"I already know it," he said before he hung up.

Did the whole county know where I lived? But I had more immediate issues. "Dermot's going to help. He wants me to move you to my house. Are you good with that?"

Worry filled his eyes. "I hear your farm is like Sweden."

"Sweden?" What? Then I realized what he meant. "You mean Switzerland?"

"Yeah, one of those places."

I shook my head. This was news to me, but I'd touted myself as neutral back at the parley I'd set up for Buck Reynolds and James a month ago—an impression I'd done my best to reinforce. It stood to reason my land would be considered neutral too. The real question was if all the criminals would honor that. I wasn't sure being in the thick of the Fenton County crime world was smart, but I'd jumped in headlong a month ago.

I was still confused about where the boy in front of me fit into the Fenton County criminal world, but we'd sort that out later. "Can you walk?" Then a new thought occurred to me. "How'd you get here, anyway?"

"I had a friend drop me off." He tried to get to his feet, then let out a loud cry of pain and fell back to the floor.

"I have another idea." I called Neely Kate.

"What's wrong?" she asked.

"Why do you think something's wrong?"

"Why else would you be calling me from just outside the house?"

"Actually, I'm in the barn, and I have a situation."

"Who's out there this time?" she asked.

It was a logical conclusion. "His name's Marshall Billings, and he has a gunshot wound in his leg. Dermot is on his way to fix him up."

"*Dermot?*"

I knew it was a lot to take in at once. "I don't think he can walk, so I need you to drive my truck back here. We can put him in the back and haul him down to the house."

"On it." I knew I'd have plenty of explaining to do later, but she hung up.

Marshall didn't look convinced this was a solid plan, but he kept quiet as he watched me. "Are you gonna turn me in?" he asked. "I know you're friendly with the chief deputy sheriff."

"I don't even know what you did," I said. "So what would I turn you in for?"

He gave me a tight nod, not volunteering any information.

"I'm gonna need you to push that gun away from you," I said. "Out of reach. I don't have a weapon, and I'd feel a lot better about helpin' you if I wasn't worried about getting shot."

He looked surprised, but he shoved the gun away willingly enough. Then, as though exhausted from the minimal effort, he leaned his back against the wall and closed his eyes.

So many questions floated through my head. "What made you think to come here?"

He opened his eyes to a squint. "Everyone's talkin' about the Lady in Black. How you brought down J.R. Simmons and brokered a peace between Skeeter and Buck. I figured you were my only hope."

I heard the truck engine roar to life, and Muffy turned her attention to the barn doors. I swung the already-ajar door open wider and then walked back toward Marshall, trying to figure out how to get him on his feet.

"You're not what I expected," he said, watching me.

"And what did you expect?"

"Someone tougher. Meaner."

My truck headlights bounced on the field between my house and the barn as the truck got closer.

"Well, you can't always believe what you hear," I said, although what he'd heard sounded pretty accurate.

"A lot of guys are nervous about you," he said.

"Why?" I asked. "Because they think I work for Skeeter Malcolm?"

"No, because it looks like you don't."

That surprised me—first, that they finally believed I was neutral, and second, that it made them nervous.

Neely Kate made a U-turn and then backed up so that the tailgate was close to the barn door. The driver's door opened, and she was out in a flash.

"Where is he?"

I gestured to the back corner of the barn. "Neely Kate, meet Marshall. Marshall, Neely Kate."

Neely Kate gave him a perplexed look. "How'd you end up here?"

"I was looking for the Lady in Black."

Neely Kate's mouth dropped open. The fact that our address was so widely known had clearly caught her off guard too, but that was a conversation for later.

We quickly got him up on his one good leg, an arm over each of our shoulders, and helped him hobble to the truck bed. He cried out when we hauled him up and slid him back enough so his legs weren't hanging over the tailgate. I stayed in the back with him while Neely Kate drove to the house, pulling up to the back door.

When she emerged from the truck, she said, "There are fewer steps back here, and I figured we could put him on the kitchen table."

I hadn't thought of either of those things. "Good idea."

I hopped down, and after some maneuvering, we got Marshall down from the truck and up the steps into the kitchen.

He leaned on my shoulder while Neely Kate hastened to clear off the table. We had just gotten him positioned on top of it when I heard a knock at the front door.

"I'll get it," Neely Kate said. "I'm gonna go grab some towels anyway."

Marshall's face was covered with sweat, and his shirt was pretty damp. All the jostling must have irritated his wound because his towel was soaked with more blood than it had been before.

My anxiety shot up again, catching me off guard and making me feel panicky and out of control. But I told myself I didn't have time to dwell on it. I needed to attend to Marshall.

"I'm gonna get you a drink of water," I said, worried about dehydration. He'd lost an awful lot of blood and he was starting to shake.

"Hold off on that," Dermot said as he walked through the swinging kitchen door.

I spun around to face him, relief washing through me. "Thanks for comin'."

He gave me a tight grin as he pulled out a kitchen chair and set his black bag on it. "I can't turn down a request from Lady."

He could and we both knew it. "Well, thanks anyway. We just got him settled on the table. All the jostling around made his wound start bleeding more. Neely Kate went to get some clean towels."

"Good thinking," Dermot said, looking the boy over. "Do I know you?"

Marshall watched Dermot with fear-filled eyes. "No, sir."

"What's your name?"

"Marshall, sir."

I noticed he didn't offer his last name this time. Was it a purposeful omission?

"What are you doin' at Lady's farm, Marshall?"

"Lookin' for Sweden," he said, his voice growing faint. His face was pale, and his eyes started to close.

"Sweden?" Dermot asked absently as he pulled on a pair of gloves before he took an IV pouch and tubing out of his black bag.

"He means Switzerland," I said, getting really worried. "Is he going to be okay?"

"We're about to find out, but I want to start an IV first." He looked up at me. "I'm gonna need your help."

"I'm not a nurse, Dermot."

Dermot held my gaze. "And I'm not a doctor, but we're both gonna do what we need to do to save this boy. Together."

Chapter Five

"Yeah." I nodded, feeling sick to my stomach as Dermot scrubbed Marshall's wrist with an alcohol wipe and slid a needle into his vein. The out-of-control feeling was back, and I swallowed my apprehension.

"We need something taller than the table to set this IV bag on," he said as he taped the needle to Marshall's skin. I pointed wordlessly to the high-backed chair at the head of the table, and he taped the bag to the back of it.

Next he grabbed a vial and a syringe out of his bag and injected something into the kid's IV. "Morphine," he said, looking up at me as he tossed the syringe into the kitchen sink. "Let's hope it works."

"I've got 'em," Neely Kate said as she burst into the room with an armful of fresh towels.

"Just in time," Dermot said as he pulled a pair of scissors out of his bag. "I'm about to cut his jeans open and get a look at the wound. I have a feeling I'm gonna need a few of those. Neely Kate, drop that load on that counter and bring a couple of those over here." He reached into his bag and pulled out a couple of gloves. "Which one of you is stronger?"

Neely Kate and I both looked at each other.

I said, "Neely Kate" as she said, "Me."

"Okay, Rose, you put these on. You're my surgical assistant. Neely Kate, your job is to help hold him down. Lay on him if you have to."

"Okay." She sounded nervous.

I quickly donned the gloves as Neely Kate put two folded towels on top of Marshall's stomach.

Dermot started with the uninjured leg and cut his pants all the way up to the waistband. Then he switched to the other leg, cutting the material until he reached the wrapped towel, which was now completely soaked with blood. "Neely Kate. I'm gonna need a big bucket or bowl."

"I can get the mop bucket, but it's not clean."

"That's okay," Dermot said, wiping sweat off his forehead with the back of his forearm. "We're gonna use it for bloody towels. Marshall's already inconvenienced you ladies enough without causing any more mess than necessary."

Neely Kate quickly ran into the broom closet and returned with the bucket.

"Set it on Rose's left side," Dermot said.

"Okay." She set the bucket next to me, casting a terrified glance up at me as she rose. Right or wrong, I felt better knowing we both felt out of our league, but my anxiety was mushrooming, and I knew it had nothing to do with the roles we'd be forced to assume and everything to do with the large amount of blood.

This isn't Merv. He's not going to die.

"Okay," Dermot said. "Let's do this. Rose, I'm going to hand you this bloody towel so you can drop it in the bucket. Then we're gonna roll him off the jeans and drop them in too."

I swallowed and nodded. Could I do this? Did I have a choice?

"Hey," he said gently. "You're doin' great."

"I haven't even done anything yet."

He grinned. "Then let's get to it."

He quickly unwrapped the towel and handed it to me.

Marshall cried out from having his leg jostled. Neely Kate pressed down on his shoulders to hold him down.

I dropped the heavy towel into the bucket, still trying to get control. I closed my eyes for a brief second and visions of Merv filled my head. I could practically feel my bloody clothes sticking to my skin as his dead body crushed me into the ground.

I gasped and opened my eyes with a jerk, but the blood-soaked towel at my feet taunted me.

I'd spent a week and a half trying to ignore my nightmares, but standing over Marshall's bleeding leg was shoving it all back in my face.

"Rose," Neely Kate said.

I turned to face her.

"Honey, are you okay?"

I blinked. This wasn't like me, and this absolutely was not the time to fall apart. "Yeah. Bad memories."

Dermot gave me another glance as he finished cutting the jeans off. Then, having clearly decided I wouldn't faint on him, he rolled Marshall toward me and tugged the denim out from underneath him, jerking it free and handing it to me. Grabbing a clean towel, Dermot dabbed the oozing wound on Marshall's leg. "It looks like the bullet's still in there. I'm gonna have to dig it out."

"Okay."

"Keep pressure on his leg while I get some tools out."

I took over pressing the towel into the wound while Dermot stripped off his gloves and dug into his bag again. The boy moaned and his entire body shook.

Dermot opened a package and laid a paper cloth on the table next to Marshall's leg. He dumped stainless steel tools from sterile bags onto the cloth, along with several packages of sterile gauze. He uncapped a bottle of alcohol and handed it to me. "When I tell you to, you're gonna pour this over his wound, got it?"

I nodded, my mouth dry, but I forced out, "Yeah."

He opened a pair of sterile gloves and donned them. "Marshall, this is gonna hurt like a son of a bitch, but I need you to stay still."

Dermot lifted his gaze to Neely Kate. "Be ready to hold him down. I suspect it will be a lot like riding a bucking bronco before this is said and done."

"Okay," she said with wide eyes.

"Rose, remove the towel and pour the alcohol on there."

I lifted the towel, swallowing hard when I saw the raw, bloody wound beneath, but I poured the liquid onto it without flinching.

Marshall screamed and tried to sit up, and I threw my weight onto his shin to pin his leg down.

"Dammit," Dermot said, "I can't give him more morphine or he'll overdose." He glanced up at the kid's face. "Marshall. I know it hurts, dude, but I need you to cooperate." Then he said under his breath, "It's only gonna get worse."

The next five minutes were terrifying as Dermot dug out the bullet. Marshall was hoarse from screaming, and Dermot ran out of sterile gauze to soak up the blood. But finally, Dermot was satisfied he hadn't left anything behind and stitched the wound shut. By then, Marshall had passed out from pain and blood loss.

"Okay," Dermot said as he stripped off his bloody gloves and bandaged the wound. "Now we wait and see."

"He might not make it?" I asked in surprise.

"He's lost a lot of blood and the wound was pretty dirty. I'll give him some IV antibiotics, and we'll hope for the best." He pushed out a breath. "I need a drink. You got anything?"

I glanced at Neely Kate. "We've got beer, wine, and some whiskey."

He walked over to the kitchen sink and started to wash his hands. "What kind of whiskey?"

"Jameson," Neely Kate said.

He nodded his approval. "You got a bedroom down here?"

"No," I said, "they're all upstairs."

"We can either put him on your sofa or the three of us can haul him upstairs."

My mouth dropped open. "You're not gonna take him with you?"

"I can't," he said. "And before you ask, it's for the same reason I didn't bring anyone with me. I did this as a favor to you, but I owe that kid nothin'. I don't want to get wrapped up in whatever trouble he's brought down on himself."

"Dermot!" I protested. "You're a nurse. It's your duty to help him."

"And I did, but I have no idea why that boy's lyin' on your kitchen table, and the fact that you called me instead of Malcolm has me worried. We just reached a truce, and I don't want to rock the boat—not over a kid I don't know anything about."

"He could die, Dermot."

"Then call an ambulance if it looks like he's on death's door. My part's done. And I'm counting on your relationship with Malcolm to save my ass if he holds it against me."

"I don't have a relationship with Skeeter Malcolm," I grumbled.

"And I'm King Tut." He gestured toward the kid on my table. "Where do you want him?"

I looked at Neely Kate, wondering how we'd gotten into this mess.

"The second guest bedroom," she said. "We can tie the IV bag to the cast-iron headboard."

He pushed out a breath. "Second guest bedroom it is. Let's get this done so I can get my drink."

In the end, Neely Kate and I were of little help, so Dermot tossed the kid over his shoulder and carried him upstairs. The two of us trailed behind, me holding the IV bag. We got him settled in the bed—with several towels under his leg to protect the sheet and mattress.

Dermot put antibiotics in his IV bag as well as a narcotic to help with his pain. Then Neely Kate tied the bag to the bed, and we headed back downstairs. Like it or not, we had a houseguest.

Neely Kate grabbed the glasses, I grabbed the whiskey, and we carried everything out to the front porch. Sighing, I settled into one of the wicker chairs and poured drinks for myself and Neely Kate. She and Dermot sat down too, one on either side of me.

Dermot took the bottle out of my hands and gave himself a generous pour, then lifted his glass. "To the Lady in Black, may her reign be long and peaceful."

I stared at him in disbelief. "What?"

"You have to know you're a legend now." Then he drained his glass and poured more before setting the bottle on the small wicker side table. "That boy won't be the last to show up at your front door—or barn, as the case may be—seeking sanctuary."

"He knew where I lived. And so did you," I said, cradling my glass in my hands.

"It's not a secret, Rose. A lot of us have known since we found out who you really are. We know Crocker tracked you down here. And a lot of us have good memories." He held his glass next to his face and unfurled a finger to tap his temple.

"Are we in any kind of danger?" I asked.

"I suspect not. Most men consider you … Sweden." A huge grin spread across his face. "I think they like the idea of a safe haven, but …" He took another sip. "I have no idea how that kid got shot, and whoever did it might be lookin' for him. They might not appreciate your offer of sanctuary. How'd he get here?"

"He said a friend dropped him off."

"We just won't let anyone know he's here," Neely Kate said.

"I suspect that ship has sailed," Dermot said, taking another sip. "He's a kid, which means his friend probably is young too. That means they're stupid. The friend's gonna talk. You need to be prepared to protect yourself." His gaze turned serious. "You should call Malcolm and have him send some men to stand guard."

"No," I said. "Marshall begged me not to call Skeeter, and besides, using his men to protect me kind of defeats the whole purpose of bein' neutral."

"Why didn't he want you to call Malcolm?"

"I don't know, but he got pretty freaked out when I suggested it."

Dermot tapped his glass thoughtfully, then turned toward me. "So now the question is what are you gonna do when Skeeter Malcolm or his men show up at your doorstep to haul that kid off?"

I already knew what I'd do, but that didn't mean I liked it.

"So basically we're up crap creek," Neely Kate said.

I took a sip of whiskey as I stared out into the yard, feeling unsettled. This was what I'd wanted, right? To be a mediator in the turbulent crime world and help achieve the kind of lasting peace that would keep Fenton County citizens safe.

And, if I were honest, to keep James safe too.

Dermot set down his now-empty glass of whiskey. "That sounds like an issue for you ladies, so I'll let you work it out." He got to his feet and picked up the bag. "Change his bandage twice a day for the first few days and give him the antibiotic I left in the kitchen. If he gets a high fever that won't come down with ibuprofen, then call an ambulance." He paused. "But they're gonna want to know who cleaned up his wound and my name better not enter into it."

I'd only met Dermot a few weeks ago, but he'd always struck me as a respectful man. Still, the look on his face and the hard edge in his voice let me know his tolerance wouldn't extend to being named in a police report regarding Marshall Billings.

A new fear washed through me. I'd been so concerned with helping Marshall survive the night, it hadn't occurred to me that I might be aiding and abetting a criminal. A quick glance at Neely Kate told me she'd already considered the possibility. She didn't look any happier than I felt.

"No one will ever know you helped us," I said firmly. "Not even James."

Dermot's eyebrows shot up. "He'll guess that it was me."

"I won't lie to him," I said, "but I won't confirm it either."

Wearing a deep scowl, he stared at me for a moment before nodding. "I guess that's the best I can ask for, but if this becomes a habit, we'll need to rotate duty." Then he turned around and left.

Neely Kate and I watched quietly as he got into his car. "What did he mean by that?" I finally asked as he drove toward the county road.

"I think he means the next time someone shows up with a gunshot wound, we need to call someone else."

"You mean *if* someone else shows up."

She gave me a deadpan look.

"This is my fault," I said. "I was stupid enough to think I could be neutral and there wouldn't be any repercussions."

Neely Kate offered me a soft smile. "For what it's worth, I think it's a good thing."

I released a sharp laugh. "You think it's a good thing there's a teenager with a gunshot wound lying in the upstairs bedroom?"

"No, I think it's good that people aren't associatin' you with Skeeter Malcolm." She turned to face the yard, lifting her glass to her lips. "And besides, we saved that boy's life. The reason he came here was because he was certain the Lady in Black would help him. He'd be dead if he didn't think he'd find refuge with her. That has to count for something."

She was right, and I had to admit I felt a mixture of pride and relief. I hadn't saved Jeanne, but Marshall could be a different story. "Are you going to tell Jed?" I asked.

She took a sip, then lowered her glass. "I haven't decided yet."

"You don't want to lie to him."

"I *won't* lie to him," she said emphatically. "For once I've got a really great guy I'm crazy about, and I don't want to screw that up." She turned to me with tear-filled eyes, imploring me to understand.

"I would never purposely do anything to hurt your relationship," I said. "If you feel like you have to tell him, then you have my blessing, but that boy showed up here seeking sanctuary. That means I can't hand him over to anyone."

"Even Skeeter?"

I pushed out a heavy breath. "Especially Skeeter."

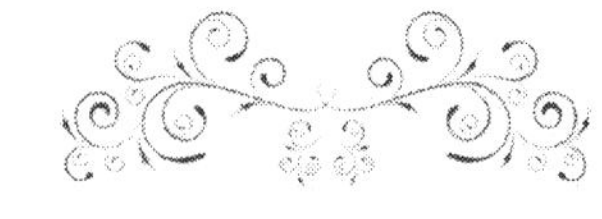

Chapter Six

=

Neely Kate and I took turns checking on Marshall that night. He started running a fever at around four in the morning, so I gave him his first dose of antibiotics and some ibuprofen, along with a pain pill. At least none of my recurring nightmares had bothered me.

After I got up and ready around seven, I peeked my head in his room to find him sleeping. When I walked down to the kitchen, I found Neely Kate sitting at the table, staring out at the barn while nursing a cup of coffee with Muffy lying on the floor next to her. The room smelled like eggs and bacon, and the sight of the gold notebook open in front of my friend made me smile.

"I hope you got some sleep after I took over," I said, grabbing a mug out of the cabinet.

"Yeah," she said absently. "Hey, I moved the towels to the dryer. All the blood stains came out."

"Thanks." I poured a cup of coffee and sat down across from her. "Are you mad at me?"

Her gaze jerked to mine in surprise. "Why would you think I'm mad?"

"Because of Marshall. You're quieter than usual."

She shook her head. "No. I'm just thinkin' about … things."

"Like Kate?"

She gave me a tight smile.

Muffy got up and moved next to me, putting her front paws on my legs for attention. I picked her up and put her on my lap, absently stroking the back of her head. "You don't have to tell me anything. I just want you to know I never want to be a burden to you. So if what happened last night upsets you and you don't want to be around this … I understand."

"You mean move out?" she asked bluntly.

A lump filled my throat, and I nodded. I hated the thought of being out here alone, especially if random strangers took to showing up at night, but I didn't want her to be uncomfortable.

She gave me a smirk as she lifted her cup to her lips. "Don't think you can get rid of me *that* easily. I love livin' here with you and Muffy."

"And we love havin' you here too, but I understand if you change your mind."

Muffy had perked up at the sound of her name, and as though confirming my statement, she leaned over and licked Neely Kate's hand.

Neely Kate cupped the side of her neck and rubbed behind her ear. "I'm not gonna change my mind."

"But you and Jed …" I took a breath. "He's such a great guy, and he makes you so happy. If things keep goin' the way they are, you'll want to live with him."

She dropped her hand to the table. "I don't see that happenin' anytime soon, so you've got nothin' to worry about."

But she was frowning now, which had me worried. "Did you tell Jed about our guest and it didn't go well? Is that why you're upset?"

"What?" she asked in surprise, then slumped back down in her seat. "No."

Something was clearly bothering her, but I let it go. She'd tell me when she was ready.

Muffy must have sensed it too because she watched Neely Kate for a second and then gave a soft whine before stretching out across my thighs.

"We have a pretty light schedule at the landscaping office again," I said. "So we should have some spare time to deal with all the nonsense going on. We need to figure out a plan to work on Patsy's case. Did you call the motel owner?"

"Yeah, Bill said Carol Ann rented the room on Saturday night."

"Saturday night?" I asked in surprise. "Patsy made it sound like Carol Ann showed up at her front door earlier than that."

"We need to figure out where she was stayin' before she rented that room," Neely Kate said.

"She might have been staying with her mother," I said. "Patsy mentioned that her aunt Lucille was tired of Carol Ann being a freeloader."

"So we need to talk to Lucille Nelson." Neely Kate wrote something in her gold notebook.

"You know who she is?"

"Kind of. Nothing helpful."

"We know that Carol Ann was murdered sometime between the end of the church picnic and when Patsy called me at seven. We need to see if she has an alibi."

"If she had an alibi, do you think she would have called us?"

"Well, no, but we still need to know what she was doing."

Neely Kate nodded, then jotted something down. "We have to talk to Calvin."

Her husband could give us tons of information. If he was willing. "You think he'll talk to us?"

"Sure. We're the ones tryin' to prove she *didn't* do it."

"But if he's foolin' around, maybe he wants her to go down for this," I said. "She'll go to prison, and he'll be free to do whatever he wants."

Neely Kate shook her head while writing in her notebook.

"No?" I asked. "Why not?"

"Because Patsy makes a killin' in real estate. More than he does. If she goes to prison, no more money."

"Why does Patsy stay with him if not for the money?"

She shrugged. "She says she loves him. Go figure. Love makes you do crazy things." The look she gave me made it all too clear what she was thinking, but she spoke her mind anyway. "You have to be smart, Rose. You have to know that startin' something with Skeeter Malcolm is the worst idea ever."

I pressed my lips together and didn't comment. We'd had this conversation already. More than once.

"I know you don't want to talk about this, but a relationship with him will be nothing but heartbreak."

"I know …"

"Yet you haven't told him no yet."

My eyes pleaded with hers. "I …"

"Love him?"

"Yeah," I said quietly, "I think I do."

She grabbed my hand and squeezed it tight. "Then you need to look long and hard at the life you'd be livin'," she said softly, "because it won't be the fairy tale you're wantin'."

"I've given up on fairy tales, Neely Kate. Mason broke me of that."

A soft smile lit up her eyes. "You're a liar. You're the biggest believer in fairy tales I know. Look at the kid upstairs." She pointed to the ceiling. "Most people would have turned him away or called the sheriff. They sure as shooting wouldn't have assisted with his surgery. You want to save him. You want to turn him to the straight and narrow, and truth be told, you want to turn Skeeter Malcolm to the straight and narrow too. I think we both know that's what you're holdin' out for, but it will never happen."

"How do you know?" I asked before I could stop myself. "Jed's changing for you."

"Jed and Skeeter aren't even close to the same man," she said, although not unkindly. "Can you imagine Skeeter Malcolm workin' a nine-to-five job, or any job for that matter?"

While he made more money on his legitimate businesses than his dealings in the criminal world, he'd made no bones about his unwillingness to leave that life behind. Part of me was willing to accept that if only I could have him, but I couldn't deny that I wanted what Neely Kate had, even if Jed hadn't quite figured things out yet. I wanted us to have a real chance.

"I should tell him no," I said in a whisper.

"I just want you to be happy, Rose," she said, meeting my eyes and holding them. "You keep tellin' *me* that I deserve a man who is there for me through it all, the good and the bad, but so do *you*. And we both know that Skeeter Malcolm will never be that man. Not only is he incapable of it, but he plain doesn't want it."

There was no denying she was right. If we were together, I'd always be worried someone would find out. Yet I still couldn't make myself pick up the phone and tell him no.

Maybe that *did* make me exactly like Patsy Sue Clydehopper.

Neely Kate reached out and squeezed my hand, and I knew she'd said her piece.

"What about Marshall?" she asked. "We can't babysit him all day."

"Crappy doodles," I said with a sigh. "You're right."

"I'm sure he has a cell phone," Neely Kate said. "He can call us if he needs us."

I set my coffee cup down and Muffy perked up. "If he's going to stay here, we need to set some ground rules. But first I need more answers. And I'm going to go get them."

"Sounds like a good idea to me," she said, getting to her feet. "I made him some scrambled eggs and bacon. I'll take them up with you, and we can ambush him together."

"He probably needs to go to the bathroom," I said.

She made a face as she walked over to the toaster. "I'm not goin' in there with him."

"Surely he can pee by himself."

Her cringe suggested she had her doubts. Great. I wasn't helping him pee either.

Marshall was dozing when I opened the door, but his eyes cracked open when we walked into his room, Muffy following behind us. She wasn't growling, but she wasn't relaxed either.

"We brought you some breakfast," Neely Kate said, "but you have to earn it first."

"Neely Kate," I admonished under my breath.

She jerked her gaze to mine. "What? We need to know what he's doin' here, bleedin' on your guest bedsheets."

"I'll pay for the sheets, Lady," he said with a sheepish look.

"You'll do no such thing," I said. "That's nothin' a little bleach won't fix, but I *do* need to know what happened to you."

He pressed his lips together and gave a tight shake of his head. "You're better off not knowin'."

"I take it you're running from Skeeter Malcolm," I said, trying to sound tough.

"If I can just stay here for a few days, I promise I'll leave and won't come back. I'll even leave you plenty of money for your inconvenience."

"And where did that money come from?" Neely Kate asked with her hand on her hip.

"I can't say."

"And can you say which bad guy's gonna show up at our front door lookin' for ya?" she asked.

He looked torn, then finally said, "I thought you were neutral. I thought you were Sweden."

"Switzerland!" Neely Kate said in exasperation, but I knew she was more frustrated by his failure to talk than his weak grasp of geography.

I couldn't help wondering if I should try to force a vision. It would be the smart thing to do. But what if he was right? What if I *was* better off not knowing anything? I could legitimately plead innocence—with both James and the sheriff's department, if it came to that.

I pushed out a breath. "We have to go into town to do some work, which means we have to leave you alone. Here are the rules if you're gonna stay with us. One, you don't tell anyone you're here. Two, don't go callin' your buddy who dropped you off to come hang out with you. Three, you stay in your room and don't answer the door should someone come callin'."

He frowned. "My friend ain't comin' back, if that's what you're worried about. Rusty done left town."

"Without you?" Neely Kate asked in disbelief.

"He couldn't take me with him. I was bleedin' all over his truck."

"No honor among thieves," Neely Kate grumbled, and the look on Marshall's face suggested she wasn't far off.

"I'm going to leave your cell phone," I said, "but I mean it. No callin' *anyone* except for me or Neely Kate."

"Yes, ma'am."

"And I'm gonna need your number before I go."

He gave it to me, and Neely Kate and I both texted him so he'd have our numbers.

"We'll help you get to the bathroom before we go," I said, "but we draw the line at goin' in there with you."

His face turned red. "Yes, ma'am."

"Okay then," I said. "Let's get this over with."

His IV bag was empty, so I steadied my nerves and pulled out the needle. After covering the needle wound with a bandage, I checked his not-so-small wound. Thankfully, I'd gotten over my initial reaction, and I could examine it without feeling like I was going to have a panic attack. The fact that he wasn't covered in blood probably helped. After I rebandaged him, Neely Kate and I helped him hobble to the bathroom.

He shut the door, and we waited in the hall while Muffy sat in the open doorway to his bedroom, watching us.

"I have a bad feeling about this," she said, casting a glance at the door.

"I'm not any more excited about it than you are, but what are our options? Kick him out? Where's he gonna go?"

"So he's our new roommate?" she whisper-hissed.

"No. I don't know …" We were definitely in a pickle. "One day at a time. We'll leave him today and see how it goes."

Her lips pressed tighter, but she didn't say anything.

A few minutes later, he emerged, his face so pale I was terrified he'd pass out before we got him back to bed.

"Try not to get up while we're gone," I said, tucking the covers around him. "If you pass out on the floor, I have no idea how long you'll lie there until we get home."

Neely Kate had run downstairs and returned with his phone and a few other things, including a charger for his phone, setting them up on the bedside table.

"Where's my gun?" he asked, his gaze darting from the phone up to me.

"Somewhere you can't find it," I said. Like in a lockbox in the basement.

"I need it."

"No guns in my house," I said.

"Tell that to the guys comin' after me."

"I will if they show up. You came here because this place is neutral, right? Others will respect that too." He didn't look convinced, so I added, "If I didn't allow guns at the parley between Skeeter Malcolm and Buck Reynolds, I'm sure not allowing them in my own house."

Marshall wisely kept his mouth shut.

Neely Kate pointed to the bedside table. "There's food, water, a thermometer, and medicine. You should be good until we get back with more bandages."

"How long will you be gone?" he asked, looking scared.

"I don't know," I said gently. "But I meant what I said. Don't let anyone know you're here."

"I've got no one to tell." He blinked to hold back tears and I felt sorry for him. What had he done to end up in this situation?

"I'm gonna leave my dog here," I said. "Her name's Muffy and she'll let you know if someone shows up unexpectedly." Then I added, "Plus she's good company."

Muffy was standing next to me, and he gave her a wary look. "Your dog don't like me."

"She's a good guard dog, and you were trespassin'. But now you're a houseguest, and she'll do her best to keep you safe." I glanced down at her and made a motion toward the bed. "Go say hello, Muffy."

She leapt up onto the bed, skirting his bad leg and walking up to his chest.

Marshall watched my tiny dog with a look of terror as she sniffed his neck and face, but then she licked his cheek, and he pushed out a breath and closed his eyes.

"See?" I said. "She likes you. No more fuss over Muffy."

"Thank you, Lady."

I nodded, and Muffy moved to the end of the bed and sat, watching the door as though realizing her duties were about to begin.

THIRTY MINUTES LATER, Neely Kate and I stopped by our landscaping office to pick up the folders for the two clients we had for the day. We'd missed seeing Bruce Wayne, who had likely headed out to a job site a good hour or so earlier. After making a few phone calls during the drive in, Neely Kate found out from the rumor mill that the sheriff's department was looking for Patsy, and Reverend Baker had been sent home from the ER with a lot of pain medication and muscle relaxers.

"So we need to set up interviews with Calvin, then Patsy's mom and her aunt Lucille," I said as I unlocked the office door.

"But we'll have to work the interviews around my lunch with Violet and the kids."

"That shouldn't be a problem," Neely Kate said. "While we're here, I'll get phone numbers for all of the people we need to talk to. We'll probably have to stop by Hebert Manufacturing to talk to Calvin. I heard he went into work today."

"I guess there'd be no point in stayin' home," I said.

"I guess not."

"After I confirm with our clients, I'll start an internet search on Marshall."

"Good idea."

Neely Kate sat at her desk and booted up her computer to look for the phone numbers. I had just finished confirming our client appointments for the morning and had started Googling Marshall when the office door opened, and Joe walked in with a drink tray with coffee cups.

Neely Kate gave him a dark look before returning to her task on the computer.

"Good morning, ladies," he said in a cheerful voice, only I knew him well enough to know it was a little forced.

"Hey, Joe," I said, worried about why he was here. The fact that he wasn't yelling was a good sign.

He handed me a coffee cup, then set the tray on Neely Kate's desk and sat down next to it. "Neely Kate, I think we both said some things we regret."

"Speak for yourself," she said, keeping her gaze on the screen. "I meant every word."

"Okay …," he said, rubbing the back of his neck. "*I* said some things I regret."

Neely Kate kept typing.

"I screwed up, Neely Kate. I'm sorry."

Her gaze lifted to meet his and tears swam in her eyes. "I think you should go."

"Neely Kate …"

"You made your choice, Joe," she said, her voice breaking. "And you chose wrong."

"It's not about choosing," he said. "It was painting, Neely Kate. I figured you wouldn't mind."

She turned back to her screen and resumed her typing.

"I'll cancel with Dena."

"Don't bother. I've already made plans."

He shot me a glance, then turned back to her. "I'm sure Rose won't mind if you cancel."

"They aren't with Rose," she said with an uppity air. "It just so happens I have a date."

His mouth dropped open as though his jaw had become unhinged. "A date? *With who?*"

I stared at her with equal amazement. What was she doing? Did she really plan to tell him about Jed?

"No one you need to concern yourself with. In fact, I've been seeing him for longer than you and Dena have been together, and it never once interfered with me seeing you. But if that's the way things are gonna be, I guess I don't have to worry so much about juggling my schedule."

Joe's eyes widened, and I could see he was struggling to figure out what to address first.

"You need to go," she said. "I have to get my work done if I'm gonna be done in time for my date tonight."

Joe got to his feet and walked over to my desk. "Who's she seein'?"

I cast a nervous glance toward my best friend. "I'm not at liberty to say."

He leaned his hands on my desk. "Not at liberty to say? Why won't either of you tell me?"

"Because it's none of your doggone business!" Neely Kate shouted, still refusing to look at him.

I got up from my seat and gestured toward the door. "I think it's best if you leave."

He started to protest, but I flicked my eyes to the door—a silent promise that we'd talk—and he nodded. Before leaving, he walked back over to his sister and squatted next to her. "Neely Kate," he said softly. "Would you please look at me?"

She ignored him, the clacking of her keyboard the only sound filling the room.

Joe pushed out a sigh, then said, "I'm new to this whole brother thing." He shook his head. "Yeah, I know Kate's my sister, but we never got along, and truth be told, I was a terrible brother to her too. I know I've screwed up several times over, but I'm not goin' anywhere. You're stuck with me. And we all know I'm thickheaded sometimes, but I'm gonna get this right with you. I swear." He stood and leaned over to plant a kiss on top of her head. "If you persist in workin' with Kermit Cooper on the Patsy Sue Clydehopper case, please be careful, okay? There was another murder last night close to the Columbia County line. Not more than a few miles from your house. I don't think it has anything to do with Carol Ann Nelson's death, but we can't be too careful."

Then he grabbed his coffee cup and headed out the door. I followed behind him.

He headed down the sidewalk, stopping when he was out of sight of the office. He looked devastated. "What if I've lost her?"

"You haven't lost her," I said. "But there's no denying she's deeply hurt. If it had only happened once, she would have forgiven you—and she obviously did. How many times have you canceled on her because of Dena?"

Embarrassment filled his eyes, and his gaze flicked to the courthouse across the street. "Three times."

"*Three?*"

"I know …," he said, pushing out a frustrated sigh. "I screwed up."

Three times in less than two weeks? No wonder Neely Kate was pissed. "You broke her trust, and she doesn't trust easily, Joe."

"I know." He looked devastated as he stared at the office entrance.

"Just give her time," I said. "But don't betray her again, because I'm pretty sure she won't give you another chance."

He nodded. We stood there quietly for a moment before he turned to face me. I'd expected this. "Who's she seein'?"

Chapter Seven

I wasn't about to answer him, and it occurred to me that Neely Kate was more pissed than I'd realized. Why else would she have told Joe something that was sure to make him ask uncomfortable questions?

"What?" he finally asked, shuffling his feet a little. "Don't you know who she's seein'?"

"That's Neely Kate's business to tell you, not mine."

"Why hasn't she told me before now?"

"You'll have to ask her that."

He was silent for several seconds. "I screwed up big time."

"Bigger than you know," I said, then crossed my arms. "People have a habit of running out on her, Joe. Her momma, her boyfriends, her stupid husband."

"I didn't run out on her, Rose," he said defensively. "I postponed painting my house."

I shook my head in disbelief. "Do you seriously still see it that way, or are you just tryin' to find a way to make yourself feel better about all of this?"

He started to say something, then wisely shut his mouth.

"She treasures every moment you spend together, and if you don't feel the same way, then maybe you should just leave her be before you hurt her again by picking some woman you just started dating over your sister."

"Is this over Dena?" he asked, starting to get ticked. "Are you jealous of her?"

I stared at him in disbelief. "*Are you serious?*"

Contrition filled his eyes.

I dropped my arms and took a step toward him. "Look," I said with a sharp edge. "I realize that you're still gettin' used to paying for your mistakes, but you need to admit to your screwup and try fixin' it, not find someone else to blame."

He sobered. "You're right."

I pursed my lips. "Well, that's a good start."

He took a second, then said, "Are you two really working to prove Patsy Sue Clydehopper is innocent?"

"Looks like we are."

His mouth twisted to the side. "I don't like it, but I guess there's nothing I can do about it." When I didn't say anything, he said, "And you're workin' with Kermit Cooper?"

"Of course we are."

He shook his head with a frown. "I'd still like to know how that arrangement came to pass. You realize he's the laziest PI in the history of PIs?"

I lifted my eyebrows. "You don't say."

He pushed out a breath and rubbed the back of his neck. "You two are dead set on becoming PIs?"

I almost told him that Neely Kate was the one who was fixated on it, but that would be a half-truth. She'd dragged me into it, sure, but I'd come to realize that I liked it. "Yeah," I said with a smug grin. "We are. And turns out we're pretty good at it." There was something else I needed to ask him about, but I had to keep it casual. "What were you saying about a guy getting killed north of us?"

"A guy was shot right off the country road, a few miles north of you. Looks like he was run off the road and shot trying to crawl away from the accident."

I covered my mouth with my hand while my stomach roiled. "Who was it?"

"We don't know yet. He didn't have any ID on him, but his truck matched the description of a getaway car at a robbery yesterday."

"What kind of robbery?"

"A pawn shop. Ripper Pawn."

That place was owned by Hugh and Kip Wagner, and until very recently, Kip Wagner used to run with Buck Reynolds. This had to be related to Marshall's injury—maybe he'd been injured in the same incident, or maybe the dead man was his friend who'd supposedly fled the county. But while I was relieved James hadn't been a part of it, there was no getting around the fact that it was a sad situation, and one that might get Neely Kate and me into a boatload of trouble. "It sounds so cold-blooded."

"It was. But like I said, I doubt it has anything to do with Patsy Sue and Carol Ann."

"Do you think Patsy killed her cousin?" I asked.

He gave me a wistful look. "Do you remember when we were first together, and you were dead set on proving Bruce Wayne innocent of murder?"

"Yeah," I said softly. "How could I forget?" We'd been so happy then.

He swallowed, looking sad as he said in a low voice, "And do you remember what I told you when you suggested the murder victim's bookie might have killed him?"

I blushed at the memory. We'd been naked in bed. And unbeknownst to me at the time, the bookie had been Skeeter Malcolm. "You told me to be careful about making assumptions. Just because something fits the empty spot doesn't mean it belongs there."

"That's right. Too many people are arrested on sloppy police work based on the easy assumption."

"So you think Patsy's innocent?" I asked.

"I don't have enough evidence to make a determination one way or the other, but you two need to be careful lookin' into Carol Ann's murder. Patsy's a loose cannon. You should get another client." Then he hastily added, "Not that I'm tellin' either of you what to do."

Months ago, I would have blasted him for trying to control me, but now I realized he was genuinely worried about me and Neely Kate and wanted us to be safe. Maybe that was because he'd changed too. Back then, he wouldn't have kindly requested that we be careful. He would have blown up.

"Look at us," I said with a mischievous grin. "We're growin' up."

He laughed. "It's about damn time, don't you think?"

"Yeah."

"Joe!" Dena shouted from across the street. "I've been waiting on you for ten minutes." Dena stalked across the street, took a good look at me, and her eyes narrowed. "I thought you were goin' to make peace with Neely Kate, not have a cozy chat with Rose."

Joe's eyes flew wide as we both realized how this might look. We stood about a foot and a half apart, deep in conversation.

"Dena," I said, "it's not how it looks."

"And how *does* it look?" she asked with both hands on her hips.

I shot a panicked look at Joe, terrified of saying the wrong thing and getting him into more trouble. "Dena, I realize things got a little tense yesterday, but I'd really like for us to get along."

"Things got tense?" she asked with cocked eyebrows. "I'm not sure what you're talkin' about, but if you felt some tension, then maybe you need some time away from Joe."

I shot a stunned look up at Joe, unsure of what to say, and from the look on his face, he was equally at a loss.

"Oh, my stars and garters," Neely Kate exclaimed from in front of our office. "Will you listen to yourself, Dena? Threatened much?" Then, as though she couldn't bother to waste another moment on the woman, she turned her back and shut the door. "Come on, Rose. I got the files we need from your desk. Our first client is waiting." She walked to the passenger side of the truck, her arms loaded with both of our purses and a tote bag.

"I'm sorry, Joe," I whispered as I passed him, walking toward the truck. When I climbed inside, Neely Kate was fuming, and I was pretty sure that Dena wasn't the only one she was ticked at.

"Why were you talkin' to Joe?" she asked once we were on the other side of the square.

I wasn't going to lie. "We were talkin' about you. And the guy who was murdered a few miles from us. And Patsy."

"What about me?"

"I told him he screwed up big time." I took a breath. "Look, you have every right to be ticked at him, but he's devastated that he hurt you. You should give him a second chance."

"He's already done it three times, and I'll bet twenty bucks he'll do it again." Her voice was tight.

"And how do you know that?"

"Because of how he reacted when Dena attacked you. He didn't defend you. He just let her blast you for no good reason."

"We *were* standin' close," I said. "I guess I understand why she jumped to that conclusion."

"Was something goin' on?" she asked.

"No! Of course not! We were talking about …" I took a breath. "Joe told me he was worried about us workin' this case, but he didn't demand we stop, and I thanked him for his concern. Then we laughed at how much we've both grown up since we were able to settle things civilly rather than lashing out like we would have done a few months ago. We probably looked relaxed."

"She's barely been dating him two weeks, and she's already jealous of who he talks to. Either she trusts him or she doesn't, and I'm not falling for any cockamamie stories about trusting him but not the women he's with." She shook her head, getting angrier by the second. "Joe's lettin' her control him. He's found himself another Hilary."

"What? How can you say that?" I asked in shock. "Dena's nothin' like Hilary!"

"Hilary tried to run his life. And now Dena's doin' the same thing and don't you deny it," she said with plenty of attitude. "The next time he has plans with me that don't suit her, he'll cancel again. Mark my words."

I wanted to protest, but I could see she might be right, not that I was happy about it. "I hope you're wrong."

"Hmph," she grunted. "What did he say about the guy who'd been shot?"

"That his truck was run off the road a few miles up the county road from us. He was shot as he was crawling away from the wreckage, murdered in cold blood—"

"Oh my word!"

"I know, but Joe said his truck matched the description of a getaway car used to flee a robbery at Ripper Pawn. Which is owned by Kip Wagner, not James."

"Did he tell you the guy's name?"

"He said he didn't know it, that he didn't have any ID on him."

"Do you think it might have been Marshall's friend?" Neely Kate asked.

"The thought crossed my mind, but I didn't have much time to look into Marshall. He went to Fenton County High School and was in Future Farmers of America. He got a ribbon for entering a calf into a competition. That's as far as I got."

"Not exactly screaming that he's a criminal."

"Exactly," I said. "Joe's pretty sure it's not related to Carol Ann's murder. He also thinks Patsy's unbalanced."

"I *know* she's unbalanced," Neely Kate said. "But she's still innocent."

"Okay," I said. "It's on us to prove it. Did you call her husband yet?"

"Yeah, Calvin says he can see us in his office at 11:34. According to him, she never came home last night."

"Eleven thirty-four? Why the odd time?"

"I don't know, but he told me that we couldn't arrive a minute sooner. He even synchronized our watches."

"But you don't have a watch," I pointed out.

She shot me a grin. "What he doesn't know won't hurt him."

We got through our two appointments in plenty of time and parked in front of the building of Hebert Manufacturing at 11:30.

"Are we really going to wait out here until 11:34?" I asked.

She shrugged. "That's what he said. Not a minute sooner." Then her eyes lit up. "But I think my watch just broke. Let's go see what happens if we show up early."

We headed down a hall toward the offices, and when we entered, I was surprised to see a larger room with eight desks, lined with several offices with closed doors. The only person in sight was a woman who looked like she was in her fifties, although from the appearance of her tiny-waisted dress, she hadn't let herself go. The frown on her face made it clear she wasn't happy to see us. The nameplate on her desk read, *June Goldman, Secretary*, and it was placed square in front of the office that said, *Calvin Clydehopper, Executive Vice President.*

The clock on the wall read 11:32.

"There's *two* of you?" she asked in dismay.

I glanced at Neely Kate, then back at her. "Is that a problem?"

"How can you be so brazen?" she demanded.

"I think there's been a misunderstanding," I said. "We have an 11:34 appointment, ma'am."

She became even more outraged. "Mr. Clydehopper is currently goin' through a personal tragedy. Shame on you girls for tryin' to take advantage of that."

Neely Kate stared at her in disbelief. "How are we takin' advantage of him when we have an appointment?"

"Then why don't I see it on the books?" the older woman asked.

"I don't know," Neely Kate said. "Why don't you ask Calvin since he's the one who made the appointment?"

"I make all the appointments now," she said. "Patsy insists they come through me, and I didn't put you in the books, so run along and find some other man to dally with." Then she made a shooing motion.

I realized she thought we were there to fool around with Calvin in his office. After the wave of nausea passed, I plastered on what I hoped was an official-looking expression and lowered my voice. "Ma'am. I'm Rose Gardner, and this is Neely Kate Rivers. Patsy hired us to help find out who killed her cousin."

Her outrage faded slightly. "I thought the sheriff's department was looking into it."

"And they are," I said in my best reassuring tone, "but the more hands on deck, the better, right?"

Neely Kate leaned forward and said in a subdued tone, "So as you can see, it's very important we speak to Mr. Clydehopper."

Her eyes grew to the size of silver dollars. "You think *he* did it?"

"We're just askin' routine questions, ma'am," Neely Kate said in a tone that made her sound like someone on a cop show.

"In fact, can we ask you a few questions first?" I asked.

Her hand lifted to her chest. "Me?"

"Yeah," I said, making my tone breezier. "When we walked in, you thought we were up to no good with Calvin. Why?"

"Well …," she said, looking flustered. "Everyone else is gone, for one thing."

"Where are they?" Neely Kate asked.

"It's Monday. They're at the weekly staff meeting."

"Why aren't *you* there?" I asked.

"I used to go, but Patsy asked me to stay in the office whenever Calvin's in."

"And screen who has access to him?" I asked.

Her face flushed. "He just can't help himself."

"So you treat him like a three-year-old at daycare?" Neely Kate asked in disbelief.

I shot her a dark look, but she ignored me.

My best friend put a hand on her hip. "Honey, I know a thing or two about men, and here's one thing I know—if they want to cheat, they're going to cheat. You standin' guard isn't gonna stop him."

A hard look filled the woman's eyes. "Like I said, I don't see your name on the books. No appointment, no access." She'd clearly decided our detective story was a ruse. Did women actually lie to get access to Calvin?

Calvin's office was only six feet behind her, and I considered storming past her and barging in, but we needed to handle this differently than we would have in the past. We were professionals now.

Apparently Neely Kate had other ideas. "Calvin Clydehopper!" she shouted. "You get your keister out here right now!"

Seconds later, his office door burst open, and he stood in the doorway with wild eyes. "What?"

June Goldman looked like she wanted to wring our necks. "It looks like your 11:34 appointment is here."

He blinked rapidly, his gaze darting from his secretary to us before returning to his office. "Come in."

He turned around to go back inside, leaving us to follow.

"Keep the door open," June barked.

"You're not the boss of me, June!" Calvin shouted. "I can shut my office door if I want to!" Since I was the last one to enter the room, he shot me a challenging look. "Shut the door."

"*Don't you dare!*" June shouted.

I was more scared of June than Calvin, but we needed answers, so I didn't want to piss him off. "How about I split the difference and leave it halfway open?"

"A quarter," Calvin grunted as he sat in the chair behind his desk.

I did as he asked, relieved that June didn't protest, but then the next thing I knew, she burst in with a stenographer's notebook and a pen, her reading glasses perched on the end of her nose.

"I'll just take a few notes."

Calvin looked fit to be tied, but wisely kept his mouth shut.

"Calvin," I said, doing a poor job of hiding my exasperation, "when was the last time you saw Patsy Sue?"

"After the picnic," he said, shuffling a stack of papers on his desk, clearly flustered. Then he gave Neely Kate a pointed look. "Why do I have to tell all y'all this when I already told the sheriff deputy?"

"Because," Neely Kate said, "like I told you on the phone, we're workin' for *Patsy*."

"Why on earth would Patsy hire y'all to find her cousin's killer? She *hated* Carol Ann, and I mean hated with a capital 'H.'"

I frowned. This wasn't exactly helping Patsy's case.

Neely Kate shifted her weight. "By chance, did you happen to mention that to the sheriff's deputy?"

"I told him they didn't get along, but that was no secret. Anybody who didn't know must have figured it out at the picnic yesterday. But I didn't tell the cops that she *hated* her. I'm no fool. I know my wife's the prime suspect."

Seemed like an intelligent man would realize why a "prime suspect" would hire a pair of detectives to clear her name, but I doubted he'd thank me for saying so.

"Do you think she did it?" Neely Kate asked.

He leaned back in his chair and pulled a white handkerchief from his pocket and dabbed his forehead. "Patsy Sue's capable of a great many things, but cold-blooded murder's not one of them." He tucked the handkerchief back into his pocket.

"You said you saw Patsy after the picnic," I said. "I take it you both went home?"

"Yeah. We were covered in pies and fried chicken. We needed to shower and change, but Patsy was none too happy with the idea of messing up Baby Spice. She didn't want grease and pie filling on the leather seats, so we called an Uber."

My eyebrows shot up. "Henryetta has Uber?"

Neely Kate leaned closer to me and said as an aside, "Officer Ernie drives it on his off days to earn some extra money."

"But Officer Ernie was on duty," I said, casting a glance at her. "He was in the thick of it."

"Literally, from the sounds of it," Neely Kate added.

"Yeah, he was," Calvin said. "He needed to change too, so he dropped us off before he went home."

"Wait," I said, holding up a hand. "You said you took an Uber. Did he charge you for the ride?"

"Yeah, but he gave us a discount on account it was in the back of his police car and not his Trans Am."

I was pretty doggone sure that was against the law, but I'd figure out what to do with that piece of information later. "Okay, so Ernie took you home and then what?"

"Patsy was a-hollerin' the whole way home. Ernie asked her to keep it down, but she wasn't havin' any of that and told him off too."

I almost felt sorry for the officer. The Clydehoppers lived on the edge of town. He'd probably spent a good fifteen minutes in the car with them.

"Then what happened?" Neely Kate asked.

"We fought over who got to take the first shower, and Patsy won. Again."

"I know for a fact that you have two showers in your house, Calvin," Neely Kate said with a glare. "You could have taken one downstairs."

I shot a glance to Neely Kate, wondering how she knew about this other shower and its location, but shook my head. Who was I to question her mystical powers?

"You said she won again," I said. "Does she usually win?"

He pointed to his secretary. "Exhibit A. Patsy hired her to guard my office."

I wondered what kind of pull Patsy Sue had that she could influence the hiring decisions of a company neither she nor her husband owned. "So Patsy took the shower first and you waited," I said. "Then you took one after her."

"Yeah," he said with a sheepish look, staring down at his desk. He fiddled with the corner of a stack of papers.

"You called Carol Ann while Patsy was in the shower," Neely Kate said in an accusatory tone. "And Patsy caught you."

His gaze jerked up. "I had to make sure she was okay."

"And was she?" I asked, trying to soften my question.

"She was upset, of course. Patsy has a way of gettin' under her skin."

"And smashin' pie all over the outside of it," Neely Kate said under her breath as she scribbled in her notebook.

Calvin looked properly chastised, but Neely Kate looked like she had a bone to pick, and we wouldn't get in his good graces if she carried on accusing him of cheating on his wife.

"Neely Kate, why don't you go outside to ask June some questions while I talk to Calvin about his afternoon with Patsy."

Her mouth gaped as she jerked her head to face me, but then she cast a quick glance at Calvin, who already looked pink-cheeked and irritated. Understanding filled her eyes. "Yeah. That's a good idea. Let's go back to your desk, June."

"I'm not leavin' him alone with this woman."

I could understand her distrust of Calvin—obviously he'd used his office for all his rendezvous—but now she was besmirching *my* character. "The only interest I have in Calvin Clydehopper is what he knows about Patsy." Then I softened my tone. "June, if you're acting like Calvin's guard dog, then you obviously care about Patsy, right?"

"I had no idea she was a suspect."

"We want to help clear her name. That's all. If you let us do our jobs, we'll get to the bottom of this a whole lot sooner."

She nodded and dabbed the corner of her eye with a wadded tissue she pulled from her pocket. "Okay."

I gave her a warm smile. "Good. Now you two go get started."

June walked out first with Neely Kate following behind. She cast an apologetic glance at me as she shut the door.

I sat down in the chair in front of Calvin's desk. "Calvin, I have no idea what kind of relationship you have with your wife. Honestly, it's none of my business, but there are certain things I *need* to know to help Patsy."

He cast a glance at the door. "I don't want this gettin' all over town."

"I promise we won't take what we learn from you and gossip about it."

He watched me for a moment as though waiting for some cartoonish confirmation that I was lying. After a few seconds, he nodded and swallowed. "If it will help Patsy …"

I gave him a smile of encouragement.

"Patsy and I have never had a … traditional marriage."

"How so?" I asked, cringing. I hated being intrusive, but I suspected these were things I needed to know.

"We used to have an open relationship. Patsy knows I like a little variety and she used to tolerate it. In fact, she used to go to Little Rock and seek out a few relationships of her own. But she's become less tolerant."

"Hence June," I said.

"Exactly." He looked up at me with pleading eyes. "Carol Ann didn't mean anything to me."

"But you slept with her anyway?" I asked, working hard to keep the accusation out of my voice.

He looked down at his desk and nodded. "She was … fun."

"When did Patsy find out?"

"Yesterday when Carol Ann sent her two photos of us."

"She sent them after you got home from the picnic?" I asked.

"Yeah. My phone call only riled her up. She said she wanted the whole world to know about us. The next thing I knew, she'd sent Patsy those photos."

"What time was that?" I asked.

"About three."

That didn't sound good, especially since Patsy hadn't called me until after seven. That was four hours unaccounted for. "Carol Ann checked into the motel on Saturday night. Did you know that?"

His cheeks turned pinker as he nodded. "I went to see her Saturday night. That's when she got the photos."

Oh crap. "And something in the photos told Patsy they'd been taken recently."

"Yeah. She recognized my …" He coughed. "Tie."

"How did she—oh …" I felt my cheeks flush. But this was no time for modesty. I might have just figured out who'd supplied the murder weapon. "What did the tie look like?"

His head jerked up and anger filled his eyes. "What difference does it make?"

"Humor me," I said with a soft smile. I didn't want to tell him the real reason. As far as I knew, the sheriff's department hadn't released the cause of death. "I want to verify with Patsy Sue that's what she saw. Just dottin' the i's and crossin' the t's."

He cleared his throat. "It was blue. With white whales on it."

This case had just gotten a whole lot more interesting.

Chapter Eight

I tried to hide my reaction. Was Calvin the real murderer? But if so, why would he have told me about the tie and the photos? And why wasn't he using Patsy as a convenient scapegoat? "Did Patsy know Carol Ann was at the Broken Branch Motel?"

"I don't know. She didn't find out from me."

"Could she have scrolled through your texts?"

He shook his head. "I deleted them as soon as they came in." He paused. "Well, she sent the photos to me too, and I kept them. I figured Patsy had already seen them. The harm was done."

That meant Patsy must have found out where Carol Ann was staying from someone else. Who? Carol Ann herself?

"I take it Patsy wasn't too happy."

He grimaced. "No. She came tearin' out of our bedroom, angrier than I've ever seen her, throwing around a bunch of things ..." Guilt filled his eyes. "She said she was gonna kill us both, but she didn't really mean it," he said emphatically.

"Do you know when Carol Ann got back into town?"

"Uh ... early last week. I saw her twice before Saturday."

"Where did you see her? Another motel?"

His face flushed. "Not exactly."

I narrowed my eyes. "What does that mean?"

"I met her out by the lake. On a side road."

"So you don't know where she was staying before Saturday night?"

"I didn't think to ask. I just knew she was back in town."

"Did she tell you why she was back or what she'd been up to?"

The crimson on his cheeks deepened. "Uh … we didn't do much talkin', if you know what I mean."

I gave a short nod, averting my gaze. "Did you know that Carol Ann was takin' photos of you on Saturday night?"

He shook his head. "No. I'm not that stupid. I'm not sure how she managed it, but they weren't selfies."

Oh, mercy. I couldn't believe what I was about to ask. "I'm gonna need you to send them to me."

"Why?" he asked in panic.

"Because I want to see where she might have hidden the camera. Maybe it caught footage of whoever killed her."

He hesitated for several seconds, a war raging on his face, but finally released a loud groan and pulled out his phone. "I'll send them in an email."

"Okay," I said, then gave him my email address.

He tapped into his phone. After nearly half a minute of tapping, he set it down on his desk and my phone buzzed with an incoming email. I opened the email to ensure it had attachments, then closed it before they could load.

"So after Patsy threw her fit, what happened next?"

"She left."

"And that was around three o'clock? Did you see or talk to her after that?"

"No."

"Do you know where she is now?"

"I don't know. Is that all?" Calvin asked, retrieving his handkerchief again. His face was covered in beads of sweat, and damp spots were spreading under the armpits of his blue shirt. He looked like he'd run a half marathon. "The office staff's about to return."

I was about to leave—he'd clearly told me all he intended to—but then realized I hadn't gotten Calvin's alibi. "What were you doin' after Patsy left?"

"I took a nap and watched some TV."

I tried to hide my disbelief. How had he taken a nap after that? "And how did you find out that Carol Ann was dead?"

"When the sheriff's deputy showed up at my house last night looking for Patsy."

"Do you happen to know which deputy it was?"

He grimaced, but it was obvious he didn't want to think about it. "Uh … Randy?"

I perked up. "Randy Miller?"

"Yeah. That was it."

That could work out in my favor. I was actually friends with Randy. I pulled a business card out of my purse—not the glittering ones Neely Kate had made that said Sparkle Investigations, but a plain white card with my name and number and the name of Kermit's agency—and slid it across the desk to him. "If you think of anything else you think might be helpful, will you give me a call?"

He picked up the card and put it in his desk drawer. "Yeah. Sure thing."

I found Neely Kate in front of June's desk, her mouth hanging open. A young woman was telling Neely Kate a story while June shot daggers at her back.

"And there Calvin was on his hands and knees, his drawers at his ankles, and the girl was sitting on his back like he was a pony while she smacked his butt cheek with a riding crop. And then you'll *never* guess what she did with that thing …"

"And we don't want to know," I quickly inserted.

Neely Kate gave me the stink eye. "Speak for yourself."

"We don't actually need to know all the details about Calvin's flings," I said.

"Flings?" the young woman asked with a raised eyebrow. "Is that what he's calling them?"

"You disagree?" I asked.

"That's enough of this nonsense," June said, her steely eyes staring down the young woman. "Don't you need to get back to the meeting?"

The young woman looked properly chastised as she picked up a notebook and pen from a desk and hurried toward a hall close to the exit.

The tension on June's face faded slightly. "Calvin has had a wandering eye for years. But his … indiscretions … have been a lot shorter lately."

Something about her choice of words struck me. "When we first arrived, you thought we were here to have a … fling with Calvin. Why?"

"Women just show up sometimes. But they're different from the ones he used to bring around. I'm sure they're prostitutes." She tsked.

Neely Kate's eyes widened. "You thought we were prostitutes?"

June had the good sense to look embarrassed. "They would show up during the staff meeting."

"How did he get these prostitutes to drop by?" Neely Kate asked. "Last time I checked, there wasn't an app for that."

"I'm not sure," the older woman said, curling her upper lip. "I never asked."

I handed her a business card. "If you think of anything that might help Patsy, give me or Neely Kate a call."

She nodded.

Neely Kate and I headed out to the truck, remaining silent until we were shut inside the cab.

"I hope you got more information than I did," Neely Kate said, "because other than the prostitute twist, I got squat."

"You'll never believe what I found out." I told her about the photos and the tie.

"I knew Calvin had a wandering eye, but I had no idea he'd been with so many women. It certainly makes the prostitute angle even more likely," Neely Kate said. "How many women in this town would *want* to sleep with him?"

She had a point. "I suppose with the tight rein June and Patsy have on that man, it's the only way he can get women."

She snorted. "Plus, he looks like a pasty sack of flour."

There *was* that.

"So," Neely Kate said, "other than the fact that Calvin could potentially be a suspect too, we've got diddly to clear Patsy."

Looked like it.

Chapter Nine

"How about you drop me back at the office before you go eat lunch with Violet?" Neely Kate said. "I'll grab some lunch with Jed and see if he'll take me to see Patsy's mother and aunt."

"What if someone sees you together?"

She shrugged. "I'm tired of hiding him. I've got nothin' to be ashamed of."

"What about Joe?"

Her face hardened. "I'm *done* carin' what that man thinks."

"Neely Kate …"

"No. He made it clear *who* his priority is."

The stubborn look on her face made it clear there would be no swaying her decision. "Well, just be careful."

She hesitated. "If more guys turn up, it might be a good idea to have someone we can call for help, for backup. We both know and trust Jed. Even if he's still with Skeeter, he wouldn't betray us."

No, he'd proven that before. "You're right, but don't tell Jed why yet. And see if he knows anything about the guy who was shot close to the county line."

A grave look washed over her face. "Yeah."

I parked on the side street next to our office. "I'll let you know when I'm done. If you're still meetin' with Patsy's mother and aunt, I'll do more diggin' into Marshall, but first things first. I want to ask Randy Miller about the case. I'll put in a to-go order at Merilee's for Violet and the kids, then give him a call while I'm waiting."

"Okay," she said. "Be careful."

"You too." I sent Violet a text to let her know I was running behind but would be bringing food over, to which she immediately responded, BLESS YOU.

Neely Kate and I both hopped out of the truck. She headed into the office while I walked across the street to the café. After putting in the order, I walked across the street to the park bench in front of the courthouse to make my call.

"Rose," Randy said when he answered. "How are you?"

"I'm good. What's new with you?"

"Things are good. Well, better than good. I'm datin' someone right now."

I squealed with excitement. "Really? Who?"

"Margi Romano."

"Romano … is she any relation to the new vet, Levi Romano?"

"Yeah, she's his sister. She's gonna help him run his office, but she's been here for about a month. I met her at the DMV when she was changing her license."

"That's weird," I said. "We dated a few times, and he never mentioned his sister had moved here too."

He paused, obviously unsure of how to respond to that. "So what can I do for you?" he asked.

I cringed, feeling guilty. "I'm sure you've heard Patsy Sue Clydehopper hired us to clear her of murdering her cousin."

He chuckled. "I hope you got your money up front, because she's gonna be needin' it for bail."

"So you found her?"

"No, but we will," he said with an assurance I wasn't sure I liked.

"I'm wondering if you can help me with a few things."

"You can ask. No guarantee I'll answer."

"Fair enough," I said. "First, was strangulation with that tie the cause of death?" We'd been running with that assumption, but I was reminded of my conversation with Joe that morning. It was just that: an assumption.

"The state coroner hasn't said yet."

I wasn't surprised. I'd learned from Mason it usually took a few days. "But what theory are y'all runnin' with for the cause of death?"

He laughed. "You know I can't tell you that."

"Okay," I said, "tell me this. Did you find any hidden cameras in the motel room?"

He was silent for a moment. "What makes you ask?"

Did that pause mean they'd found some and he didn't like that I knew or that they hadn't found any because they hadn't thought to look? I was going with the latter. I pulled the phone away from my ear, put him on speaker, and opened up my email from Calvin. "I have my sources. I take it you didn't look."

There was a long pause before he said, "No."

"If I give you a point in the right direction, maybe you'll feel up to sharing information with me sometime in the future," I said, then braced myself as I opened the photos. Oh, lordy.

No wonder Patsy Sue had lost it. I squinted, trying to see as little of the action as possible. "I suspect there's a camera still hidden in there. Look at the top left corner of the photo of the big deer, over the dresser."

"How do you know about the camera?" he asked, turning serious.

"Like I said, I have my sources. This was a freebie, but if that camera helps ID the killer, I'm hoping you'll let me know before you announce it to the media."

"Yeah. If we find something, I'll let you know."

"Thanks." I hung up and headed back into the café. The food was ready, so I paid and was heading out the door as Dena was heading in.

I tried to hide my surprise at seeing her, unsure how to act. Before Joe, I would have told her hello, maybe exchanged some pleasantries before continuing on my way. But it was obvious that Dena had issues with me, and I wasn't sure talking to her at the entrance to downtown Henryetta's most popular restaurant was the best idea.

She made the decision for me. "Rose," she said in a curt tone.

"Dena, about this morning …"

She lifted her chin. "There's nothing to discuss."

"But I know you—"

"I said there was nothing to discuss," she snapped, then pushed past me toward the counter.

I walked out onto the sidewalk, worried I'd just lost Dena as a friend.

ASHLEY AND MIKEY were waiting at the door when I arrived, and they ran out to meet me.

"We're hungry, Aunt Rose!" Ashley said as I got out of the truck. "We didn't think you were *ever* goin' to get here!"

"Well, I'm here now," I said with a grin.

Violet was lying on the sofa, propped up with pillows and covered with an afghan. I had to hide my surprise when I saw how pale she looked. But I forced a huge smile and held up the takeout bags.

"I brought your favorite from Merilee's."

She grinned. "Her pot roast?"

"Of course." I went into the kitchen and set the bags on the counter, and the kids followed behind. "Hey," I said enthusiastically, "how about we have a picnic?"

"We just had a picnic yesterday, Aunt Rose," Ashley said.

"That one was outside. This one will be inside."

She wrinkled her nose. "An inside picnic?"

"It'll be fun. Can you get something to drink for you and Mikey? I'll get a blanket."

"Okay."

I grabbed a quilt out of the linen closet, but I had second thoughts when I saw Violet dozing. Her eyes cracked open as I reentered the living room and squatted next to her. "Maybe you'd rather I take the kids outside so you can nap."

She smiled and reached for my hand. "No. Let's have our inside picnic. There'll be enough time for sleepin' later."

A knot lodged in my throat, and I didn't know what to say to that.

"It's okay, Rose. I know I'm dyin', and Ashley knows it too. There's no point hidin' it."

I swiped a tear from my cheek. "It's just takin' some getting used to."

"You'll have a lifetime to get used to it. Let me have what I want."

I laughed at that. "You've been gettin' what you want for practically your entire life."

A twinkle filled her eyes. "So why stop now? Spread out the blanket already."

Ashley and Mikey helped me spread out the quilt, and the three of us sat on the floor while Violet stayed on the sofa. The kids ate their chicken strips and macaroni and cheese, while Violet picked at her pot roast and vegetables. Finally, she handed the takeout container to me, looking like she was about to pass out.

"Vi," I said, trying to hide my worry. "Why don't you take a nap?"

"Okay," she said, "but I want to go out in the backyard to do it."

I gave her a look of surprise.

"You can lay the quilt under the mimosa tree. Ashley said there was a nice breeze. I thought the kids could play in the little wading pool and the sprinkler."

"Okay, kids," I said as I got to my feet. "You heard your momma. Go put your swimsuits on and let's go outside."

Twenty minutes later, I helped Violet outside to the blanket I'd spread under the tree. Mikey and Ashley were running through the oscillating sprinkler on the opposite side of the yard, but I noticed Ashley had her eye on us as we headed for the quilt. Violet's arm was so thin, I worried I'd break it if I held on too tight. She practically collapsed onto the quilt, and I helped situate a pillow under her head.

"Are you comfortable?" I asked. "The ground's so hard."

"Stop fussing over me," she said softly as she turned her head to watch her children. "Now lie down with me."

"You're using this dyin' thing to your full advantage to boss me around," I teased as I sat beside her. It was silly, but I figured it would make everything the smallest bit better if I could make her laugh or even smile.

"At least it's good for something." She turned back to give me an ornery grin. "Now lie down next to me like I asked."

"Don't you want me to watch the kids?"

"They're fine," she said. "They're in a fenced yard. They're not going anywhere."

I did as she requested, leaving six inches between us, but as soon as I was settled, she reached out and laced her fingers through mine.

"The mimosa flowers are so pretty, don't you think?" she asked. "Such tiny, tenacious things." She paused and squeezed my hand. "A lot like you." She turned to face me. "I'm countin' on your tenacity, Rose."

I stared at her in confusion.

"Mike's gonna give you a hard time after I'm gone. He's gonna do his best to keep you away from the kids, but I need you to fight for them. I need you to make sure they don't forget me … and that they always know how much you and I love them. Will you do that for me?"

My mouth dropped open. "Violet …"

"Rose. Please. I need you to fight him. Will you do it?"

"Yes. Of course. I hated stayin' away from them while you were in Texas. Of course I'll fight for them."

"Thank you," she said with so much relief it made my heart hurt. "I'm having an attorney draw up a new will, but I'm worried he'll contest it." She gave a tiny shake of her head. "He's worried you're associating with criminals. I told him that all of that's behind you, but he won't listen to reason."

I swallowed, knowing I needed to come clean, but I couldn't find the words.

"But there's more to it," she said. "There's something else goin' on with him, but I don't have the energy to figure out what it is."

"Something *shady*?" I asked in disbelief. Sure, I knew he'd done something foolish when he was young and stupid, but hadn't he learned his lesson?

"Shady?" she chuckled, then started to cough. Her coughing continued and didn't stop.

I wrapped an arm around her back and helped her sit up. When she continued to cough, I snatched up the water bottle I'd brought out earlier and handed it to her.

She took a sip and her coughing settled down. I rubbed her back, my gaze settling on Ashley and Mikey. They'd stopped playing and stood watching their mother with fear in their eyes.

"Your momma's okay," I said.

Violet nodded. "Aunt Rose is right," she said in a quiet voice. "Go back to playin'."

They reluctantly turned back to the sprinkler, but I continued to rub soft circles on her back.

"I don't have long, Rose," she finally said, keeping her gaze on the kids, who were now shrieking with laughter. "I'm usin' everything within me to hang on until the will's done and signed, but after that …"

My hand froze and panic rose up inside me. "No."

The corners of her mouth tipped up, but she refused to look at me. "Your denial won't stop it from happenin'."

"I can't believe you're just givin' up, Vi. Get a second opinion. Let's go to the Mayo Clinic. I'll take you."

She turned to face me, grabbing my hand. "No, Rose. No more doctors. I wasted so much time and put you through unnecessary pain for nothin'."

"I'll do it again," I insisted, my voice breaking. "I'll give you as much bone marrow as you need."

She lifted her hand to my cheek and her thumb swiped away a tear. "I know you will, but the chances are so slim, Rose. Ten percent. I lost months with my babies. Why would I give up more time for a measly ten percent?" Her chin quivered. "Them seein' me like this is bad enough. I won't put them through anything worse." Then she lowered back down onto the blanket, tugging me with her.

We lay on our backs, our hands linked again as we stared up at the tree canopy over our heads, and I couldn't help wondering how much time she had left and what she planned to put in her new will.

VIOLET HAD BEEN NAPPING for nearly an hour under the tree. The kids were ready to go inside, so I kissed Violet on the forehead and took them inside to change. I put Mikey down for his nap, and then Ashley and I grabbed a chapter book and took it into the backyard. We settled in a hammock under the mimosa tree, several feet from Violet.

Ashley snuggled into my side and started to read quietly out loud while I listened in amazement. I couldn't believe how well she read for a six-year-old, and somehow I'd missed it—all because Mike had kept the kids from me.

She stopped reading and looked up at me with her big blue eyes, looking so much like her mother it stole my breath.

"I've missed you, Aunt Rose."

"I've missed you too. I'm sorry I didn't do a very good job of spending time with you lately, but I promise it won't happen again. I'm here whenever you need me."

Ashley pressed the back of her head into my chest. "My momma's dyin'."

My arm tightened around her. "I know. How do you feel about that?"

"Sad."

"Me too." I glanced down at her and tucked a stray strand of blond hair behind her ear. "You know, your momma is my big sister."

"I know that, Aunt Rose," she said as though I was a fool.

"Just like you're Mikey's big sister. Your momma used to look out for me and make sure I was okay. You could do that for Mikey." But even as I said it, I worried I was putting too much pressure on her. "You need your brother, Ashley, and he needs you. You'll always need each other, even when you're bigger. Even when you fight."

"Until we die too," she said with a frown, then lifted her hand to my cheek. "You won't have a sister anymore."

A burning lump clogged my throat and my eyes stung with tears. "No," I whispered, "I won't."

"Mikey and me will be here for you too, Aunt Rose."

I squeezed her tightly, and her arms slid around my chest and back.

She started to cry, and I held her until she settled down, stroking her back and hair. When I snuck another glance over at Violet, she was watching us with tears in her eyes.

"Thank you," she mouthed.

I nodded as tears streamed down my own cheeks. I wasn't sure I could do this, but I didn't really have a choice.

A little while later, Ashley and I helped Violet up and into the house, getting her settled onto the sofa again.

"You go on back to work," Violet said. "I'm gonna take a good long nap, and Mike will be home any minute now."

I glanced around the living room, wondering if I should stay.

"I can tell what you're thinkin'," Violet said. "Go back to work. Maybe you can come back in a day or two."

"Yes, of course. But I can start some laundry before I go," I said. "Or start dinner for tonight."

"I've got a freezer full of meals from the church, and Mike got the laundry caught up last night. We're fine, Rose."

"Okay." I gave her a kiss goodbye, but she held me close when I started to pull away.

"You're wrong, you know," she murmured. "People can't help loving you, Rose. They're drawn to you, and even if they fail you, I'll always be with you."

I hurried for the door, giving Ashley a quick hug, then bolted for the truck before I broke down into tears again.

Chapter Ten

Since I'd been gone nearly three hours, my first thought was to check on Neely Kate. I checked my phone and found several messages. She said that she and Jed were having a hard time tracking down Patsy's mother and her aunt, so they'd switched their focus and were looking for her sister down in Pickle Junction.

I wasn't sure what else to do for Patsy's case, so I decided to work on Marshall's. I was half-tempted to drop by the pawn shop and see if I could find any clues there, but I didn't want anything tying me or Neely Kate to this mess. We needed to fly under the radar. The question was whether to go back to the office or out to the farm to check on Marshall, but that was quickly answered when I listened to the rest of my voice messages. A client who was due to have her backyard landscaped in a few days had called asking for yet another substitution. I needed to head back to the office to figure out the cost difference as well as the availability of the plants.

After sorting it all out and calling Bruce Wayne to let him know about the changes, I settled in at my desk to dig up more information on Marshall.

I'd already figured out that he attended—or used to attend—Fenton County High School and had been in FFA. The *Henryetta Gazette* published the high school's honor roll every semester, but Marshall's name had never appeared on the list. Based on the little information I found about him, it didn't look like he played any sports either, and his Facebook profile only had sporadic posts. Most of the public posts showed him at FFA events. In one of them, he was standing next to a dead deer and holding a shotgun.

Basically, I'd found squat.

I was staring at my computer, about to shut it down and head home, when my phone rang and Neely Kate's name appeared on the screen.

"How's Violet doin'?" she asked first thing.

"Not good," I said, fighting the urge to cry. "Not good at all."

"Would you rather Jed and I work this case instead?" she asked. "Then you can spend more time with Vi."

I sucked in a breath. I was tempted. "How about we play it by ear? I offered to stay and help with laundry and start dinner, but she practically kicked me out, saying Mike had gotten the laundry caught up and the church had given them plenty of meals."

"Okay …," she said reluctantly. "But if you change your mind, the offer stands."

"Have you had any luck?"

"We finally got ahold of Patsy's sister, Poppy, but the two don't get along. She's also not close to Carol Ann, so she has no idea when she first got back to town. While we were there, Poppy got ahold of her momma and she agreed to meet us tomorrow morning at ten. She's gonna convince Carol Ann's momma to come too."

"That's great. We need to work on Patsy's alibi," I said. "We should try calling her again."

"I already did and she didn't answer."

"Huh. So we're temporarily stalled."

"Maybe. Jed and I have one more place to try, but I'm callin' about something else. Marshall called me a little while back."

My heart skipped a beat. "Is everything okay?"

"He said he's running a high fever and wants one of us to come home."

I kept thinking about Dermot saying the kid might not make it. "I should go check on him. Maybe I'll call Dermot too."

"I already called him, although he wasn't happy to hear from me. He called in a stronger antibiotic under your name."

"He did? He's not a doctor."

"No, but he's a nurse practitioner, so he can do that. Slight problem, though." She hesitated. "He called it into the Piggly Wiggly."

I groaned. Last winter I'd been banned from the Piggly Wiggly, and I hadn't tried to go back since. "Can't we get him to call it in somewhere else?"

"I already asked him, and he said it's the only pharmacy that takes his prescriptions without askin' questions."

"Well … it has been over a half year. Maybe they forgot."

"Yeah," she said with a forced exuberance. "I bet they have."

"Liar." I'd had a couple of incidents at the grocery store. The last one had ended with me being arrested for vandalism and evading an officer. In reality, I'd recognized a potential bank robber from one of my visions. When I took off running after him, my cart got tangled with Officer Ernie's and my frozen turkey knocked down a display of cans like a bowling ball. Mason had gotten the charges dropped, but as far as I knew, the ban still stood.

"Okay," she said, lowering her voice. "Wear the hat I left in the backseat of your truck and sneak in and out. No one will even notice you. If you make a beeline to the pharmacy counter and get the drugs, then who cares if you get caught on the way out?"

She sounded a lot more confident than I felt. "Yeah. You're right."

"Thatta girl." She rushed on. "As soon as Jed and I get done chasin' one more lead, we'll head home."

"Actually," I said, turning off my computer, "if you and Jed want to go out to dinner or something, don't rush home on my account. I'd already planned on spendin' the evening alone."

"But you'll be stuck with Marshall."

"There's no reason for both of us to babysit him. At least one of us can have fun tonight."

"I feel guilty leavin' you."

"Please," I said. "The only reason he's at our house right now is because I insisted on pullin' the Lady in Black out of mothballs. If I need you, I'll call."

"We could come hang out with you."

"I'm plannin' on curlin' up on the sofa with Ben & Jerry's and a movie."

"Now I really need to stay home," she said. "It must have been awful with Violet. I don't want to leave you alone."

I rubbed my forehead. "It was rough, but selfishly, that's not the only thing that has me down."

She paused for a moment. "Skeeter."

My chest ached. "I know I'm gonna have to tell him no, Neely Kate. Mike's gonna fight me on seein' the kids, and Violet begged me to fight for them. She's even changin' something in her will to make sure he can't keep me away. But if word got out that I'm seein' him …"

"Mike will have grounds to keep you from them."

"Yeah," I said, sounding as dejected as I felt.

"Maybe I should come home, Rose."

"I'm already livin' under a mountain of guilt. Don't add more to the pile."

"Jeanne."

I didn't say anything. I didn't need to.

"It wasn't our fault."

"I know," I lied. "I'm gonna go get Marshall's medicine and then get to the farm to check on him. You kids have fun," I added in a teasing tone.

"Rose …"

"I'm fine. I promise."

WHEN I PULLED into the Piggly Wiggly parking lot, I parked in the back, worried if I parked too close to the door, someone would see the landscaping company's logo painted on the side. Leaning over the backseat, I'd expected to find the ball cap Neely Kate had been using on job sites, but the hat in the back was floppy, straw, and had a wide brim decorated with a pattern of clear and pink rhinestones. While a floppy hat would do more to hide my face, the rhinestones were sure to be noticed.

I jammed it on my head and grabbed my purse, then made my way toward the closest doors, my heart hammering in my chest. Why was I so nervous about getting kicked out of this stupid grocery store? Shoot, I'd been nearly kicked out of Walmart a few weeks ago. This was nothing.

Filled with a new confidence, I walked through the door as bold as I pleased, but I wasn't eager to tempt fate, so I tugged the brim down a little as I grabbed a handbasket and passed the cashiers.

So far, so good, I thought as I headed down the produce aisle, toward the aisle with bandages at the back of the store. Fighting the floppy brim to see, I grabbed a few boxes of large square gauze bandages, a couple of rolls of medical tape, and a large tube of antibiotic ointment for good measure. I was about to go pick up the prescription when I saw an endcap of dog toys and treats. I hadn't gotten Muffy a new toy in ages, and I figured I'd get her a reward for babysitting Marshall all day. I picked a stuffed squirrel that made crinkling noises and a bag of chew sticks, then headed to the counter.

There were a surprising number of customers for a late afternoon on a Monday, but I figured that would work in my favor. Nevertheless, I still wasn't happy to see there was someone in front of me at the pharmacy counter.

"Can I take this with soup?" an elderly man asked the woman ringing him up.

"The medication says to take with food," she said, giving her attention to the register.

"But soup's not food," the elderly man said. "It's liquid."

The clerk looked exasperated. "It's food. Besides, soup usually has chunks of meat and vegetables."

"But I like the tomato kind. There's no chunks."

The clerk gave the man a hard stare. "It's food."

"But—"

Transferring my basket to my left hand, I approached the elderly man and shifted the hat back on my head so I could give him a warm smile. "I think the pharmacy tech is telling you that you just need to have something in your stomach when you take your pills."

"Then why didn't she just say so?" he demanded, then squinted his eyes.

"I've been tryin' to!" she said in a loud voice.

"I think this is just a simple misunderstandin'," I insisted, then flashed the clerk a smile. If I stood up for her, she'd hopefully be more lenient if she recognized my name.

The older man stared at me like I was a circus oddity. "Why are you covering your face with that hat?"

My face flushed. "I work outside in the heat. A lady should shield her face from the sun."

"You're in the damn store," he grumped. "No sun in here."

I took a step back. So much for offering my help.

He finally took his bag and hobbled away, and I walked back up to the counter and lowered my voice. "I'm here to pick up a prescription."

"Name?" the clerk asked.

"Rose. Rose Gardner."

Her eyes went round. "Aren't you …?"

I leaned on the counter and pleaded. "Can you give me my prescription? Please."

She shook her head, her eyes wide. "I've heard about you."

She stared at me as though I was the boogeyman. What on earth had they been saying about me?

"Look," I said. "There was a mistake when the prescription was called in here, but I don't want to cause trouble. If you'll just give me my medicine, I'll be on my way. I promise not to come back."

She gave me an apologetic grimace. "I'm gonna have to call security."

Piggly Wiggly had security now? "Didn't you take an oath to do no harm?" I asked. "Isn't withholding medication doin' harm?"

She started pressing numbers while shaking her head. "That's the Hippocratic oath, and I ain't no doctor."

"Are you willing to risk a lawsuit?" asked a man as he approached the counter. All of the breath left my chest when I recognized his voice. "My client is entitled to her medication."

I lifted the brim of my floppy hat, stunned to see I hadn't had an auditory hallucination.

Mason Deveraux stood at the counter next to me, wearing dress pants and a long-sleeved button-down shirt that was open at the collar. But he wasn't looking at me. His full attention was on the clerk.

"Client?" the woman asked. "Lawsuit?"

"Everyone is entitled to health care," Mason said.

"That ain't true," she said, starting to recover. "Just last week my momma's doctor of twenty years kicked her out on account of she ain't got no insurance and she was behind on her payments."

Mason glanced down at her name tag before shifting his gaze up to meet hers. "Stephanie ...," he said in a softer voice. "May I call you Stephanie?"

She nodded, looking anxious.

"It's obvious what happened to your mother is a travesty, so why not try to right a wrong by giving Ms. Gardner her medication?"

"I'm not supposed to."

He leaned closer and lowered his voice. "This country was built by men and women who stood up for the downtrodden.

You, Stephanie, can take the first step in standing up for patients' rights. All it takes is giving this poor woman her medication."

She mulled over his words for a moment, then cast a nervous glance behind her before asking, "Are you picking up medication too?"

"Yes. For my mother, Maeve Deveraux."

Her mouth twisted to the side. "I suppose if I just happened to pick up her medication while I was gettin' yours, it might not be so bad."

Mason gave her a dazzling smile. "That would be greatly appreciated."

It was apparent she was mesmerized by his smile because she walked backward a few steps before bumping into a shelf and rattling a bunch of bottles. Realizing what she'd done, she spun around and disappeared in the back.

Mason turned to me, and I stared up at him as though I was seeing a ghost. Tears stung my eyes. I couldn't believe he was standing here next to me after all these months.

He watched me, emotions wavering in his hazel eyes, but none that I could read.

Why was he here? Was he back? I was blindsided by his sudden appearance, and I wasn't sure how to handle it.

"Hey," he said, lowering his voice to barely above a whisper.

There were so many things I wanted to tell him—I'd imagined this day for the past five months—and depending on my mood, the conversation had either gone very well or very badly. So I was surprised that the first thing that popped out of my mouth was, "You left a box behind."

He blinked in surprise. "What?"

"A box of your stuff," I said. "The movers forgot to put it in your truck. Didn't your momma tell you? I told her to tell you." I was rambling, but I couldn't help myself.

He reached out and grabbed my hand. "Why don't you go wait in your truck, and I'll get your prescription and bring it to you."

"Uh …" I considered protesting and telling him I didn't need his help. Not anymore, but he'd just proven that I did, and it chafed. I pulled my hand away.

"Rose," he pleaded, and I wasn't sure if he was pleading with me to let him get my antibiotic or … more.

In the end, I knew I couldn't handle seeing him here. Not like this.

Dropping my gaze, I reached inside my purse. "I'll leave you money to pay for it, but I don't know how much it costs." I fumbled to get out my wallet, but my hands were shaking too much.

"Rose," he said, choking on my name. "I'll pay for it. You can reimburse me later." He took the basket from my hand. "I'll take care of these too."

I nodded because I didn't trust myself to speak, then practically ran toward the entrance. The stupid hat brim was blocking my view, and I nearly crashed into a woman's cart.

"Look where you're goin'!" the woman snarled.

"Sorry," I said, fighting tears.

I ripped the hat off, lest I crash into someone else, but I immediately regretted my mistake.

"Oh my God! Rose Gardner is in the store!" someone shouted.

Suddenly, lights started flashing on the ceiling and a loud, piercing siren went off.

"Security to the front," a voice said overhead.

I ran for the entrance, making it through the sliding doors just before a security guard showed up in the opening.

"If you come back again, we'll have you arrested for trespassing."

"Don't worry," I shouted over my shoulder. "I have no plans to come back."

I hurried to my truck and fumbled with the key as I started the engine. Once the air-conditioning was going, I rested my hands on the steering wheel.

Mason was back.

Tears streamed down my face, and for the life of me, I couldn't figure out what I was crying about. But one thing was for certain—Mason would come out of that store soon, and I wasn't going to let him find me like this.

I sat up and grabbed several tissues from my purse, then wiped my face and blew my nose. I stuffed them back into my purse when I saw Mason approach my truck with two bags.

He rounded the hood and opened the passenger door. "Can I get in for a moment?"

"Uh … sure."

He gave me another look, obviously hearing the hesitation in my voice, then got inside and shut the door.

I pulled out my wallet. "How much do I owe you?"

"Don't worry about it, Rose."

"No," I said, my back stiffening. "You've already done enough. How much do I owe you?"

"I didn't have your insurance information, so the antibiotic was expensive."

I pulled out all the bills I had—which wasn't much—out of my wallet. "How much?"

"Just give me twenty dollars, and we'll call it good."

I grabbed the bag and found the receipt. $86.91. I counted out my bills, coming up nearly forty dollars short.

I shoved the money at him in frustration "I'll pay you the rest later."

His hand gently covered mine. "Rose. It's okay."

Anger flooded through me, and I jerked my hand away. "I don't need you anymore, Mason Deveraux. You made damn sure of that when you left me."

Sadness washed over his face. "I know, and I'll regret it until my dying day."

"What are you doin' here?"

"Picking up my mother's medication. Just like I told Stephanie."

I shook my head. "Not that. Here in Henryetta. How long have you been here?"

"I literally just got into town. Mom and I are going out to dinner, but she mentioned she needed to pick up a prescription, so I offered to do it for her."

"So you're here visiting your mother?"

He hesitated. "It's an added bonus. I'm here on official business."

"Attorney general business?"

He looked surprised. "Yeah."

"I'm still friends with your momma," I said. "She told me things. Including the fact you've been datin'."

His eyes widened as his cheeks turned pink. "Oh."

"You can do whatever the heck you want," I said in a snotty tone. "You broke up with me. That means we can both do whatever the heck we want."

"Does that mean I can't ask you why Tim Dermot prescribed you antibiotics?" he asked, his voice rough.

"You have no right to snoop into my life, Mason Deveraux! What were you doin' spyin' on me?"

"I wasn't spying on you, but I confess I was worried about the amount and size of bandages you purchased, so I looked at the prescription. I care about you, Rose. You can't fault me for that."

"Care about me?" I shouted, knowing that I sounded like a crazy person, but I couldn't stop myself. "Where the hell have you been for the last five months, Mason? Where were you when I went to Houston in April and donated bone marrow for my sister? I was alone and *terrified.* I needed you. Where were you then?"

Tears filled his eyes. "Rose. I had no idea."

"No. How could you since you abandoned me? I lost just about everything to save you, and you thanked me by deserting me."

Anger flashed on his face. "Don't you pretend you only did it for me. You did it for him too."

"Him who?" Then I realized what he was saying. "You mean James Malcolm?"

His mouth dropped open. "You call him James now?"

"I called him James before you ever left," I said in the most hateful tone I could muster.

His gazed turned hard. "So you were sleepin' with him before I left too?"

I gasped, more hurt than if he'd accused me of murdering someone. "Get out! Get the hell out of my truck!"

"So you're admitting it?" he demanded, not budging.

To my irritation, a tear spilled down my cheek and I angrily swept at it. "You pretty much asked me the same thing last winter, Mason, and the answer is the same as it was back then. No. *No.* I never cheated on you. And if you were too stupid to see I was so in love with you that I couldn't entertain the notion of sleepin' with anyone else, then you didn't deserve me. And if you begrudge me for becoming the Lady in Black when I kept doin' it to save your life, then that's two strikes against you. Get out."

"You're still doin' it, aren't you?" he asked, sounding pissed.

"Doin' what?"

"You're still the Lady in Black."

I shook my head, hating to lie, but Mason was no longer my boyfriend. I couldn't count on him to cover for me. So I went with option three. "You can't just break my heart and expect to walk back into my life. Get out."

He snatched the prescription from my bag. "I know about Tim Dermot, Rose. You're workin' with him now? What happened to Malcolm?"

Crap. Crap. Crap. "Are you askin' me in an official capacity?"

His countenance changed. This was no longer my scorned ex-boyfriend; this was the by-the-books assistant DA I'd first met last summer. "Should I be?"

I grabbed my cell phone and pulled up my contacts.

"Who the hell are you callin'?" he asked in exasperation.

"My attorney."

"*Carter Hale?* So you have him on speed dial? How often have you used him since I left?"

I lowered the phone and stared at him in disbelief. "Do you really think so little of me now?" I asked, tears flooding my eyes again.

Why was I crying over this man? Why was I giving him the power to hurt me after he'd already hurt me so much?

His shoulders slumped, and contrition filled his eyes. "Rose. I'm sorry. I didn't mean that. You just …"

"Get under your skin," I finished for him, still pissed.

"No." His voice broke. "Make me feel so damn much."

Now I really started to cry. I'd loved him so much I'd willingly risked my life and my reputation to keep him safe. I'd become the Lady in Black, a decision that was still making waves in my life. And while I understood Mason's horror that his girlfriend had lied to him and joined forces with the man he was trying to put behind bars, I'd always expected him to come to his senses soon after breaking up with me.

I knew how he was when he got angry. He would blow his top, then storm off to cool down. But in the past he'd always come back. He'd apologize—and so would I—and we'd be stronger than before. I realized now that I'd always expected him to come back. I'd pined for him for months, but he had never once called or texted. Never checked to make sure I was okay.

He put a hand on my arm. "Rose, I'm sorry. This wasn't how I planned to see you again."

I shoved his hand off. "You planned how you'd see me again? *You* planned?"

A sheepish look washed over his face. "I didn't mean it like that."

"What exactly did you *plan*?"

He grimaced. "I'd planned to call you and see if we could meet in person and discuss … things."

"Like your presumptions about my involvement in the criminal world?"

His eyes hardened. "No. But we can discuss that if you'd like."

I grabbed my checkbook out of my purse and found a pen.

"What the hell are you doing now?" he asked.

"I'm making sure I don't owe you a damn thing." I scribbled the amount of money I owed him on both lines.

"Rose," he sighed as I signed my name.

I didn't say anything as I filled in the payee line with *Mason Deveraux, the man who doesn't deserve me,* then ripped out the check and handed it to him. "This conversation is done."

He glanced down at the check. "You're right," he said, meeting my eyes. "I don't deserve you. Maybe I never did."

I stuffed my checkbook into my purse. "I've got an appointment I'm goin' to be late for."

But he didn't move to get out of the car. He was still for a second. Then he said, "I'm sorry, Rose. I'd like to see you again before I leave. Maybe cooler heads will prevail."

I grabbed the steering wheel and stared out at the parking lot, not committing one way or the other. Part of me wanted to tell him to go screw himself, yet part of me held back. I couldn't figure out why. Did I still have feelings for him, or did I want to keep him around as a friend like I had with Joe?

He started to open the passenger door, then stopped. "Are you okay?"

I turned to him, pissed anew. "How can you ask me that after *this*?"

"Not after our … talk," he said, looking chagrinned. "The bandages … the antibiotic … are you okay?"

"It's a little late to be askin' me that now, isn't it?" I asked, feeling like I'd run a marathon.

"Nevertheless …"

"I'm fine, not that you have any right to know."

"I meant what I said. I still care about you, Rose."

I shook my head, refusing to look at him. "Carin' about someone is being there when they are at their loneliest and most broken. Not only were you not there, but you're the one who broke me."

He got out but didn't close the door. "You're wrong," he said softly. "You may have thought I broke you, but you're stronger than ever. And I still love you. I've wanted so badly to call you or text you or get in my goddamned car and drive here to see you, but I stopped myself every damn time," he said, getting worked up, his voice tight. "Do you know why?"

I couldn't stop myself from turning to look at him in anticipation of his response.

"Because I was still pissed at you for breaking us. For putting me in the position of possibly destroying my career." Tears filled his eyes. "But mostly, I was pissed at myself for being a goddamned hypocrite. I let you save me and then I condemned you for it." He took a breath. "You're like a mirror, Rose. Anyone who gets close to you gets a reflection of who they truly are, and I didn't like what I saw. So I left because I wanted to become the man you needed me to be."

A sob rose up in my chest.

"When I left, I knew I'd probably lost you for good, but I still hoped to win you back someday." He paused. "Stupidly, I still do." Then he shut the door and strode over to his car.

I watched him get in and drive away, then leaned my head against the steering wheel and broke down into tears.

Chapter Eleven

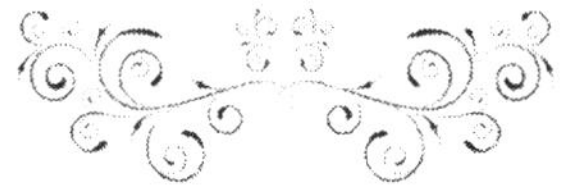

After I'd cried for another minute, I pulled myself back together and drove home. Muffy greeted me at the front door, but she released a little whimper as she smelled my legs. Could she smell Mason? Could she sense my sadness?

I let her out and left the door cracked for her to come back in before I headed upstairs. I was worried about what I'd find in the guest bedroom, and I didn't want her to be stuck outside if it took a while to set things to rights with my houseguest.

"Marshall?" I called out as I topped the stairs.

He didn't answer.

Terrified, I entered the guest room. He was in bed, but blood was streaked clear across the wood floor.

He turned his head to face me, looking paler than before. Sweat beaded on his forehead and upper lip. His bandage was soaked, and blood had dripped down his leg to the sheets beneath him.

"I'm sorry about the mess," he said, his voice weak.

"Don't you worry about that," I said, trying to keep my tone light as I tried to figure out where best to start. The most worrisome issue seemed to be his fever, so I grabbed the thermometer and stuck it in his mouth, then ran into the bathroom and grabbed some clean towels and several wet washrags.

The thermometer beeped as I entered the room, and I tried not to freak out when I read the number: 102.5.

I'd intended to use the washrags to clean up the blood, but I folded one and put it on his forehead and the other on his throat. "We've got to cool you down."

Rather than protest, he sank back into the pillows and closed his eyes.

"When was the last time you took any ibuprofen?" I asked.

"About an hour ago," was his weak reply.

Crap. "What about your antibiotic?"

"I already took two."

"I got you a new one. This one's stronger than penicillin." I unscrewed the cap of the medication bottle and handed him a pill along with the nearly empty cup of water. "Take this."

He swallowed it and finished off the water. "Sorry I'm so much trouble."

"We'll discuss that later," I said, pulling off his bandage to look at his stitches. "The good news is you didn't bust your stitches. Small miracle indeed. What were you doin' out of bed?"

"I had to pee," he said with a sheepish look.

We *had* left him in bed for a long time. "Sorry. I should have come to check on you sooner."

"I don't want to be a burden," he said hastily.

That ship had sailed, but I didn't see any reason to point it out. "Hopefully this antibiotic will kick in and you'll be back to yourself in no time. Do you know what you'll do then?"

"No."

"Did you have anything to do with the pawn shop robbery?" I asked, deciding to just come out with it.

He tried to hide his reaction, but I saw the fear flash in his eyes before his lips pressed into a thin line.

I put a hand on my hip. "If you're gonna stay, then I need to know why you're hidin' out here."

He still didn't say anything.

I thought about threatening him, but his face was flushed from fever. Now was not the time. "I'll let it go for the time being, but if you don't tell me by tomorrow morning, I'll call the sheriff's department to come pick you up."

Fear flickered in his eyes again, but he kept his mouth shut.

I pushed out a sigh. "Are you hungry?"

"Yes, ma'am."

"I'll bring you up something to eat. Then I'll clean the floor."

I headed downstairs and let Muffy in before I went into the kitchen and fixed my houseguest the last of the meatloaf and mashed potatoes. When I got back upstairs, Marshall was dozing, so I set the plate on the bedside table. I was taken aback by how young and innocent he looked. This was no hardened criminal. He struck me as a kid who'd gotten in over his head.

A kid who came to me because he had nowhere else to go.

"What am I gonna do about you, Marshall Billings?" I murmured under my breath. Surely his family was looking for him. I considered digging deeper to find his address and reach out to his family. But if the people who'd shot him were watching them, they might trace him back to me. For now, I'd wait. Tomorrow I'd need to press him for answers, but I was going to make sure he was protected. I wouldn't let the same fate that fell on Jeanne happen to Marshall.

I headed downstairs to the kitchen to get something for dinner. I'd clean up the floor later. In the meantime, I was alone again, and now my mind had even more to mull over.

Mason.

Thinking back on my conversation with him, I knew I could have handled it better. Fewer tears and more backbone, and that made me angry with myself. Why had I reacted so badly? Did I still love him? Was it even possible to love two men at once?

After I fixed a plate, I went into the living room and turned on the TV, loaded up Netflix, and lost myself in a movie. I could think about Mason later. But the exhaustion from lack of sleep and crying caught up with me, and I found myself dozing on the sofa with Muffy snuggled up to me.

My dog's low growl was the first sign of trouble.

I roused and brushed my hand along her back, thinking she'd seen a squirrel out the window, but I quickly realized the movie was over and it was dark outside.

At the sound of truck engines—*multiple* engines—I jerked upright, jumped to my feet, and ran upstairs to Neely Kate's bedroom to get a look at the front yard through the sheer curtains covering her windows. Two pickup trucks were barreling toward the house from the county road. They started honking their horns and driving in circles, kicking up dirt and grass.

I called Neely Kate, hoping she'd answer, but Jed answered instead. "Rose. What's goin' on?"

"Someone's here."

"*Who's* there?" he asked in a hard tone.

My heart leapt into my throat as I raced to my bedroom. After putting Jed on speakerphone, I tossed the phone onto my bed and started digging through the closet. "I promised James

I'd call him if I was in trouble, but there's no time. Make sure he knows, okay? I don't want him to think I fell back on my promise."

"Trouble? What kind of trouble?"

I found the box of casings, opened the shotgun, and began loading the chamber. "There are two pickup trucks carrying guys with shotguns circling my front yard."

After snatching up the gun, the casings, and the phone, I hurried out of my room and poked my head into Marshall's and found him wide-eyed and terrified. "You stay in this room no matter what. You got it?"

"Who are you talkin' to?" Jed demanded.

"I thought you said no guns were allowed in your house," Marshall said as he eyed my gun.

"That applies to everyone who doesn't live here," I said before bolting for the stairs.

"Rose," Jed growled. "What the hell is goin' on?"

I ran down the stairs, calling out, "Muffy?" in an undertone. She didn't answer, and I prayed she was hiding in the kitchen and hadn't figured out a way outside. Though hiding wasn't exactly her style.

I dropped the box of shotgun shells on the coffee table and moved to the window. Several men had fanned out across my yard.

"Lady in Black!" a man shouted from the front yard. "You have something we want, and we're here to collect it."

I took a deep breath, my heart beating so hard I was sure it was about to fly out of my chest. "Jed—"

"I heard him. What do you have?" he asked as calm as could be.

"Now's not the time to discuss it." I glanced around for Muffy but still didn't see her anywhere. She hadn't followed me upstairs.

"Do you know who's at your front door?"

"I haven't gotten a good look at them yet, but if I had to guess, I'd say they belong to Kip Wagner."

"Wagner?" Then he cursed a blue streak. "Does this have anything to do with the pawn shop robbery?"

"How would I know?" But I knew I didn't sound all that convincing.

"You are the most damned stubborn …" His voice trailed off. "You go into your basement and lock the door. Use the bolt I installed."

After I was kidnapped a couple of weeks ago, Jed had made Neely Kate and me a sort of panic room in the basement. He'd installed brackets to hold two two-by-fours to reinforce the door to a small room my father had used as a dark room.

"I can't find Muffy," I said. "I don't know where she went, but she was the one who alerted me to the trucks." I glanced around again and called out her name in a low voice. No answer.

"She's a smart dog," Jed said. "She'll hide, and you need to do the same. I'm already on my way."

"I suspect you're a good twenty minutes out, Jed." What if they came in and snatched Marshall—and me—before he got here?

"I can be there in fifteen." Then he hung up.

As I stuffed my phone into my pocket, I kicked myself for not telling him more, but it was too late now. I backed up into the kitchen, taking a peek at Muffy's dog bed in the corner.

Empty. Where was she?

"Lady, I ain't got all day," the man shouted from the front of the house, and I recognized the voice this time.

It *was* Kip Wagner. That just plain pissed me off, and my anger burned through my fear. If I cowered behind this door, I'd look like a scared little girl. I was the freaking Lady in Black, and damned if I was gonna let him treat me with disrespect in my own yard. Damned if I was going to let him kill Marshall either.

Cocking the shotgun, I marched up to the front door and opened it with my foot, using more force than I'd intended. The door slammed into the wall, startling a few of the waiting men. I strode onto the front porch with the shotgun lifted under my arm and trained directly on Kip Wagner.

"Mr. Wagner," I called out in contempt I didn't need to feign. "I see you didn't learn your lesson about respect a month ago."

"You can parade around in your dresses and your hats," he said with a sneer, "but we all know you're just a little girl playin' dress-up. And this time you don't have Malcolm or Carlisle backin' you up."

I lifted the gun higher and trained it on his crotch. "Does it look like I'm playing dress-up now?"

I heard the shifting of a half dozen weapons. My heart was lodged in my throat, but I knew I couldn't show any kind of weakness. If I did, this would all be over for me and Marshall.

Wagner held both hands out to his sides, taking his aim off me, and said in a cajoling tone, "Just send out the guy, and we'll be on our way."

"It doesn't work that way, Wagner. My farm is neutral, and you're breaking the rules by bein' here."

"Rules? What rules?"

"Let me spell them out for you—I'm neutral. *My land* is neutral. If someone comes to me seeking sanctuary and I choose to grant it to them, they get it."

He laughed. "So Malcolm's protecting him. Why?"

"Malcolm doesn't know he's here. He has no idea I have him."

Kip Wagner's eyes lit up with possibilities. I knew it might have been foolish of me to admit it, but I had to prove I wasn't James' puppet.

"Before you go thinkin' you can just shoot me and be on your way, Malcolm knows you're currently on my property, and so does Dermot," I lied, figuring they would both find out soon enough from Jed. "They've both recognized my neutrality and will destroy you if you so much as touch me."

Indecision wavered on his face. Then he said, "Fine. You can keep the kid, but I need the file."

"I don't know anything about a file."

"The damn file they stole out of my safe. Just hand over the file, and no one needs to get hurt." Then he grinned. "Well, any *more* hurt."

"I don't know anything about a file," I repeated. "But if I come into possession of it, and you can prove it's yours, I'll be happy to return it."

He cursed, then aimed his gun at me. "You lyin' bitch!"

I curled my finger around the trigger of my own weapon. "I've become a pretty good shot, Mr. Wagner. Neely Kate makes me practice for an hour every day. Guess what her favorite target is?" When he remained silent, I said, "I hear a man can live if his testicles get shot off. I guess it stands to reason. Bulls get castrated and do just fine." I shot him an evil grin. "And you always did remind me of a bull, so I'm sure you'd be just fine too … if you can learn to overlook the fact that I castrated you."

He growled, and his face turned beet red.

"Now here's what we're gonna do," I said. "Your men are going to lower their guns and get back into their trucks. When I give the word, you're gonna do the same, and then all y'all are gonna get off my land. Have I made myself clear?"

"She's bluffin'," one of his men sneered.

"Are you willing to take that chance?" I asked, still aiming at Kip Wagner's crotch. "Because I assure you that your boss will live, and I suspect he's going to take his wrath out on the person who cost him his manhood. I suspect it won't be pretty."

No one else said anything.

"Okay, now that everyone knows the plan, I'm gonna give you five seconds to get in your trucks. One." I paused. "Two."

"Do what she said!" Wagner shouted, lifting his arms. "Go!"

"Three."

His men lowered their guns and grumbled as they got back into their trucks, while Kip Wagner stood his ground and gave me a death stare.

"You can get in now," I said. "Slowly. And while your family jewels might be shielded by the door, your head will not be, and that's my next best shot." I gave him another grin.

He cursed as he headed to the door.

"Today's lesson is about trespassing," I said, "but the next lesson will be about respect, Mr. Wagner, because if we're going to have future interactions, you will treat me with respect or face the consequences."

He got inside the passenger side of his truck, then shouted out the open window, "Don't mistake me for Buck Reynolds. I ain't treatin' you like a princess."

"I don't need you to treat me like a princess," I said. "I just need you to treat me with respect. It's really not that difficult of a concept."

"I'm gettin' my file, one way or the other," Wagner spat out, hatred simmering in his eyes. "And *no one* is standin' in my way. You have twenty-four hours." Then he banged on the side of the truck and they all took off, their horns blowing as they went. I realized I was in a vulnerable position—I'd lost my primary target, but I wasn't about to go scampering into the house. Part of getting that respect was making them think I wasn't scared of them … even when I was about to pee my pants.

As soon as the sound of their engines faded, I sank to the porch and began to shake.

Muffy shot out of the bushes and ran straight for my lap.

"How did you get out here?" I asked in dismay, shaking even more. "They could have shot you." I held her close and tried to take slow, deep breaths, willing my heart to slow down. She reached up and licked my cheek while I rubbed behind her ears. "Thanks for the warning."

I was still sitting there when I heard a car pulling onto the property, the headlights shutting off. I knew it was probably Jed, but I still set Muffy down and got to my feet, my shotgun ready if I needed it.

The dark sedan sped toward my house, spinning to the side as it came to a stop. The driver's door opened within seconds, and my heart sank when I realized how wrong I'd been.

It wasn't Jed, and now I would have hell to pay.

I was about to face James Malcolm's fury.

Chapter Twelve

"What the hell are you doin' on your goddamned front porch?" James shouted, red-faced as he marched around the front of his car toward me. He wore a shoulder harness and had a revolver in his hand.

I couldn't ignore the little flip-flop of my heart at the sight of him. Seeing him only made me realize how much I'd missed him. Nevertheless, I couldn't let him show up and start bossing me around. I dropped my shotgun to the wooden porch floor, then stood on the top step, holding my ground. "What are you doin' here?"

"*What am I doin' here?* Jed told you to barricade yourself in the goddamned basement!" he shouted, pointing to my open front door.

Muffy hunkered down and growled.

"You're scarin' my dog," I said.

"Scarin' your dog? You scared the ever-lovin' shit out of *me*!"

I lifted my chin. "I'm sorry I scared you."

He gave me a lingering look, emotions shifting like storm clouds behind his eyes, and then shifted his gaze to the road. "I swear to God you're nothin' but trouble," he growled.

"I said I'm sorry!"

He holstered his weapon and bounded up the steps toward me. The anger emanating from him gave me a moment of pause, but I realized it wasn't directed at me. As soon as he reached me, he pulled me into his arms and gave me a punishing kiss.

Without thinking, I linked my hands around his neck and sank into his chest, desperate to be close to him.

He pulled back and cupped my face with both hands, holding on tight as he searched my face. "Are you okay?"

"Yes."

"Don't lie to me, Rose." His voice was deep and raspy with emotion.

"I'm fine. I swear. They never touched me. They never even stepped foot on my porch. I'm fine."

"They? Who was it? What did they want?"

So Jed had only told him I was in trouble, not the nature of my predicament. How much was I willing to tell James?

Before either of us could say anything else, another car turned onto my drive. I registered it as Jed's sedan, but only after James had placed himself in front of me and pulled out his handgun and pointed it at the car.

When he realized it was Jed, he reholstered his weapon. Jed and Neely Kate hopped out and Neely Kate ran for me, pushing James aside so she could pull me into a hug.

"Are you okay?" she asked, crying. "Did they hurt you?"

"No," I said, giving her a squeeze. "I'm okay."

"What happened?" she asked.

I cast a glance up at James, weighing my options. How much did I want him to know? If he knew about the file, would he want to go up and question Marshall? My feelings for him aside, I wouldn't have let Dermot up there to question the teen, so that meant I couldn't let James or Jed do so either.

"It was a misunderstanding that's been resolved." I glanced at James and then Jed. "Thank you for your concern, but everything's fine now."

James' faced reddened. "If you think that I'm gonna drive away without an explanation after hearin' you were taking gunfire from two truckloads of men, then you've lost your damn mind. Start talkin'."

"Was it Kip Wagner?" Jed asked in a stern voice.

"*Kip Wagner?*" James demanded. "What the hell was *he* doin' here?" Then his eyes narrowed. "Does this have anything to do with the robbery at his pawn shop?"

"Why would I have anything to do with that?" I asked. "*I* didn't rob it!"

He continued to stare at me, but then Jed asked, "Who were you talkin' to while I was on the phone?"

I tried to look innocent. "What?"

"Who were you talkin' to?"

I put a hand on my hip and said with plenty of attitude, "Maybe I had company."

"Who was it?" Jed asked.

"And where the hell are they now?" James demanded.

I stared up at him in defiance. "We aren't in a relationship, James Malcolm. You don't have the right to ask me about the minute details of my life." But even as I said the words, I wished I could take them back. Not only were they untrue, they were unfair. James was going to want an answer in a matter of days, and our kiss aside, I had no idea what to tell him. I couldn't bear to say no, and I couldn't accept the cost of saying yes.

Something flickered in his eyes, and his jaw looked like it was chiseled in granite. "I'm gonna ask you one more time who was at your house when Wagner showed up."

I cast a quick glance at Neely Kate, but it was long enough to catch Jed's attention.

"Neely Kate," Jed said. "What do you know about this?"

Her eyes flew open in a panic.

"You can tell him," I said gently. "I swore to you that I wouldn't let this get in the way of you and Jed."

Still, she glanced up at Jed with indecision.

Jed's expression softened. "Whatever it is, Neely Kate, you can tell me."

She cast another look at me before turning back to Jed. "There's a kid up there."

"A kid?" Jed asked in confusion, then concern. "Rose's niece or nephew?"

She shook her head, still looking uncertain. "No. Not a *kid* kid, more like a teenager."

"Why do you have a teenager upstairs?" James demanded, but a look of understanding washed over his face as he finished his question. "That kid robbed the pawn shop. That's why Wagner was here."

I crossed my arms and kept my mouth shut.

James blew up. "Why are you harboring a kid who ripped off Kip Wagner? What the hell were you thinkin'?"

I flung my arms down and balled my hands. "*Excuse me?*"

His eyes narrowed. "Don't play dumb with me, Lady. You know exactly what I'm askin'."

I cocked my head to the side. "Oh, I *heard* what you were askin'. What I'm wantin' to know is what makes you think I owe you an explanation?"

"You've got to be shittin' me! How about the fact I had to drive out here to save your ass!"

"News flash!" I shouted, stomping in front of him and glaring up at his furious face. "You didn't save me! I saved my own daggum self!"

"Why is that kid hidin' in your house?" he asked, his voice low and deadly.

"He got shot," Neely Kate said in a rush. "Rose found him in her barn. He was lookin' for sanctuary."

"You have a wounded kid in your house?" James asked, his voice rising. "What the hell makes you think you're qualified to help him?"

"Dermot," Jed said. "They called Dermot." Neely Kate gasped, and he added, "This is why you were talkin' to him earlier, isn't it?"

She didn't answer.

If Neely Kate had shared that piece of information in the hopes of getting James to cool down, she was about to be sorely disappointed.

"Let me get this straight," James said, his voice a low rumble of fury. "Instead of calling me for help, you called Tim Dermot."

When he put it that way, I could see why he was upset. "Are you capable of diggin' a bullet out of someone's leg?"

His jaw twitched. "Is that what Dermot did? Dug a bullet out of the kid's leg? And then Wagner showed up to collect him? Is the kid still up there?"

Neely Kate stiffened. "Oh, my stars and garters! Did Wagner take him?"

I turned to face her. "No. Wagner left with exactly what he came with: nothing."

"And how'd that happen?" James asked. Then he glanced down at the shotgun I'd laid down on the porch. His gaze jerked back up to me. "Are you *shittin'* me?"

"You held off two truckloads of gun-totin' men on your own?" Jed asked, his voice tight.

"What else was I supposed to do?"

"Hide in the goddamned basement!" James shouted, his voice booming in the night air. "That's what Jed told you to do!"

"Keep your voice down!" I shouted. "Or Joe's gonna hear you all the way over at his property and come over and investigate!"

He started to say something, then swallowed hard and turned away from me, staring out toward the road. "Who's in your house, Rose?" he asked in a deadly calm voice.

His tone scared me. He'd sooner die than physically hurt me, but if he thought someone else had brought harm to my door, he wouldn't hesitate to protect me. This type of calm always came before a storm.

I held my tongue.

He spun around to face me. "If you don't tell me, I'm goin' in there to find out."

I moved to stand in front of the door. "The hell you are."

His face was devoid of expression, but the set of his jaw told me how furious he was.

I stood my ground. "You either respect and trust me or you don't, James Malcolm."

"That has nothing to do with it!"

"It has *everything* to do with it!"

He stared me down for several seconds before taking a step backward. "Do you even *know* this kid?" he asked in a quieter voice.

Only then did I realize how much I'd scared him. "No."

"I don't understand," he said, "why you would risk your life for someone you don't even know." Then he shook his head, pushing out a long breath. "That's not true. I *do* know." But he didn't look happy about it.

"How'd you get Wagner to leave?" Jed asked.

I was probably about to set James off again, but he deserved to know the truth. And so did Jed and Neely Kate. "I met them on the porch with my shotgun and told them to leave."

"He knows the kid is here?" Jed asked.

"He guessed it, but I didn't confirm it."

"How?" James asked. "What would make him guess the kid is here?"

"The teenager shot and killed a couple of miles from here," Jed said. "I bet he was part of it."

"So why didn't Wagner show up last night?" James asked. "Why wait twenty-four hours?"

None of us had an answer.

"I still don't understand how you got Wagner to leave," Jed said. "You told me there were a dozen guys with guns. Did the kid help you?"

"No … he can't walk on his own. It was just me—no shots fired. I had my gun trained on Wagner and told his men if they made a wrong move, they'd have to face his wrath since they'd be responsible for him losing his manhood."

"That's my girl," Neely Kate said, beaming with pride.

The tips of Jed's mouth turned up into a reluctant grin, but James kept his expression neutral. "You're holding something back."

I held his gaze, uncertain of whether I wanted to tell him about the file. What if he used me to get it? It wouldn't be the first time. He'd tried to manipulate me into handing over an expensive necklace that rightfully belonged to Buck Reynolds, though part of that had been an attempt to push me away emotionally.

"I think that's enough questions for tonight," Neely Kate said. "It's time for both y'all to go."

Jed stared down at her as though she'd declared he should run off and become a nun. "If you think I'm leaving you here with some criminal in your house, knowing that Kip Wagner and his men could come back at any time, you've lost your mind."

"Take her with you," I said to Jed, knowing that everything he'd said was true. I'd gotten us into this mess. She didn't deserve to be stuck in it.

"If you think *I'm* goin' *anywhere*, you've both plum lost your minds," Neely Kate said in a huff. "If Wagner and his band of merry fools comes back, I'm gonna be standin' there next to you."

"*Neither one of you* will be facin' Wagner and his men," Jed said. "I'll be here to deal with it."

I started to protest, but stopped. Neely Kate and I had discussed him staying earlier today. Still, I had to verify a few things first. "If you stay, you go nowhere near that kid."

He didn't answer, but I'd push him on it later.

"Also, I need to know that you're good and done with James. You bein' here won't do me much good if everyone thinks you're tied at the hip to him."

James looked furious, but Jed gave a sharp nod. "I'm no longer working for him, but we've worked together for long enough that most people will go on considerin' us allies no matter what." He paused. "But I know someone else who can come stay with you two and look after the kid." His brows lifted. "Just to be clear. If you two are here, then I'm not going anywhere, but this guy might be a good addition. He's the perfect face of neutrality."

"Witt." Neely Kate said her cousin's name in a breathy voice, then shook her head. "No. I'm not putting him in that position again."

"I agree," I said. We'd asked Witt to help us a couple of weeks ago when we were working for Reynolds to find Scooter Malcolm, but Neely Kate's cousin was on parole. "We've already put Witt in enough danger. I won't put him in any more."

Jed already had his phone out. "How about we let him decide for himself?" He walked down the porch steps toward his car as he placed the call.

Jed had Witt's number programmed into his phone?

Neely Kate looked nervous, and I hated that I was once again putting her and her cousin in danger. I was sure this would be one more strike against me with Witt. Though he'd willingly helped us last time, he'd made a point of telling me how much he hated seeing his cousin in danger. He'd made it clear that he wasn't about to put up with it for much longer.

I knew he'd try something, but it didn't take a fool to see that Neely Kate wouldn't take orders from anyone, which meant there would be an epic showdown.

"Neely Kate," I said as I moved closer to her, "maybe you should just go with Jed."

Her eyes flashed with outrage. "Are you *kiddin'* me?"

"I don't want to get between you and Witt."

"How would you get between us?"

I hesitated. I wasn't about to tell Neely Kate about Witt's promise to protect her from me if the need arose. "I got us into this mess. Me and the Lady in Black. I refuse to drag you in any deeper."

Her face hardened with determination. "I'm not leavin' you, Rose."

"Rose is right," James said. "Go with Jed, Neely Kate. I'll stay with her."

Neely Kate started to protest, but I beat her to it. "You are *not* staying with me, James Malcolm."

"Why the hell not?" he demanded.

"For the exact reason Jed's calling Witt—which I still don't approve of—because if I'm going to look neutral, then only neutral people can help me guard the boy."

"Let me make this perfectly clear," James said in a cold voice. "I'm not protecting that kid. I'm protecting *you*."

"You're only proving my point."

"Witt's on his way," Jed called out as he turned to face us, pocketing his phone.

I shook my head. "This is a bad idea. Witt will need a gun to stand his ground against anyone who shows up at the house, which would be a direct violation of his parole."

"Hopefully it won't come to that," Jed said, sounding more lighthearted than I would have expected.

James held my gaze. "Why did Wagner leave, his threatened manhood aside?"

And here we were again. I needed to decide if I trusted James not to use me again. I made a split-second decision to take the risk, although I wondered if it was my risk to take. "He wanted a file. He said it had been stolen from his safe in the robbery."

"What was *in* this file?"

"I have no earthly idea, but he wants it back. He says he'll be back in twenty-four hours to get it."

"Does the kid have it?" James asked.

"I have no idea. I didn't even know the file existed until Kip Wagner asked for it, and I haven't asked him yet."

"Then *I* will." He started to move around me, but I grabbed his arm.

"If you walk through that door, you and I are officially done, you understand me?"

James' entire body tensed. "You would choose that kid over me?"

"No, *you* would be choosing to disrespect me and my attempt to be neutral."

"You are deluded and naïve," he snarled. "My world doesn't work that way."

"*Deluded and naïve?*" I said in a hard tone. "You think I don't have firsthand experience with the way your world works? Have you forgotten that I've spent *months* in it? That I was so good at gettin' close to your suspected traitors and findin' out their secrets with my visions that you offered me a partnership? Was I deluded and naïve *then*?"

Holding my gaze, he hesitated before he said, "You're deluded and naïve if you think I'm going to drive off and let you get killed over some two-bit kid who stole a file from Wagner's safe. So I'm going to grill that boy until he tells me what's in the file and where it is."

"Jed, Neely Kate. Go inside," I said, keeping my focus on James.

"Rose …," Neely Kate said softly.

"Go inside and take Muffy with you. This needs to be a private conversation."

James' eyebrow lifted slightly. "You don't want your dog overhearin' our conversation?"

"Muffy's an excellent judge of character, and I'd hate for her opinion of you to be marred by the discussion we're about to have."

Neely Kate gave me one last look, then said, "Come on, Muffy."

Muffy gave a soft whine as she followed my best friend and Jed inside.

As soon as the door clicked shut, James' face softened. "I'm goin' to take it as a good sign that you're worried about preservin' my character with your dog."

I didn't crack a smile. "I know you don't understand why I insist on remaining neutral, but you have to admit that it's actually helped you a few times. We were able to broker a truce with Buck Reynolds, and it helped me find Scooter."

His scowl was back. "Merv made sure I found my brother."

"But he planned to kill you *and* me, and it was my cooperation with Reynolds and Dermot that *saved* me."

His certainty wavered.

I took two steps toward him and rested my palms on his chest. Feeling his hard muscles under his shirt sent a shiver of desire down my back, but I reminded myself this wasn't the time or place. "I know you're scared for me. But I need to do this, James."

"It's a fool's errand, Rose, and you know it."

"Trust me."

"And let you get yourself killed?" he asked in a low tone. "You have to know you were lucky tonight. Damn lucky."

"I know."

"I don't know if I can continue to watch you do this. I'm not sure I can be part of it."

Something in my chest tightened, and I took a step back. "Then you're no better than Mason. He wanted the fruits of me bein' the Lady in Black without the stench that came with it."

His anger was back. "I am *nothin'* like that man."

"No," I said, "but the comparison stands all the same."

He turned away from me and walked to the end of my porch, staring out into the hayfield that bordered Joe's property. "This is all my fault," he said in a broken voice. "This is like a damned runaway freight train, and I don't know how to stop it."

"What are you talkin' about?"

He slowly turned to face me. "You." He flung his hand toward the house. "*This.* I forced you to go to that goddamned auction last November to help save my sorry ass. I didn't give two shits about how it would affect you. Hell, I thought it was funny I had that arrogant son-of-a-bitch's girlfriend in my pocket."

His words stung, but I wasn't surprised. Why wouldn't he have felt that way at the time? That auction, which had earned him his position as king of the underworld, marked the first time I'd used my visions to help him. I'd brought information to James, hoping he could do me a favor in return, but I'd had a vision of him dying at the auction. None of the details had come through, however—like who would do the deed or when—so he'd insisted I go to the auction with him. And so, with a hat and a dress and a veil, the Lady in Black had been born.

I held his gaze, unflinching.

He continued. "And now you're stuck in a disaster of my creation. You wanted to stop being Lady, and I wouldn't let you."

My irritation softened. "Sure, you coerced me in the beginning, but I chose to continue. To help you."

He shook his head with a bitter laugh. "So you could save that sorry bastard who left you as soon as he was safe."

"Even so, it was by choice. You didn't coerce me."

He kept his gaze on the tree line for a moment before turning to face me. By then, his melancholy had been replaced with determination. "I can't change my previous selfishness, but I'm damned by it now." He strode toward me and cupped both sides of my face with his hands. "Let me claim you. Then I can give you my full protection."

"You and I both know that will make me more of a target, not less. This is the safest way—to appear neutral."

He dropped his hands and took a step back. "I will *not* let you pay with your life for my own greed."

I gave him a soft smile. "I'm too stubborn to let someone kill me."

He released a laugh, but it sounded forlorn. "I almost believe that."

"Good." I took a breath, steeling myself, then said, "Now you need to go."

He gave me a look of pained surprise.

"I've missed you more than you can possibly know," I said, "but the longer you stay here, the more danger I'm in. What if Wagner finds out you're here and thinks I've given this mysterious file to you? I assured him that if I found it, I'd give it to him, but we both know he doesn't trust my word."

His brow lowered. "You shouldn't have told him that."

"If it's his file, then of course I will. Just like I gave Buck Reynolds back his necklace."

He moved next to me, close enough for his chest to touch mine. His voice was a low growl. "And what if whatever's in that file is harmful? What if it's a hit list? What if it's dirt on me? Worse yet, what if it's something that could hurt Neely Kate? Would you be so willing to give it back then?"

I stared up at him in horror, but the look on his face wasn't gloating. It was sympathetic.

"Livin' in the gray area's not so easy, is it?" When I didn't respond, he wrapped me in his arms, placed a gentle kiss on my forehead, then got into his car and drove away.

Chapter Thirteen

Jed and Neely Kate were sitting on the sofa when I walked inside.

"Everything okay?" Neely Kate asked with a worried look.

Everything was far from okay, but I suspected that wasn't what she was asking. "James left of his own volition. He wants to claim me to protect me, but I told him that I'll be safer if I continue to paint myself as neutral." I turned my gaze to Jed. "What's your opinion? Do you think I'm as deluded and naïve as James does?"

He gave me a long look. I trusted his opinion more than anyone else's on this situation. James was too close to be objective, and while Jed was close, he was also far enough removed to hopefully keep most of his feelings out of it.

"No. I think you're right. You'll have a definite target on your back if he claims you. Most people would give pause before doin' something, but we all know the world is full of ruthless people. Fenton County's no different than anywhere else. Men are starting to recognize your neutrality—that much is obvious if the boy showed up lookin' for sanctuary. We just need to give it time."

I nodded. "Thanks." I pushed out a breath, then glanced toward the stairs. "I'm going to ask Marshall some questions. Want to come help me?" I asked Neely Kate.

She hopped up. "Definitely."

I turned my attention back to Jed. "You are to stay away from this kid. Can you abide by that rule?"

He gave me a hard stare. "For now."

I put a hand on my hip. "What's that mean?"

"It means that if a situation arises that requires me to talk to him, I will." When I started to protest, he held up his hand. "Rose, I plan to abide by your rules, but I refuse to swear that I'll have absolutely no contact with him. I'm not gonna paint myself into that corner. I promise I'll only do it as a last resort."

It was hard to argue with that. "Are you plannin' on spendin' the night?"

He shot a look at Neely Kate and then glanced at me. "If you'll allow it."

I gave him a tight smile. "I'd prefer it."

"Good," he said with a brisk nod. "You girls head up and see what you can find out, and I'll wait for Witt."

The mention of Witt's name made my stomach twist. I dreaded facing him.

We headed up the stairs. Since the clock on the living room wall said it was close to eleven o'clock, I expected to walk into a dark room, but Marshall had turned on the bedside table lamp and was curled up in his bed, clutching his cell phone.

"We'll take that," Neely Kate said, snatching it from him.

"That's mine!" he protested.

She ignored him as she started tapping and scrolling on his screen. Then she held it up and pointed it toward him. "What are these two calls? Becky called an hour ago and you called her back." Her gaze jerked up to his. "You weren't supposed to have contact with anyone."

"She's my girlfriend." He looked scared. "She left me a voicemail and told me it was important for us to talk. So I texted instead."

"What was so important?" Neely Kate asked.

"She told me that Rusty, the friend who dropped me off here last night, was murdered. She was worried about me."

"And did Becky want to come see you?" Neely Kate asked, still holding up the phone.

His gaze dropped to his hands. "Yeah."

Neely Kate gave me a look of disbelief, then turned back to Marshall. "And you told her where you were." When Marshall started to protest, she shook her head in disgust. "I know you did. It wasn't a question. Was the plan for her to come right away?"

"She said she was coming tomorrow morning after you two left for work."

"I thought we told you no calls and no visitors," Neely Kate said.

"I know, but she's scared, and I get lonely here all by myself." He cringed and shot a glance at me. "No offense to your dog."

I nodded. "No offense taken, but you're gonna have to call her and tell her you'll get evicted if you have any visitors."

"I was gonna leave with her. We talked about goin' to Little Rock," he said. "But now she won't answer my calls, and I'm scared for her." He sniffed, obviously distraught. "She don't know *anything*."

My heart softened. "Marshall, how old are you? The truth this time. I know you were in Fenton County High School last spring."

His gaze flicked up to me then back down. "I'm eighteen, I swear. My birthday was last month."

I grabbed the chair in the corner and dragged it next to the bed. When I sat down, I said, "Look, I'm not sure if you heard everything that happened downstairs, but Kip Wagner showed up looking for you, and I risked my life to keep you safe. So in exchange, you're gonna tell me everything you know, startin' with how you got shot."

"I can't."

"Can't?" Neely Kate said, giving him a look that made him shrink into the bed. "You mean *won't.* You showed up in our barn lookin' for help, and we gave it to you, no questions asked, and now you refuse to tell us what you know." She sucked in a breath, then looked at the phone screen. "Do you have Kip Wagner's number in your contacts? No," she said with a frown. "No worries. I'm sure we can find it and tell him to come haul your booty away."

"No!" he protested. "Don't call him!"

"Then start talkin'."

"Okay!" he shouted in a panic. "Okay! But you gotta make sure Becky's okay. You gotta protect her."

"We don't *gotta* do nothin'," Neely Kate said, keeping up her bad-cop routine, but I heard her voice waver.

I resisted the urge to sigh. "Okay, here's what we're gonna do. You tell us everything you know, and we'll check on Becky."

"No!" he shouted, rising off the bed. "That's not good enough! You have to protect her!"

"Marshall," I said in a gentle tone, "I can't guarantee anything. I suspect Kip Wagner and his friends got to her and found out where you were from her." When I thought about the timing of his call to her and Kip Wagner's drop-in visit, I was nearly certain of it. "For all I know, they're holding her hostage to get you to cooperate. Or …" I hesitated, wondering if I should tell him the next part, but he needed to understand the severity of the situation. Lord knew I should have been more straightforward with Jeanne. I certainly shouldn't have made promises I couldn't keep. "Or she might be dead."

I had another suspicion, but I had a notion he wasn't ready to hear it yet.

"No!" he wailed.

"But we'll look for her, okay?" Neely Kate said, caving when she saw his anguish. "That's all we can promise." He nodded, and she added, "But the more you tell us, the better our chances of findin' her. So start spillin'."

He nodded at her again and wiped his face with the back of his hand. "It was Rusty's idea to rob the pawn shop."

"Why?" I asked.

"He's always wanted to live life on the wild side … well, I guess he used to want to, on account of he's dead now." Then he teared up again.

"Rusty's dead because of his own stupidity," Neely Kate said. "And you got shot for the same."

The boy's eyes flew wide, but he didn't argue.

I needed to keep this confession moving. "You know about Skeeter Malcolm and you know about the Lady in Black, so you already have a foot in Fenton County's seedy underbelly. Who are you loyal to?"

He stared at me, still wide-eyed.

"Come on," Neely Kate said. "It wasn't a hard question."

He swallowed, looking nervous, before he said, "I'm not."

"You're not what?" Neely Kate asked.

"I'm not loyal to anyone."

"I suppose it's possible," I said to Neely Kate. "Look at Witt."

Neely Kate put her hand on her hip and narrowed her eyes at the boy. "Yeah, but he's not old enough to know about the crime world unless he's loyal to someone in it."

"I'm not," he insisted.

"Okay," I said. "If you're not loyal to anyone, then how do you know those things?"

"Rusty. He's the one who knew things. He'd been hangin' out with Wagner's guys. I guess he was loyal to him."

Neely Kate snorted. "He couldn't have been very loyal if he robbed the guy."

"Rusty said Wagner had something he needed, and he said if he got it, Skeeter Malcolm would finally listen to him."

That caught my attention. "Listen to him about what?"

"About lettin' him join his group."

"If Rusty wanted to join Skeeter Malcolm's group," I said, "then why wouldn't you let me call him?"

"Because I've heard how mean he is." He nodded toward me. "And I heard about you too. Rusty said you had a special arrangement with Malcolm, but you sided with Reynolds a few weeks ago, which made everyone think you might be neutral."

"You didn't hear this yourself?" I asked.

"No," Neely Kate said, turning to face me. "Because Marshall here wasn't hangin' out with Wagner's men. Everything he's heard is secondhand from Rusty, who was hangin' out with them and braggin' to his buddy."

"Is that true?" I asked.

He gave me a sheepish look and nodded.

I sat back in my chair and collected my thoughts. "Why did you agree to help Rusty rob the pawn shop? You had to know it was a fool's venture."

"I did it for Becky."

"Becky?" Neely Kate asked in surprise. "Why would you rob a pawn shop for your girlfriend?"

His face flushed. "She was livin' with this guy, and she wanted to get away, but she needed money to do it."

Neely Kate's face lost color.

I gave her a curious look, then leaned forward. "If she was livin' with a guy, how is she your girlfriend?"

He lowered his gaze, his face turning a deeper shade of crimson. "She isn't exactly my girlfriend—*yet*. She said she can't be my girlfriend so long as she's living with Bubba. So I told her I'd get the money to help her escape." He was silent for a moment, then added with some attitude, "We weren't stupid. We knew robbin' the pawn shop would be hard. That's why we robbed it on a Sunday afternoon on account of no one's there."

"Surely Kip Wagner has cameras," I said.

"He does, but we wore ski masks."

"You forgot about the cameras in the parking lot," Neely Kate said. "I bet he got your license plate number."

Marshall shook his head. "We took off the plates, and we weren't driving either one of our cars."

"Then how'd he know you robbed him?"

"I don't know," Marshall said, his voice shaking.

"Okay," I said, "let's back up. Rusty tells you he wants to rob the pawn shop, and you agree, knowin' Becky needs help."

"Not exactly," he said. "At first I said no, *no way*, but he kept askin', and *then* I realized Becky needed my help ..."

"And you said yes," I finished. Men the world over had been known to do stupid things for women.

"I couldn't stand to see her hurt anymore."

"Hurt?" I asked in surprise. "You mean physically hurt?"

He nodded. "She showed up at the convenience store with bruises, but last week they were really bad. I couldn't stand to see her hurt anymore, so I called Rusty that night and said I was in."

"Convenience store?" I said in confusion.

"That's where I work. She'd been comin' in every day for the last month, always at the same time. After a while, we started talkin' and she told me the reason she always comes in at the same time is because that's when Bubba isn't watchin' her. She said she wished she had a man who would be sweet to her." He swallowed. "I guess I always knew I didn't stand a chance with her. She's beautiful, and she's twenty-two—what would she want with a kid like me? But I still wanted to help her."

"We'll find her," Neely Kate said with a determination that caught me by surprise. "But we'll need to know where you worked, where she lived, and anything else that can help us."

His mouth sagged. "You will?"

"Yeah. I promise."

"Neely Kate," I said in a stern voice.

She shot me a defiant look—not in a hateful way, but more of an *I'll do this with or without you* way. Of course if she felt this strongly about it, I'd help her, no questions asked. I just couldn't figure out why it was so important to her … and then I felt like a fool.

I'd bet my truck she'd been in a similar situation back in Ardmore.

"I work at the Stop-N-Go, and I don't know for sure where she lives. She don't have a car, so she walks to the convenience store every day from the apartments about a quarter mile down the road."

"Did you ever see her boyfriend?" I asked.

He shook his head. "No. She said he didn't know she visited the store as often as she did."

"His name is Bubba?" I asked.

"Yeah."

"Does she have a job?" I asked.

"None that I knew about. I asked her a few times, and she said Bubba doesn't like her to leave the apartment."

"Do you have a photo of Becky on your phone?" Neely Kate asked. "We can use it to ask around about her."

"Yeah," he said, then opened his photos and showed us a picture.

Becky was a tiny girl with shoulder-length dark hair and a few scattered freckles. She would have been pretty in a girl-next-door way if not for the vacant look in her eyes.

Neely Kate took a long look, her expression distraught.

"We need you to send that to us," I said.

He tapped on his phone, and mine buzzed with the incoming text. "Can you think of anything else that might help us?"

"No," he said, lying back on his pillow and looking exhausted.

I gave Neely Kate a warning glance before I said, "We'll do everything we can to find her, but right now, we need to know what you and your buddy pulled out of the safe."

"A whole lot of nothin'," he said. "Rusty thought there would be more money in there, but there was only a couple hundred dollars and a bunch of papers. He stuffed everything inside a pillow case. Then we smashed a few cases and grabbed some jewelry and cells phones to sell."

"Where'd you go?" I asked.

"To Rusty's grandma's house. She was at some church picnic, and then she was goin' over to a friend's house. She rode with her friend, so we left Rusty's truck at her place and took her car to the pawn shop. The plan was to split the loot, get

Rusty's truck, and head home, but Rusty said he had something to sell first. He told me to stay at his grandma's place while he took care of it. Said we shouldn't be seen together."

Neely Kate and I exchanged looks.

"Those papers he took from the safe have to be the file Wagner is lookin' for," I said. I turned to Marshall. "Who'd he go meet?"

"I dunno."

"Think hard, Marshall," Neely Kate said, sounding gruff. "I suspect your life might depend on gettin' those papers back."

Terror filled his eyes. "I dunno." He ran a hand through his hair. "Uh … he made a call, but I don't know who to. Then he said he had to take the papers to the buyer and left."

"What time was that?"

"I dunno exactly. I was scared, and it all kind of ran together. Maybe four? Maybe six?" Then he held out his hand to Neely Kate. "He called me. I'll look it up."

She handed him his phone, saying, "Don't try to delete anything, or we'll drive you to Ripper Pawn and drop you off on Kip Wagner's front step with a bow tied around your neck."

He looked scared to death as he opened his phone, and he seemed to be careful as he scanned his calls. "Here," he said, holding it up. "He called me at 5:05 and said his buyer had fallen through, but he was on the west side of town, so he wouldn't be back for at least a half hour. He said he was bringing food."

"You trusted him?" she asked. "You trusted that the buyer didn't go through?"

He looked surprised. "Why would he lie?"

"To keep the money," she said.

He adamantly shook his head. "No. Rusty wouldn't do me wrong like that."

"Then why didn't he take you with him?" Neely Kate asked. "And no, I'm not buyin' his excuse of not bein' seen together. You could have ducked down in the back."

Marshall didn't answer.

"So he came back a half hour later with food?" I asked.

"No, closer to an hour."

"And did you talk to anyone while he was gone?" I asked. "Did anyone know what you two were up to?"

He shook his head. "Only Becky."

"Did you call or text her while you were waiting for Rusty?" I asked.

"Yeah, I texted." He gave me a pleading look. "She knew what we were doin', and she'd heard about the robbery on the news. She was scared for me and sent me a text askin' if I was okay. So I told her I was fine, we'd gotten some loot, and I'd be back in town soon."

"Did she know where you were?" I asked.

He ducked his head. "Rusty told me not to tell, but she was scared, so I told her not to worry, I was at Rusty's granny's property on the east side of town."

"So Rusty showed up with food," Neely Kate said, "and then he took you back to town?"

"No, he said we should hang out for a bit. He looked really nervous and could hardly choke down his burger. I asked him what was wrong, and he said he thought Wagner was onto us. He thought we ought to leave town. I told him I wasn't leavin' without Becky, but he said I couldn't go into town to get her. We needed to head to Little Rock."

"What happened then?" Neely Kate asked.

"Well, the only reason I agreed to this whole mess was to help Becky, so I sure as hell wasn't leaving without her. I made a dash to his truck, but he tackled me. And as we were rollin' around in his yard, a truck showed up and started shooting at us."

"Wagner's men found you?" I asked.

He nodded. "I guess so. I got shot, but Rusty dragged me into the truck and took off."

"How'd you get away?"

"I don't know. I was freakin' out, but I think he lost them on his granny's property. When the coast was clear, he brought me to you. He said you'd take care of me." Tears filled his eyes. "He saved me and got himself killed. I can't believe he's dead." He swiped a tear from his cheek.

"Where's the loot?" Neely Kate asked.

His tone turned bitter. "He took all the stuff with him, but I didn't realize that until today. I risked my life and got shot for nothin'."

It was hard to argue with that.

"You're tellin' the truth?" Neely Kate asked. "Rusty took everything?"

He nodded but avoided eye contact. "I don't know how I'm gonna be able to save Becky now."

"Marshall," I said gingerly. "Somebody told Kip Wagner that you were at Rusty's granny's farm, and he also found out you were here at my house. Both instances involved you tellin' Becky where you were. Are you sure she's on the up-and-up?"

"Why would she want to rat me out when I was tryin' to help her?"

I shot a glance to Neely Kate, who didn't look happy with my line of questioning. "I don't know. It just seems like an awfully big coincidence."

"I think we need to talk to Becky and hear her side of the story," Neely Kate said. "We're gonna need her number."

"I have a better idea," I said, then held out my phone to Marshall. "We're gonna need your phone."

Chapter Fourteen

Chapter Fourteen

Marshall was reluctant to hand over his phone, but Neely Kate finally convinced him.

"Becky might not answer if the call or text comes from someone she doesn't know," she said. "She'll be more likely to answer if it's you."

Fear filled his eyes. "She didn't rat me out. I swear it."

"I believe you," Neely Kate said. "But if someone's watchin' her, she might be in danger."

Neely Kate placed another unanswered call to Becky while I took his temperature. I was relieved to see it had gone down. We told him to get some sleep, and Neely Kate promised to start looking for the girl first thing in the morning.

"Are you gonna bring Becky here?" he asked.

"I don't know what we're gonna do," I said.

"If we find her and she wants to come, yes," Neely Kate said emphatically. "The fact that her number doesn't go directly to voicemail is a good sign."

I had major doubts about Becky—and her failure to answer seemed like an indication of guilt—but now didn't seem like the best time to address them.

When we headed downstairs, Witt was standing in the living room talking to Jed. The moment he saw Neely Kate, he jogged over and engulfed her in a bear hug. "What trouble have you gotten yourself into now?" he asked in a teasing tone, but the look he gave me let me know he was none too pleased.

"The usual," she said before pulling free. "Thanks for coming."

"If you need help, I'm there, NK," he said in a serious tone. "You know that. Always."

"I know." She reached up on her tiptoes and planted a kiss on his cheek. "Are you hungry? We still have some leftovers from Rose's picnic yesterday."

Witt laughed. "I saw the whole thing on YouTube, although I guess it's not so funny when you take into account that Patsy Sue went and killed her cousin later."

Neely Kate put her hands on her hips. "She did no such thing."

"How on earth can you say that?" Witt asked in disbelief. "Isn't it obvious?"

"And that's why our client hired us," Neely Kate said. "Because everyone thinks she's guilty, never mind that we're all innocent until proven guilty."

"It didn't help that we found her standing over the dead body," I muttered.

"Is that why I'm here?" Witt asked. "How's Wagner tied up in Carol Ann Nelson's murder?"

"He's not," Neely Kate said, heading for the kitchen. "Totally different situation. Wagner is Lady in Black business."

Witt's dark look returned, but Neely Kate missed it since he was facing her back.

"You're seriously tryin' to prove that Patsy Sue Clydehopper is *innocent*?" he asked with a chuckle.

"Yep." Neely Kate pushed open the kitchen door, and Witt followed her in.

"Find out anything helpful?" Jed asked. He was seated on the sofa and Muffy was curled up on his lap.

"Possibly," I said, flopping down in the armchair. "But I think we should wait for Neely Kate and Witt before we discuss it."

He gave a short nod.

I glanced toward the closed kitchen door, and when I heard the cousins' muffled voices, I said, "Jed, I'm about to ask you a few things that will likely have you tellin' me to mind my own business, but I'm gonna ask them anyway."

He looked amused. "Shoot."

I suspected he wouldn't be grinning when I was finished. "Why does Neely Kate keep goin' up to Little Rock to see Kate?"

Sure enough, his smile fell. "You should be askin' *her* that question, not me."

"Believe me, I have, and she refuses to tell me." I paused. "Joe knows. He confronted her with it on Sunday night. Did she tell you that?"

"Yeah."

"But he didn't seem to know about you goin' with her. I know you drive her up there, but does she visit Kate alone?" I couldn't stand the thought. Kate Simmons was a manipulative witch who'd been stringing Neely Kate along by claiming to have details about her missing mother. But from what I could gather, Kate mostly just taunted and tormented my best friend for her own sick amusement.

"No. I go with her." Jed paused, then lowered his voice. "But that's not public knowledge. Skeeter has a person in the hospital who lets us in through the back door. I have no idea how Joe knows about our visits. Maybe Kate told him."

"But she didn't tell Joe about you?" I asked. "Because I know he would have grilled her about you."

He made a face. "Kate considers me a curiosity. She looks forward to our visits. She probably told Joe about Neely Kate to make her life more difficult. Joe's gonna be unhappy she's visiting, but he can't stop her. But Kate's not gonna tell him about me because she wants me to keep comin'."

"So Kate's playin' some sick game?"

"When is she not?" Jed asked. "But I have no idea what she's up to this time."

I narrowed my eyes. "How and why does James have a person in the psych ward in Little Rock?"

Jed crossed his arms. "I guess you'll have to ask him that."

"Why do I think I won't get a better answer out of him?"

"That's between the two of you."

"Have you really quit workin' for him?" I asked.

"I no longer take orders from him, and I'm lookin' to become a fine, upstanding citizen of Fenton County."

But that wasn't exactly an answer. I still heard Neely Kate's and Witt's voices in the other room, so I broached my next subject. "I know you helped Neely Kate in Ardmore. I … I need to know if she was mistreated by a man there."

He made a face, clearly uncomfortable. "Rose, you'll have to talk to Neely Kate about this."

"Believe me, I've tried, so I'm asking you: was she mistreated by a man? I only ask because Marshall told us he was stupid enough to rob the pawn shop hoping to get enough money to help a girl he met at the convenience store he works at. She's livin' with a man who controls her, and Marshall's hoping to help her escape. Neely Kate looked shaken when

Marshall mentioned it, and she seems to have taken a personal interest in the girl." I waited for a reaction, but he didn't say anything. "I suspect she's going to dump Patsy's case to go look for Becky. I'm good with that, but I don't want her doin' it alone. I want you to help her—if you're open to it."

"Of course. I care about her, Rose. I'd *never* let anything happen to her."

I nodded, pleased by the fierceness of his reply. It felt good to know she had someone to look out for her. "Thank you."

The kitchen door burst open, and Witt walked through carrying a plate of fried chicken and potato salad, along with some biscuits. He sat down in the armchair next to mine while Neely Kate handed a plate of the leftover fried chicken to Jed and then sat down next to him. "I figured you'd want some too."

He smiled down at her, his face soft and tender as he leaned over and gave her a sweet kiss.

She smiled up at him, and my heart nearly burst with happiness for her. Neely Kate deserved every bit of joy she had coming her way. While Jed didn't seem to know what Neely Kate's sister was up to, I couldn't think of a better person to protect my best friend. I'd just have to trust him for now.

Neely Kate and I then proceeded to tell Jed and Witt what we'd found out from Marshall.

"We need a plan for tomorrow," I said, looking at Neely Kate. "I take it you want to search for Becky."

Her face hardened. "I know we're supposed to be helpin' Patsy, but if Becky's in danger—"

"Neely Kate," I said softly. "You don't need to convince me. I think it's a good idea. You look for Becky, and I'll take over on Patsy's case. But the only way I'll agree to all of this is if you take Jed or Witt," I said, not wanting to let her know Jed and I had already discussed it.

"I'll take her," Jed said.

"You mean you'll go with me," she said in defiance.

Jed's brow lifted. "I'd love to let *you* take *me* if you'd let me get you another car. Your piece of crap isn't goin' anywhere."

Witt was strangely quiet considering he was the guy who usually worked on Neely Kate's piece of crap. Last I'd heard, he was trying to get money together to start his own mechanic's garage since his old boss had suddenly closed shop several weeks ago.

"Okay," I said. "Did your other lead on Patsy pan out?"

Neely Kate nodded eagerly. "We tracked down a cousin who had some information on Carol Ann. Charlene, a relation on her father's side."

"Oh?"

"She insinuated that Carol Ann had been back for longer than anyone suspected. I got the impression she'd been back longer than a month. More like two."

I tilted my head. "Wait. Patsy and Calvin made it sound like Carol Ann just got here last week."

"That's because she'd been living under the radar down in Big Thief Hollow. According to Charlene, her own mother didn't know she was back."

Big Thief Hollow was about a half hour south of Henryetta. "Why would she hide something like that?"

Neely Kate shrugged. "Charlene said Carol Ann was working on setting up a new business, but she had no idea what it was."

"She hit Patsy up for money last week. Maybe it was for her business. I'll take over the meeting you set up with her mother's side of the family tomorrow. Anything else?"

"We dropped by Patsy's real estate office too, but nobody knew anything … or at least that's what they said. I got the impression they weren't being straightforward with us."

I lowered my phone. "I just don't get it. If Patsy wants us to help clear her name, why not just tell us what she was doin' after the picnic on Sunday afternoon? Why all the secrecy?"

"Sounds like she's up to something devious," Witt said. "Something that's likely to incriminate her for a whole different reason. Which is why she hired you all to find the killer." He leaned back in his chair. "Ten to one she'll be spittin' nails when she finds out you've been investigatin' her and not really lookin' for the killer."

Neely Kate leaned forward and planted her hands on her hips. "Are you gamblin' again?"

Witt's face flushed. "What makes you ask that?"

"You just said 'ten to one.'"

He waved his hand to the side. "Everyone says things like that."

"But it's different when it comes from a guy who's gotten into trouble gamblin'."

"I ain't gamblin', Neely Kate," he said, getting riled up. "Now lay off."

It was clear Neely Kate didn't want to let it go, but she sat back on the sofa and Jed wrapped his arm around her shoulders.

Witt seemed eager to change the subject. "So, let's return to the kid for a moment. Who was his buddy's contact for selling the papers from the safe?"

"And why were they important?" Jed added. "Too bad we don't have Rusty's phone."

"Do you remember Rusty?" I asked him. "Marshall said James turned him away."

Pursing his mouth, he shook his head. "No, but I did turn away the kids who showed up wantin' to work for us after the Simmons mess in February. Skeeter disagreed, but he deferred to me in the end."

"Sounds like it didn't do any good," Witt said through a mouthful of fried chicken. "The kid got dirty anyway."

"I can sleep at night," Jed said. "I had no part in soilin' 'em."

I watched their exchange in silence. James had shared parts of his business with me in the past. One thing he and Jed had never seen eye to eye on was new recruits. Jed was dead set against bringing in green kids, hoping he could keep them from a life of crime, while James insisted they'd be better off joining his men if they were intent on getting involved. In the end, he'd deferred to Jed.

"I know you two are gonna look for Becky," I said, "but you don't have much to go on."

"We got the name of the convenience store he works at," Neely Kate said, "and we know she lives in the apartments down the street. He said she walked there."

"It would help if we could ID her," Jed said.

Neely Kate held up Marshall's phone and showed them her photo. "Rose had Marshall send a copy to her phone too."

I turned to Jed. "Any thoughts on the file Rusty stole?"

Jed rubbed his chin. "Could be any number of things. Since Reynolds and Wagner had a parting of the ways, Wagner's been looking to build his drug business. Maybe it's a list of out-of-state suppliers."

Witt dropped a thoroughly gnawed piece of chicken onto his plate and picked up another. "Last I heard, Wagner was building his prostitution business."

"James said there wasn't a prostitution service in the county," I said, surprised. "But one of the issues Wagner brought up at the parley was prostitution. James said he'd never allow it."

"That doesn't mean Wagner dropped the idea," Jed said. "It's not like we followed through on makin' sure he let up."

Neely Kate turned to face Jed. "What if the file was a list of clients?"

He shook his head. "Havin' a few pimps is one thing, but runnin' a prostitution ring is another. We knew about the pimps. If it had grown any bigger, we likely would have caught wind of it."

"Well, Calvin Clydehopper's secretary is certain he's hirin' hookers," Neely Kate said, then filled them in on what we'd discovered.

"I'm still not sure I buy it," Jed said when she finished.

"Then where's Calvin's never-ending supply of girls coming from?" Witt asked as he picked up his third piece of chicken.

"Somebody needs to pay Clydehopper another visit," I said.

Jed gave me a dark look. "I'll take care of it tomorrow."

"It's gonna look suspicious if you're askin'," I said. "Besides, you're supposed to find Becky with Neely Kate."

"I don't like the idea of you quizzing Clydehopper on your own."

"I'll go with her," Witt said before he took a bite of his biscuit. "I can put Marshall down in your safe room for a little while."

"I don't need a babysitter to visit Calvin," I protested. "He's as harmless as they come."

He shrugged. "I've got nothin' goin' tomorrow besides watching the kid. I can meet you there and we'll go in together."

Jed nodded. "I like it."

"Thanks, Witt," Neely Kate said, stifling a yawn. "I'll feel better if you're with her."

"No problem," he said. "Rose and I need to catch up anyway." The look he shot me let me know exactly what he planned for us to catch up on.

Chapter Fifteen

Jed and Witt discussed guard duty, and in the end they decided Witt would sleep downstairs on the sofa, and Jed would stay in Neely Kate's room, which happened to be at the top of the stairs.

We got bedding for Witt, and it was well after midnight by the time I headed to bed. I called Muffy to come with me, but she refused to budge from her spot at the end of the sofa.

"What's up with Muffy?" Witt asked.

"I think she wants to pull guard duty too," I said. "She's pretty good at it. She's the one who alerted me to Kip Wagner and his cronies showin' up."

Witt ruffled the fur on the back of Muffy's neck. "Then it looks like I have company."

A quick check on Marshall told me he was sleeping and his fever had broken. One less thing to worry about.

When I got to my room, I plugged my phone in. I noticed that I'd missed a text, and I sucked in a breath when I saw who it was from.

Mason.

I SHOULD HAVE LET YOU KNOW I WAS COMING TO TOWN. I'M SORRY TO HAVE BLINDSIDED YOU AND EVEN SORRIER FOR HOW THINGS WENT. I'D REALLY LIKE TO SEE YOU AGAIN, ROSE. YOU DECIDE THE TIME AND THE PLACE. EVEN IF IT'S ONLY TO TELL ME YOU NEVER WANT TO SEE ME AGAIN, I DON'T WANT TO LEAVE THINGS LIKE WE DID. I'LL BE STAYING WITH MY MOTHER UNTIL THURSDAY MORNING.

Did I want to see him again? I was too exhausted to think about it.

I had trouble getting to sleep without Muffy curled up at my feet. I rolled onto my side to face Mason's old spot, placing my hand on top of the covers. Getting over Mason had been ten times worse than getting over Joe, and truth be told, I wasn't sure I had completely recovered. But part of it was undeniably that I missed spending my life with someone. There was no denying the feelings James stirred inside me, but even if he and I were in a relationship, I doubted he would sleep over at my house. The risk of people finding out would be too great. I'd have to stay over at his house, and even then, it would likely only be a few nights a week.

Was that really what I wanted?

I finally drifted off to sleep, but my dreams were troubled. I dreamed of Jeanne telling me that I'd killed her, and of Kip Wagner and his men shooting their way into my house and killing Marshall in front of my eyes. And then Merv was standing in front of me once again, my hand firmly in his as a bullet pierced the side of his head. We fell into darkness until he crashed into me and a thick, warm liquid spilled over my body. Merv's blood. I kicked and thrashed as I tried to get free, but it only made more blood pool around me, rising higher and higher. I began to scream as the blood started to cover my face.

I bolted upright in bed, my body drenched in sweat.

"Rose," Neely Kate said, stroking my arm. "It's okay. It was only a dream."

I gasped for breath as I turned to see her sitting beside me. "I'm sorry I woke you."

"It's okay," she said, running her hand over the side of my head.

I shook my head. "No. It's not okay."

She pulled me into a hug, my chin resting on her shoulder as she rubbed my back.

"I think you should talk to Jonah," she said in a soothing tone. "Maybe he can help you work through this."

I had to wonder if she was right. My friend Jonah Pruitt, who also happened to be the pastor of the New Living Hope Revival Church, had helped me work through my breakup with Joe, not to mention the lingering trauma from years of my mother's abuse.

"Just consider it, okay?" she asked.

I nodded.

"Let's lie down," she said, tugging me down to the pillows. "Try to get more sleep."

I did as she asked, and to my surprise, she lowered herself down next to me, over the covers, resting her hand on my arm.

"Go back to bed, Neely Kate. I'm fine. I'm sorry I woke you."

"Let me just stay here for a few minutes, okay?" she asked. "Jed's downstairs, pacing the living room floor, and I can hear him. I might get some sleep if I'm in here with you."

I didn't totally believe her, but I was grateful that she was here. My breathing slowed down, and I felt myself begin to relax.

"Do you ever look at your life and wonder how you got here?" Neely Kate whispered.

I rolled to my side to face her. "You mean because of what happened tonight with Kip Wagner?"

"Not just that." She gave a tiny shake of her head. "I'm not explainin' it right." She paused. "I mean like me and Jed. Never in a million years did I think I could get a guy like him. Sweet. Devoted." She grinned. "Sexy as hell."

I grinned back.

Her smile faded. "Sometimes I think he's too good to be true. That any minute he's gonna come to his senses and change his mind."

"Oh, Neely Kate," I gushed. "I've seen the way that man looks at you. He's not gonna change his mind."

"But he still won't sleep with me. Maybe he just feels sorry for me after …"

"After?"

"What he found out about me in Ardmore."

"Well …," I said. "I'm not sure what he found out about you in Ardmore, and I know you're not ready to tell me, but he looks like he's more smitten with you every day. I suspect he's just old-fashioned."

"I hope so."

"He cares about you, Neely Kate. I can see it plain as day. That's not pity. It's …" I almost said love, but as far as I knew, they hadn't exchanged the L word yet. I was going to let her find that one out on her own. "He likes you."

She was quiet for several seconds before I said, "I saw Mason today … Well, I guess yesterday."

She jolted in shock. "*What?*"

"Shh!"

"Don't worry about wakin' Marshall," she said. "I peeked in on him before comin' in here, and he was out cold." She grabbed my hand. "Why didn't you tell me?"

"There wasn't a right time."

"When? What happened? I need details!"

"I was at the Piggly Wiggly pickin' up Marshall's antibiotics, and before I knew it, he was standin' beside me, helpin' me get the prescription like he was ridin' in to save the day."

"What's he doin' here? When did he get back into town?"

"Yesterday. He said he's here for work. He wants to see me again before he leaves on Thursday."

"Do you want to see him?" she asked.

"I don't know. Our conversation didn't go well … I'm not proud of the way I behaved. I think maybe I'd like a chance to make it right."

"I don't know how you reacted," she said, "but if you told him off, he totally deserved it."

I grinned. "I did, but that's not the part I'm ashamed of."

"What on earth did you do?"

"I cried."

"Oh, honey …," she said, squeezing my hand. "*That's* nothing to be ashamed of. You had to be in shock. And he hurt you."

"He told me he wants me back, Neely Kate."

"What?" she whisper-shouted. "You're kiddin' me."

I didn't say anything.

"Do you want *him* back?"

I closed my eyes. "I don't know. I don't think so. There's no denyin' that I loved him, but he hurt me, and I've changed. I'm not the woman he fell in love with. I'm not even the woman he left."

"What about Skeeter? Are you gonna tell him no?"

"I know you're right, and I'll never get what I want in a relationship with James. There's so much stacked against us."

"So you're gonna tell Skeeter no?"

I hesitated. "I suppose I should."

"That's not a no, Rose."

I grimaced. "It's not a yes either."

"I shouldn't have pushed you so hard on this earlier. The thing is, I'm not really sure what to tell you. I want to tell you to follow your head, be smart, but following my head is what got me married to Ronnie. I want to tell you to follow your heart, but that's what convinced me to go to Ardmore after I graduated."

"But you think I should walk away from him, right?" I asked.

"It was wrong of me to try tellin' you what to do. All I can tell you is that I listened to my instincts with Jed. He makes me a better person. He makes me believe I'm not worthless."

"Oh, Neely Kate. You're not worthless."

"Jed helps me believe that." She took a breath. "I think a good man loves you for who you are, but isn't threatened when you grow."

"Yeah, maybe you're right." So where did that leave Mason?

"Roll over and I'll scratch your back," she said. "That'll help you go to sleep."

I did as she suggested. When I felt her sharp nails scratching through my thin T-shirt, I nearly sighed with contentment. "Thank you," I whispered, already getting drowsy. "I don't know what I'd do without you."

"Good thing you'll never have to find out."

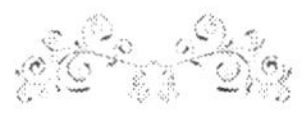

I WOKE UP a few hours later, surprised it was a little before seven. Neely Kate was still sleeping, but she'd gotten under the covers at some point. I slid out of bed and took a shower and changed into a pink sundress with tiny pink rosebuds.

Neely Kate was awake when I came out of the bathroom, and she looked surprised when she saw my dress. "Are you canceling your appointment this morning?"

"I figured I'd focus on Patsy Sue and Marshall today. I don't think the client will mind. She seemed pretty flexible."

I walked over to my dresser and dug out my small handgun and leg harness from my underwear drawer.

Neely Kate sat up in bed and watched me. "You hate wearin' your gun."

"After last night, I think it's a good idea, don't you?"

"Yeah," she said reluctantly.

"Did you and Jed come up with a plan to look for Becky?" I asked as I propped my left foot up on the bed.

"We're goin' to canvas the apartment complex. If we don't find her, hopefully we'll find someone who knows her, then take it from there."

I nodded. "You take as long as you need."

"I know you don't trust Becky."

"Neely Kate," I said as I started to strap the holster on my left thigh, "you have to admit it's suspicious that she's the last person Marshall contacted both times he was ambushed."

"For all we know, her abusive boyfriend was eavesdropping."

"I realize that's a possibility," I said as I buckled a strap. "But even if that's the case, we still need to be careful."

She didn't respond.

"Look," I said, holding her gaze, "it's easy to see Becky's tugged at your heartstrings, but we don't know for certain that she's innocent."

Anger flared in her eyes. "We don't know that she's guilty either."

"Agreed. We don't know enough to make a decision one way or the other. We need more facts in both cases."

"I know that, Rose," she said, getting irritated.

I glanced up from tightening the strap on my thigh. "Neely Kate, I'm not the enemy here. I just don't want you to get hurt if it turns out Becky's been selling Marshall down the river."

Contrition washed over her face. "I know. I'm sorry. It's just …"

"You knew someone like her?" I asked.

A sad smile twisted her lips. "Yeah."

"Well, I hope she's who Marshall thinks she is."

"We just have to find her," Neely Kate said.

Marshall was still sleeping when I checked on him. Then Neely Kate and I headed downstairs together.

Jed and Witt were in the kitchen, each with a cup of coffee, and Muffy was curled up at Jed's feet. She hopped up when she saw me and came running over. I squatted and rubbed her head. "Any trouble after I went to bed?" I asked.

"None," Witt said. "You headed to work?"

"Yeah. I have some plans I can work on until I go to meet Patsy's mother."

Jed turned his seat to face me. "Don't forget to call Witt so he can go see Clydehopper with you."

I stood and moved to the coffee maker, grabbing a travel mug from the cabinet. "I'm not sure when I'm going to go see Calvin, but I'll give you a heads-up when I know, Witt."

Jed watched me with narrowed eyes. "Don't forget to call him, Rose."

I got the creamer out of the fridge, looking down at Muffy. "I can't take you with me today, girl. You get to stay with Uncle Witt today."

"Rose …," Jed warned.

"I said I'll call him," I said with a groan as I poured the creamer into my mug then put it back. "I'll let him know when I know."

"Uncle Witt?" Witt groaned in disgust, but Neely Kate and Jed chuckled.

I gave Witt the evil eye as I screwed the lid on my mug. "You better be nice to my dog today. If she tells me you were anything but, there will be hell to pay."

"Like your dog's gonna tell on me …"

"You'd be surprised what that dog's capable of," Jed said

Neely Kate was still standing by the door to the living room, so I kissed her cheek as I walked past her. "Be careful today," I whispered. "Be careful with your heart." Both of us knew I wasn't talking about Jed.

I LIKED WORKING at the office in the early mornings. There was hardly anyone milling around the square, and it was quiet enough for me to get plenty done.

I'd already worked up a landscaping plan for one of the clients I'd interviewed the previous day when the bells on the door chimed. I glanced up, half-expecting to see Joe with another peace offering for Neely Kate, so I was surprised when I saw Maeve Deveraux.

"Maeve," I said in astonishment as I got out of my seat. "Hey."

"Good morning, Rose," she said as she walked toward me with a look of hesitation. "Sorry to just drop in like this. Am I interrupting?"

First, I was constantly dropping in on her at the nursery, and on more than a few occasions, she'd watched Muffy for me. And second, Maeve might be Mason's mother, but I considered her a dear friend. Still, there was no getting around the fact that the breakup had affected my relationship with Maeve in a negative way. Mostly, we didn't know how to spend quality time together without reminding each other that we had lost the same person. I wasn't the only one Mason had left behind when he moved to Little Rock. Maeve had moved to Henryetta to be near her son, and now she was alone.

"Don't be silly," I said, pushing my chair back from my desk. "You're never interrupting."

"I wasn't sure how you'd feel about seeing me after you ran into Mason yesterday."

I grimaced. "He told you what happened?"

"Not everything, so please don't worry about him breaking any confidences, but he told me enough for me to know it caught you by surprise, and for that I'm terribly sorry."

"Maeve," I said. "Why on earth are you sayin' you're sorry? This has nothing to do with you. It's between me and Mason."

"I had a day's notice that he was coming. I should have warned you, but what with Violet and the nursery bursting at the seams with business … well, it just slipped my mind. I'm sorry."

I stood and walked over to her and pulled her into a hug. "It's not your job to warn me. Besides, I'm a big girl."

She gave me a tight squeeze before releasing me. "I know, but it might have made things easier."

I thought about it for a moment, then said, "You know, I'm not sure which would have been better. If I'd known he was coming to town, I probably would have been paranoid about running into him. So maybe it worked out better this way." I glanced at the clock on the wall. "What are you doin' downtown this early?"

Her face flushed. "Mason took me to Merilee's for breakfast."

My stomach clenched. "Oh." I forced a smile. "That must have been lovely for you, Maeve. I know how much you've missed him."

She nodded, tears filling her eyes. "That's part of the reason I stopped by. I don't want to worry you, but I thought you should know that I'm at least considering something."

I resisted the urge to stiffen my back, but I suspected I knew what she was going to say … and it hurt. "Considering what?"

"Moving back to Little Rock."

I nodded, trying to keep my emotions at bay as I backed up and sat on the edge of my desk. "I see."

"I'm not sure you do," she said, wringing her hands.

In all the time I'd known Maeve, I'd only seen her this anxious one other time, and that had been over the threat to Mason's life. "Maeve, I understand. Truly I do. I haven't been very good at keeping in contact with you. I know Neely Kate and Joe have been better, but they've both been distracted lately …"

"Rose," she said softly with a warm smile. "It's not up to you to make me happy. It's up to me."

"I know, but—"

"But nothing. And I haven't been lonely. I've kept busy with the nursery and my activities. Of course I wish I saw you more often, but I understand how painful it's been." She smiled. "We've discussed it ad nauseam."

I grinned back.

"I'm only considering it because of Mason. He's lonely. He misses me and, well …"

"He's your son." And her daughter had been murdered over a year ago, so he was also her only child. Her husband had died when Mason was in college, and they only had each other now.

"Yes," she said. "One day when you have a child, you'll understand."

"I think I understand now."

The look she gave me was full of warmth. "Of course, I wouldn't leave you high and dry with the nursery. Anna's been doing a wonderful job, so I'm sure she could take over my duties. We'd just have to hire someone to replace her. In fact, business has picked up so much, we might consider hiring a seasonal worker to help out until the end of fall."

I nodded, but truthfully I hadn't even considered the nursery. I was sad she was leaving because I didn't want her to go, pure and simple. "Maeve, you're the last person I would accuse of leaving me high and dry."

"I probably wouldn't leave right away. Maybe just take off some weekends to go up to Little Rock. I know you have your hands full with Violet and all."

I nodded, looking away so she wouldn't see the tears in my eyes. I'd taken her for granted all these months. I'd expected her to be waiting for me when I was ready to jump back into our friendship, only a part of me had never considered Maeve a friend at all. I'd considered her to be the mother I'd never had but always wanted. And now I could be losing her.

She closed the distance between us and hugged me. "I haven't made a decision yet. I want to think about it, but I promise you'll be one of the first people I tell if I decide to move."

"Okay."

She pulled back and lifted my chin. "I'll still be here for you, Rose, even if I'm not in Henryetta."

I nodded, not trusting myself to speak.

"Before I say my next piece, I want you to know I'm not trying to meddle."

I grinned through my tears. "You're not a meddler."

"You may think differently when I'm done." I waited while she took a breath. "Mason knows your conversation went badly yesterday. He hadn't planned to see you. You hadn't planned to see him. You were both caught off guard, and I suspect he may have said some things he regrets. He feels terrible. He won't discuss his feelings for you, but I know he'd like to see you again before he goes back to Little Rock." She paused. "I'm not going to ask you to see him. That wouldn't be fair. I'm only telling you this because I think he wants to make things right."

"Thanks, Maeve. I'll consider it."

She kissed my cheek. "That's all I ask. I'll love you no matter what you decide."

A lump filled my throat, and I couldn't push out the "Me too."

I was losing everyone. I'd lost Mason. Violet was dying. Maeve was thinking of moving away. Neely Kate would spend less and less time with me now that she had Jed. I told myself I had James, but even if I decided to take the risk of being with him, I wouldn't have him. Not really. We couldn't have lunches like Mason and I used to do. Or go out to dinner. Or be seen together at all for that matter. He couldn't come to the hospital while I sat in the waiting room, anxious for news about my sister. He couldn't spend time with my niece and nephew. He couldn't stand by my side at Violet's funeral.

That last thought cracked me open.

"Rose."

Tears were streaming down my face, and I was barely holding myself together. "I'm fine."

"I don't think you are."

I swiped my face, irritated at all the tears I'd leaked over the past twenty-four hours. But my sister was dying—shouldn't that cut me some slack? "I was thinking about Violet."

"How's she doing?"

"Not good," I said, my voice breaking. "She doesn't have much time. Maybe weeks." Then I began to cry in earnest, gut-wrenching sobs that consumed my entire body.

My legs gave out and I lowered myself to the floor. Maeve got to her knees next to me and wrapped her arms around me. She rocked me and smoothed my hair, and the thought of losing her—of losing *this*—made me sob even harder.

We sat like that for several minutes until I started to settle down, and as I came to my senses, profound embarrassment washed through me.

"I'm so sorry …"

"Whatever for?" she asked in admonishment.

I gestured to her tear-soaked and snot-covered shoulder. "Exhibit A."

She reached up and cupped my cheek, staring into my eyes. "How many times have you cried since you found out that Violet was dying?"

"Like this? None."

A soft smile lit up her face. "Then I'd say you were due. I'm honored you felt safe enough with me to help you through it."

"I'm going to be alone, Maeve," I said, starting to cry again.

"Oh, sweet girl. You're not alone. You have so many people who love you. I promise you that." Then she pulled me into another hug. "If I move, I won't go until you're ready."

I wanted to tell her I'd never be ready, but that was selfish, so instead I said, "Thank you, but I could never ask you to stay."

"It's a good thing I wasn't asking for permission," she said with an ornery grin.

"You sounded like Neely Kate just now."

She laughed. "I'm going to take that as a compliment."

I realized we were both still sitting on the floor, so I got up and offered Maeve a hand to help her to her feet. She waited while I went into the restroom to wash my face—what little makeup I'd put on was now smeared all over my face.

When I emerged, Maeve wore a guilty look. "I'm sorry if anything I said upset you. In hindsight, I realize this wasn't a good time to bring up my possible move."

I gave her a wry grin. "There'd never be a good time to bring that one up, and besides, I don't want you to tiptoe around me."

"I don't want to be one more person hurting you," she said. "You've had too much pain in your short life. Be kind to yourself, Rose." Then she gave me another hug and left.

More unsettled than ever, I watched her walk across the street toward her car.

Chapter Sixteen

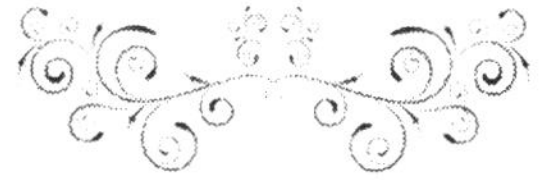

On the drive to Patsy's mother's house, I tried to call Patsy for the twentieth or so time. When I didn't reach her, I called Neely Kate.

"Made any progress?" I asked when she answered.

"We've knocked on a lot of doors at the apartment complex, and so far no luck. But the apartment manager's supposed to show up at eleven, so we're hopin' he can tell us something."

"Good idea," I said. "Did you check on Marshall again before you left the farm?"

"Yeah, his fever's still gone, and he has more color in his face. Witt said he'll make sure the boy gets fed today."

"Let me know when you find something," I said.

"You too."

I pulled in front of Blanche Stoneman's house a few minutes before ten, surprised to see four cars in the driveway. A teenage girl appeared in the doorway before I could knock on the door.

"Are you Neely Kate Rivers?"

"No, but I'm her partner, Rose Gardner. Neely Kate got detained with something else."

"Is that girl one of those lesbians?" an older woman shouted from behind the girl.

"No, Grandma," the teen said, rolling her eyes.

"She said she was somebody's partner," the older woman called back. "That's what they call their lovers on all those TV shows. They call 'em partners."

The teen gave me a sympathetic look. "I apologize in advance for Great-Grandma Bluebell."

Bluebell? Was she serious?

But I didn't have time to ask because the teen stepped to the side and let me in.

It felt like a walk-in freezer when I entered the house. Two older women who looked like they were in their sixties were sitting on the sofa and an even older woman was sitting on a dining room chair with a four-footed walker in front of her. I suspected the woman with the walker was Miss Bluebell. Her next words confirmed it.

"Do you know those boys on that show?"

I shook my head in confusion. "I'm sorry. What show?"

"You know, that show on Netflix. The one with all those gay boys."

I stared at her in disbelief for a second. "No. I'm sorry. I don't."

"Oh, for heaven's sake, Grandma!" a woman shouted from the other room. "We've already told you that not all gay people know each other!"

"How am I supposed to know that?" Miss Bluebell shouted back. "The ones on TV all seem so friendly." She looked up at me. "Are you sure you don't know them?"

"No," I said, trying to hide a grin. "And your granddaughter's right. I'm not a lesbian."

"Oh. Well, that's too bad," she said as she waved her hand in dismissal. "I've never met one before."

"Granny," the teen groaned. "I've already told you that you've met gays and lesbians before. You just didn't know it."

"That's a doggone shame," the elderly woman said. "Now that I've stopped condemning them to eternal damnation, I'd like to talk to one. They've got their own parade with a rainbow flag. I've always liked rainbows."

A woman who looked like she was in her late thirties appeared in the doorway to the kitchen, holding a dish towel in her hand. She gave me an apologetic look. "I'm so sorry about my grandmother." She gestured to the girl next to me. "Nicki there introduced her to the internet a few months ago, and now we never know what she's gonna say."

I grinned. "That's okay." I turned to her grandmother. "I don't happen to be a lesbian, but I like rainbows too."

The older woman frowned, clearly not appeased. "Well … I guess that has to count for something."

The teen leaned into my ear. "Granny just discovered tolerance at the New Living Hope Revival Church. Now she's trying to learn about the LGBTQ community."

"That's great," I said. "It's never too late for a change in your heart."

"That Reverend Pruitt is a miracle worker," the girl said.

"Jonah Pruitt is a godsend to this town," Miss Bluebell said, pointing her finger at her great-granddaughter. "I kept tryin' to get Patsy to go to his church with me, but she's too busy sinnin'."

So much for tolerance.

"She goes to church, Granny," the woman in the kitchen said. "That's where she got into a fight with Carol Ann."

Her face scrunched up in disgust. "It didn't stop her from sinnin', now did it?"

Miss Bluebell had a point. "What about Carol Ann?" I asked. "Did she come to church with you?"

The elderly woman's eyes narrowed. "How could she have come to church with me? She was only in town for a few days, and the picnic was on Sunday."

"I'm confused about when she got back," I said. "Do you know what day?"

The woman in the kitchen doorway wiped her right hand off with the kitchen towel. "Where are my manners?" She held out her hand. "Poppy. I'm Patsy's sister. Can I get you something to drink? A slice of coffee cake?"

"No, thank you."

"I thought Neely Kate was comin' with you," one of the women on the sofa said.

I turned to give her my attention, suspecting that one of the two sofa sitters was Patsy's mother. "Neely Kate got caught up in something else. I hope y'all don't mind that it's just me."

The woman made a face that suggested it wasn't ideal, but she didn't complain.

Poppy walked into the living room and gestured to the woman who'd asked about Neely Kate. "This is my mother, Lily. And next to her is her sister Lucille."

Lucille gave me a blank stare, looking like she was still in shock.

"I'm so sorry for your loss, Ms. Nelson," I said.

She nodded, and tears filled her eyes. "She always had a penchant for runnin' on the wild side. I guess I shouldn't be surprised this was how she left us."

"Nevertheless, I'm still sorry."

Poppy motioned to a worn and stained pale blue wingback chair by the door. "Rose, why don't you sit over here?"

"Thanks," I said as I took a seat and pulled a stenographer's notebook from my purse. "First of all, I want to thank y'all for meeting with me. I know this has to be a stressful time."

All five women nodded, and I realized I was sitting with four generations of Patsy Sue's family.

"Patsy called us and said you and Neely Kate would likely be comin' by," Poppy said in a gentle tone. She'd planted herself on the sofa between Lily and Lucille. "She told us that she'd hired you to help solve Carol Ann's murder."

"Yes." Okay, not exactly, but finding Carol Ann's killer was the surest way to clear her name. "When was the last time any of you talked to Patsy?"

They all shot glances to one another. "Yesterday morning," Lily said. "Right after word got out around town that Carol Ann was dead."

"Do you happen to know where she might be?" I asked.

Lily shook her head. "I have no earthly idea."

"Does she happen to own a lake house, or any other property she might be stayin' at?"

Lily shook her head. "I know she has some rental properties, but they're all filled with tenants."

I couldn't tell if she was lying, so I decided to move on. "Miss Bluebell mentioned that Carol Ann hadn't been in town long. Do y'all know when she came back?"

"Last Thursday," Poppy said. "She showed up at all our houses askin' for money."

"How much did she want?"

"Five thousand dollars."

My eyebrows shot up. That was a lot of money.

"I laughed in her face," Miss Bluebell said. "I'm living from one Social Security check to the next. I ain't got any extra to give. And even if I did, I sure wouldn't have given it to a girl who just frittered her money away."

"Granny," Poppy admonished. "Think about poor Aunt Lucille."

"*What?*" her grandmother demanded. "Just because the girl is dead don't make it any less true."

Poppy cringed. "Nevertheless, Grandma …"

"Where do you think she was before she came back?" I asked.

"Out in California," Lily said, "tryin' to become famous."

"I heard she wanted to be an actress," I said.

"Ha!" Miss Bluebell said. "It was a way to a means."

"So she wanted to be an actress to become famous?" I asked.

The older woman nodded. "The last we heard, she was tryin' to get on reality TV shows. She got on a few small ones no one's ever heard of like *Bowling with Frogs* and *Night Fishin' with Gators in the Swamp*. But last we heard, she hadn't been on one of them shows in a couple of years."

"Huh," I said as I wrote the information down. "So she was out in LA before she came back?"

"She was in Atlanta the last two years," Lucille said in a soft voice. "She said it was easier to get acting jobs there on account of all the production studios filming shows there. I'd hoped to see her more since she was so much closer, but if anything, I saw her less. But I think she spent a few months in Vegas after Atlanta."

"And when was the last time you saw her, Miss Lucille?"

"Thursday," she said, looking down at the tissue balled up in her hand.

"And when was the last time you spoke to her or saw her before that?"

"Well … she called me about two weeks ago. She told me she was workin' on a new opportunity that was different than anything else she'd done. She told me this one was perfect for her and it would finally bring her back home to me."

That fit with what Neely Kate had found out from her other cousin—that she'd been working on a business opportunity. "Do you happen to know what her new business was?"

She shook her head. "She said it was a secret. That if word got out, the competition would try to stop her."

"Competition?" I said, writing that down. "She didn't give any hints about what the competition might be?"

"No."

"What about where the business might be located?" I asked.

"Why are you askin' all these questions about a business that's never gonna happen?" Lily challenged. "My daughter is fightin' for her life, and you're talkin' about Carol Ann's pipe dream?"

"Fightin' for her life?" Miss Bluebell snorted. "Patsy's doin' what Patsy does best—lookin' out for Patsy." She pointed her finger at Lily. "There's no loyalty in that one. Not even to her husband."

There was so much information here for me to dig deeper into, but I ran the risk of alienating half the people in the room with every question. "I'd like to circle back to Patsy in a bit, but first I have a few more questions about Carol Ann's business."

The older woman looked pissed.

I turned back to Lucille and asked in a soothing tone, "Do you happen to know where she planned on opening it?"

She shook her head. "She said she didn't need a storefront. She could work out of her home, only she didn't have one yet. She was workin' on that too."

"Do you know what part of town? Or if she was hopin' to rent or buy?"

Lucille shook her head. "I don't know. She was so secretive about it."

"What does all of this have to do with Carol Ann bein' murdered by her cousin?" Miss Bluebell asked.

Everyone in the room gasped and tensed.

"What?" the older woman demanded. "I know all y'all are thinkin' it."

I rested my elbows on my knees and leaned closer as I held the older woman's gaze. "First of all, Neely Kate and I are tryin' to prove that Patsy Sue *didn't* murder her cousin."

She snorted. "Well, that's a fool's errand."

"Nevertheless, we're gonna try. Which means part of our job is to help figure out who *did* kill Carol Ann and why." When she didn't respond, I added, "If Carol Ann was opening a business and worried about competition, then there's the chance that the competition might have found out and killed her."

Everyone gasped except for Nicki, who was sitting on the floor next to her great-grandmother's chair. Nicki didn't look shocked at all. I definitely needed to talk to her later.

"Does the sheriff know that?" Lucille asked.

"I suppose it depends on what you told them," I said. "The more information they have, the better." The looks on their faces told me they hadn't thought it important enough to share.

"Carol Ann was stayin' at the Broken Branch Motel, but she checked in on Saturday night. Did any of y'all ask where she was stayin' before that?"

They all shook their heads.

"Did she ask to stay with you, Miss Lucille?" I asked.

"No. She doesn't like stayin' with me, and I don't like the late hours she keeps." Then she started to cry. "I guess she's not keeping any hours now."

"Did she have any friends she might have stayed with?" I asked.

Lucille shook her head and shrugged. "As far as I know, she burned most of her bridges years ago."

"What about other relatives?" I asked. All the women gave me blank looks, but Neely Kate had said she'd found one of Carol Ann's cousins. "Anyone on her daddy's side?"

Disgust washed over Lily's face. "Those fools live down in Big Thief Hollow."

"I take it y'all don't get along with them?" I asked.

"No," Lily bit out.

"Where is your ex-husband, Miss Lucille?" I asked.

Lily let out a harsh laugh. "Husband? Carol Ann's a bastard."

My eyes shot open, and Poppy let out a loud protest. "Momma, you can't go around sayin' things like that!"

"Why not?" she countered. "It's true."

I turned to Lucille, trying to ignore her sister. "So you had Carol Ann out of wedlock?"

She nodded. "She's my only child. Or I guess she was …"

I really wished I was conducting this interview with her alone, but Lily was beginning to seem like a bully. I doubted she would have allowed a one-on-one interview, and no doubt she would have given her sister endless grief had I insisted on it.

Poor Lucille had been through enough. "What happened to Carol Ann's father?"

"He died in prison," Lily blurted out in contempt. "Doin' fifty years for murder."

Lucille looked up at me through tear-filled eyes. "He didn't do it. He was framed."

"Neil's family is nothin' but white trash," Lily said. "It's no wonder Carol Ann turned out the way she did."

"Momma!" Poppy said.

Lucille turned toward her sister and slapped her hard across the cheek. The loud smacking sound made me startle.

Lily jumped to her feet. "You're just as white trash as the rest of 'em! Get out of my house!"

"Momma!" Poppy protested while Nicki looked on with wide eyes.

"Stop it right now," Miss Bluebell snapped. "Both y'all, stop it *right now*."

"My daughter is accused of murdering that white trash fool," Lily shouted at her mother. "So why are we wasting time talkin' about her white trash family?"

"Miss Lily," I said. My tone was a bit harsh, but she was starting to piss me off. It was easy to see where Patsy had gotten some of her negative personality traits. "I already told you why we're trying to find out who killed Carol Ann. Patsy can't bring herself to tell us what she was doin' on Sunday afternoon, so it's the only good avenue we have to investigate. And besides"—I gave Lucille a soft smile—"it will help Miss Lucille find some semblance of closure."

"Sit your ass down, Lily," Miss Bluebell said. "We're gonna help this woman find Carol Ann's killer. Even if it's your sorry daughter."

The other women looked startled, but Nicki glanced up at her great-grandmother and giggled.

"What?" the older woman asked. "You never heard the word ass before?"

The expressions on everyone's faces suggested they weren't used to hearing it from her.

"Carol Ann has some cousins down in Big Thief Hollow," Lucille said with more determination in her eyes. Slapping her sister seemed to have given her more backbone. "They're Neil's brother's girls."

"And where's Neil's brother?"

"He's the one Neil murdered," Lily said in disgust.

I expected Lucille to crumple from her sister's harsh tone, but the fierceness in her eyes said she was done with her sister's bullying. "I don't know how many times I have to tell you that Neil did not murder his brother. And before you start gloatin', maybe you should take a moment to reflect on the fact your daughter is facin' the exact same situation."

Lily clamped her mouth shut.

Lucille sat up straighter. "Neil came from the other side of the tracks. He was tryin' to make a better life for himself—and me. We were planning on gettin' married, especially after we found out about Carol Ann. Neil had been helpin' his brother with something illegal—"

"Drugs," Lily said in a self-righteous tone. "He was dealin' drugs."

Lucille shot her a dark look. "He planned to tell his brother he was done, but it didn't go well. Chuck said he'd never let Neil leave. The next night Chuck was dead, and Neil was arrested for his murder." She paused. "And I was left to raise our baby alone."

"I'm so sorry, Miss Lucille." Nowadays, plenty of women raised their babies alone, but I could only imagine the insults and judgment Lucille must have faced forty years ago. The fact that her sister seemed to be gloating about it didn't sit right with me.

"Was Carol Ann close to her cousins in Big Thief Hollow growin' up?" I asked softly.

Lucille glanced up with confusion in her eyes. "No. She never saw them. Their mother blamed me for bein' widowed, so we never had anything to do with that side of the family."

She obviously didn't know that Carol Ann had been in contact with them. I considered mentioning it, but I didn't want to give Lily any more information she could use to hurt her sister, and I doubted that Lucille had anything helpful to offer. Carol Ann had purposely kept the last couple of months from her. I wanted to find out why before bringing it up. "Did you and Carol Ann get along?"

I'd come into the interview thinking they hadn't—everyone had been quick to say they were tired of being used for money—but everything she'd said about her daughter had been loving.

She flopped her hand over in a nervous gesture. "We had our spats, but for the most part we got along."

"Carol Ann loved her momma," Poppy said with a tearful look. "She hated disappointin' her."

Lucille looked startled. "What?"

Poppy's mouth tipped up into a sad smile. "She knew she was all you had, and she hated that she didn't do more to make you proud. She hated that she was weak."

I focused my attention on Poppy. "When was the last time you talked to Carol Ann?"

"Last Thursday. She asked me for money too, but I don't have that kind of money."

"But you gave her *some*?" I asked.

She nodded with an embarrassed look. "A few hundred dollars. It wasn't much, but she was so desperate to make this new business work."

"She didn't give you any more information about the business?"

"No."

"And you gave her money anyway?" Lily demanded.

Instead of addressing her mother, Poppy turned to me. "She was really tryin' this time. I could see it in her eyes. She and her momma just needed to catch a break."

"Do you know where she was stayin?" I asked.

She shook her head. "No."

"And before last Thursday, when was the last time you talked to her?"

"About two months ago. That was the first time she mentioned her business—but she wasn't asking for money that time. She just told me she was workin' on it."

"She was in town?" I asked.

"No. Maybe she was in Atlanta. Or Vegas? I lost track of where she was livin', but she didn't say."

Lily snorted. "I don't believe for one minute she didn't ask you for money."

"Well, she didn't," Poppy said in defiance. "She called to say she was tired of hurtin' her momma, and she was finally goin' to do something that would make her proud."

I cast a glance toward Lucille, who was now silently weeping.

I really wanted to be done with this toxic environment, but I hadn't finished questioning them. "I know that Carol Ann asked Patsy for money. Do you know who else she hit up?"

"She didn't ask me," Nicki said.

Her great-grandmother shot her an ornery grin. "That's because you don't have a pot to piss in."

Lily's mouth dropped open in outrage. "Momma. You have got to stop goin' on the internet!" She glanced around the room, her face becoming blotchy. "This family is goin' to hell in a handbasket!" Lily shouted, then pointed her finger at her mother. "And you're in the driver's seat!"

"You know what you need?" Miss Bluebell asked. "You need a joint. Weed's legal in several states now."

Lily froze and looked so horrified you could have pushed her over with a pin. And while everyone else looked momentarily stunned by her announcement, they were soon stifling giggles.

It was time for me to take charge. "Look, it's obvious y'all have a lot of family business you'd like to attend to, so if I could ask a few more questions, I'll be more than happy to get out of your hair." When no one protested, I asked, "Does anyone know what Patsy was doin' between three and seven on Sunday afternoon?"

They remained quiet.

"Do you know of anyone who held a grudge against Patsy? Someone who might want to set her up?"

They were quiet again, but I could see they were putting more thought into this question.

"She made some enemies in her business," Poppy said.

"Fools who were jealous of her success," Lily said.

"Her *questionable* success," Poppy said.

"You hush your mouth!" Lily shouted. "You're jealous of her too."

"How can I not be, Momma? When you constantly shove my face in how wonderful she is and what a disappointment *I* am."

Nicki stiffened during the exchange. Her great-grandmother put a hand on her head and began to stroke her hair soothingly as she gave her daughter a dark glare.

"Poppy," I said. "Why do you say *questionable* success?"

"Patsy's always braggin' at family dinners about all her land deals. But I have a friend who says Patsy ripped her off."

"Ripped her off how?"

"Patsy purchased the land for a lot less than it was worth."

"And you made sure to bring it up at Thanksgivin' dinner, didn't you?" Lily asked. "Right there in front of everyone, you accused your sister of fraud. But you keep leaving out the part that exonerates your sister."

"What's that?" I asked.

"Patsy used an appraiser to come up with how much the land was worth. Poppy's friend is delusional."

Poppy made a face. "Well, my friend's not the only one who's pissed at her. Several people tried to bring a lawsuit against her, but Judge Berger refused to hear it."

"See?" Poppy's mother said. "Even the judge said she was on the up-and-up."

"Judge Berger is as crooked as they come," Poppy scoffed. "He was arrested for bribery charges."

"Everyone knows he was set up."

I resisted the urge to groan. Talk about denial. Judge Berger was the same corrupt judge who'd set my bail at a million dollars last winter after J.R. Simmons got me arrested on trumped-up charges.

"Poppy, do you think you can get me a list of the people you know who might have held a grudge against Patsy?" I pulled a business card out of my purse and handed it to her.

"Yeah." But she didn't look too sure, and I realized why. Giving me the information might help prove her sister didn't kill Carol Ann. And it looked like Poppy would love nothing more than to see Patsy Sue behind bars.

I got to my feet. "Well, if there's nothin' else you all have to share with me, I'll be on my way. But feel free to let me know if you think of anything."

The women all nodded, but Poppy was the only one who got to her feet. "I'll walk you to the door."

I cast a glance at Nicki, remembering her reaction to my suggestion that Carol Ann's competition might have killed her to get in the way. "Hey, Nicki. My niece's birthday's comin' up. Do you think you could walk out with me so I can pick your brain about what teenagers like these days?"

"Sure."

Poppy opened the front door and held it open for me. "Thanks for your help," I said.

She grimaced. "Yeah. Sure. I'm not sure what good we did."

I smiled. "You just never know."

Nicki followed me and shut the door behind her. As soon as we reached the driveway, she said, "That was pretty much the lamest excuse you could have made to talk to me alone." Then she grinned. "Good thing my family's not the brightest."

I chuckled. "I guess I wasn't so subtle. I wanted to ask you what you know about Carol Ann's business."

She shoved her hands into the front pockets of her short jean shorts. "Not much more than what you learned in there."

"But something more …"

"More like who she was doin' it with."

"Her cousins on her father's side?" I asked.

She nodded.

"Neely Kate talked to one of them last night. Sounds like Carol Ann was in town for a lot longer than your family knows."

Nicki glanced back at the house before answering me in a much lower voice. "I know she'd been in town for at least two months. I ran into her down in Big Thief Hollow, but you can't tell my mom. I skipped school to go down there."

I almost asked her what she'd been up to, but I knew the sheriff's department had been trying—and failing—to stomp out the thriving drug market in that town. "When was this? The middle of May?"

Nicki nodded. "She was stayin' with one of the Big Thief Hollow cousins. She asked me not to tell anyone that I saw her. I told her she had a deal as long as she kept quiet about me."

I hesitated before asking my next question, but considering the profession of Carol Ann's cousins' deceased father, it needed to be asked. "Do you know if Carol Ann was using drugs?"

She stared at me like I'd just caught her letting out a loud, stinky fart.

"It might help me find out who killed her."

"Oh, I know who killed her," Nicki said. "Patsy's guilty as sin. I can't believe you're defending that bitch."

She glanced at the house, and I saw Lily glaring at us through the big picture window.

"Just so you know," she said with a grin. "When Grandma Lily grills me over our conversation, I'm going to make this whole gift story sound lame as hell."

Chapter Seventeen

I called Neely Kate as soon as I pulled away from the house. "Any luck finding Becky?" I asked.

"The manager's running late, so we haven't talked to him, but we found a neighbor who remembers her. He said he sees her walk to the convenience store nearly every day in the early afternoon. He pointed out the apartment he thinks she lives in, so we're watchin' the door while we wait for the manager. What about you?" she asked. "Find out anything useful?"

"You wouldn't believe what I found out." I spent several minutes filling her in on both Carol Ann and Patsy.

When I finished, she was quiet for a moment. "What do you think she was up to?"

"Honestly," I said, "I would have said she was jumping into the drug business, but why would she tell Poppy she was doin' something her mother would be proud of? Carol Ann's daddy got thrown into prison because he messed with the drug trade, or at least Lucille thinks so. She would *not* be happy."

"Yeah, that's throwin' me off too."

Since I didn't know where I was going next, I pulled into a convenience store parking lot. "Her cousin in Big Thief

Hollow didn't know anything specific about Carol Ann's business?"

"No, she only mentioned it in passing. She made it seem like no big deal."

"Or she was bein' super secretive about it. How'd it come up in the conversation?"

Neely Kate was quiet for a moment. "Come to think of it, Charlene's mother's the one who mentioned it. She kind of played it down."

"Sounds like we need to have another chat with Charlene."

"Yeah …"

"Did you know anything about Patsy cheatin' people in her real estate deals?" I asked.

"I've heard rumors. I know there was a lawsuit filed against her that got dismissed, but the people who sued her weren't the most trustworthy citizens of Fenton County. I figured it was a wash."

"Yeah, but Judge Berger's the one who threw out the case. Plus, you said Patsy's office staff acted weird. There's something fishy going on with her. All the more reason for me to talk to Calvin again."

"Agreed, but when are you plannin' on seeing him?" Neely Kate asked. "Witt had to leave Marshall in the panic room while he went to talk to someone about renting garage space for his mechanic shop. He won't be able to go with you until later this afternoon."

"Huh." I didn't want to wait to go see him. I'd built some momentum, and I would hate for it to grind to a halt now. I heard the beep of a text message and saw James' name on the screen.

WE NEED TO TALK. CAN YOU MEET ME AT THE SINCLAIR AT NOON?

My heart skipped a beat. What did he want to talk about? Was this about Marshall or about us? Maybe he'd decided to end things before I could give him an answer. Maybe the whole situation had begun to seem like too much of a gamble.

"Rose," Neely Kate said in an insistent tone. "Are you still there?"

"Yeah," I said. "Sorry. I got distracted. Call me if you find something. Maybe we can meet Charlene after you wrap things up there."

"Yeah," she said. "Be safe."

"Yeah. You too."

I checked the time and saw it was eleven thirty. If James had decided to end it, I'd rather know now than spend the rest of the day in suspense. I texted him: OKAY.

I could see the bubble telling me he was typing. After several long seconds, he sent: SEE YOU THEN.

Considering how long it had taken him to send those three words, I knew he'd originally planned to say something else, but Lord only knew what. I found myself pressing the back button so I could look at the list of my texts. Mason's name sat there like a bomb waiting to go off. No matter what happened with James, I felt like I had to put this business with Mason to rest. If nothing else, I needed closure—my talk with Maeve had shown me that.

I also needed to understand how much of James' appeal came down to how different he was from Mason, who'd always seemed so safe, solid, and reliable. Turned out he'd been none of those things, but in fairness to him, he'd expected me to be a much sweeter, more innocent version of myself. James represented everything Mason was not—dark, wild, and ruthless.

I pulled up my conversation with Mason and, before I could think on it too hard, typed, OKAY. I'LL MEET YOU.

Since my food intake for the day had been limited to coffee and a protein bar I'd found in my desk drawer, I was starving. I swung by a sandwich shop so I could eat while I drove.

I might not feel like eating after my conversation with James.

I pulled behind the abandoned gas station five minutes early and drove back farther than usual so I could park in the shade. After lowering the tailgate, I sat on the edge, then took a deep breath and drew out my phone. Mason had already responded, and the time stamp indicated he'd done so immediately.

DINNER AT JASPERS?

My breath caught in my throat. I wasn't sure I could handle dinner with him. It was too much like a date, and besides, I was pretty much guaranteed a date with Kip Wagner around ten p.m. HOW ABOUT COFFEE INSTEAD?

He seemed to hesitate before responding. I CAN COME OUT TO THE FARM IF YOU'D LIKE.

Then a few seconds later, he sent: AND PICK UP MY BOX.

The absolute last place I wanted to meet him was at the farm—Marshall, Jed, and Witt aside. There were too many memories of him there that I'd spent months trying to purge. HOW ABOUT IN MY OFFICE?

His response was much quicker this time: WHATEVER MAKES YOU COMFORTABLE. I CAN'T GET AWAY BEFORE FOUR. I CAN TEXT YOU.

I stared at his message before I sent: I HAVE APPOINTMENTS OUT OF THE OFFICE THIS AFTERNOON. TRY TO GIVE ME AT LEAST FIFTEEN TO TWENTY MINUTES' NOTICE.

OKAY.

I stared at the phone, trying to decide how I felt about seeing him again.

Anxious. Apprehensive.

Nevertheless, it still seemed like a good idea. I couldn't seriously think about starting a new relationship before reassuring myself the last one was good and dead.

I heard an approaching car engine, then saw James' black sedan drive around the corner. My breath stuck in my chest as James got out, keeping his gaze on me until he stood directly in front of me.

The dark look in his eyes pulled at something deep in my core, and I stopped myself from sucking in a breath to clear my head. Part of me didn't want to clear my head. I liked this feeling of standing on a precipice with him.

I found myself asking that same question again. Were my feelings for James real, or did I want him because he was the exact opposite of Mason Deveraux?

Still, as I stared up into James' face, practically sitting on my hands to keep from touching him, I knew that no easy explanation encompassed this man or my feelings for him. James knew my flaws as well as my strengths, and yet he wanted me anyway. No, it was more than that—he considered some of my flaws to be strengths. He was the first man who'd seen my full potential and encouraged me to live up to it. If I were honest with myself, that's how I felt about him too. I saw his flaws, yet I also saw the better man hiding underneath them all, the one he didn't show the world.

Was it enough?

He spoke first, his voice husky. "You're makin' it damn hard for me to focus on why I asked you here."

Reveling in the knowledge that I could distract him, I said just as huskily, "Maybe that's not such a bad thing."

"Does that mean you have an answer to my proposal?"

His question was like being doused by a bucket of cold water. I glanced down, feeling slightly ashamed.

"So it's a no?" he asked in a much colder tone.

"No, it's not a no, but it's not a yes either." I stared back up at him, my eyes pleading with him to understand.

He moved closer, his face softening. He reached up and cupped my cheek, his fingers sliding deeper into my hair, then curling around the strands.

A white-hot heat flared up inside me, and I sucked in a breath of surprise and need. One touch had me wanting to sleep with him right here on my truck bed in broad daylight. "I'm scared of this."

"Of what?" he asked, his voice so low his chest rumbled. His hand loosened its hold on my hair, but only so it could slide behind my head and wrap around more strands. Pulling a little tighter this time, he held my face upturned. "Us?"

"You make me forget myself. You make me into someone else. Someone more wanton."

He grinned at that, but it was more of a predatory grin than amused. "Wanton?"

I tried to look down again out of embarrassment, but his grip on my hair tightened, holding me in place as the playfulness faded. "Don't ever be ashamed of who you are with me. I love you *wanton*."

I wanted to look away, but his gaze held mine, refusing to relent.

"You are the sexiest woman I've ever known," he said, and I felt the feather-light touch of his hand on my left side, his fingers lightly sliding over my ribs, drifting up to the curve of my breast.

Another wave of heat washed through me and I relaxed, letting his hand hold up my head.

He stepped between my legs, pushing them apart, but then he stopped, and his hooded eyes widened into a look of concern. "You're wearing a gun."

"I thought it prudent after last night."

As he shifted from seducer to protector, his hand fell away from my side and he loosened his grip on my hair. "Did you have any problems after I left last night?"

It was hard to stifle my disappointment at losing his touch. "No. And none today. But my encounter with Wagner made me realize I needed more than a Taser for protection."

Wearing a grim look, he nodded as he let go of my head and took a step back. "Do you want me to assign someone to watch over you?"

"No. I suspect Wagner won't try anything until tonight."

"And what do you plan on doing about his ultimatum?"

"I can't give him what I don't have," I countered.

His voice turned rough. "True. But he's gonna show up with guns blazin' anyway."

I offered him a half-smile. "I'm still workin' out how to avoid that."

"I'm gonna be there when he comes, Rose."

"At my farm?"

"Did he tell you he'd meet you somewhere else?"

"No." Part of me wanted to protest that it would destroy my attempts to look neutral if he showed up, but I was smart enough to know that while I might have held Wagner off last night, there would be no repeat performance tonight. I didn't want a shootout at my house, and men like Wagner only respected and bowed to threats that were stronger than him. He'd make doggone sure he came back with more force this time, which meant I had to be prepared too. "Okay. You can be there."

He nodded, relief filling his eyes. He took another step back. "You're not the only one who loses control, and as much as I want to take you right here, that's not why I asked you to meet me."

He was putting distance between us to talk. I grinned. "Then why *did* you ask me to meet you here?"

"We need to set some ground rules."

"What does that mean?"

"If you're going to continue to be in dangerous situations, we need to make sure you're protected."

"You mean you'll send your men to protect me."

He paused, and it was obvious he wasn't excited to have this conversation. "Not just mine."

I squinted at him. "What does that mean?"

He paused again, his entire body taut with tension. "Dermot's men too."

I stared at him in disbelief. "Dermot?" I shook my head. "He'll never agree to that."

His dark gaze held mine. "He already did."

In that moment, I could see exactly what this cost him. He'd sacrificed his pride and risked his reputation, all for the sake of keeping me safe because I wouldn't let him claim me. He'd put everything on the line.

I shook my head, wanting to say something but not knowing what to say. No? Thank you? I'm sorry?

His mouth spread into a soft smile. "It's okay, Rose."

"It's not," I said in a thick voice.

He moved closer and stood between my legs again, wrapping his arms around my back. When he looked down at me, his smile had fallen away and the look in his eyes suggested an emotion I'd only seen a time or two before. Love. Not that he'd ever admit it. "You were right. The best way to keep you safe is for you to be neutral. Dermot recognizes that too. He's none too thrilled to get into the middle of a spat with Wagner, but he believes in you enough to risk it."

"*Why?*"

"Because he thinks you can help bring about the kind of peace this county hasn't known for decades."

"Me?"

His hand slid behind my head again, his fingers curling around my hair in a light hold. "You."

I tried to shake my head, but his hold made it a tiny movement.

"It comes with a price though," he said reluctantly.

"What does he want you to do?"

"Not me," he said, and the pain in his gaze let me know how much it killed him to say this. "You. He wants you to agree to have visions for him."

"How does he know about my visions?" But even as I asked, I knew.

"The night Merv kidnapped you."

I'd managed to send Jed a text that night, telling him that Merv was kidnapping me, and he'd called Dermot as backup. Dermot had shot Merv to save me, and he'd been there in the aftermath, when James had dragged me out from underneath Merv's body—and also out of my vision of death. I'd been a freezing mess, unable to warm up, and too shaken to hide my visions from anyone present in the warehouse. It wouldn't have been difficult for him to piece things together. All he would have needed to do was ask a few well-phrased questions.

Mouth gaping, I stared up at him.

"He's open to negotiation." He swallowed. "I told him it wasn't my talent to barter."

I pushed on his chest, backing him up so I could slide down from the tailgate and take several steps away. I felt trapped and confined, but it had nothing to do with James. "I'm not sure I can agree to that."

"I know it's not ideal, but I suspect he's open to a limited arrangement. I can insist you'll only do it if you're accompanied by Jed or one of my men you trust."

I shook my head. "No, you don't understand …"

Until last night, I hadn't seen or communicated with James since the morning after Merv's death. He had no idea my visions had stopped. Neely Kate was the only one who knew.

"I'm not sure I can do that."

"I do understand. You have no idea how hard this is for me to even suggest it."

I turned to face him. "Believe me, the enormity of that isn't lost on me."

"Offer him a vision. I swear we'll make sure you're safe when you do it. I'll even be with you if you want."

I took a step closer. "James, it's not my stubbornness that's keeping me from considering it."

"Then what is it?" he asked, confused now.

"Because I haven't had a vision in nearly two weeks."

He stared at me, his eyes wide. "You mean since you almost died."

"Yeah."

"They're gone?" he asked in disbelief.

"The spontaneous ones."

"You can't force a vision either?"

"I haven't tried."

He waited for me to elaborate.

I started to turn around again, but he snagged my arm and spun me to stand in front of him. "Why haven't you tried?"

"I spent my entire life wishing the things away. Why would I want them back now?"

"You're serious?"

"Those visions made me an outsider. Now that they're gone, maybe I'll finally fit in."

His face went blank.

"You're only upset because you can't use them," I said, sounding more bitter than I'd intended.

"I'm upset that you still see yourself as that scared woman who walked into my pool hall a year ago."

Tears stung my eyes. He was right. Some days I still saw myself that way. I'd made so much progress, yet sometimes I still felt like that scared girl who'd been berated for twenty-four years by my mother's sharp tongue.

"Your visions don't define you, Rose, but they've played a part in the woman you've become. And I wouldn't change a hair on your head."

"So you think I should force a vision?"

"Only you can decide what choice to make, but your visions have done a lot of good." He paused. "You of all people know that. What are you *really* afraid of?"

I stared up at him, realizing he was right. That hadn't been the real reason. "What if I try to force a vision and they're gone for good?"

"What if they're not?"

"I'm not ready to face this yet."

"That's not the way of the Lady in Black. She faces her fears head-on." A smile played on his lips. "She threatens to shoot hardened criminals in the family jewels."

"Maybe she needs a little longer to figure this one out."

"I'm not sure you have that much time."

He was right, but I still wasn't ready to face it. Maybe I wasn't the badass Lady in Black after all. Maybe Kip Wagner was right. Maybe I'd been playing dress-up all along.

"It's okay," he said, tugging my chest to his and wrapping his arm around my lower back. "But I need you to know that the visions have nothing to do with how I feel for you."

It wasn't until he said the words that I realized that had been one of my fears too. "Thank you."

"You still need to negotiate with Dermot."

I tilted my head back to look up at him. "You think I should negotiate with something I'm not sure I have?"

"I think you should assume you still have it until you prove otherwise."

"You and I both know how badly this will go if I can't force a vision for him. It could mean my death." I shivered at the thought. Dermot might be nice to me now, but I had no idea how he'd react to the notion he'd been double-crossed.

James' eyes hardened. "All the more reason to have Jed or me with you."

"I thought you said I could pick one of your other men."

"That was before I knew about the change in your visions."

I should force one now and get this over with. James was right. I needed to face this head-on. "This is stupid. There's one way to resolve this, and it needs to be done." I pulled out of his arms. "Give me your hand."

He looked momentarily confused but quickly caught up to speed, taking my hand in his. We both knew I could have forced a vision in his arms, but for some reason, I felt more comfortable this way. Thankfully, he didn't fight me on it.

"What do you want me to see?" I asked in a low voice.

He looked down at me with warm eyes, a gaze he only showed to me. "Let's make it easy. Look for what I'm gonna have for dinner."

I shook my head. "That's not the Lady in Black way. She goes big or she goes home."

He grinned, and his hand tightened around mine. "That's my girl."

"I'll look for what happens tonight with Wagner."

He didn't answer, just held my hand tighter.

I closed my eyes, about to ask that very question when I heard a loud bang, a sound that reminded me of a gunshot. Suddenly, I was back in that warehouse, hearing the gunshot that had killed Merv. Feeling his body crush mine to the concrete floor. Being covered by his blood. My eyes flew open in panic.

James pulled me to his chest, wrapping his arms tight around me, and it was then I realized I was shaking.

"It's okay. A car passin' by backfired."

But it wasn't okay. It was far from okay. "I need to try again."

"Just give yourself a couple of minutes," he said in a soothing tone. "A couple of minutes isn't gonna make a difference one way or the other."

I glanced up at him, realizing how much he'd changed too. Last November, he would have pushed me anyway, fear or no fear. I wasn't sure if this was a positive development or not. Nevertheless, I was grateful for the reprieve. I suspected being afraid could hinder my abilities even more. It had certainly affected me that way when Merv had practically held a gun to my head to force a vision.

"Why don't you sit down?" he said, already guiding me toward the truck bed. "There's something else I need to talk to you about."

"Okay."

I put my back to the tailgate, reaching my arms behind me to hop up, but James put his hands on my waist and lifted me as though I weighed nothing. He set me down and left his hands on my hips, watching me with a look I wasn't used to from him.

"Why do you look so worried?"

He hesitated a moment, then said, "Mason Deveraux is in town."

Was he worried that I'd be happy to hear the news? Or worried it would upset me? "I know," I said softly. "I saw him yesterday."

His eyes hardened. "You saw him?"

"Not purposely, if that's what you're thinkin'. I ran into him at the Piggly Wiggly late yesterday afternoon."

"I thought you were banned from that place."

I rolled my eyes. "Does everyone know?"

"I'm not everyone, Rose," he said in a dark tone.

I lifted a hand to his face and stroked his cheek with my fingertips. "No. You're not." I dropped my hand to my lap. "I was picking up a prescription, and they didn't want to give it to me … because of the ban and all, and Mason was suddenly there, cajoling the pharmacy tech to give me my prescription anyway."

"I don't need the details," he said in a gruff voice, his fingers digging into my hips.

"It's important you know that I didn't plan it. I had no idea he was even going to be in town until I saw him."

"And?" he asked.

I lifted my eyebrows. "Are you askin' me if I want him back?"

He didn't answer.

"We talked in my truck afterward." I held his gaze. "And we're talkin' again this afternoon in my office. Our conversation didn't go well yesterday, and I need for it to end differently."

He started to pull away, but I grabbed his wrists and held his hands in place.

"I know you don't understand, but I have to do this. It's the only way I'll really be free of him."

"Do you want to be free of him?"

I lifted my chin and gave him a look of defiance. "He doesn't deserve me."

"Neither do I," was his gruff response.

I relaxed my hold on his tense arms and placed my hands on his chest, feeling the hard muscles underneath.

He froze, staring at me as though he wasn't sure what to do, a rare look for him.

"You see me for who I am and you're still here," I said, my hands sliding up to his shoulders. "That means more than you know."

"You mean because you lost your visions?" he asked, parting my legs as he stepped closer.

"Before that." I tilted my head back to look up at him. "Last winter. You saw the real me before anyone else. You believed in me before anyone else."

"So you're here with me because I saw you first."

"No … but part of the reason is that you saw me … and you liked what you saw. You didn't try to change it." I leaned my head back to look up at the clear blue sky. "I'm not explaining this right."

His face lowered to my neck, and I felt the lightest touch of his lips to my skin.

My body tensed as if I'd been shot with a jolt of electricity.

His hand at my hip snaked around the small of my back, hauling my groin hard against the bulge in his jeans.

I gasped and tried to lower my head to look at him, but his face had moved lower, his mouth and tongue blazing a path to the top of my sundress.

His other hand rose from my hip to the strap of my dress, slowly tugging it and my bra strap down over my shoulder. His mouth remained on my skin as his finger hooked over the fabric of my dress and slowly tugged it down, exposing my nude-colored bra.

I held my breath in anticipation.

His hand cupped my breast, his finger sweeping up to find my nipple.

I gasped again as heat shot straight to my groin, and he tugged me tighter to his bulge. I lifted my leg to wrap it around his waist, but the gun in its holster was in the way.

As though reading my mind, he pushed the thin fabric of my dress up my thigh until the gun was exposed. He lowered both hands to unstrap the harness and drop it onto the truck bed. He reached under my dress and tugged my panties off, and I had half a mind to stop him. Anyone could drive back here and see us, but I knew the chances of that happening were slim to none. And if nothing else, I knew James would never put me in danger. He might lose his head when he was with me, but his concern for my safety would always trump his own needs.

He dropped my panties next to my holster and then returned his attention to my sundress, pulling the strap on the other side down and easing the fabric all the way off. My bra came off next, and he tossed it aside.

I sat in front of him naked except for the thin swath of fabric at my lap, while he was completely clothed. Reaching for the hem of his shirt, I lifted the fabric slowly, exposing his abs and his chest as though I was unwrapping a gift, taking in the sight of every ripple of muscle. When I got to his shoulders, he took over, tugging his shirt over his head and tossing it close to my bra.

I unfastened his belt before shifting my focus to unbuttoning and unzipping his jeans. I started to pull them down, but he grabbed my hands and stopped me without explanation.

Staring down at me with a hunger that stole my breath, he lowered his mouth to mine and showed me how much he wanted me. I wrapped my arms around his neck, clinging to him as his lips and his teeth and his tongue devoured me. I kissed him back with my own hunger, fueled by the growing ache deep inside me. By the time he lifted his mouth, I was gasping for breath, my body burning with need. Without thinking, I reached for his jeans, tugging at the heavy fabric, but his mouth had lowered to my breast, pushing him out of reach and making me lose focus as the fire in my groin grew hotter.

I cried out as the ache spread, desperate to be satisfied.

He moved to my other breast, giving it the same attention as he had the first, which was why I was surprised when his finger slid inside me with the gentlest of touches. I shuddered and pushed into him.

I moved both hands to his hips, sliding my fingers between the fabric and his skin and pulling the fabric down over his hips enough for him to spring free. Smiling, I wrapped my hand around him and stroked.

He rose up, staring down at my face with his finger still inside me. His thumb stroked my bundle of nerves while his finger worked its own magic. I gasped again, and he grinned as he wrapped an arm around my upper back, holding me up as he lowered his mouth to my breast to resume what he'd started.

Soon he had me writhing and panting, until I was close to begging him to give me what I needed, but the small part of me still capable of reason knew it wouldn't be fair to him unless I made something perfectly clear.

I grabbed his face with both hands and jerked him up to face me. "This isn't a yes. Not yet. I need more time. There's so much to think—"

His eyes darkened. "I know."

Then his hand slipped out from between my legs. I thought he'd changed his mind until he grabbed my leg and pulled it up to his waist, sinking deep inside me with one hard plunge.

I arched my back and moaned, pushing against him.

He set a frenetic pace, but I matched it beat by beat, until I'd climbed so high that I was sure I'd pass out from the lack of oxygen. And then I exploded into a million pieces, losing myself as we came together and wave after wave of pleasure washed through me. The pleasure was overwhelming, but I was never once scared I'd lose myself because James was holding me tight in his arms.

I opened my eyes and found him staring down at me in wonder. I grinned. "You never cease to amaze me."

He laughed. "I think that's supposed to be my line."

I lifted up and placed a soft kiss on his lips, and he kissed me back, his passion tamed into gentleness.

His face lifted and the tenderness in his eyes startled me. "You don't have to say yes, Rose. You have so much to lose. If I were a better man, I'd rescind my offer." A wicked grin lit up his face, but I saw the darkness in his eyes, the regret and self-loathing. "But I'm not a better man, and I want you. I want every part of you I can get."

A new fire sprang to life inside me at his words. "You know I want you too. Surely you have no doubt of that."

His fingers dug into my hip and hauled me closer to him. "No, that one thing I'm sure of."

I laid my cheek on his chest, my heart aching. What was I going to do?

Chapter Eighteen

James broke away first, pulling up his pants, then walked around to my driver's door and looked inside. I'd already put on my bra when he came back with several napkins. I tried to take them from him to clean myself, but he silently refused, taking over the task instead. I let him, and he then slid my panties up over my feet and pulled them into place. I started to fix my dress, but he brushed my hands away, gently slipping the straps over my shoulders and placing a kiss on my collarbone. This might be our last time together. If this was what he wanted, I'd willingly give it.

After he put his shirt back on, he strapped the gun holster to my thigh, his fingers tracing my skin after he'd secured it in place.

"So you're workin' Patsy Sue Clydehopper's case," he said, placing a feather-light kiss on my inner thigh.

My breath stuck in my throat, and he glanced up at me with a grin.

"I hear things," he said. "What I can't believe is that you're tryin' to prove her innocence."

"Neely Kate thinks she *is* innocent."

"And you?" he asked, his hand trailing higher and sending a shiver through me.

"I can't think when you do that," I said.

His grin spread, but he stood and sat on the truck bed next to me, wrapping his arms around me and snugging me to his side.

"So you're working this case for Neely Kate's benefit?" he asked.

I couldn't see any harm in telling him the truth. "And mine. Between worrying about Violet, dealing with Mason, and trying to figure out my answer for you, I needed the distraction."

"You truly think she might be innocent?" he asked in disbelief.

"I haven't formed an opinion yet. I spoke to her family this morning and found out some interesting information."

He glanced down at me, waiting.

"Her family thinks Carol Ann got into town last week, but her niece and a cousin from her father's side both claim she's been back for a good two months."

He nodded.

"You knew that?" I asked, turning more to face him. "Why would you know about Carol Ann Nelson?"

"Because Carol Ann had big aspirations."

"Her business," I said.

"You found out about that?"

"I know she was asking her family for money to help seed it, but no one seems to know what it was. I suspected it had something to do with drugs given the connection to Big Thief Hollow, but then Patsy's sister said Carol Ann was tryin' to make her mother proud."

"She wanted to open a club."

I blinked in surprise. "A club? What kind of club?"

"A gentleman's club."

"What? How would that make her mother proud?"

He laughed. "*Some* mothers would be proud."

I suspected Lucille Nelson wasn't one of them. Then it hit me. "Do you think she was raisin' money to buy Kip Wagner's file?"

He looked surprised by that. "First of all, we don't even know what's in Wagner's mysterious file. Second, why would Carol Ann Nelson have hooked up with some teenage kid to mastermind the robbery? And third, a club is different than a prostitution ring."

"But she could have run a prostitution ring from a club."

"It would be pretty damn stupid of her. Simmons would be breathin' down her neck at the first sniff of it. And that doesn't even touch on the first two points."

"You said you knew she was trying to open a club. That would cost way more money than her family would be able to give her."

"That's why she came to me. A mutual acquaintance introduced us."

"You had a business meeting with Carol Ann Nelson?" For some reason, the thought bothered me.

"I wouldn't exactly call it a business meeting. A guy I know dropped by with Carol Ann in tow. He asked to speak to me, so I went out to see to him and agreed to meet with them in my office as a courtesy. The meeting lasted all of five minutes. I told her I'd be a fool to help her open something that would be direct competition to my own club, and even if *that* wasn't an issue, she had a shit business plan. I told her to find something else to do."

"How long ago was this? Why doesn't Jed know about it?"

"Because she came in while he was in Oklahoma with Neely Kate."

"So three weeks ago … What was she doin' the first month or so she was here?"

"Who knows? I suspect Carol Ann wasn't all that driven."

Still, a month was a long time to do nothing. It seems like she'd have had something to occupy her. I suddenly wondered how long she'd *really* been sleeping with Calvin. "She was having an affair with Calvin Clydehopper."

He grinned and shook his head. "Why am I not surprised?"

"What makes you say that?"

"The guy has a holier-than-thou attitude and a closet full of skeletons. Clydehopper's on the city council, and he voted to zone Wagner's pawn shop, something that goes against his previous voting record. I suspected Wagner has something on him, but I've never found out what."

"Could the information in Wagner's file be dirt about Calvin?"

He thought for a minute. "Maybe, but I doubt it. It wouldn't be valuable enough."

"What if Wagner's providing prostitutes to Calvin?"

His brow furrowed. "What makes you say that?"

"Well, Calvin's secretary thought Neely Kate and I were prostitutes when we walked into his office yesterday. She said young women just drop by and disappear in his office for a bit before going on their way. Calvin's secretary hinted that a lot of women had come and gone, and we both know Calvin's not good-lookin' enough to have that many cute girls droppin' by his office for sex. If he's getting prostitutes, they have to be from somewhere."

James grimaced.

"Wagner admitted he was ticked about your no-prostitution policy. What if he's had a ring going for the past few months and you didn't realize it?"

He didn't look too happy with the question. "That would mean I have a serious breach in my information network."

I thought for a moment. "Could be the file's a list of his usual girls. What if Carol Ann knew about it? Maybe she found out that those boys were gonna break into the pawn shop, and she hit her family up for money to help buy the file from them? The timing's right."

"How much was she hittin' them up for?"

"Several thousand dollars."

He considered it. "I suppose it's possible. She came to me about her business. It's not outside the realm of possibility that she made the rounds and approached Wagner too. She may have gleaned something about the file while meeting with him, but honestly, it's a stretch."

I had to agree with him.

He was silent for a moment. "Patsy, on the other hand … if he had information on her, I can see why he'd want it back."

"You know something about Patsy Clydehopper?"

"Let's just say there's a reason she's the most successful real estate agent in Fenton County."

"Patsy's sister said her friend accused Patsy of ripping her off. Do you know what she's been up to?"

"Look," he said, holding me tighter. "You're puttin' me in a tricky situation."

"You've done illegal real estate deals with her?" I asked in disbelief. Of course, I had no reason to be surprised. He'd done all kinds of illegal deals, some of them much worse than this.

He stared down at me, holding my gaze. "Are you sure you want to know?"

Did I? If I said yes, I'd be opening one of the remaining doors that stood between us, but I suspected I didn't want to know everything about the criminal stuff … but how would a relationship between us work if we kept so many secrets?

"Hey," he said softly, putting a finger under my chin. "Relax. I haven't. But we've done plenty of legit business together. She even helped me buy the land that I built my house on, although she had no idea who she was really selling it to. I haven't had any illegal transactions with her, but I know that she's orchestrated quite a few of them. She's approached me with a few of those deals before."

"Like what?"

He lightly stroked my arm. "She'll get an appraiser to artificially inflate or deflate the worth of a property, depending on who she's dealing with. Let's say she wants to make a huge profit, she'll get the appraiser to mark up the value and the bank will grant a loan to the buyer. Or if she's wantin' to buy property cheap, she'll have the appraiser lower the value so she can scoop it up at a literal steal."

Which sounded like the exact pickle Poppy's friend had found herself in.

He paused, then added, "I know she had some big deal going with Denny Carmichael."

I shook my head. "I don't know him."

"He's a meth supplier. Carol Ann's cousin in Big Thief Hollow works for him, so it's possible Carol Ann hit him up for cash too. If you girls decide to pay him a visit, you need to take Jed and make sure he's visible. Denny won't mess with him."

"He's dangerous?"

"He has the potential to be if he thinks someone's threatening his capitalist ventures. He's protective of his secret cook, and he'd beat the shit out of anyone who tried to put an ID on him. Or her. I don't condone Denny's enterprise, yet I know people use it."

"So you let him?" I asked, sounding as accusatory as I felt. It was one thing to condone pot—which I knew he did—but meth was the kind of drug that screwed up people's lives and killed them.

"Choose your battles, Lady," he said in a low tone. "People use that shit to escape their miserable lives. I'm workin' on a project that's goin' to help make their lives less miserable, and then hopefully Denny'll go out of business when no one wants the shit he's sellin'."

I stared at him, my mouth gaping open. "You believe that?"

Sadness filled his eyes. "Not entirely, but someone taught me to dare to dream." He kissed me. "So I am."

I stared at him in awe. He meant me. "What's your project?"

He grimaced, looking uncomfortable. "Patsy Sue is helping me buy a factory on the west side of town. If she doesn't end up in jail, I have a deal lined up with a small appliance manufacturing company. They'll move a plant to town, and I'll provide the land and help refurbish the factory in exchange for a share of the profits. I asked for a ten-year commitment. Good payin' jobs with salaries our people can actually live on."

"You have the money to make that kind of arrangement?" I asked in amazement.

"The bank's helpin' me out, but yeah."

I wrapped my arms around his back and pressed my cheek to his chest. "You're a good man, James Malcolm."

"It's not entirely altruistic," he grunted. "I'll be making a very nice profit."

But I knew better than to think money was his only motivation.

He rested his cheek on my head, and we sat like that for nearly a minute, just soaking each other in as the leaves rustled over our heads. I reminded myself that this was what life would be like with him—stolen moments. As wonderful as they were, would it be enough?

James shook me out of my musings. "So what do you plan to do next in your investigation?"

"Talk to Calvin again. I want to see what he knows about Patsy's business deals. It could be that a wronged client set her up for Carol Ann's murder."

"You believe that?" he asked in disbelief.

"After talkin' to you, no. But since he was sleepin' with Carol Ann, he might know more about her business transactions. I'll kill two birds with one stone."

"Good thinkin'. Quiz him about the prostitutes too. If he was really usin' them, see if you can find out who was supplyin' them."

"I think I'll call Dermot and see whether he knows if Carol Ann approached Buck Reynolds. Reynolds would have been in charge three weeks ago."

"He'll want to negotiate," he said with a low rumble of warning in his chest. "You haven't tried to have another vision yet."

"I'll try again before we go." I leaned the side of my head into his chest. I hadn't felt this peaceful in weeks, and I wasn't willing to let it go quite yet.

"If you're going to be neutral, then the more support the big dogs show you, the more accepted you'll become." He paused. "But it pushes you deeper into my world, Rose. And there will come a point when you'll step into something so rank it'll be enough to get you in trouble with the law. I think you should take more time to think about it."

"I'm already there, aren't I?" I asked. "Hiding that kid up in my guest bedroom?"

"It will be much worse than that, Lady. Much worse."

I almost asked him what that could be—I'd already done all kinds of things the law would frown upon—but I knew he was right. There were much worse things than what I'd done or been exposed to. Much worse. "So let's say I changed my mind," I said, thinking out loud. "What happens to the kid? I'm sure as Pete not handing him over to Wagner."

"Dermot and I could work out an agreement," he said, sounding far more hopeful than I'd expected.

"And what would happen to the next kid who runs into trouble?"

"I doubt it will be a kid next time, Rose. It'll be a hardened criminal, demandin' help from you with a gun pointed at your head."

He might be right, but I knew that Marshall Billings would be dead right now if he hadn't shown up in my barn. He might be criminally naïve, but he wasn't a bad kid. He didn't deserve that. "When did you find out about the murder north of my farm?"

"About a minute after the 911 call. I have someone monitoring the sheriff's office. I make it my business to know about *every* murder in the county."

"Did Daniel Crocker know about every murder?"

His brow furrowed. "Daniel Crocker was an egotistical megalomaniac."

"So I take it that means no."

"No. He did not."

That didn't surprise me. James was nothing like his predecessor.

He studied me for a moment. "Is Jed still givin' you lessons in self-defense?"

His question caught me by surprise. "Not since he and Neely Kate got back from Oklahoma."

"Ask him to start them up again. If you persist in this, Wagner won't be the last asshole to mess with you. I'll feel better if I know you can handle yourself, especially when the next criminal shows up at your door or barn. In fact, I'm surprised he hasn't started up again to protect Neely Kate. Especially after her trip back to Oklahoma. I heard she was pretty upset over her last visit with Kate up in Little Rock."

James knew about her visits to see Kate? And how did he know the last one had upset her? One thing was obvious—he might decide it was need-to-know information unless I let him believe I knew as much or more than he did. "Yeah. I guess Kate gave her a hard time."

"Kate keeps dangling something from Ardmore over her head, and I heard she delivered a piece of news on Sunday that threw Neely Kate for a loop. Did she tell you what it was?"

I stared up at him in a daze. Neely Kate had told me she'd taken care of everything in Ardmore, whatever it had been. She hadn't shared any of it with me. How did James know?

Jed.

Jed was still reporting to him. Why?

I could continue to pretend I knew what he was talking about or share what little I knew and hope he did the same. "She barely told me anything about her trip to Ardmore. I know she was goin' back to confront something awful from her past, but when she got back, she told me it was taken care of."

"Jed told me pretty much the same, no details. I figured it meant he'd found something grisly from her past and helped her take care of it."

The blood rushed from my face. "What does that mean exactly?"

"I don't know," he said. "But Jed's buttoned up tighter than a scuba diver in a wetsuit."

"Do you think Kate really has something on Neely Kate?" I asked. "Or do you think she's just jerkin' her around?"

"Jed's concerned, so she must have something. I've had someone watchin' Kate for a while now. I thought I'd figured out how she was getting information in and out, but she must have found another way."

"Why are you having Kate watched?" I asked.

He watched me for a moment, then gave me a gentle kiss. "This is one of those 'don't ask, don't tell' situations."

That had me stumped. Why was he watching her? Then it hit me. She was J.R. Simmons' daughter. She must have something James wanted.

His phone buzzed in his pocket, and he pulled it out and checked the screen. "It's Reacher."

"Who's Reacher?"

"Jed's replacement," he said as he answered the phone.

I'd never heard of Reacher before, and it made me uncomfortable that some man I didn't know was James' new right-hand man.

James' side of the conversation involved a lot of one-word sentences, and something about a game. When he hung up, he frowned. "I've got to get back. There's a baseball game on Friday that's got half the county in a tizzy, and we're overrun with bets."

"Okay. I need to get back to town to interview Calvin again."

He took my hand in his. "You want to try havin' a vision before we go?"

Did I? What if I couldn't have one? I'd be freaked out and James would probably feel compelled to stay with me until I settled down, but I didn't want to put that burden on him. I for sure didn't want to feel like a weak, helpless woman.

"No," I said. "Not now. I'll try with Neely Kate tonight."

"Dermot's gonna want an answer before tonight."

"I know. I'll figure it out." I gave him a sad grin. "Who knows? Maybe a vision will burst into view when I'm talkin' to Calvin and I'll find out why Patsy's car is called Baby Spice."

His face twisted into a grimace that suggested that would be a nightmare.

"I'll figure it out," I repeated.

He nodded, then leaned down and kissed me with the same tenderness as before, but soon the kiss heated up and I found myself clinging to him again. He lifted his head, studying my face. When he saw my expression, he grinned. "A business tip: Whenever possible, leave the person you're negotiating with a taste of what they want so they'll be more willing to compromise."

I chuckled. "This was a business lesson?"

"A lesson with benefits." He hopped off the tailgate, then grabbed my waist and helped me down. "Be careful, Rose," he said as he walked me to the driver's door of my truck.

He didn't wait for a response. He gave me another kiss, leaving me even more breathless this time. When he released me, the look on his face didn't look so amused. He looked like he'd lost his best friend. Without a word, he walked over to his car and waited for me to pull out. Only then did he drive away.

Chapter Nineteen

Twenty minutes later, I pulled into the Hebert Manufacturing parking lot. I knew Neely Kate wanted me to wait for Witt, but this was Calvin Clydehopper. James hadn't even insisted I bring someone with me. I could handle this on my own.

I pulled out my phone, turned on my recording app, then blanked the screen so Calvin wouldn't realize I was recording him. Since my dress didn't have pockets, I had to hold it in my hand unless I tucked it in my purse, and I was afraid that would muffle the recording.

June was surprised to see me when I walked in, and the two other secretaries glanced up from their work. One of them was the woman who had told Neely Kate about Calvin's pony performance.

"Mr. Clydehopper's busy," June said, but she looked nervous.

"Then it's a good thing this will only take a few minutes."

She stood, and I ignored her protests as I walked around her desk and opened his office door.

Calvin was on the phone, but his eyes filled with fear when he looked up at me. "I've gotta go," he mumbled, then hung up and got to his feet. "Rose, do you have any word on Carol Ann's killer?"

I shut the door behind me and locked it, muffling June's protests. "Why do you look so scared to see me?"

He did a poor job of looking confused. "Huh?"

I ran through a short list of what could have upset him. One, the sheriff's department had figured out it was his tie wrapped around Carol Ann's throat, a real possibility since I'd told Randy about the camera. Or two, he knew about Kip Wagner's missing file.

I walked up to his desk and lifted my eyebrows. "Who were you talkin' to?"

He waved his hand a little too wildly. "Oh … you know … work stuff."

"Kip Wagner work stuff?"

His face lost color and he sank down into his chair.

I stared down at him. "You're gonna tell me everything you know about Kip Wagner's new side business."

He tried to look indignant, but he didn't quite pull it off. "I don't know what you're talkin' about."

"The way I see it, Calvin Clydehopper, you have two choices. You can tell me *or* the sheriff's department what you know. Because if you don't tell me, I *will* get Joe Simmons to send someone sniffin' in your direction."

He swallowed and splayed his hands on his desk. "I swear, I don't know what you're talkin' about."

I stared at him for a few seconds. Was he really clueless or just doing a very bad job of trying to throw me off? There was one way to find out.

I turned around to head for the door.

"Wait!"

I spun back around.

He held up his hands. "Don't go."

"You have something to tell me?"

"You can't tell the sheriff's department."

I nodded slightly. I wouldn't tell them a thing, but the audio recording on my phone might find its way into Joe's inbox depending on how this went down.

Indecision wavered in his eyes before he sat back down in his office chair.

I sat in one of the chairs in front of his desk and set my phone in my lap, screen down. "Tell me how you became a client of Kip Wagner's prostitution ring."

Calvin's face paled and a fine sheen of sweat covered his forehead. "What?" he squeaked out. "Prostitutes? You think I have to buy my women?"

"Yes, that's exactly what I think you've been doin'," I said, "and I know Kip Wagner's been supplyin' them."

He opened his mouth to say something, then promptly closed it.

Sometimes I loved it when I was right. "How long has it been goin' on?"

He swallowed and seemed to give it some thought before he said, "What does this have to do with who killed Carol Ann?"

"I'm not at liberty to share the details of my case, but if you want me to help clear Patsy's name, then you need to tell me what you know." When he didn't argue, I repeated, "Tell me about the prostitutes."

He pulled out his handkerchief and wiped off his forehead. "Wagner and I have … an understanding."

I studied him for a moment. What kind of understanding could Calvin Clydehopper have with someone like Kip Wagner? How had they hooked up in the first place? Then it hit me. This wasn't a new thing, and as a city councilman, Calvin had more influence over the Henryetta police than he did the sheriff's office. "You've been workin' with Kip Wagner for some time now," I said. "How long?"

"What?" he asked in a meek voice.

"How long?"

He swallowed again, his tie bouncing with the movement.

"Look, Calvin, I'm pretty busy, so maybe you could cut all the malarkey and just tell me what I need to know."

Reaching up to loosen his tie, he said, "I want to hire you too."

I hadn't expected that. "What?"

"If I tell you all of this, I need to hire you to protect me."

I shook my head. "We work with a detective agency, Calvin, not personal security."

"If I tell you, then I'm a dead man walkin'."

"Then maybe you should tell the sheriff's department." I wasn't sure I wanted to hear his confession, not if there really was a chance he'd be murdered for spilling his guts. I'd been down that road with Jeanne, and I could barely live with myself. I didn't want to add Calvin's spilled blood to my guilt, even if he was less than innocent. It wasn't my place to play judge and jury.

He opened his bottom drawer and pulled out a short bottle and a glass. He poured an amber-colored liquid into the glass, then held up the bottle. "Where are my manners? Would you like some?"

"No, thanks."

He screwed the cap back on and set the bottle on the desk. "Suit yourself." He took a long drink from the glass. His hand shook, but he seemed to have more confidence when he set the glass back on his desk. "I'll only say this once, and I'd rather tell you than anyone else."

"I still can't protect you, Calvin. You have to know that before you say another word."

He reached into another drawer and pulled out a handgun.

My heart leapt into my throat as he set it on the desk. "There's no reason to pull out a gun. I'm certain we can work this out."

"That's not for you," he said, taking another generous gulp from his glass. "Now what do you want to know?"

I kept my eye on the gun. Did I really want to know? If he didn't tell me, I was fairly sure he wouldn't tell anyone else. It could help catch Carol Ann's killer, maybe even clear Patsy Sue. And if it provided enough evidence to get Wagner arrested, all the better. But the gun on his desk reminded me that Calvin could pay a very steep price to tell me his story. I wasn't sure I was willing to play a part in it.

He finished off the drink and slammed his empty glass on the desk. "Ask your damn questions!" he barked.

I jumped at the loud thud and took a breath. God forgive me if Calvin paid for this with his life. "How is it that you and Kip Wagner came to a … business arrangement?"

His mouth tipped into a wry grin. "He approached me with an offer I couldn't refuse."

"Women?"

He reached for the bottle. "At first."

"How long ago was this?"

"About a year ago. He'd heard I had 'a restless nature,' he called it. He offered to help me meet beautiful young women for a finder's fee."

"A finder's fee? Like an escort service?"

He poured more alcohol into his glass. "Only I didn't escort them anywhere. I met them at a motel."

"How long until Kip asked for a favor?"

He grinned and held up the bottle. "See, I knew you were a smart girl."

"How long?" I repeated.

"He let me marinate in the mess for a good six months … supplyin' the girls, supplyin' the place. Even supplyin' the cocaine after a while … to take the edge off, Marietta said."

"Marietta?"

"She was my favorite," he said in a wistful tone, staring out the window.

"What happened to Marietta?"

He ignored me for a moment, then turned back to face me. "She was my lesson about what happens when you cross Kip Wagner."

My blood turned cold. "What happened to her?" I pressed.

He shook his head. "He wanted to open that pawn shop, but the council wasn't sure they wanted it in that part of town. He insisted I use my influence to push it through."

I hadn't paid any attention to Henryetta zoning issues. I barely paid attention to anything official regarding Henryetta. "Did you?"

"I tried to convince Fred Jones to vote with me and Nan Hutchins to approve it, but he wouldn't budge. It didn't pass the first go-round." He paused and took a generous gulp. "I made damn sure it passed the second time."

"Because Kip Wagner did something to Marietta?" I asked, my words coming out in a breathless whisper.

"He said Patsy would be next."

"What happened to her, Calvin?" I asked with more force.

"Nothin' good." He picked up the gun, and I was suddenly grateful I'd brought my own, not that it would do me much good. Calvin could shoot me before I ever got mine out.

"So Kip started the escort service a year ago?" I asked, deciding to let the issue of what happened to Marietta sit for a bit.

"No. He offered me special services—'as a friend,' he'd always say—but then a few months ago, he told me he'd started branching out. He wanted to open a club on the north part of town. I told him he was crazy. If he wanted a club, he needed to put it out of city limits like Malcolm's Bunny Ranch, but he wouldn't listen. He said he was better than Malcolm, and he was gonna make it happen … with my help."

"A gentleman's club?" I found it difficult to believe it was a coincidence that Carol Ann had wanted to open one too.

"Yep." He punctuated the word by finishing his drink and pouring still more liquor into the glass. "But it never made it to a council meeting. Wagner refused to face the embarrassment of getting his club shot down like his first attempt at the zoning for the pawn shop. He told me he'd wait until I had more council members in my pocket before he filed the paperwork. But he got impatient."

"He threatened you?"

"Not exactly. He embarrassed me. He started sending prostitutes to my office."

So June hadn't been wrong.

"Patsy found out and sicced June on me as a watchdog. Patsy knew her from the real estate office, but there'd never been any love lost between them, so I was kind of surprised at Patsy's choice."

"You didn't turn the women away?" I asked.

He shrugged, the movement sloppy. The slurring of his next words proved the alcohol had started taking effect. Or maybe he'd gotten a head start. "They were already here."

"Where does Carol Ann fit into all of this?" I asked.

"All of what?"

"This mess with Kip Wagner?"

He shook his head and took another drink. "As far as I know, she doesn't."

"Are you sure about that? Really sure?"

He studied me for a moment. Then his brow lifted slightly. "I'd had a few conversations on the phone with Wagner while she was with me." He shrugged. "She could have put things together."

"Does he know you were sleepin' with her?"

"What?" he protested in mock outrage. "How can you suggest I would do such a thing?"

"You already told Neely Kate and me this morning, Calvin," I said in disgust. "Are you drunk already?" Then I narrowed my eyes. "And as an elder at the First Baptist Church, what are you doin' drinkin' in the first place?"

"The first rule of bein' a church elder is knowing that what you do outside the church has nothin' to do with your duties inside."

Apparently that was his excuse for all of the adultery too. "How long?"

"About a month."

"Do you know how long she'd been back in town?"

"A month? She called me and told me she needed to see me. So I met her at a motel down in Big Thief Hollow."

"And you slept with her then too," I said, trying to keep the judgment from my voice.

He gave me a salacious grin that just looked gross on him. "There wasn't any sleepin' involved."

It took me a second to ask, "What was her excuse for askin' you to meet her?"

"She didn't need an excuse. This wasn't the first time."

That caught me by surprise, although I wasn't sure why. "When was the first time?"

"Back in high school. Carol Ann got a little thrill knowin' she was sleepin' with her cousin's boyfriend."

That sounded sad and pathetic, but it also explained her using her grandmother's fried chicken recipe against Patsy Sue at the picnic. I wouldn't have been surprised to learn Patsy liked to rub her success in other people's noses. "How many times did you sleep with her after that?"

"Pretty much every time she came back to town."

"Does Kip Wagner know you were sleeping with Carol Ann?" I repeated. When he gave me a blank look, I said, "She was strangled with your tie, Calvin. He could have set you up as punishment for not pushing hard enough for his club." And maybe got her out of the way at the same time.

He waved around his glass, sloshing liquid onto his blotter, and then set it down unsteadily. "Well … shit." The cops clearly hadn't told him that part.

Another thought occurred to me. "Calvin, are you sure you haven't heard from Patsy since yesterday?"

He shook his head, then nodded it. "No, I mean yeah … I mean I haven't."

"Is that odd? She's in trouble. Is she so independent she wouldn't contact you? Is it possible she suspects you?"

He shook his head, tears filling his eyes. "I don't know."

"And you have no idea where she could be?"

He shook his head.

"Calvin," I said, wondering if this was a good idea or a bad one. "Could Kip Wagner have snatched Patsy to punish you? Maybe Carol Ann was the warning?"

He glanced up at me, tears spilling over his lower eyelashes.

"You have to tell the sheriff," I said. "Patsy's life may be on the line."

He shook his head. "I can't."

"Calvin!"

He poured himself another drink. "You can't tell them either."

"If you expect me to keep this to myself when they could be questionin' Wagner—"

"No," he said firmly. "I told you I was only sayin' it once."

"Then you leave me no choice, Calvin," I said as I stood, gripping my phone tight in my left hand. "I'm telling the sheriff's department myself."

He picked up his gun and pointed it at me. "I can't let you do that, Rose."

I tasted bile. I was being held at gunpoint for the second time in less than twenty-four hours, but in all honesty, I was more scared of getting shot by Calvin. His shaking hand made him a wild card. I considered trying to reach for my own gun, but I suspected I'd never pull it out in time.

"I'm walkin' out of this office, Calvin, but I won't head straight for the sheriff's department. I'll give you an hour to do the right thing, and if you haven't, I'm tellin' them everything I know." Then, without waiting for an answer, I headed for the door.

Chapter Twenty

I didn't waste any time making a beeline out of his office. June yelled at me as I walked past her, then hopped up and ran inside to check on Calvin. I heard her shouting Calvin's name as I hurried through the outside door.

I made it to my car, then drove out of the parking lot, half-expecting Calvin to shoot at me from his office window. When I was several miles away, I pulled into the parking lot of the Chuck and Cluck and called Neely Kate.

"Any luck finding Becky yet?" I asked, not ready to spill my guts yet—metaphorically or otherwise. She and Jed had been looking all day. Surely they had something by now.

"We *just* talked to the manager," she said. "He says he's seen her, but he only deals with Bubba. Jed convinced the manager to tell him where Bubba works, so we're headed there now to ask him about Becky."

"Could she be hiding in her apartment?"

"The manager wouldn't let us in, but after Jed convinced him that Becky might be in danger, he did a walk-through and confirmed she wasn't there. I'm just hopin' Bubba will talk."

"Good thing Jed's gonna be there to help convince him."

"Yeah," she said, sounding more optimistic than when I'd first called. "Have you made any progress?"

"I talked to James, and he knew about Carol Ann's business. Turns out she approached him about helping her fund a new gentleman's club."

"Why didn't Jed know about it?" she asked defensively.

"He said she came in while you two were in Oklahoma." When she didn't respond, I said, "But I just found out that Kip Wagner was wanting to open a club too."

"Skeeter knew about that?"

"No. Calvin did."

"Witt got away already to meet you?"

"No. I went on my own—but before you start scolding me, let me tell you what else I found out." I told her everything that had transpired, including walking out of Calvin's office with a gun trained on my back.

"He could have shot you in the back, Rose!" Neely Kate protested.

"I *know*," I groaned.

We were both quiet for a moment, before she asked, "Are you really gonna wait an hour to tell Joe?"

"No." Jeanne's murder had been a painful reminder that I wasn't qualified to make these life or death decisions. I couldn't handle feeling responsible for Patsy's possible death too. "I can't wait that long. It could mean the difference between saving Patsy's life."

"And Becky's."

"Yeah, her too."

"Joe's gonna be pissed," she warned.

She had a point. "Then I'll call Deputy Miller. I need to find out if the camera tip paid off."

"Be careful, Rose."

"I plan to." As soon as she hung up, I searched my phone for Randy's number. He didn't answer, so I left a message for him to call me back ASAP. I was about to suck it up and call Joe when a call from Dermot showed up on my screen.

What was I going to do about his offer?

"Hey, Dermot," I said when I answered.

"I had an interesting chat with Malcolm earlier."

So much for pleasantries first. "He mentioned it."

"Are you open to an agreement?"

I decided to stall. "What did you have in mind?"

"If I send my men to stand with Malcolm's tonight, you work for me for a month."

"*A month?*"

"I'm riskin' a lot, Lady. I'm takin' over Reynolds' position, and I'm runnin' the risk of lookin' weak if I stand with Malcolm. It might come across as me followin' Malcolm's orders. I know he rules the land, but we still have autonomy."

I was getting irritated. I liked Dermot well enough, but I suspected he was taking advantage of the situation for his own gain. "There's no way in Hades I'm workin' for you for a month."

"Let me remind you that I came when called to operate on that kid. I could have charged you for that."

He had a point, but there was no way I was agreeing to a full month. "When you say work for you, what do you have in mind?"

"You know," he said, but he didn't sound as sure of himself.

"I want to hear you say it."

"Your visions thing."

My heart sank. He *did* know. "Just so I'm understanding this correctly, you want me to have visions for you for a month? How do you plan to make that work?"

"How does it work for Malcolm?" he asked in defiance. "I've given this a lot of thought since the night Chapman died. When the Lady in Black was in Malcolm's meetings last winter, you were reading his men and his enemies."

Crappy doodles. Why had I acknowledged that I had visions? How much should I tell him now? "You realize very few people know about this?"

"You mean your talent? I figured. I've never heard anyone mention it. I put things together when Malcolm was trying to warm you up after the … meetin'. Then his brother spilled the rest while he was helpin' me clean up."

Clean up meant dispose of the body and erase any trace that a murder took place. "What did he tell you?"

"Enough. I know you were havin' a vision for Merv when I shot him. You got stuck in it."

Well, crap on a cracker. "How many people have you told?"

"No one. I'm not stupid. If everyone knows about your talent, it's no longer as valuable."

I breathed a sigh of relief, but I wasn't off the hook yet. "Why didn't you mention it when you were at my house a couple of nights ago?"

"Because sometimes you have to bide your time. I knew you'd need a favor. The question was when I'd make my proposal."

"I still don't understand why you didn't make your request two nights ago. I needed your help and you wanted mine."

"Because you weren't really askin' me to help you. You were askin' me to help the kid. I needed to wait until you really needed something." He paused and I heard the grin in his voice. "And it's finally happened."

"No, thank you," I said.

It took him a full second to ask in disbelief, "Excuse me?"

The fool obviously didn't know me very well. I would have been much more inclined to make a deal to help someone else than to save myself. "Did I not make myself clear? I do *not* accept your offer."

"You're not gonna negotiate?"

"Here's the thing, Mr. Dermot: I'm a businesswoman. I may be new to the whole business world, but I do my homework. I've been reading a lot of business books, and one thing I've learned is that if someone presents you with an offer so outrageous that it's insulting, you don't counter. You ignore it, which means you're lucky you got a 'no, thank you.' I should have just hung up."

"I'll tell everyone your secret."

"And who's going to believe you? I'll deny it until I'm blue in the face, and so will Skeeter Malcolm. Besides, if you hope to change my mind, you won't want the secret out."

He was silent again for a good five seconds. "Well played, Lady. Well played."

I didn't respond. No need to gloat.

"I'd like to rescind my offer and make a new one."

"I'm listening."

"Five visions. No time limit."

That was more reasonable, but it still made me nervous, especially since I still wasn't sure I could pull off what I was offering. "Before I'd ever agree to such a thing, measures would have to be taken to ensure my safety *and* to keep my secret."

"What kind of measures?" he asked, sounding leery.

"I'll need a bodyguard of my own choosing."

"Why?" he asked. "I've seen you handle yourself, and I plan to be there every time I use you."

I sure as Pete didn't feel like telling him that I was momentarily out of it whenever I had a vision, let alone that I always blurted out something about whatever I had seen. As my bodyguard, Jed had always found ways to help cover for me. "I'll only agree to this if Jed Carlisle is with me."

"*Carlisle?* I thought he quit Malcolm."

"He did, but he was my bodyguard when I was Lady last winter, and I trust him implicitly. No Jed, no chance of me entertainin' a deal."

He was silent for a moment. "How the hell will I explain him bein' there?"

"Your problem, not mine."

"So you'll agree to five visions?"

"What do you plan on havin' me see?"

"What did you see for Malcolm?"

"What I did for James is between me and him, just like my visions will be between me and you *if* I agree to do this."

"And Jed Carlisle," he added with a sneer. "There might be things I don't want him seein' or hearin'."

"Not my problem."

"Then I'm not sendin' any men to help you."

"That's your choice, Dermot, especially since I never said I'd agree to a deal in the first place. I only wanted to hear your terms and for you to know mine."

After five seconds of silence, I realized he'd hung up. And I hadn't had a chance to ask him if Carol Ann had approached him for money.

I started to call Randy again, but the last thing I needed was the department on my back. I decided to make the call anonymous. While I still needed to talk to him about the camera, I could call about that later.

The convenience store across from the abandoned fertilizer plant still had a functioning pay phone, so I headed that way. Once I was parked, I grabbed a couple of quarters and walked over to the phone on the side of the building.

After I dialed the anonymous tip line, an automated message directed me to leave a message. I lowered my voice an octave in an attempt to disguise it. "I have some information about Patsy Sue Clydehopper. See if Kip Wagner knows anything about her disappearance as well as Carol Ann Nelson's murder." I quickly hung up, wondering if I'd taken the right route. Would the sheriff's department take my call seriously? Would they give it more weight if I'd called Randy or Joe directly?

Still mulling it over, I walked back to my truck, trying to decide what to do next. I should have asked Dermot if Carol Ann had approached him about the club, but it was too late now.

Maybe it was time for me to follow up with Carol Ann's cousin in Big Thief Hollow. Too bad I didn't have anything to go on other than the first name Charlene.

After I got my truck started, I sent Neely Kate a text.

CAN YOU GIVE ME THE FULL NAME AND ADDRESS OF CAROL ANN'S COUSIN ON HER DADDY'S SIDE?

She called seconds later.

"Rose, Jed and I can go when we wrap things up here."

"Are you still trackin' down Becky's boyfriend?"

"Yeah, but he's not at work, and when we showed Becky's picture around, no one recognized her."

"So none of them have ever seen her? Did they know she was livin' with him?"

"The guys who work next to him know he has a new girlfriend, but that's about it. The receptionist said he'd been arrested for domestic abuse with his previous girlfriend. In fact, the receptionist was a little afraid of him."

I didn't like the sound of that. "Do they have any idea where Bubba could have gone?"

"None. Apparently it's unlike him to miss work, let alone not call in."

I chewed on the information she'd shared. "What does Jed think? Could Bubba be tied up in the robbery or the file?"

"He says it's too soon to speculate."

I glanced at the time. It was nearly three o'clock. "So what are you and Jed plannin' to do now?"

"Bubba's supervisor gave us the address of Bubba's parents. We're gonna go talk to them. What are you gonna do?"

I twisted my mouth as I stared at the clock. I was supposed to meet Mason in an hour or so, and my stomach was in knots. "I was thinkin' I could go see Charlene by myself if you're still tied up."

"I don't think it's a good idea for you to go alone. Let's do that together tomorrow."

"I thought you were workin' on findin' Becky?"

"I am, but it feels like we're about to hit a dead end. We'll go to Big Thief Hollow together."

"Okay," I said, running a hand over my head. "Maybe we could bring Jed. I'd like to pay Charlene's dealer a visit too. See if Carol Ann asked him for money."

Neely Kate was quiet for a moment. "That's a good idea. I'm sure he'll agree."

"In the meantime, how about I go to Patsy's real estate office and question them with the new information I've gotten?"

"What new information?"

Crap. I hadn't told her about my meeting with James or any of the information he'd given me. "I'll tell you tonight, but I'm not sure when I'll get back to the farm. I'm meeting Mason at the office sometime after four."

"Are you sure that's a good idea, Rose? You were pretty upset talkin' about him this morning."

"I think I need to, Neely Kate. I need to see him without all the freaking out and crying."

"Yeah, I understand. I've spent many a late night thinkin' about what I'll say if I ever see Ronnie again, and in all of the scenarios I've come up with, I'm cool as a cucumber when I calmly tell him off."

I sighed. "I know I handled it all wrong."

"That's not what I'm sayin', Rose. I'm sayin' that in my head, I'm super cool and collected when I confront him because it's a daydream. But if I ever ran into him out of the blue, I doubt I'd be so calm. You're prepared this time. You can say all the things you wish you'd said yesterday. Just be careful with your heart. You've spent months gettin' over him. Don't let him steal your progress."

NO ONE WAS HAPPY to see me at Clydehopper Realty. For one thing, they were all in a tizzy over the fact that Patsy Sue was still missing, and they were struggling to pick up the pieces of her ongoing business deals. And for another, I was asking harder questions than Neely Kate and Jed had asked the day before.

"I don't like what you're insinuating," Bobby Tucker, Patsy's most senior realtor said. He'd pulled me aside upon realizing my line of questioning wasn't necessarily beneficial to the firm. I'd asked some of the other realtors about Patsy's lawsuit and how appraisers were assigned in real estate deals.

"I'm not sure I understand," I said, playing innocent. "I'm merely askin' questions about the real estate business."

He narrowed his eyes, not buying my act. "I thought you and Neely Kate were tryin' to clear Patsy's name, not run it through the mud."

I cocked my head. "How is askin' questions about how she does things runnin' her name through the mud?"

He stammered, realizing he'd backed himself into a corner.

"I promise you, Mr. Tucker, I have a reason for my questions, and I also promise that Neely Kate and I really are trying to find out who killed Carol Ann." Even if it turned out to be Patsy.

He nodded, but he still didn't seem very happy.

"I know that Patsy upset a few people. Do you think you could get me a list of people who might have been upset enough to do something drastic?"

"Like what?"

"Patsy might be in danger," I said. I truly was worried that Kip Wagner might have snatched her to get to Calvin, but I still felt like we needed to pursue this angle too.

"The sheriff's deputies never mentioned it. They hardly asked any questions at all."

"That's because we're goin' at this from different angles, so I'd really appreciate it if you could get me that list."

"I'm about to go to a closing," he said. "The Lebowskis have had their closing moved twice. They'll never stand for a third change, especially if it's of my doin'. The soonest I can get a list to you is tomorrow morning."

"I suppose that will have to do." I gave him my card and told him to email me the list, then walked out to my truck. I pulled my phone out of my purse to see if I'd missed any calls and saw a text from Mason.

I CAN BE AT YOUR OFFICE AT 4:30. DOES THAT WORK FOR YOU?

Part of me wanted to tell him no, that I'd changed my mind. But I went with my gut. I needed to see him. I needed the closure.

SEE YOU THEN.

I was only ten minutes from my office, so I had plenty of time to go by the coffee shop and get a cup of coffee. Since I hadn't gotten much sleep the night before, I needed the caffeine boost. But first I called Deputy Miller.

"Rose," he said when he answered. "I've been meaning to call you. Thanks for the tip about the camera."

"So you found one?"

"No … but we found the telltale signs that one had been there. It adds a whole new dimension to the case."

"Come up with a cause of death yet?" I asked. The obvious answer was that she'd been strangled with Calvin's tie, but nothing about this case had gone as expected.

He was silent for a moment. "Strangulation."

"Thanks."

"Is that it?" he asked, and I could tell he was interested in what I might have. "Any other questions?"

I pulled into a parking space in front of the landscaping office. I was dying to know if anyone had given any serious attention to my anonymous tip, but obviously I couldn't ask. "There's an appointment I need to get to. Thanks for the chat."

"Rose. Wait."

I turned off the engine and sat back in my seat. "Okay."

"Have you heard any whisperings of Kip Wagner's involvement in all of this?"

I couldn't help smiling, but I kept my voice neutral. "In regard to Carol Ann's murder? No. But I did hear his pawn shop was robbed. Do you think the two are related?" Had they made a connection before my call? Or had my message spurred this new line of thought?

"No," he said, keeping his voice neutral too. "We got a tip we're running down, but if you'd heard anything to help us …"

"I haven't heard anything that can help you tie them together," I said, which I told myself wasn't really a lie. I did know things about Wagner, just nothing that explicitly tied him to Carol Ann. Well, nothing but a hunch, and I'd already shared that with them anonymously. "And don't worry. I'll keep the tip to myself too."

"Thanks."

I still had a few minutes, so I hurried down to the coffee shop. Just as I opened the door to go in, I heard Joe calling my name from across the street.

"Rose!"

I let go of the door and turned to face him, my stomach turning flips. Had he figured out that I'd made the anonymous call about Kip Wagner? I decided to play innocent. "Hey, Joe."

He headed across the street to join me, and the serious expression on his face only worried me more. "How's Neely Kate?"

Some of the worry bled out of me. He was still upset over Neely Kate. "She's still mad, but she's keepin' busy with our investigation."

"How's that goin'?" he asked, but I could see there was something else he wanted to tell me. He was working his way up to it.

"Slow."

He nodded. "Randy's sayin' the same thing on his end, although he told me he got an interestin' lead that might prove more helpful than we could ever dream." He swallowed, then lowered his voice. "Rose, there's something you need to know." He shook his head. "Maybe you already know, but I wasn't sure, and I don't want you to be blindsided."

I braced myself. "What?"

"Mason's in town."

I stared up at him in disbelief. Joe was warning me that Mason was back? The worry in his eyes told me that he was sincere. He didn't want me to accidentally run into him. "I know."

He gazed at me for a second, looking a bit chagrined. "I'm sorry if I overstepped."

I shook my head. "No. I didn't know he was comin'. I found out exactly how you hoped to keep me from finding out—by running into him yesterday afternoon." I put my hand on his arm. "Thank you for tryin' to protect me. It means more than you know."

He smiled down at me, but his eyes were sad. "I know how much he hurt you when he left." He leaned closer. "He was a fool, Rose, and you deserve better than that."

His words stunned me. There was no gloating in his statement. Only sorrow and empathy. I would have thought he was using this to make another go at restarting a relationship with me, but he was dating Dena. "You don't even know why he left."

"Because you embarrassed him," Joe said in a tight voice. "He was the assistant district attorney, and you were playin' with criminals behind his back."

I glanced away, unable to face him. Joe had it half right. "Does everyone think that?"

"I don't know what everyone thinks, but I know Mason Deveraux." He paused as though he was weighing his words. "He's here on official business. Did he tell you that?"

I nodded. "But not what."

He paused, glancing back at the imposing stone courthouse before turning back to face me. "He's here to rip this place apart, brick by brick."

My breath caught in my throat. "What does that mean?"

"He's got a solid foothold in the attorney general's office, and he definitely has the man's ear. He knows enough about how this county is run that he's presented a case to his boss to start a formal investigation into the county government. He's about to start burnin' it all down to the ground."

I stared back up at him. "You mean he's gonna expose the corruption?"

"That and more."

A cold chill washed through my body. "What does that mean?"

His dark gaze held mine. "He's about to go after the crime world too."

I swayed, not realizing I'd become dizzy until Joe grabbed my elbow to steady me, holding my gaze the entire time. He was watching me for a reaction, and I'd just given him a doozy of one.

"I have no idea what your part is in that world. I've heard rumors that the Lady in Black has resurfaced, and we both know your role as Lady last winter wasn't just a pretense to bring down my father."

The Lady in Black had fallen on the law enforcement officials' radar since the day after Thanksgiving, when rumors had floated around that a woman in a black dress paired with a hat and veil had shown up at the auction to decide the fate of who ran the criminal underworld in the county. Everyone knew she'd stood at Skeeter Malcolm's side. I'd heard whispers of it from Mason and his team of officials. They'd been intent on finding her.

And now Mason was back in town with the full knowledge of my true role as Lady, and the knowledge that James and I were friends.

He'd seen the prescription with Dermot's name.

I stared up at Joe, wide-eyed. "Do you think he's comin' for me?"

His mouth gaped in shock. "Why would he come for you?"

I took a step back, trying to think things through, but I was so thrown off I no longer felt capable of logic.

His mouth closed and the skin around his eyes tightened. "You think he'd come after you to hurt you?"

Would he? I shook my head. "No. He told me he's sorry for how he ended things. He told me he wants me back."

He blinked, obviously taken aback. "Do you want *him* back?" Then he shook his head, his jaw tight. "No. Don't answer that. I have no right askin'. I'm sorry."

I didn't answer. I was still trying to process what he'd told me.

"So then you already know he's movin' back."

"*What?*"

"Oh." He looked pained. "I figured he would have told you."

I shook my head. "No. You must've gotten it wrong. He told me he was staying until Thursday morning, and he only told me that because he wanted to talk to me again before he left."

Joe didn't say anything.

He had to be wrong. "Maeve told me she was considering moving to Little Rock to be closer to him. She told me this morning after havin' breakfast with him."

Pain filled his eyes, and I realized I should have softened *that* piece of news. Joe and Maeve had formed a special friendship last fall. He had been her daughter's boyfriend over a year ago, although they had never met before. Joe had broken up with Savannah to go back to his toxic on-again, off-again girlfriend Hilary. When Savannah had announced she was pregnant, Hilary had convinced Joe it was a lie she'd made up to get him back. J.R. Simmons had had Savannah killed to make sure he didn't lose control of the situation.

Although Joe hadn't known her murder was his father's doing until last February, he'd always blamed himself for her death. Maeve had offered him something he couldn't seem to give himself—forgiveness—and he'd latched onto it and her like a drowning man.

He swallowed, his eyes glistening, then cleared his throat. "Maybe he didn't share his plans with her. In fact, he acted like he wasn't plannin' on stayin' until about an hour ago, but knowin' Mason, I figured it was an act. That he'd maneuvered the conversation to make it look like it was the mayor's idea, not his."

"What are you talkin' about? What happened an hour ago?"

"The mayor asked him to work with a county task force, which means he'll need to be here full-time. Mason said he had to clear it with his boss, but they were so eager to clean up the corruption, he was sure the attorney general would approve." He was still holding my arm, and his grip tightened. "Rose, maybe you should sit down. You look pale."

So much for being the Lady in Black. She never would have felt like passing out over a dramatic situation with an ex-boyfriend. But this was more than Mason moving back to Henryetta.

This was Mason going after Skeeter Malcolm.

I knew it in my bones. In Mason's eyes, James had done this to me. To us. He'd forced me into this role, and now he was going after the man for ruining both our lives.

I opened my mouth to say something, but then I closed it. I couldn't talk openly with Joe. Not about that.

"Rose, you're really worryin' me. Let's get you back to your office, okay?"

I nodded dumbly. I needed to get myself together, but my mind was racing over all the incriminating information Mason had on both James and Jed.

There were reams of it.

Chapter Twenty-One

Joe held my arm until we were in my office. The afternoon had heated up, but I hadn't realized it until the air-conditioned air hit the beads of sweat on my skin. But then again, the sweat was just as likely from nerves as it was from the weather.

I shook him free once we were inside, and I headed for my office chair.

Joe disappeared into the back, then squatted in front of me with a cold bottle of water. "Here. Take a sip of this."

The fridge in the back was a new addition. Neely Kate had bought it from a woman whose son had refused to go back to college in the fall. I'd given her the twenty bucks from the business account, figuring it might be nice to store food and drinks. Joe had helped Neely Kate move it in back when things had been better between them.

He started to unscrew the cap for me, but I took it from him, irritated with myself for acting so helpless. "I can do it, Joe," I said softly.

After I took a sip, he asked in a soothing tone, "What has you worried, Rose? What does Mason have on you?" Down on one knee, he was a little shorter than eye level.

"Everything."

"Everything you did as the Lady in Black last winter?"

I stared at him wide-eyed. Joe was my ex-boyfriend and now my friend, but he was also the Chief Deputy Sheriff of Fenton County. I'd do best to remember that.

But he must have read my thoughts in my eyes. "I'm here as your friend right now, Rose. I'll help you."

"You'll help me against Mason?"

His eyes hardened. "You bet your ass I will."

Why would he do this? If Mason was really on a witch hunt like Joe suspected, he could potentially dig up dirt on him too. Joe had plenty of skeletons in his closet up in Little Rock, and they had always irritated the snot out of Mason. If Joe helped me, he could be putting himself in the line of fire.

I shook my head. What was I thinking? This was Mason, my sweet Mason who had been so gentle and tender with me, even after he'd discovered my awful secret, even when he'd ripped my heart to shreds by ending us.

Mason would never hurt me.

Right?

I took another sip of water, then lowered the bottle to my lap. "I think we're overreactin'."

"You do?" he asked, his disbelief evident in his eyes.

"Why would he pretend he wants to get back together if he's plannin' to prosecute me?"

"He might be usin' you for information, Rose."

"This is Mason we're talkin' about, Joe. *Mason.*"

"You didn't see the man I saw in Little Rock, Rose. He wasn't the man you know now."

My heart stuttered. "How so?"

"Little Rock Mason was cold and calculating. No defense attorney wanted to deal with him in the courtroom. When you started dating him, he became a gentler version of himself. More compassionate." He paused. "But the man I saw in that meeting this afternoon was more like the Little Rock version of Mason Deveraux. Ruthless. Driven."

A shiver ran down my back. He'd told me that before, but Mason himself had admitted that I'd softened him. Surely he hadn't reverted to his old ways so quickly. "No. I don't believe he would hurt me. He said he still loves me. I think he might go after everyone else, but he would never intentionally hurt me." But I had no doubt he would go after James and Jed, and if he used what he knew from last winter, I wasn't sure there was any way to untangle me from the mess.

"What if you turn him down?"

"What?" I asked, certain I'd misconstrued his question.

"You said he wants you back. What if you tell him no?"

"No, I can't believe he'd try to hurt me. Not even then."

"But he might drag you into court to testify."

And I could easily imagine what I might be asked to testify about.

The bell on the front door dinged and Mason stood in the doorway, wearing a pale blue dress shirt—its sleeves rolled up just below his elbows—and a pale yellow tie. His gray dress slacks clung to his hips, and six months ago the sight of him would have made me breathless. Now I was breathless for a different reason.

Mason's face hardened as his gaze landed on Joe, who was still kneeling in front of me. "Didn't waste any time getting to Rose, I see."

Joe got to his feet. "What difference does it make to you, Deveraux? You left her months ago."

Mason's hard gaze turned to me.

I put my hand on Joe's arm. "Go. Let me deal with this."

The look on Joe's face told me that was the last thing he planned to do.

"Joe," I said, my voice softening. "Please. We'll talk later."

He hesitated, then leaned closer, whispering, "Be careful what you say, Rose. He's here as the person in charge of the task force investigating the corruption in the county. Every word can be used against you."

I stared up at him, trying to hide my shock and disbelief. After giving me one last look, he stalked toward the door, stopping next to Mason.

"You've already hurt her enough, Deveraux. Think about that before you hurt her any more." Then Joe went out the door, slamming it behind him hard enough to make me jump.

With Joe gone, Mason relaxed a bit and took a few steps into the room. "What did he tell you?"

"That you're movin' back to Henryetta."

He looked pained as he said, "I didn't know when I spoke to you yesterday or I would have warned you."

"But you suspected."

He didn't respond.

"Have you told your mother yet?" When I saw the questioning look on his face, I added, "She's considering movin' to Little Rock to be closer to you."

Confusion swam in his eyes. "But she loves it here."

"She loves you more."

That sobered him and he advanced toward me, stopping at the edge of my desk. "What else did Joe tell you?"

"That you're heading a task force."

His mouth pinched. "He had no business telling you *anything*."

"He's my friend. He wanted to warn me so I wouldn't be hurt."

"Or maybe he's trying to get between you and me. Again."

My anger flared. "I've been single for months, and he hasn't once tried to make a move on me. In fact, he has a girlfriend. He's over me."

"Joe Simmons will never be one hundred percent over you."

I could have argued, but I was too tired. I sat down in my seat and glanced out the window.

"May I sit with you?" he asked quietly.

I didn't like the idea of him getting too comfortable, but I also didn't want to stare up at him. It would make me feel even more out of control of the situation. "Yeah."

He grabbed Neely Kate's chair and rolled it over to my desk. As he situated it mere feet from me, I was bowled over by a sudden stream of memories of Mason in this office. Mason helping me set up the office when I'd decided to break away from the nursery. Mason bringing me food on his lunch break and the two of us eating at my desk. Mason telling me that my betrayal had been too much for him to bear and he was moving out. Memories both happy and bittersweet, and now I had one more to add.

Maybe meeting here had been a bad idea after all. Maybe there was nowhere we could comfortably meet.

"What else did Joe tell you, Rose?" Mason finally asked, his voice soft.

I couldn't look at him. My mind was still racing over Joe's suggestions. "That's all: that you're in charge of a task force to root out corruption in Fenton County, and that you're moving back."

"I am. I hadn't planned on it. I'd only planned to come down every few weeks, but the mayor called my boss this morning after our initial meeting, and my boss is trying to get the paperwork accelerated to make it happen. It's not official yet, but it will be by the time I leave on Thursday." He paused, and when he spoke again, his voice was tight. "Rose, will you please look at me."

I slowly turned to see his anguished expression.

"This is not how I wanted you to find out, Rose. I wanted to be the one to tell you."

"Joe says your task force is goin' after the crime world too."

He studied me before he said in a careful tone, "You and I both know the judges and officials in this county have been bought. Yes, I'll be goin' after the people who bought them off."

"And others."

"I freely admit that I plan to clean up the county."

"Do you have any specific people in mind?" I asked, thankful my voice didn't shake.

He gave me a piercing look. "Are you askin' about anyone specific?"

I narrowed my eyes and tilted my head to the side. "I'll take that as a yes."

"And so will I," he said, sounding irritated. Then he shook his head and leaned forward with his elbows on his thighs. "I don't want to fight with you."

"You're the one with a personal vendetta."

Scowling, he sat back up. "What's that mean?"

"You plan to go after Skeeter Malcolm, and we both know it."

Arrogance tightened his features. "If he's part of any wrongdoing, then yes, I will be going after him."

I pointed my finger at him. "It's more than that and we both know it. You're wanting to punish him for his part in the whole J.R. mess last winter."

He pressed his lips together. "Are you intent on helping him?"

"He saved my life, Mason," I said with a sigh. "He made it possible for me to save yours. Doesn't that count for something with you?"

He stood and walked toward the front of the office. For a moment I thought he was going to up and leave, but he stopped at the windows and stared across the street. "We both know I've spent my career prosecuting criminals." He turned back to look at me. "A year ago, we were both on the same page with that."

I stood too, still not wanting to have to look up at him. "You think the world is black and white, Mason. I helped you see the gray. Have you forgotten it?"

He slowly spun to face me. "The gray starts to get messy. The lines begin to erode. There is right and there is wrong, and it was foolish of me to overlook it."

I took several steps toward him. "What happened to the man who started a program helping kids who got in trouble with the law? The old Mason would have written them off, but the man I knew thought there was a way to help them. Is that man gone?"

He gave me a defensive look. "Not gone, Rose. Just more jaded."

"Because of what happened in February when we took down J.R. Simmons?" I asked, moving closer.

He didn't answer. He didn't have to.

"And me," I added, my words dripping with sorrow. "You're more jaded because of me."

He turned from me again, staring at the courthouse.

"Yesterday you told me you always thought you'd come back here to apologize," I said, overcome with grief. "But that was never going to happen. Not really. So instead, you came back to get revenge. You're gonna destroy the very thing you think stole me from you."

His head spun back, a fire in his eyes. "I love you, Rose. By God, I wish I didn't, but I still do." He took a breath. "But I won't let that love blind me to the job I'm supposed to do—the job that was assigned to me." Suddenly, all the anger fled from him, leaving him a broken man. "Regardless of what you think, I didn't ask for this. I tried to decline this assignment, but I was told to take the job or resign. What was I supposed to do?"

I stared up at him, slack-jawed as tears filled my eyes.

"I lost you, the only woman I ever really loved. All I have left is my work."

My heart was breaking. "Mason …"

He reached for my hand, and I didn't resist. I'd missed him—I'd missed us—and now he was standing in front of me offering the very thing he'd snatched from me. "I don't want to hurt you, Rose. That's the last thing I want."

"What if I said yes?" I asked as a tear tracked down my cheek. "What if I said I wanted you back? Would you still do this?"

He watched me for a moment, pain washing over his face. "Those are the conditions? I can have you back, but I'd need to drop this assignment?"

He tried to pull away, but I tightened my hold on his hand, some desperate part of me still clinging to the hope I could have my life with him back. "You were fired from your job before, Mason. You were lookin' at doin' something else. Some other kind of law. You could still do that."

His mouth twisted into a sad smile. "You told me I'd be bored to tears. You were right."

"Then get your old job back as the assistant DA. I'm sure you could."

"Get a job in the department I was sent to clean out?" he asked, sounding incredulous.

"Do it from the inside."

He shook his head. "You and I both know how corrupt this county government is. There's only one reason you're trying to keep me from doin' this." He snatched his hand from mine. "Him."

I started to protest, but he was right. I hated the corruption in this county. It had very nearly sent me to prison for my mother's murder. There was only one reason I was fighting him on it, or rather one person. James would and *had* risked everything to keep me safe while Mason wasn't willing to give up anything.

"Are you sleepin' with him?" Mason asked in a cold voice.

I had to be very careful with my answer … and my reaction. "You have no right askin' who I'm sleepin' with."

His hazel eyes turned cold. "So you are?"

"Who are *you* sleepin' with?" I asked in a hateful tone.

"That has no relevance in this conversation."

"The heck it doesn't!" I shouted. "You're demanding to know who I've been with since you abandoned me. If you expect an answer, then I have every right to know who you've been with."

"This is not even close to the same thing, Rose, and you know it!"

"The hell it's not! I've dated one man, Mason. *One man* since you left. The new veterinarian, Levi Romano, and I sure as Pete didn't sleep with him. Now you tell me who you've dated." It was a lie of omission, and I felt horrible for it, but I certainly couldn't tell him the truth. Not unless we really got back together, but it was pretty clear there was little chance of that happening now.

His anger faded some. "Rose, my dating life isn't—"

"So you *have* slept with someone else?" I asked, realizing the truth hurt worse than I'd expected. Maeve had told me he was seeing other people, but it felt different to hear it from him.

He must have heard the pain in my voice because his face softened, and now he looked like the Mason I'd loved. The man I'd risked my life to save. "My lack of denial doesn't mean it's true," he said, his voice thick with emotion.

"Exactly," I said, though his words didn't feel validating. Maybe because he'd guessed correctly.

"He loved you, Rose. There was no denying that. I can't believe he didn't swoop in to win you as soon as I left."

I shook my head as fresh tears fell from my eyes. "He wouldn't have done that, Mason. He respected me too much." I felt better knowing that part wasn't a lie. We'd remained friends, but he'd never pushed that boundary. Not once. I'd been the one to do it a month ago.

His anger was back. "I don't believe that for one minute."

My reaction wasn't anger. It was regret. "That only shows how little you know him."

He started to speak, then wisely shut his mouth.

"We both know what I did to save you. And we both know that you left me because you were pissed off, pure and simple. Sure, you told me I needed space to grow, but we both know your anger drove you to it."

He didn't correct me.

"With one breath you tell me you've missed me, and with the next you say that you expected Skeeter Malcolm to put the moves on me in your absence?" Then it hit me. "It was a test. *You were testing me?*"

Guilt filled his eyes. "Rose, I had to be certain."

"Certain of what? That I loved you?" I placed my palm on his chest and shoved hard. "Get out of my office."

"Rose …"

"You told me to move on, Mason," I said, struggling not to cry. "I moved on by dating the new vet."

Why wasn't I angry? All I felt was profound disappointment and grief.

Was it because I'd failed his test?

No. I had never thought of James as anything other than a friend until months after my breakup with Mason. James could have made a move and taken advantage of my vulnerability, but he hadn't. Quite the opposite. He'd tried to push me away, insisting I was too good for him.

But Mason couldn't know any of that. If he so much as caught a whiff of my involvement with James, he'd go after him with a vengeance.

"I'm sorry, Rose. I had to be sure."

I shook my head and turned from him. "We're done. Go."

"If I could change things …"

"You wouldn't change a thing, because it still kills you that I collaborated with the very man you vowed to put behind bars. I understood it back then, and I still do. But I never once gave you reason to believe I'd be anything less than faithful."

"How can you say that?" he demanded, his voice rising. "You paraded around for months as his lover!"

"I was not his lover!" I shouted. "Pretend or otherwise! I was always presented as his business partner."

"I'm sure those men bought that," he spat out.

I took a breath to ease the ache in my heart. "You're right," I said in a calm voice. "They didn't at first. But they did by the time they left my presence."

Indecision flickered in his eyes. "I'm supposed to believe that?"

That pissed me off. Now he was calling me a liar. "I earned those men's respect. Hardened criminals respected me, Mason. *Me.* Not because I'd done anything even remotely criminal. Because I *demanded* it. So I'll be damned if I'll let you make me feel like I'm some worthless slut." I flung my hand toward the door. "Now. Get. Out."

"Rose."

"Go!"

He started for the door and stopped with his hand on the doorknob. "This wasn't how I wanted this to go."

"You keep sayin' that, yet it still keeps happening. But how could you expect it to go any differently?" I asked as the truth hit me hard.

"What do you mean?" he asked in a quiet voice. Cold and collected.

"You don't respect me. You lost every ounce of respect for me the moment you found out that I'm the Lady in Black. You still loved me, but you didn't trust me, and you sure didn't respect me. I crossed the line you've always held so sacred, and I did it to save you. You hated that you were beholden to me for it. You hated James for agreeing to help me. You couldn't be with me, but letting me go for good made you an ungrateful asshole." I made a shooing motion. "Go. Be free of it. I'm not holding it over your head. You're the only one holding you captive."

He was silent for several seconds. "Maybe you're right. Maybe I lost all respect for you, but you know what stood out to me the most in your pretty speech?" He paused. "You said '*I'm* the Lady in Black'—present tense, not past." His face hardened. "You better get your house in order, Rose, because you don't want to be standing in the way when I bring everything down."

Chapter Twenty-Two

Jed's car was parked in front of the house when I got back to the farm. Muffy met me at the door, and I squatted to rub her head.

"What smells so good, Muff?" I asked, realizing my stomach was rumbling.

"You're just in time," Neely Kate called out from the kitchen. "I'm makin' BLTs."

I leaned in closer to Muffy and whispered, "Surely she can't mess those up, right?"

She looked at me as though to say, *Don't count on it.*

The previous winter, Neely Kate had become enamored with food shows that required the contestants to create unique dishes with even more unique ingredients. Bruce Wayne and I—and even Mason—had been subjected to a host of very bad dishes. She'd since gone back to the Southern comfort food her granny had taught her how to make, but she'd begun to roll out her "gourmet" cooking to impress Jed. The fact that Jed choked it down instead of running for the hills was a sure sign of how crazy he was about her.

I scooped up Muffy and headed to the kitchen, surprised to see Marshall sitting at the kitchen table with Jed, while Neely Kate stood in front of the stove. Marshall was wearing a T-shirt that looked to be Jed's, based on the way it swam on him, and a pair of athletic shorts, most likely also Jed's, which hung to his knees, covering his bandage.

"How are you feeling, Marshall?" I asked, giving him the once-over. His face had more color today and he seemed to have more energy.

He bowed his head. "Better, thanks for askin', ma'am."

"Jed helped me bring him downstairs," Neely Kate said as she flipped some bacon in a cast-iron skillet. "We wanted to ask him more questions about Becky, plus we figured he was goin' stir-crazy upstairs."

I doubted Jed could care less if the kid was going stir-crazy, but I was sure he wanted answers. "Good idea."

"Where's Witt?"

"He'll be back later tonight," Neely Kate said. "He was goin' to see if he could catch wind of what Wagner might have planned tonight."

While I suspected that was true, he'd probably also purposefully made himself scarce after hearing about Neely Kate's plan to cook.

Neely Kate's focus was on the skillet, but Jed had leveled a good, long look at me. Based on the set of his jaw, I realized something was wrong.

"Rose," he finally said, "when I took Muffy out a bit ago, I noticed the screen to one of the basement windows is loose. I wanted to point it out to you so we can get it secured."

Neely Kate glanced over her shoulder. "You don't need to show it to her, Jed. We can just get it fixed."

"No," I said, still holding Muffy in my arms. "Muffy got out the other night when Kip Wagner and his men showed up, and I forgot in all the craziness. I want to see if she could have used that window."

"Okay …," she said, sounding suspicious. She had a right to be. I knew Jed had an ulterior motive. He had something to tell me.

We went out the back door and rounded the corner to the side of the house. Sure enough, the window screen had been jostled loose, leaving a big enough space for Muffy to get out. But the broken window was much more concerning.

"Do you think Muffy could have done this?" I asked.

"No."

"I wonder how long it's been like this."

"Good question. I checked out the basement, but I didn't find any sign of someone snoopin' around. And there's no glass on the inside. The glass shards are lyin' in the grass." So maybe he *had* asked me out here to examine the window.

"So someone or something broke out," I said. "Not in."

"I still don't think it was Muffy. She would have been cut up, and I looked her over. There's nothin'."

I frowned. "One more thing to worry about."

"If it's all right with you, I'm going to see about getting it fixed tomorrow."

Crossing my arms as I studied the window, I nodded. "Yeah. Thanks."

"I know you saw Skeeter today."

I stared up at him, trying to decide how he'd found out and if I was about to get a lecture. "And …?"

"He told me he's concerned about you girls' safety, and he wants me to start up your self-defense lessons again."

I nodded. "He suggested the same to me."

"It's a good idea. We can even work on some of it here on the farm."

"We'll just have to warn Joe if we do target practice," I said, my stomach twisting with anxiety. "Otherwise, he'll worry if he hears the shots."

"Something else is bothering you," he said. "I can see it in your eyes, but I didn't think it was a good idea to bring it up in front of the kid."

"You're right, but Neely Kate needs to know too, so I'll wait to tell you both."

"Hey!" Neely Kate called out. "You two get in here! Dinner's ready!"

WE ALL PICKED at our food, even Neely Kate, who seemed reluctant to admit that her Bacon, Lentil, and Tomato sandwiches with mint jelly had been a horrible idea. Marshall, on the other hand, wolfed it down.

Even if the food had tasted halfway decent, I would have had a hard time choking it down. Jed had told us that James and several men would be over at around eight to help stand watch for Wagner. I broke the news that Dermot and his men would likely not be coming but refused to give the reason at the dinner table.

But then it hit me that we were dealing with a bigger issue, one of my own making. There was about to be a possible shootout at my farm in about three hours. Given that the sheriff's department was on overdrive, they'd likely show up on Wagner's heels, especially since I'd given them the nod about him. Even worse, Mason Deveraux would jump on it like a flea to a dog.

When we finished, Jed helped Marshall into the living room and turned on the TV, then came back into the kitchen under the guise of helping us clean up, even though the work was mostly done by the time he came back in.

"Jed," I said in a low voice. "I think we should call the whole thing off."

"What are you talkin' about?"

"James and his men can't come out here. It's too dangerous."

He scowled. "We've been in dangerous spots before."

"That's not what I'm talkin' about." Although it was pretty sad that a potential shootout wasn't our worst problem. "If there's a shootout, then you and James and his men can't be anywhere near here. And neither can Marshall."

"You expect us to leave you girls here like sitting ducks?" he asked as though I'd lost my mind.

I shook my head, hating what I was about to say. "No. We won't be here either." This was going to make it look like I was running from my problems, like I was weak, but I sure didn't want to go to jail again.

"While I'm finding it hard to disagree with you, I'm curious what made you change your mind," Jed said.

"I called in an anonymous tip that Wagner might be responsible for Patsy Sue's disappearance and Carol Ann's murder. Joe hinted at it later. Which means they're watchin' him. We don't want to fall on their radar."

"They can trace that to your phone," Jed said.

I rolled my eyes. "I called from a pay phone. But there's another issue on top of that one." I paused. "Mason."

"What about Mason?" Neely Kate asked.

"I found out that he's the head of a task force set up by the attorney general. He's here to root out corruption, with the mayor's approval, but he thinks it stems from the crime world, and he plans to root it out there too. If there's a shootout and James, or Jed, or anyone associated with them is involved, Mason's gonna lock them up faster than we can say Rumpelstiltskin."

Neely Kate paled. "I thought he was only in town for a couple of days."

"This afternoon he told me that his plans have changed. He's movin' back."

Her eyes flew wide. "Oh … what does that mean for you and …"

"We're not getting back together, and after our discussion this afternoon, there's little chance of him wantin' me back."

The surprise on Jed's face let me know that neither James nor Neely Kate had filled him in on our meeting.

"I'm sorry, Rose," she said in a soft tone.

"I'm not." I didn't have time to deal with my feelings for Mason.

"Why isn't Dermot comin'?" Jed asked. "Skeeter said you were workin' out a deal with him."

"I found his terms unacceptable." And now that I knew the truth about why Mason was in town, I had to wonder if I should be trying to work something out with Dermot at all. If he were smart, he'd stay as far from me as he could get.

"Have you told Skeeter?" Jed asked.

"About which part? Mason's witch hunt or Dermot?"

"Both."

"Neither. I haven't had the opportunity." I definitely intended to tell him about Mason. I was just trying to figure out the right way to do it.

Jed scratched his chin. "Then if you're not opposed, I think I'll see if Skeeter is open to lettin' us use a safe house. The sooner we get out of here, the better."

I took a moment to think it over one last time, then nodded. Our lives weren't worth the risk. "Okay."

Jed headed out the back door, and Neely Kate took my hand.

"Are you okay?" she asked.

"No," I said with a shaky voice, "but I will be."

"Is part of it that you're upset you're not gettin' back together with Mason?"

Was it? I was hurt over his opinion of me. I was upset that he was going after James, but was I upset that we were done for good? "I think I'm upset that I can't go back to my life last fall … when Mason and I were so happy and in love, but there's no stuffing that genie back into a bottle. I'm not that person anymore, and we both said some things this afternoon that we can't take back."

Neely Kate bristled. "He said some ugly things to you?"

"I'm sure he didn't like what I had to say to him either."

"And *I'm* sure he deserved every word."

Jed walked back in the kitchen door, stuffing his phone into his front jeans pocket. "I think we're safe here for tonight."

"Why?" Neely Kate asked.

"You were right. Wagner's bein' held for questioning," he said. "The sheriff's department just showed up at the pawn shop and invited him to the station. He wasn't arrested. But he showed up at the station an hour later with his attorney in tow. We should be safe for tonight."

"But what makes you think that?"

"Joe will have his men watchin' him after he leaves the station. They won't get anything from him there, but they'll keep a close eye on him in case he scurries off to do something stupid. So if he does show up here, Joe's men will be all over it, but chances are that he'll lie low. At least for a day or two."

I nodded.

"I doubt he'll think the call came from you, so he's still just holdin' you accountable for the file … which we still don't know the first thing about."

"I need to tell James about Mason. In person."

Jed watched me for a moment, then gave a sharp nod. "Agreed, but he's not in Henryetta right now."

I blinked, sure I'd heard him wrong. "He was planning to come over to face Kip Wagner."

"He was, but as soon as he found out Wagner was at the sheriff's department, he left town."

"Where did he go?"

He remained silent for a moment, then said, "You'll have to ask him."

I planned to.

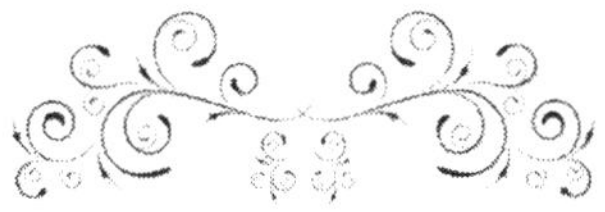

Chapter Twenty-Three

I sent James a text that I needed to talk to him when he got back into town. He texted that he'd be back the next afternoon, but to call him if there was an emergency.

After another sleepless night, Neely Kate and I headed to the office the next morning, with Jed following behind us. He'd gotten word that Wagner had been released around ten o'clock the night before, and a couple of James' men had parked at the entrance of my property all night, standing guard.

We had two clients on the schedule, and we decided to drop by Big Thief Hollow to talk to Carol Ann's cousin after our last appointment in Pickle Junction. Jed followed us to the first client, but he had to leave for a meeting of his own. He told us to hole up and give him a call if we got into any trouble.

"Rose. You have your gun?" he asked.

I fingered the fabric of my skirt. "Yeah."

"I have mine too," Neely Kate said, clutching her large purse to her side.

He grinned. "I know. I'm countin' on it, but I'm hopin' you don't need to use it."

I hoped we didn't need to use them either.

After our second appointment, I decided to stop by Bruce Wayne's job site since we were five minutes away. He'd been so busy I hadn't seen him in nearly a week.

Bruce Wayne gave us a wave as we walked up. "I didn't expect to see you two," he said with a grin. "I heard you're workin' the impossible—tryin' to prove Patsy Sue Clydehopper is innocent."

I chuckled, but Neely Kate didn't look amused. I suspected she was having major second thoughts about taking this case … not that she'd admit it.

"We had a potential landscaping client down here," I said, "but now we're on our way to Carol Ann Nelson's cousin's house to ask her more questions."

Bruce Wayne's grin fell. "The drug dealin' cousin?"

"That's the one," Neely Kate said.

"Does Jed know you're goin' there?"

Neely Kate shot him a defiant glare. "I don't need his permission."

"I didn't mean to insinuate that you did. It's just I know he's kind of protective of you."

Her expression softened. "Jed was with me when we visited her once already. He'd pitch a fit if he thought it was dangerous." Then she added, "Not that I'm askin' for permission from anyone."

He gave her a slight nod.

"So you know about Carol Ann's cousin, huh?" I asked.

He hesitated. "Yeah, I've heard a few things."

"Like what?"

"She's a small-time dealer, but I hear she's makin' a move to go big time."

I shifted my weight. "Carol Ann was supposedly tryin' to open a gentleman's club. Had you heard anything about that?"

He shook his head. "Nope."

"Does her cousin have enough money to help her out?"

Bruce Wayne laughed. "Charlene barely has enough money to pay rent. All the money she makes goes straight to her drug habit. Likely as not, her ambitions are just a pipe dream."

"Do you know who her dealer is?" I asked. "I hear it's a guy named Denny Carmichael."

Bruce Wayne's expression hardened. "You do *not* want to mess with Denny, Rose. He's bad news."

"I was told I'd need backup."

"At the very least," he said. "But if I had my druthers, you'd stay away entirely."

"Good to know."

A middle-aged woman stepped out of the house, shading her eyes as she looked over at us. "Rose? Is that you?"

"Hey, Mrs. Garcia," I said. "I wanted to drop by and see how things are goin'."

"Isn't it beautiful?" she gushed. "I love how you put the rose bushes over here, but now I'm wondering if we need another couple of bushes at the corner."

"Let me come take a look," I said, wandering over to her.

I spent five minutes talking to her about her options and her general thoughts about Bruce Wayne's crew of five men. (She loved them.) She went back into the house, and one of Bruce Wayne's men leaned closer to me.

"Miss Rose."

I gave him a smile. "Hey, Tillman. I hope you're keepin' hydrated in this heat." I'd given Bruce Wayne free rein to hire his crew. I didn't know most of the men very well, but I knew Tillman better than the rest. He and Bruce Wayne had been friends in the old days, before they'd both cleaned up their acts.

While Bruce Wayne had been a drug user, he'd mostly stuck to pot. I knew Tillman had used some harder stuff, but he'd been clean for nearly a year.

He laughed. "This heat ain't nothin'. It sure was hotter last week."

"Well, nevertheless, we don't want you gettin' heatstroke."

Neely Kate was texting when I approached her, and Bruce Wayne had already gotten back to work. I told him about the extra rose bushes our client wanted.

"I can call the nursery and make sure they have them on hand," I said.

"That's okay," Bruce Wayne said with a grin. "I'll call and ask Anna."

I smiled. Anna was Bruce Wayne's girlfriend, and she made him happier than I'd ever seen him. It warmed my heart to see him beam like that. "Okay, but if you need me to run over there and get them, let me know. Neely Kate and I might be workin' a case right now, but *this* is our bread and butter. We've got to keep the landscaping clients happy."

"Thanks, Rose."

Neely Kate glanced up from her phone. "Charlene's at the rec center. We're pickin' her up there."

I leveled my gaze with hers and asked in a flat voice, "We're meeting her at the Big Thief Hollow rec center? Do I need to remind you of what happened the last time we were there?"

When Neely Kate and I had been lookin' for her cousin, Dolly Parton, last December, we'd gone down to Big Thief Hollow to talk to her cousin's best friend. Turned out that Tabitha held a huge grudge against Neely Kate for snatching up Ronnie and marrying him. She'd attacked Neely Kate and things had gotten so heated the sheriff's department was called.

Next thing I knew, Neely Kate and I were in handcuffs until Joe showed up to set us loose. I did *not* want a repeat.

"Tabitha probably isn't there. We'll be fine."

Why did I have my doubts?

We loaded up in my truck and talked about how we'd approach the interview with Charlene.

"Let me do most of the talkin' on this one," Neely Kate said, looking through her massive purse. "It might be better since I've already talked to her."

"Good idea," I said. "We need to focus on what she knows about Carol Ann's business. If she told someone she was gonna pay them back and the investment fell through, they may have decided to kill her and Patsy just stumbled upon the body."

"Yeah, good point."

"Also," I said, a new thought hitting me, "we need to find out if Carol Ann stayed with her cousin until Saturday, and if so, why did she check into the motel?"

"And where did she make her fried chicken for the church picnic?" Neely Kate said, still sorting through her bag. "She couldn't have made it in a motel."

"Another good point." I cast a glance at her. "What are you lookin' for?"

She looked up at me with wide, innocent eyes. "Nothing."

My own eyes narrowed. "What's goin' on, Neely Kate?"

"Nothing. You're sure paranoid today."

I considered pressing her, but I knew I wouldn't get it out of her. I'd have to bide my time.

There were only a few cars in the rec center parking lot when I pulled in. I shot Neely Kate a look, still worried about her suspicious behavior. "What's Charlene doin' here, anyway?" The last time we'd been here, Neely Kate's cousin's best friend had been teaching a senior citizen belly dancing class as part of her community service.

"She's takin' an art lesson. It gets over at noon."

"Huh." Based on the few cars in the lot, it must have been a small class.

Neely Kate grabbed her floppy hat out of the back and stuffed it on her head.

"Is Tabitha here?" I asked, but she got out of the truck and walked toward the entrance.

"What?" she asked, playing innocent.

I pushed the door closed as she tried to open it. "We're not goin' in there until you tell me why you're tryin' to hide your face."

She gave me an exasperated look. "Charlene didn't want to meet us, but her sister didn't want to pick Charlene up from her art lesson, so she said *we* could pick her up and bring her home and have a chance to ask our questions. Kill two birds with one stone." She gave me a cheesy grin.

My gaze pierced hers. "Let me get this straight: Charlene doesn't know we're pickin' her up? How do you propose to get her in the truck?"

"Pearl told her she was sendin' an Uber and gave her the description of your truck."

"Then why are we goin' inside?"

"Because I'm not sittin' out here for ten minutes if Charlene's not even here. Pearl could have lied."

"Huh."

Against my better judgment, I let Neely Kate open the door and followed her inside.

The class was fuller than I'd expected. Several long cafeteria-type tables had been set out, and twenty women and a few men were scattered around with canvases and palettes of paint.

A man was standing on the stage at the far end of the entrance, and the only stitch of clothing he had on was a white cloth wrapped around his groin like a diaper.

"What in the Sam Hill …?" Neely Kate blurted out in a low whisper.

A few of the people closest to us turned around and shot her a glare.

I leaned in close. "Obviously it's a painting class with a live model."

"So they asked some old flabby guy to wear a *diaper*?"

She had a point.

"Do you see Charlene?" I asked.

"It's hard to see around this hat," she said, lifting the flap and lowering it after she took a peek.

"Can I help you?" a woman in her sixties called out from the front of the room. She wore a long, flowing purple and red floral caftan dress paired with a black caftan robe, and her pure white hair was swept up into a beehive updo wrapped in a purple cloth. The welcoming smile told me she wasn't going to kick us out … yet.

"We heard about your painting class and decided to check it out," Neely Kate said, walking toward her but keeping the brim of her floppy hat covering the side of her face. "We didn't realize you used a live model."

"I'm Sagittarius, the art guide."

"Art guide?" Neely Kate asked.

She winked with a conspiratorial grin. "One can't actually *instruct* someone to paint or draw, can they? I guide."

Neely Kate gave her a skeptical look. "Actually, I think one can."

Sagittarius either didn't hear Neely Kate's statement or chose to ignore it. I was going with the latter. "Painting living things is so much more spiritual, and the human body is the most spiritual of all. All that flesh and perfection …" She motioned over her shoulder toward the man on the stage. "That's why we have Dave with us."

"More like the dog from last week wouldn't stay still and everyone complained," an older woman grumbled next to me. I glanced down at her painting and refrained from gasping in horror. She'd made poor Dave look like the Hunchback of Notre Dame.

While Dave wasn't exactly an Adonis with rippling abs, he wasn't quite a hunchback either. He looked like the kind of guy whose idea of a good weekend was eating a massive amount of barbeque and putting away a twelve-pack of beer. On his own. His thinning hairline wasn't helping matters. Neither were his cracked feet and yellow toenails that had needed trimming several weeks ago. The woman next to me had exaggerated all those unfortunate features and more.

"Now, Lois," Sagittarius admonished, but even that sounded soft and breezy.

Lois shrugged and started adding ivy to her painting. At least I thought it was ivy, although there was a chance they were marijuana leaves.

"Did you bring art supplies?" Sagittarius asked, glancing behind us.

"Sadly, no," Neely Kate said as she made a slight pouty face. "We thought we'd just drop by and take a peek today."

Sagittarius motioned her arm toward her students with a dramatic sweep. "Feel free to wander around. Let your spirit lead you." The art guide glanced over at one of her guidees and started to tsk as she hurried over. "Susan! Let me help you blend together a clamshell color that will be perfect for his skin tone."

"My spirit's about to lead me out the door," Lois said.

"If you hate it so much, why don't you just leave?" Neely Kate asked.

"Court-ordered anger management," the woman said. "Gotta stay the whole time or it don't count." She shrugged again. "It beats group therapy sessions."

Neely Kate and I turned to each other with raised brows.

I leaned down to Lois, keeping my voice low. "Just out of curiosity, why aren't there very many cars in the parking lot?"

Her upper lip curled as she looked at me. "Most of us walk on account of we lost our licenses with DUIs and such, but Thelma over there drives anyway." She flung the end of her paint brush toward a middle-aged woman at the other table, sending flecks of green paint onto the canvas of a younger woman across from her.

The younger woman's gaze jerked up, her eyes blazing. "Did you do that on purpose, old woman?"

Lois' back straightened. "*Old woman?* Who you callin' an old woman?"

"Have you looked in the mirror lately?" the younger woman asked in a hateful tone as she got to her feet. She ran a hand over her ample hips. "You ain't looked like this since before they made cars."

Lois looked disgusted. "My body's doin' just fine. I don't have no trouble gettin' men in *my* bed. It's getting' them out that's the problem." She glanced back at me and Neely Kate and said under her breath, "On account of two of 'em's got bad hips."

I stared at her in disbelief.

"Hey!" the younger woman shouted. "I'm still talkin' to you, old woman!"

"Give it a rest, Kesha," Lois grumbled. "The grown-ups are talkin'."

The rage on Kesha's face didn't look like a good sign.

"Hey, Lois," Neely Kate said in a cheery voice. "If you're here for anger management, what's Kesha here for?"

Lois rolled her eyes, then said dismissively, "Manslaughter."

I grabbed Neely Kate's arm and headed toward the exit.

Moments later, Kesha launched over the table and tackled Lois to the ground. Rather than intervene, Sagittarius spun around to face them. "Oh, isn't this lovely. Art brings out so many emotions."

Dave was still on the stage, but he looked like he was ready to bolt, especially when a woman at the farthest table squirted a tube of paint onto the man next to her and all hell broke loose.

"Hey," Neely Kate said, "I see Charlene on the other side of the room."

"Come on," I said, pulling her to the door. "We'll wait for her outside."

Neely Kate lifted her phone and took a photo. "Pearl wanted proof that Charlene was here." She snapped several photos before I got her out the door and into the truck cab.

I rolled the windows back up and turned on the a/c, but we could still hear the shouts filtering out from inside. About five minutes later, I heard sirens and a sheriff's patrol car parked next to my truck. My heart sank when I saw who got out.

"Oh, crappy doodles," I muttered. "It's Deputy Abbie Lee Hoffstetter." This was bad. That woman hated us.

Deputy Hoffstetter moved to the front of my truck and put her hands on her hips, staring us down as though she could zap us with her laser eyes.

"What's she doin'? Why's she just standin' there?" Neely Kate rolled down the window and partially leaned out. "The ruckus is inside!" Then she pointed to the door.

Deputy Hoffstetter looked good and pissed. "Don't you two go anywhere or I'll hunt you down and arrest you for fleeing a crime scene!" Then she spun around and stomped inside, stumbling over the curb in her haste to reach the door.

"Can she do that?" Neely Kate asked.

"I think so," I said. "Maybe we should call Joe."

"Why?" she asked, getting worked up. "We literally had zero part in startin' that riot."

I made a face. "Well, maybe we played a tiny part."

"We were askin' questions like good investigators," she snapped. "We are *not* callin' Joe Simmons."

I pulled out my phone.

"You better not be callin' him, Rose. I mean it!"

"Calm down. I'm not. I'm texting Jed to let *him* know. Otherwise, he might hear about the riot and worry about us."

The fight bled out of her. "Oh. I guess I should have thought of that."

"Hey," I said as I tapped out the message. "I've got months and months of experience of keepin' Jed in the loop." I sent the message and looked up. "You're still new to keepin' him involved."

"I always hid this stuff from Ronnie," she said with a frown.

"And I hid it from Mason and look where it got me. It's good that Jed knows the real you and you don't have to hide it."

She studied me for a moment. "I guess it's like that with Skeeter for you, huh? Mason hated you bein' Lady, but Skeeter embraces it."

I didn't see any point in answering.

She was quiet for a moment. "Now that I think about it, other than Jed, Skeeter's the only guy who knows the real you."

I scowled. "Mason knew the real me. Turned out he didn't much like it."

"Mason doesn't deserve you," she said quietly.

Tears flooded my eyes. "Maybe so, but why does it still hurt so much to see him?"

She wrapped an arm around my back and laid her head on my shoulder. "Because your life with Mason was everything you always wanted. A successful man who loved you like crazy. Someone good, and stable, and kind." She turned to look at me, her face inches from mine. "But I think you outgrew him. I think you outgrew the you that wanted that." She dropped her arm and sat up. "If you'd never approached Skeeter Malcolm last fall, you would have been perfectly content with your quiet life, but then you were exposed to something *bigger* and you became this different person because of it."

"I screwed everything up." I leaned back against the headrest.

"No," she said softly. "You opened up a whole new world."

"A criminal world," I said derisively.

"No, Rose. Think bigger. You're the Lady in Black. Two major players in the criminal world see you as neutral. Do you know what you could do with that? What you're already doin'? You could bring real peace to this county."

I shook my head. "Dermot's pissed at me. He wants me to have five visions for him in exchange for standing with me against Wagner, and I wouldn't commit."

"Why not?" she asked. "You had visions for Skeeter." Her face fell. "Oh. You still haven't had a vision."

"No. I tried to have one with James yesterday afternoon, but a passin' car backfired. I told him I'd try one with you later, but it scared me too much to try again."

"Oh, Rose …"

"But my current dry spell aside, I gave Dermot certain conditions that he refused to agree to, and I won't budge, so no deal."

"What kind of conditions?"

I cringed. "One of them was that Jed has to be with me each time."

Her face paled. "What?" She took a second to recover. "Rose, he's not even workin' for Skeeter anymore."

"I know. Which is why he's perfect. He's neutral like me. It could help establish his neutrality quicker."

"And he agreed to that?" she asked.

Crap. "I haven't asked him yet."

"You just volunteered him for it without even askin'?"

"I'm sorry, Neely Kate. Honestly, I was just throwin' out requests. Dermot didn't go for it, so it doesn't matter anyway."

She looked good and ticked. "You still had no right to bring him in like that without his permission."

"I know. You're right. Even if Dermot agreed, I wouldn't have flat-out said yes. I would have told him I'd need time to think about it and to talk to Jed. If he'd said no, I would have figured something out."

A frown wrinkled her forehead. "Why did you suggest him in the first place?"

I pushed out a breath. I'd gone and screwed things up again. "Because I *trust* him. You have no idea how vulnerable I was last winter, alone in a room with some of the most hardened criminals in the county. You know how I get when I have a vision—I just blank out, and then there's the way I blurt out something about the vision … Jed was the only one there to protect me. Part of the reason I was so successful was because I knew he would never let anything happen to me."

"You had Skeeter," she said defensively.

I shook my head. "No. When I had my visions, it was just me, the guy I was questioning, and Jed off to the side. A couple of times I sent Jed out and handled the guy alone. But I always knew he was out there waiting if I needed him."

She pinched her lips together.

"When I was the Lady in Black, Jed was my bodyguard, not James. You know he stood between me and James' wrath when I got pissed and quit. I trusted Jed to have my back—I still do—and I know he has yours. Do you have any idea how relieved I felt when I found out he was with you in Oklahoma? There's no one alive I trust more than Jed to keep you safe … because I know how much he did to keep *me* safe."

Her eyes glistened with tears. "He would have said yes."

"What?"

She turned back to face me. "He would have agreed to protect you while you had visions for Dermot. He would have said yes, no questions asked." She sniffed. "But I don't want him to. I want him good and out of that world, and sayin' yes will drag him back into it."

My heart sunk. "I'm sorry, Neely Kate. I didn't even think of that part of it."

"I know." She took a breath. "Maybe I'm bein' hypocritical. I want him out, yet we're askin' him to help us hold off Kip Wagner and protect Marshall."

"No, I understand," I said quietly. "It's complicated. And it's all a moot point anyway. Dermot said no. He said he wouldn't know how to explain Jed bein' there. And while Dermot has helped me plenty, I don't trust him enough to protect me if a vision goes bad. So no deal."

"You need Dermot, Rose. That's the only way this will really work."

I shook my head. "Maybe this whole idea of Lady being neutral was foolish. Especially with Mason back in town and intent on rootin' out all the crime in the county. After seein' Dermot's name on the prescription on Monday, he already suspects I'm up to no good. Yesterday, when he was good and pissed at me, he told me to get my house in order before he brings everything down."

Her mouth dropped open. "He *threatened* you?"

I found myself in the odd position of defending him. "We both know Fenton County is a hotbed of corruption."

"But he threatened the woman he claimed to still love the day before?"

"What do you expect him to do? It's his job."

"He protected you last winter."

"That was different," I said.

"Yeah," she spat out in disgust. "He was sleepin' with you then."

I cringed. "Neely Kate."

"It's true. You said he told you that he still loves you, and we both know he loved you last winter. So the only difference is you won't take him back, so he's punishin' you for it."

I shook my head, but before I could protest, the doors to the community center flew open and a mass exodus of people covered in paint spilled out of the building.

Neely Kate tugged the hat brim to cover her face as one person headed straight for my truck—more like wove a curvy path—then opened the rear passenger door. I could see that it was a woman, but I had a hard time determining anything else since her face and shirt were smeared with paint. When she opened the back door and climbed inside, all I could think about was that she was going to ruin my upholstery, but I was too stunned to protest.

She gave me a look of disgust. "What are you waitin' for? Drive!"

What had Neely Kate gotten us into? "Charlene?"

"Yep, but I'm about to become Prison-Shower-Good-Times Sally if you don't hurry up and get out of here." Charlene flung her hand toward the entrance. "You better get goin' before that battle-ax gets herself together and tries to arrest me for pantsing her."

What? But sure enough, Deputy Hoffstetter hobbled out the door, her pants at her ankles and her hot pink underwear covered with cat faces flashing the world.

Neely Kate lifted her phone and snapped a photo of the deputy.

"Neely Kate!" I protested.

"Neely Kate?" the woman in the backseat asked in confusion.

"What?" she asked, taking another. "We might need these later when we get in trouble."

"In trouble for what?"

"For disobeyin' Abbie Lee, now go!"

I jerked the truck in reverse as the deputy ran toward it.

"Don't you dare think about leavin'!" Deputy Hoffstetter shouted.

But I'd already backed out and shoved the handle into drive. I glanced in the rearview mirror and saw her trying to run after us, but her pants weren't very forgiving, and she toppled face-first in a patch of grass.

I had a feeling I was going to be having some one-on-one time with my defense attorney, Carter Hale. But the more imminent threat was sitting in my backseat, shooting daggers at the back of my best friend's head.

Chapter Twenty-Four

"Neely Kate Rivers," Charlene said in a low tone. "What the hell are you doin' here?"

Neely Kate took off her hat and turned around to face the back. "Givin' you a free ride home."

"I knew it was too good to be true," she said in disgust, grabbing a towel off the floor in the back. "Pearl never gives me nothin' for free."

"Well, now that we're all here, you can answer a few questions," Neely Kate said.

Charlene started to wipe her face, muffling her words. "I already done answered your annoying questions the other day."

"I have a few more. I think you know more about Carol Ann's business plans than you let on."

"Maybe I do. Maybe I don't."

"Cut the crap," Neely Kate spat out. "Your cousin's dead and we're tryin' to find out what happened to her. Why don't you want to help?"

Charlene sobered. "You don't have to be so bitchy about it. I was just havin' a bit of fun."

"And I'm sure Carol Ann's havin' a lot of fun in the mortuary."

That shut her up.

I'd pulled up to a stop sign and realized we didn't have a destination. "Where are we goin'?"

"Turn right here," Neely Kate said.

I did as she said, then asked, "Why did Carol Ann come back home when she did?" Neely Kate was supposed to be running things, but I was hoping we could get back to the business in a roundabout way.

"She said she was wantin' to settle down. She was tired of the movie star life."

Neely Kate coughed. We were both fully aware of the extent of her "movie star life."

"She came directly to you?" I asked. I knew Neely Kate had asked her some of these questions already, but she didn't exactly seem the reliable sort. I was hoping we could compare her answers now to the ones she'd given Neely Kate before to suss out what was true.

"Yeah," she said, getting irritated. "And since we have nothin' to do with her momma, she didn't tell that bitch she was stayin' with us."

I bit my lip to keep myself from defending Carol Ann's mother. Maybe I could take advantage of her anger at Lucille and trick her with my next question. "Did she have the plan for her business when she arrived, or did she come up with it after she got here?"

"She already had the plan. She just needed to get her ducks in a row." Charlene groaned. "How many times do I got to tell y'all this?"

"Well," Neely Kate said in a smug tone, "seeing how you never even admitted to knowin' anything last time, it looks like our badgerin' is working." She put her hands on the backseat and leaned closer. "Now what was the business?"

Charlene let out a few curses, then finally said, "She wanted to open a whorehouse, only she wasn't callin' it a whorehouse. She was callin' it a gentleman's club and plannin' to have the men meet women there." She shook her head. "She'd worked at one out in Nevada and wanted to run her own and not lay on her back so much. She figured it would be easier to run one here, but it was harder for her to get the money than she expected."

I glanced at Neely Kate, who was still staring down Charlene.

"How much money did she get?" Neely Kate asked.

"Do I look like a banker to you?" she snorted.

"No," Neely Kate said. "You look like a used-up drug addict who's so stoned she took part in a riot in the middle of a painting class."

My mouth dropped open. It wasn't like Neely Kate to be so ugly, but I could see that she was good and irritated. A quick glance over my shoulder confirmed Charlene's pupils were dilated. She was definitely high.

"Why keep all this from me when I visited you before?" Neely Kate asked. "Why hide it?"

Charlene squirmed. "Who said I was hiding anything?"

"Please," Neely Kate said with a groan. "How much money had Carol Ann managed to raise?"

"Not much," Charlene finally said after a couple of seconds. "Enough to put a deposit on the building, but she was having trouble gettin' girls."

Neely Kate shot me a look, then turned back to the woman in the backseat. "We heard she was lookin' for money from her momma's side of the family a couple of days before she was murdered. Why then? Why not ask them when she first got back to town?"

"First of all, she wanted nothing to do with her slimeball cousin, Patsy Sue. I knew she was screwin' Patsy's husband because she thought it was funny. But last week, she got desperate enough to go to her for help, and when Patsy refused to invest any money into her project, Carol Ann decided to go after Patsy where it really hurt—her reputation of makin' the best fried chicken in Fenton County."

Neely Kate rolled her eyes. "Best fried chicken in all of Fenton County? Wow. Patsy's got some good PR goin' if people believe that."

"Where'd she make the fried chicken?" I asked. "Your house?"

Charlene shrugged. "She bought all the ingredients and let us have some, so why not?"

"If she made the chicken at your house, why was she stayin' at the Broken Branch Motel when she died?"

"For her big business deal on Sunday."

"What business deal?" I asked.

"She was gettin' a list of women to hire and men who wanted to screw them."

My eyes flew wide—that was the first real lead we had on Wagner's list, not to mention it was a solid connection between him and Carol Ann.

Neely Kate picked up her phone, keeping it low enough to stay out of Charlene's view, and sent a text. Who was she sending it to? Jed?

"Who was she meetin' to get the list?" I asked.

"Some kid she met while makin' a drug run for me. She'd met him several times, and somehow they'd figured out the kid could get her the list. I think they were shootin' up together and it all came out." She laughed.

"What's so funny?" Neely Kate asked.

"I'm high as shit and I'm doin' the same thing."

She had a point.

Neely Kate launched her next question. "Do you know where the list was comin' from?"

She held up her hands. "Didn't know. Didn't *want* to know."

"When did you find out about the list?" Neely Kate asked, and I could see she was struggling to hold her temper.

"A few weeks ago, although it weren't until last week she found out she could get it. But she needed money, so she got desperate enough to hit up the rest of her family."

"So where'd she get the money?" Neely Kate asked.

She gave a flippant shrug. "Beats me."

"You didn't lend it to her?" I asked.

Charlene released a sharp laugh. "I ain't no fool. Givin' Carol Ann money was like pissin' money in the toilet." She shifted in her seat. "Look, here's the thing about Carol Ann. She had lots of big ideas, but she could never make them work. I have big plans of my own, and I knew this one was destined to fail."

"And how'd you know that?" I asked in a dry tone.

"Because Sheriff Simmons would have been all over her in about two seconds flat if she tried to run a whorehouse. Callin' it a gentleman's club would be like slappin' paint on a pig and callin' it a billboard."

"Joe Simmons isn't the sheriff," Neely Kate said, sounding pissed.

"He might as well be," Charlene said. "He sure acts like it."

"Skeeter Malcolm would never have allowed it either," I said. "He has very strict rules on that sort of thing."

Her eyes lit up. "Hey! You're her, ain't ya?"

I resisted the urge to squirm and ignored her.

She got excited, scooching forward on her seat and leaning into my ear, her breath blowing the hair around my ear as she said, "You're the Lady in Black."

"She's Rose Gardner," Neely Kate said in a steely voice.

"Yeah, that's her Clark Kent. The Lady is her Superman." She sat back and leaned down into the floorboard. "Where's your costume?"

I shot Neely Kate a look of panic.

"Charlene," Neely Kate barked. "Get up right now. There's no black hat or veil back there."

She sat up, but she resumed her place behind me. A quick look in the rearview mirror showed her wide, excited eyes. "What could I do with you?"

I didn't like the sound of that.

Apparently neither did Neely Kate. "That's enough nonsense out of you, Charlene. Rose, that's her place right here."

I turned off the county road onto a gravel drive that led to a rusted mobile home with a sofa out front under a makeshift covered patio.

Neely Kate's phone vibrated, and she scanned the screen.

I pulled to a stop, and Charlene reached for the door handle. "Thanks for the ride."

Neely Kate hit the lock button. "Not so fast."

"What the hell?" Charlene blurted out.

Neely Kate unbuckled and spun all the way around to face her. "Why didn't you tell me and Jed any of this when we talked to you on Monday?"

"You didn't ask."

"That's malarkey if I ever heard it," Neely Kate said. "Why'd you *really* hide it?"

Charlene jerked on the door handle. "Let me out."

"Here's what I think," Neely Kate said. "You *did* give Carol Ann the money to buy the list."

She jerked on the door handle harder. "You're crazy! I done told you I didn't and why."

"Yeah," Neely Kate said. "You knew Joe Simmons would be all over the whorehouse, but only if it was out in the open. You wanted to take it underground."

"You're dumbass crazy," she said, still jerking the handle. "I'm not that stupid. I wanted no part of that mess."

Then it hit me. "No, but you needed more money," I said, turning back to face her. "And you caught wind that there might be something else in that file. Something you could use to get seed money."

She stopped jerking on the door handle.

"You gave Carol Ann the money so you could get the *other* part of that file," I said. "You were letting her keep the list of prostitutes and johns, and you were supposed to get the rest. It was perfect, because you knew that Kip Wagner would put it all together and Carol Ann would take the fall … only something happened after she worked out the deal."

She shot me a hateful glare. "How would I know what happened? Do you have other superpowers to go along with the hat and veil?"

Other superpowers? Was she just making a dig to save herself, or did she know about my visions? Was there something about *me* in that file?

Neely Kate gave me a worried glance, then renewed her attack. "Because I know you were in the motel parking lot the evening she was murdered."

Charlene got a wild look in her eyes. "Liar!"

"Am I?" Neely Kate asked as she handed me her phone. "Then why does the owner of the Broken Branch Motel say he saw you sittin' in that car in the parkin' lot around five thirty?" She pointed to an ancient-looking pale blue Buick parked in front of the trailer.

Sure enough, there in her text history to Bill Peterson was the photo she'd taken of Charlene at the rec center—sans paint—as well as a photo of Charlene's car parked next to a red pickup truck, something she must have taken before or after their first meeting. Neely Kate had asked him if either the woman or the vehicle had been at the motel at any time over the weekend.

He'd just texted back that he'd seen the woman in her car between five and five thirty on Sunday. She'd gotten out of the car, but he hadn't seen where she'd gone. Then, fifteen minutes later, the car was gone.

Holy moly. Neely Kate might have just solved the murder. I grabbed my phone and turned on the recorder.

Charlene jerked harder on the handle. "He's a liar. You're a liar. You're all liars!"

"You sat outside while the kid brought Carol Ann the list, didn't you?" Neely Kate asked, as calm as if she were having iced tea on a warm summer's day. "You were her backup."

"Let me out!"

"When the kid left, you went in to see what you'd purchased," Neely Kate said.

Charlene stopped jerking on the door handle again.

"What happened when you got inside?" Neely Kate asked. "Carol Ann must have pissed you off. I bet she changed the plans once she realized what she'd agreed to."

She remained silent, staring out her window at the trailer.

I picked up where Neely Kate left off. "You'd given her enough money to be part owner of the file, and then she didn't want to include you at all."

"Part owner!" Charlene shouted, nearly leaning over the seat to get to me. "*Complete* owner! I gave her *all* the money!"

"And she was claiming full ownership, wasn't she?" I asked, still staying calm.

"That bitch thought she could keep it from me!"

"So you killed her," Neely Kate said. When Charlene didn't respond, she said, "Aren't you worried about the camera Carol Ann hid behind the picture on the wall?"

Charlene gave Neely Kate a sarcastic look. "They won't see nothin'. I knew about the camera. I made sure they didn't find it." Then her eyes flew wide.

"I'm sure you were justified for killin' her," I said, trying to sound sympathetic. "She screwed you over, just like her daddy did to yours."

"Yeah!" Charlene said, getting riled up again. "I said I wanted my cut, but she laughed and told me to leave. Said she'd texted Patsy Sue to come over so she could blackmail her with them photos she had of her in bed with Calvin. She was headin' to the bathroom to freshen her makeup, just dismissin' me like I was a piece of trash. Like she was better than me. So I picked up the tie on the dresser, and then lassoed her around the neck and strangled her."

"Where's the file?" Neely Kate asked.

"It had other sorts of information about people in the county." She shot me a wicked smile. "Even you, Lady."

My breath stuck in my chest.

Charlene lifted one shoulder into a dismissive shrug. "So I found one of those people and worked out a deal."

"What's that mean?" I asked.

She grinned. "I found a buyer and sold it."

"To who?" Neely Kate asked.

The front door of the trailer swung open, and an older woman carting an oxygen tank behind her stood in the opening with a shotgun pointed at the truck.

Well, crap.

"Charlene? What's goin' on out there?"

I hit the unlock button.

Charlene grinned. "That's my cue to leave. But if you girls were smart, you wouldn't tell anyone about what I just told you. The person who bought the list wouldn't like it." Then she got out and waggled her fingers with a cocky grin. "On the off chance you ignore common sense and call the sheriff, I might have to let slip some of the information I read in that file." Her crazy eyes landed on me. "And I don't think you want that to happen."

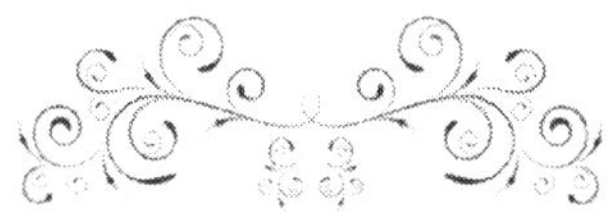

Chapter Twenty-Five

I didn't waste any time getting out of there in case the woman with the shotgun decided to use it on us anyway.

Neely Kate snatched up her phone and placed a call. "She can't threaten us like that."

"Who are you callin'?" I asked as I turned off my recording app.

"Jed."

That was a good idea.

"Jed," she said when he answered. "I've put you on speakerphone so Rose and I can both talk to you." She paused. "Charlene just confessed to murdering Carol Ann."

He hesitated for a second. "Where is she now?"

"We just dropped her off at her trailer. Her momma was standing at the door with a shotgun."

"Are you two okay?" he asked, getting worried. "Did she shoot at you?"

"No. She just stood there. Charlene was pretty cocky." She paused. "She had the file, Jed. She said there was other stuff besides a list of prostitutes and johns." She shot me a worried look. "She said there was stuff about the Lady in Black in there.

She told us if we told the sheriff about her confession, she'd share things she read in the file. She told Rose she didn't want that to happen."

"Did she happen to mention any specifics?" he asked.

"No," I said, trying not to panic. There was a list about God-knew-what floating around, and Mason was back in town to rain down justice on the county. Talk about bad timing. "But we need to find out who she sold that list to and what they plan to do with it."

"She sold the list?" He paused a beat. "She's at her trailer now?"

"Yeah," Neely Kate said.

"You girls get as far from her as you can get. I'll call Skeeter and we'll figure out how to handle this. Obviously someone needs to pay her a visit and ask a few questions."

"What will you two do after you get your answers?" I asked.

"I don't know," he said, not sounding happy about it. "But before I go, I have a good news/bad news situation," Jed said.

"Give us the good news first," I said. It felt like we sorely needed it.

"I found Becky."

"What?" Neely Kate shrieked. "Where?"

"I tracked down a friend of Bubba's and found them holed up in a hotel up in Magnolia."

"Is she okay?"

"Yeah …" He paused. "Now for the bad news … Bubba was playin' Marshall the whole time."

Neely Kate sank back in her seat.

"He found Becky's phone after the robbery and started texting Marshall to set him up. Becky didn't realize it when she called Marshall out at the farm, but Bubba was listening. He tipped Wagner off, but Wagner called him in a rage after he walked away empty-handed from the farm. Bubba was worried, so he took off with Becky."

"Was she part of it?" I asked.

"Nah, but I don't think she had any intention of goin' with Marshall."

"Yeah," Neely Kate said, getting riled up again. "Because Bubba is holding her hostage."

"This is different," Jed said softly. "This isn't …" His voice trailed off, and I realized he'd stopped because he'd almost said something they didn't want me to know about.

I had to admit that stung, but I'd deal with my hurt feelings later.

"I talked to her alone, Neely Kate," he continued. "I asked her if she needed help. I offered to take her to you and Rose. Marshall was right, she had some bruises on her arms, but she didn't want to leave him."

"I don't believe that," Neely Kate insisted. "I bet she did want to leave with Marshall, but she was too scared to say so."

"You might be right," he admitted, "but she insists she wants to stay with Bubba."

Neely Kate was quiet for a moment, but I could tell her mind was working something fierce.

Jed changed the subject. "What do you girls plan to do now?"

I glanced at Neely Kate. "I guess go back to the office. We can work on the landscape plans for our clients from this morning."

"Sounds like a good plan," Jed said. "Lie low until we have the Charlene situation contained. As soon as I finish up here, I'll head over to the office to keep an eye on you both."

Contained. Did that mean they were going to kill her? I had trouble believing they would turn her over to the sheriff. "You can't kill her," I blurted out.

"What?" Jed asked, sounding caught off guard.

"You have to turn her over to the sheriff after you get your answers."

"Rose, you realize if she has something incriminating on you, she won't hesitate to use it for revenge."

My stomach was in knots and my chest was so tight I felt like I was about to have a heart attack, but nevertheless I said, "No more killing."

He was quiet for several seconds. "I'll talk to Skeeter." Then he hung up.

We rode in silence for a minute before Neely Kate turned in her seat to face me. "I'm starvin'. Let's pick up lunch on the way."

My stomach was still performing acrobatics. I couldn't handle one more murder, even if she posed a threat to my future. But dwelling on it wasn't helping anything. "Sure."

"I guess our job's not done until the sheriff's office clears Patsy's name," she said. "So we just need to wait until Jed and Skeeter ask their questions."

"And we still need to tell Patsy something," she said. "But I guess we better wait until Jed gives us the all clear. It's not like she's beatin' down the door to find out how we're doin'."

True enough. She wouldn't even answer her phone.

We stopped at Neely Kate's favorite place—Chuck and Cluck—and picked up some congratulatory fried chicken for her. (I opted for just mashed potatoes and green beans.) We'd only been back to the office for a half hour, each of us working on a separate client's file, when I got a call from Violet.

My heart started beating double time—was she back in the hospital?—but I tried to sound calm when I answered. "Hi, Violet," I said, "everything okay?"

"I'm fine," she said, sounding exhausted, "but I'm calling to ask for a favor."

"What do you need me to do?"

"I was wondering if you could help me run a couple of errands. I'll need you to pick me up first."

"Sure, I can help you with some errands." I glanced up at Neely Kate, who had been watching me.

Neely Kate was bobbing her head, making a shooing motion.

"I can come get you now if you'd like," I said.

"That would be great."

I hung up and grabbed my purse out of my drawer. "I'm sorry to run off. Vi needs some help. She's so weak that she's not supposed to be driving."

"Of course. Go. Spend time with Violet." The *while you can* was unspoken.

"Is Jed out front yet?" I asked, tilting my head to search for his car.

"No, but he sent Brent. Don't worry about me. It's you I'm worried about."

James had sent Brent to watch over us a few times in the past.

I shook my head. "I'll be fine. If Charlene goes after anyone, it's gonna be you. She has the information in that file to use against me," I said with a wry smile. She started to say something, so I quickly added, "You're the one who figured out Charlene was at the motel." I smiled. "Good thinkin', by the way."

She beamed. "Thanks."

"We've come a long way."

VIOLET WAS WAITING at the door, and when I pulled into her driveway, she started walking toward the truck.

"Where are the kids?" I called out as I hopped out and ran over to meet her.

"With Mike's parents."

That surprised me. "I wouldn't have minded having them along."

"I wanted it to be just the two of us."

"Okay," I said as I opened the passenger door.

She was so weak she struggled to climb up inside. I grabbed her arm to help her up, resisting the urge to draw my hand back in shock when I realized she was mostly bone covered in skin.

"I can run these errands for you, Vi," I said. "Maybe you should stay home."

"I'm tired of staying in a house that's not really mine. I'm goin' stir-crazy, and even if I wasn't, I have to do both of these things myself."

She was so adamant, I wouldn't have considered arguing with her, especially because of the way she'd phrased her objection—*a house that's not really mine*. When she and Mike had gotten divorced, they'd sold their home. Violet had moved into our childhood home, and Mike had bought a smaller house. They'd reconciled at some point over the course of Violet's illness, so Mike had insisted that Violet stay in his house with the kids after returning from her treatments in Texas. This was the first time I'd heard she was unhappy with the arrangement.

I let it sit until I got both of us buckled in.

"Would you rather stay at Momma's old house?" I asked. "Or you're welcome to come stay with me out at the farm." At least after I sent my current houseguest on his way.

Her forehead wrinkled. "No, I didn't mean it that way. Honestly, the only place that would feel like home is my old house with Mike, and that's not happening." She gave me a tight grin. "I'm grateful, Rose. I truly am. I've been given a second chance with Mike, but some days I long for something familiar. Especially after spending months in that hospital in Houston."

"I totally understand." And I did. "If you ever want to just go sit in Momma's old house, let me know. I know it's not the same, but you fixed it up the way you liked it. It might be better than nothin'."

She reached out for my hand, then squeezed. "Thank you."

"Now where are we goin'?" I asked, pulling out of the drive.

"My attorney's office."

That caught me by surprise. "Your new will."

"Yes. Which is why the kids aren't with us. I didn't want to do something so morbid with them around." Only the way she said it wasn't entirely convincing. I suspected she didn't want them to know so they wouldn't tell Mike.

She gave me directions, then leaned back against the headrest and closed her eyes. They were still closed when I parked in the attorney's parking lot. I hated to disturb her, but I didn't think I could run in and handle this for her.

"Violet?" I asked softly.

Her eyes fluttered open and she glanced around. "Are we here already?"

"Yeah."

She sat up, but I could see it was a struggle. "Then let's get inside."

Violet was exhausted by the time we reached the office. I gave the receptionist her name, and the attorney, Mr. Gilliam, came out less than a minute later. He was an older man and he looked concerned at the sight of us, probably because Violet was looking so poorly, but he forced a smile on his face.

"Violet," he gushed. "So good to see you. Why don't you come in?"

I helped Violet to her feet. Then she turned to look at me. "You wait out here. I'll be fine."

I was slightly taken aback, but she didn't wait for me, just followed Mr. Gilliam into his office. He gave me an apologetic look as he shut the door.

Since I had nothing to do, I checked my phone, surprised to see a text from James.

I HEARD YOU FOUND CAROL ANN'S KILLER AND INFORMATION ABOUT THE FILE. SIT TIGHT WHILE JED AND I TAKE CARE OF IT.

Did that mean he was back in town?

DON'T KILL HER, I sent back.

A half minute later, he sent: I WON'T.

I considered asking if he planned to have someone else do it instead, but decided to let it be. I had to trust him at some point, or there would never be any chance of us working out … *if* I said yes, which would be beyond stupid with Mason back watching my every move.

Instead, I mulled over who could have possibly purchased the file from Charlene. I hadn't heard back from Wagner, so she could have sold it back to him, but I couldn't see Wagner paying money for his own file. Sure, he might have agreed to a finder's fee, but I doubted she'd killed Carol Ann for something so paltry. Someone who was a key player would want that file, if for no other reason than that Wagner wanted it. Dermot was out, and I knew James hadn't bought it. Buck Reynolds might have wanted it, but there was a player I didn't really know much about.

Denny Carmichael. And Charlene definitely knew him.

I started to text James my theory, but Mr. Gilliam's office door opened, and Violet appeared in the doorway, looking more peaceful than I'd seen her in months.

"Don't you worry, Violet," her attorney said as he walked her toward me, her arm looped over his. "I'll make sure everything is taken care of." He gave me a warm smile as they came closer. "You must be Rose."

"Yes," I said, taking Violet from him.

He glanced from my sister to me, maybe looking for a resemblance. He wouldn't find much of one. We looked as different as night and day. "When the time comes, I'll reach out to you, Rose. You won't have to do a thing."

"Thank you," I said, although I didn't feel very thankful.

The time. I knew what that meant well enough, and I didn't want to even imagine it.

Violet patted my hand. "Don't worry about a thing, Rose." Then she glanced up at the older man. "Thank you so much, Mr. Gilliam. You've put my mind at ease."

"Of course," he said. "You spend the time you have left knowin' everything's taken care of."

She nodded, then started for the door. I glanced back at her attorney with a questioning look, but he only gave a grim nod.

As soon as we were outside, I asked, "What was that about?"

"Like I said, I updated my will to make sure you could go on seein' the kids."

I glanced back at the building before I opened the truck passenger door. "That seemed like somethin' more."

"Mr. Gilliam just likes to make sure he's dotted all the i's and crossed all the t's. You don't need to worry about a thing. He'll contact you after I'm gone."

I helped her up into the truck. "Don't talk like that, Vi."

"About my death?" She gave me a sad smile. "It's comin' whether any of us wants to acknowledge it or not."

"Still …"

"I don't want to pretend I'm not dying. Knowin' I'm dying is what helps me keep the important things in focus." She laid her head back on the headrest. "Now take me to the nursery."

"Maybe we should just go back to your house, Vi."

"The nursery is the closest thing I have to home right now, and I really want to see it."

I teared up as I shut her door. We were silent on the short drive, and I was sure she'd fallen asleep again. I considered texting Maeve to let her know we were coming, but I didn't want to text and drive, and I worried I'd wake Violet up if I pulled over.

When I parked in front of the building, Violet's eyes cracked open and a satisfied smile spread across her face.

I got out and walked around to the passenger side to help her out, but the front door opened seconds after I set my feet on the ground.

Maeve hurried out. "Violet's come to visit?" she asked in surprise.

"She said she wanted to see the nursery. That it felt most like home," I said, choking on the words.

Maeve moved up next to me and wrapped an arm around my upper back, squeezing me to her side. "Then we'll give her a taste of home."

"She's weak and exhausted," I said. "She's gonna need to sit down."

A knowing smile tipped up Maeve's mouth. "We've got it covered." Then she opened the passenger door and a huge smile lit up her face. "Violet, what a wonderful surprise!"

"I hope I'm not disrupting your day, Maeve."

"Disrupting? How can you suggest such a thing? We're thrilled you're here." She glanced over her shoulder. "Aren't we, Anna?"

"You betcha, Miss Maeve."

I turned, surprised to see Anna was standing behind me with a bright smile of her own.

"Violet," Anna said, clasping her hands in front of her, "we've got a spot inside for you to sit and to rest your feet if you want. We made it special for you."

Violet slid out of the truck, and Maeve and I each took an arm and helped her inside. I gasped when I saw what Anna was talking about. An Adirondack chair had been set up in the back corner of the retail space, close to a window that overlooked the parking lot full of colorful flowers. The chair itself was surrounded by a gurgling fountain and pots bursting with brightly colored flowers.

"We even got you a footstool so you can put your feet up," Anna said with a shy smile.

Violet's chin quivered. "It's so beautiful. Thank you."

"Do you want to try it out?" Anna asked.

"I'm worried if I sit, I'll take a nap."

"There's no harm in that," Maeve said, "unless you need to get back."

"No, the kids are gone all afternoon." She glanced over at me. "Would you mind? I feel peaceful here."

"Mind? Of course not."

Violet said, "But I might be here awhile, and I know you have things to do."

"She can come back," Maeve said. "Or I can take you home. We'll work out the details later. You just make yourself comfortable."

Violet still hesitated. She was worried about me.

"If you don't sit in that chair, then I'll steal it from you," I said. "Sit."

Violet laughed, but it sounded thin and weak. "If you insist."

We helped her down into the chair, and Anna put a footstool under her feet. Violet closed her eyes and released a sigh. "This is my happy place."

"I'm so thrilled you like it," Anna said, smiling ear to ear.

"In case you missed it," Maeve said with a laugh, "this was Anna's idea."

Violet glanced up at her. "Thank you. I absolutely love it."

"Would you like a cup of tea?" Maeve asked. "I was getting ready to make myself one."

"That would be lovely."

Maeve held my gaze, then flicked her eyes to the storeroom entrance.

I followed her back there, feeling even more nervous and jittery than I had earlier, with a confessed murderer in my car and her momma holding a shotgun pointed at us. My last conversation with Mason was fresh on my mind, and I had no doubt she wanted to talk about it.

"I hope you don't mind her comin' by," I said once we were in the back room.

"Mind? We're thrilled to see you both, not to mention you both own the place."

"I know, but …"

"It sounds like she needed a taste of something familiar," Maeve said, filling the electric kettle with water from the sink. "Something like her old normal."

"Yeah."

"I know you and Mason talked yesterday afternoon." When I glanced down at the floor, she added, "And I heard it didn't go well."

"We know how to push each other's buttons," I said. "That's how we met, you know. Tempers flyin'."

She gave a sad smile. "I remember." Setting the kettle on the stand, she said, "I'm embarrassed about coming to your office yesterday morning. Obviously I had no idea that he was intending to move back to town. I caused all that unnecessary drama and worry …" She stared at the kettle. "I hope you don't think less of me."

"Maeve, how could I think less of you? You were being thoughtful by letting me know." I released a short laugh. "And as for the drama, well, my emotional breakdown was the source of most of it."

"Don't you feel badly about that."

"Well, I'm thrilled it was a false alarm. I don't want you to leave."

"Even if Mason movin' back is part of that package?"

I took a breath. "As far as I'm concerned, they are two totally different things."

"So you *are* upset he's moving back."

How much should I tell her? She knew a thing or two about the risks I'd taken last winter, and she'd given me her full support. But that had been because I was saving her son's life.

Now was an entirely different matter. "We both spoke some cross words yesterday," I conceded. "And he let me know he was unhappy with me, so yes, I'm worried about running into him, but that has absolutely no bearing on how I feel about you. However, he's your son and some of the things he said led me to believe that he won't want you associating with me, so I understand if you want to take a step or two back."

"What did he say?"

"Never you mind about that," I said. "I'm a big girl and I can take it. I just don't want you to feel like you're being forced to choose a side, because if you do, then you obviously need to choose your son."

She studied me for a long moment. "Does this have anything to do with what you did last winter?"

"Maeve …"

"Does it?"

"In a way."

She turned from me. "I'm sorry."

"You have absolutely nothing to be sorry about. We both know Mason can only see black and white when it comes to the law. There's no changin' that."

"Not true," she said, her voice wavering. "You were changing him."

"He couldn't handle what I did to save him. I understand that."

"Well, I don't." She sounded pissed. "I mean I do, but for him to be so—" She turned to face me with tears in her eyes. "I'm so sorry, Rose."

"I know you are."

"Rose," Anna called out as she walked into the storeroom. I resisted the urge to jump.

"Yeah?" I said, turning to her with a smile. "Is Violet okay?"

"She's great. Her eyes are closed, and she looks like she's floating on a cloud."

"Thank you again for doin' that for her," I said. "It means more than you know."

Anna glanced down, looking embarrassed. "It was nothin', but that's not why I'm back here. Bruce Wayne called."

I held back a mild curse. "I completely forgot about those rose bushes. Is he still at the job site?"

"Yeah. He says they can finish the job today if someone runs them over."

I turned to Maeve. "Is it really all right for me to leave Violet here? I can come back and take her home when I'm done."

"Don't you worry about it," she said with a tiny wave. "I'll handle it."

"Are you sure?" I felt guilty leaving Violet when I was supposed to be the one helping her with errands, but I also knew she wouldn't want me sitting around.

"Go," Maeve said, beaming. "You get those bushes to Bruce Wayne."

THE DRIVE TO Pickle Junction gave me time to think about what I was going to do about Mason. I had no answers by the time I reached the job site, but I sat in the parked car for a moment and sent a text to James.

I'M DOWN IN PICKLE JUNCTION AT A JOB SITE, BUT WHEN I FINISH I NEED TO SEE YOU ABOUT SOMETHING IMPORTANT.

As soon as I sent the text, I realized that tomorrow was my two-week deadline, and I still didn't have an answer I could live with. I'd worry about that later.

I climbed out of the truck and stuffed my phone into my skirt pocket as I got the rose bushes out of the truck bed. I was surprised to see that Bruce Wayne and Tillman were the only guys left on the site. Tillman was cleaning several tools with a garden hose, and Bruce Wayne was standing where we planned to plant the bushes.

"I hope you haven't been standin' there, waitin' on me," I said as I walked toward him.

He grinned. "I saw your truck at the end of the street."

I laughed. "Sorry I'm not Anna."

His grin spread wider as he reached for the pots. "I'll see her soon enough." He sobered. "I heard Violet's at the nursery now."

"She's in the space Anna set up. That was so sweet of her."

He nodded. "She put a lot of thought into it. She knows how much Violet loves the nursery and suspected she might like to spend some time there. Maybe she can't work like she used to, but Anna figured they could make it a special place for her."

My chest tightened. "You found yourself a special woman, Bruce Wayne. Don't screw it up."

He laughed. "Trust me. I won't."

He started to squat to get to work, then stopped and held the bushes back out to me. "I think you need to do this."

Anyone else would have thought he was crazy, but Bruce Wayne and I had a bond founded in the dirt. He got my connection to the earth and growing things because he felt it too.

I started to kneel, but he held up a hand to stop me and called out, "Hey, Tillman, bring me a fresh towel."

"You don't need to do that, Bruce Wayne," I protested.

"You're wearing a skirt. Can't have you gettin' your knees all dirty."

Tillman jogged over with a blue hand towel and handed it to Bruce Wayne. "Here you go."

Bruce Wayne spread it out next to the shovel and trowel, then got to his feet. "Unless you need anything else from us, we're gonna take off. I want to look over the plans for the Turnball install tomorrow. I figure you might want some time to yourself."

"You go," I said. "Let me play in the dirt." I watched them walk to their truck and take off before I knelt on the towel and started to unpot the first plant.

Violet loved the nursery, but planting things in the ground was my love. Something about burying my hands in the earth soothed my soul and made me believe everything would be okay.

Even if it was a pretty lie.

Chapter Twenty-Six

It was after three when I finished planting the rose bushes, and while I felt less anxious than I had before the dig, my hands were filthy. I washed them off with the hose while I watered the bushes, but some of the dirt was ground in. There was a convenience store about a mile away, so I decided to use the restroom there.

The convenience store was packed with people getting gas, drinks, and snacks on their way home from work, forcing me to park in the side lot. After I used the restroom, I bought a bottle of water and took a long drink as I walked back to my truck.

I stopped in my tracks at the sight of the big, beefy guy leaning against my driver's door. He had on jeans, a loose graphic T-shirt, and a pair of work boots that looked like they'd actually been used for their intended purpose and weren't some fashion fad. His arms were folded across his chest, showing off the full-sleeve tattoos on his arms. His pose appeared nonchalant, but the set of his jaw suggested otherwise.

I lowered my water bottle, giving myself a second to come up with a plan. Flee or confront him? Most of me screamed,

"Flee!" but the fed-up part of me decided to confront him and get this over with.

I walked up to him, my water bottle in my left hand, my phone and keys in my right. "Can I help you?"

"Lady, my boss wants to see you."

Lady. Crap. Was this one of Wagner's men? Or maybe Dermot's? "Who's your boss?"

He dropped his arms and stood up straighter, taking a step away from my truck. "I'm not at liberty to say."

"Well," I said as I pushed the button on my key fob to unlock the door, "when you *are* at liberty to say, then let me know and we'll see what we can arrange."

He put his hand on the door to keep me from opening it, then lifted his T-shirt a few inches with his other hand to expose part of the handgun in a holster on his belt.

That complicated things.

"What do you expect me to do?" I asked, trying to run through my options. "Get in your car and go with you to God knows where and have God knows what happen to me just because you flashed that thing? I think I'd rather take my chances out in public."

He looked stumped at that, but he still kept his hand on the door.

Pushing out a huge breath, I took a step back to look up at him. "So we're going with option two, which is me puttin' up a huge fuss to make you run away."

Confusion washed through his eyes. "He just wants to meet with you."

"I need more assurance than that, Mr. …?"

He looked puzzled, but he answered me nonetheless. "Brox."

"Why does your boss want to meet with me? Give me a little incentive to go with you."

He pulled out his phone, then placed a call and held it up to his ear. "She doesn't want to go." He grimaced, then gave me a dark look as he added, "She's threatening to pitch a fit if I try to make her. She's scared you'll hurt her."

I watched the exchange, knowing this was pointless. This was probably the stupidest idea ever, but I reached up and snatched his phone and pressed it to my ear. "Why don't we cut out the middleman? Why do you want to meet with me?"

There was a moment of silence before a deep male voice said, "We have a mutual problem."

It definitely wasn't Kip Wagner or Tim Dermot—I'd recognize either of their voices—but who was it? Denny Carmichael? "And what might that be?"

"Come meet me and we'll discuss it then."

"No, thanks. I'm not that stupid."

"It could mean helpin' Skeeter Malcolm."

That gave me a millisecond's pause, but probably long enough to do damage. "And why would that concern me?"

"Now you're insinuating *I'm* stupid."

"Give me more than that."

"Let's just say it concerns a missing file."

I stared up at the pissed man in front of me. "And what assurance can you give me that you won't put a bullet in me once we're done with our meetin'?"

"If I wanted to put a bullet in you, you'd already be dead."

Fair point.

This was probably the stupidest thing I'd done in a while, but there was a chance this could solve the Wagner problem. Besides, we needed to find that file, and I'd already decided Denny was likely my next best lead. "Fine."

"See you in fifteen minutes." Then he hung up.

I handed the phone back to the very pissed-off Brox. "I'll go with you, but you are *not* allowed to lay a finger on me. Is that perfectly clear?"

His answer was a glare. I'd take it.

He walked over to an older, bright red, two-door Mustang that was backed into a spot two spaces over. "You'll sit in back," he said, opening the driver's door.

At least he wasn't putting me in the trunk, but it was going to be awkward climbing into that car in my skirt, especially since I wanted to keep my gun holster hidden. "I'll come with you, but I need you to turn to the side a bit so I can make sure you don't get a peep show of my panties."

He held out his hand. "I'll look away, but I'm gonna need your cell phone."

I wasn't surprised, but my anxiety ratcheted up a few notches as I handed it over. Then he walked over to my truck and tossed the phone on the floorboard. "You can lock it and keep your keys," he said with an unfriendly smile, "but only if you get in the Mustang *now*."

I pressed the lock button, making the truck chirp, then started to get in, making sure he was living up to his end of the bargain. Once I was in the back, I sat in the middle, but he grunted as he pushed his seat back and climbed in. "Lie down."

I started to put up a protest, but it wasn't worth it. There would be other ways to figure out our location. My biggest concern was flashing my gun holster, but I lay on my left side, covering both gun and holster with my right thigh. As soon as I was down, he started his car and pulled out.

We spent the next ten minutes or so in silence while Brox drove us to our destination. I kept track of the turns, watching what I could see of the landscape through the tiny passenger windows. Mostly I saw trees, followed by a stretch of open sky and then a heavily wooded area that included a lot of pine trees. He pulled to a halt and turned off the engine. "You can sit up."

I put a hand on his seat to help push myself up, and he gave me a suspicious glare—had he expected more protesting from me?—but didn't say anything.

We were in the middle of the woods, parked in front of a log cabin with two small windows in front and a tiny window nestled under the top of the A-shaped roofline. There were multiple outer buildings and an older pickup and another muscle car.

As Brox opened the door and got out, I stuffed my keys into my skirt pocket to use as a weapon in case the need arose. I was sitting with my hands in my lap when he leaned down to push his seat forward to let me out.

I led with my right foot to hide my holster, then stood next to the car. "Nice place you have here."

He looked like he wanted to say something but pressed his lips together.

The front door to the cabin opened, and a man who looked like he was in his early twenties appeared. "*That's her?*"

Brox still didn't say anything. He started to reach for my arm, but I slid to the side. "No touching."

The guy in the doorway laughed. "She's got you whipped, boy."

Both of us shot him a glare.

Brox motioned to the porch, then said in a condescending tone, "After you."

Straightening my back, I walked toward the house, trying to exude a confidence I wasn't feeling. I had no idea where we were, and by allowing Brox to leave my cell phone in my truck,

I'd taken away any chance of Joe or James finding me with my phone finder app.

The man stayed in the doorway and gave me a leer. "You're a pretty one."

I lifted my eyebrows and said in a cold tone, "I'm here for a business meeting. If you're lookin' for a girlfriend, I suggest you download a dating app."

Brox busted up laughing behind me, but the doorway guy scowled in a way that told me I'd made a new enemy.

"Carey, move to the side and let her in," a man said inside. It was the voice on the phone.

Carey didn't look too happy about being told what to do, or perhaps he took umbrage with the way I was staring at him like he was an annoying housefly, but after a second he backed up into the room.

I stepped into a room so dark I could hardly get my bearings. The two windows were covered with heavy blankets that blocked out most of the light, and a window on the left side wall was covered as well. I could see outlines of a table and chairs as well as a sofa in front of the window. A figure sat at the far end of the table and another figure stood in front of the window to the left, both of them swathed in shadows.

"Did you check her for weapons?" the man to the left asked.

"Look at her," Brox said as he walked in behind me, shutting the door. "She weighs next to nothin'."

If it kept him from checking me for weapons, I was happy to be underestimated. "I'm here, and I don't want to stay here all day, so why don't we get this meeting started?"

"Have a seat, Lady," the man from the phone said.

"That's okay," I said. "After lyin' down in the backseat of Brox's tiny car, I think I'll stand."

"I don't like lookin' up at you," the man said. "I'd prefer we were at a more equal level."

"Well, considerin' I feel like I'm in a cave meeting a vampire, I'm not sure what difference it makes."

"Humor me," he said.

My eyes were adjusting to the dark, and I could see the kitchen chair at the opposite end of the table. I pulled it out and the legs scraped against the wood floor. Once I was seated, I asked, "What's with all the secrecy?"

"I'm a private man, Lady. I don't let many people see me. That makes you special."

Maybe only semi-special since I hadn't really seen him at this point, but that was splitting hairs. "You have a name for me; what should I call you?"

"Gerard will do."

So this wasn't Denny? But now that I thought about it, these guys didn't look like drug dealers. If anything, they looked like doomsday preppers. Were they one of the militia groups rumored to be hiding in the woods? Supposedly there were a couple of them. "You said you had information about a file, Gerard. How about we get to that?"

"I thought we'd start with some pleasantries first."

I drummed my fingers on the table. "If you were concerned with pleasantries, you'd turn on a lamp or two and maybe offer me a cup of tea, but since neither of those things seem to be in order, I vote that we get down to business."

"She's too mouthy," the guy by the side window said. As my eyes grew more accustomed to the dark, I could see he was in a small kitchen, standing in front of what looked to be a sink with an old-fashioned pump handle. "I don't like 'er."

"Good thing it's not up to you," Brox said. "It's up to Gerard."

"Brox is right, Tony. We've all known from the beginning that you wanted no part of this, but you were outvoted." Gerard turned to me, and my eyes had adjusted enough by now that I could vaguely see his features. He looked older, maybe sixties based on his white hair and beard. "We've heard about you, Lady. We hear you're neutral. Is that true?"

"Yes."

"Then how do you explain your connection to Skeeter Malcolm?"

I considered telling him to mind his own business, but if he was really a player in this dangerous game, then I needed to prove my neutrality. "It's no secret that I worked with Skeeter Malcolm last winter. We cooperated to bring down Mick Gentry and J.R. Simmons, but I did it for the good of the county, not for personal gain."

"But you helped Malcolm."

"We had a deal. He got me access to the people I needed to speak to, and I gave him bits of information." Then I added, "He *is* the king of the Fenton County crime world. It only seemed appropriate."

"We recognize no king," Tony said in disgust. "This is the United States of America. We threw off tyranny over two hundred years ago."

That was good to know. It fit with my impression that they were one of the militias. But they tended to stick to themselves, so why was I here talking to them about my neutrality as the Lady in Black?

"Be quiet, Tony," Brox sneered.

"Yes, Tony," Gerard said. "Be silent or leave."

Tony thought about it for a couple of seconds and then stomped toward the door, throwing it open as he left. It slammed shut behind him, but the light that spilled in gave me a much better look at my host.

I'd guessed wrong about his age. He looked a little younger than I'd thought at first, maybe late fifties. His white beard reached several inches below his chin, and his salt-and-pepper hair was several inches long and in need of a good trim. He was wearing a solid black T-shirt, and I thought I caught a glimpse of jeans before the door shut.

"I apologize for Tony's outburst. Some of us are slow to adapt," Gerard said in a sober voice. He sounded sad.

"As long as Tony leaves me be, he can be as slow to adapt as he likes."

Gerard shifted in his chair. "I heard you were no-nonsense, but I didn't expect you to be this direct."

"Because I'm a woman? And who did you hear this from?"

"I have my sources, which is how I know about Kip Wagner's missing file."

"Do you know who bought it?"

"Perhaps." He sounded amused, and I realized that as much as he hoped to appear practical, he was really all about the drama—from setting the stage to his cloak-and-dagger performance. "I thought we could work out a deal."

"What kind of deal?"

"I want to know what Mason Deveraux is doin' back in Fenton County."

"And what makes you think *I* know?"

"You used to live in sin with the man. That's why you really helped Malcolm last winter—to save him. I can't figure out your motivation now."

"I already told you. To protect the county as best I can. I saw firsthand the terror Daniel Crocker unleashed. He killed my own mother. I won't let that happen to any other innocents. Not if I can help it."

"So you propose to stop people from being murdered?" he asked, sounding amused.

"If I can, yeah. And for the record, Mason and I are not back together. He's here on official attorney general business. You'll have to find another source for that because he and I are no longer speaking."

Gerard stood. "I abhor liars, Lady."

His cold tone sent a wave of fear through my veins. "Well, good for you. You can join that datin' app with Carey over there and put it in your profile."

"I will not tolerate lies from *you*."

I stood too, because if I had to sit while he sat, then that meant I could stand when he did … and I could also reach my gun faster this way. "And how did I lie to you?"

"You know why Deveraux's here, yet you refuse to tell me."

"Let me make this perfectly clear, Mr. Gerard. Just because you ask me a question, doesn't mean I owe you an answer. In fact, I don't owe you a doggone thing."

He was standing in front of me, and I could feel the tension radiating from him as easily as I could smell the scent of wood chips and bacon in his clothes. He was trying to intimidate me, but I had to stand my ground, no matter how much I wanted to turn around and run out the front door.

"I invited you here," he said. "You came."

"You must be an alternate-facts kind of guy because we both know that's not how this played out. I didn't just hop in Brox's car and eagerly come to meet you. He showed me his gun. He refused to let me into my truck. You used force and intimidation to get me here, so don't try to paint this as if I'm breaching some nonexistent agreed-upon contract."

He held his ground, and I started debating whether to go for my gun or my keys—the keys would be easier to reach standing this close to him, but I knew *they* had guns.

"She's right, Gerard," Brox said. "She didn't agree to nothin' except discussing the file."

"Fine," Gerard spat out as he backed up. "But I'm not just gonna give the information to you. You have to earn it."

I didn't like the term *earn*. "You said you wanted information, but unfortunately, I'm unable to answer the question you asked me. If there's something else you'd like to ask, and I feel that I can answer it, I will. Otherwise, you'll have to come up with something else."

"I'm the one callin' the shots here, Lady."

"Actually, Gerard, you're not. We're workin' out a deal, and if we don't reach an agreement, then we'll go our separate ways. Now if you have something specific to ask me, feel free, otherwise I'll have Brox take me back to my truck. I'm supposed to meet with Skeeter Malcolm, Tim Dermot, and Kip Wagner in a few hours, and they won't appreciate it if I keep them waiting."

"Not Carmichael?" he asked as though he knew something I didn't.

"Did Denny Carmichael buy the file?" It had been my best guess all along, but would Gerard really have thrown his name out there if he was the buyer?

"That'll cost you."

"Name your price."

But the more I studied Gerard, the more I suspected I wouldn't be willing to give him anything. What role did he and his group of younger friends have to do with the crime world, anyway?

"I wanna know what Deveraux's doin' back in Fenton County," he repeated.

I put a hand on my hip. "And as I mentioned before, *that* is off the table."

He stared me down, and I finally said, "Okay. We're done. Brox, let's go."

"You're not going to leave," Gerard said. "You want that buyer's name too much."

"Your price is too steep. If you think of something else, give me a call. No offense, but I'm not finding your cabin getaway very hospitable." I flicked my gaze to the tall man behind me. "Brox."

Brox moved next to me and waited.

After several seconds, Gerard waved toward the door. "Fine. Go."

"Gerard!" Carey protested.

"It's within her right to walk away," Gerard said, although he didn't sound happy about it. "I brought her here to negotiate, and she's not willing to work out a deal. She'll be sorry tonight."

I hadn't heard from Wagner since he'd shown up at my house two nights ago. He'd been at the sheriff's office last night. Did Gerard have inside information that Wagner was planning to return tonight? Then I realized I'd name-dropped Wagner with the others. It was just as likely he didn't know anything.

Gerard waved to the door again. "Go."

We'd made it onto the front porch when I saw Tony running toward us from the trees. "We've got company!"

Gerard was instantly behind me, staring down Brox. "Were you followed?"

"No."

"*Are you certain?*"

"Yes! I'm sure of it."

Tony reached the porch steps. "There's a car comin'."

A dark sedan rounded the curve in the road up ahead, and I recognized the car … and the driver.

"Carey," Gerard barked into the cabin. "Get the rifles." He reached for my arm, but I scampered back several feet, pulling out my own gun and pointing it at his chest in one fell swoop.

Surprise filled Gerard's eyes, followed quickly by anger. I'd bet good money he was pissed he'd been hoodwinked by a woman.

Gerard reached for me again, but I fired the gun at the frame of the cabin door, sending wood fragments everywhere. A large splinter lodged in Gerard's upper arm.

I leveled the gun at his chest. "The next bullet's gonna be in your body, and since you seem to know so much about me, you must know I've shot and killed a few men before you."

The car came to a halt and I heard James shout, "Let her go, Gerard. Whatever you think she's done, she's no part of this."

Hate filled Gerard's eyes. Still staring at me, he shouted, "Seems like it's the other way around, Malcolm."

I heard a gun cock and saw Carey and Brox holding semiautomatic rifles pointed in the direction of James' car.

"Had I known you were gonna use those guns on me, I never would have sold them to you," James said.

"I told you I was gonna use them to protect me and mine," Gerard said. "So you shouldn't be surprised to see them given you've driven up onto our land uninvited."

"You have something that interests me," James said, his voice tight. "So I came to fetch it."

"Lady?" Gerard asked in disgust. "I can't figure out why you're all so enamored with her. She's disposable."

"Dermot disagrees."

"And you," Gerard said with a grin.

He was about to pull a stunt.

"Let me make this perfectly clear, boys," I said, thankful my voice didn't shake even though my heart was racing. "If you take so much as one shot at Mr. Malcolm, I will *not* hesitate to shoot Gerard."

"Hold your fire!" Gerard shouted, losing his grin right quick. "She'll do it."

"Okay," James said calmly. "I want you to send Lady over to me. Then we'll be on our way."

Gerard motioned behind him. "Brox, you got us into this mess, you take care of it."

Brox dropped his rifle to the porch floor and circled behind Gerard. "I'm gonna walk you to the car, Lady. You can point your gun at me if you like."

I stared up at him like he'd lost his mind.

"I'm giving you thirty seconds to get out of here," Gerard said. "And don't you *ever* come back, Malcolm."

"Don't give me reason to."

Brox backed up, motioning for me to follow. As soon as I moved past Gerard, he stepped between Carey and Tony. He motioned for me to go down the stairs, which I did backward, still keeping my gun trained on Gerard. He seemed the least disposable of the lot of them.

"Bring her to the back door," James said as I continued to retreat.

Brox stepped in front of me so we were face-to-face as I backed up to the car, so close I no longer had Gerard in my sight.

When we were about six feet from the car, James swung the back door open, and Brox leaned closer. "It's not Carmichael," he whispered. "He was throwing you off. It was someone closer to the case you've been workin' on." Then we were next to the car, and he gave me a tiny shove toward the open door.

I scampered inside, and Brox shut the door, but James was still standing next to his open door, aiming his handgun toward the porch. "Our upcomin' deal is off."

"I already paid you a down payment of half," Gerard shouted. "Two hundred weapons."

"Then I'll return it," James said, beginning to sound angry.

"All because of her?" Gerard asked in disbelief.

"And because you used my own guns against me."

"Because of her," Gerard repeated.

"If you want to see it that way, go ahead. You had no reason to take her, other than to get to me. What's your game, Gerard?"

"Why don't you ask her why she was here? Now get out of here before I change my mind."

James got into the car and shut the door, jerking the steering wheel to turn around and head out on the gravel road. "Keep your head down," he barked.

I stayed down. He was so tense he looked ready to snap in two.

"What did he mean?" James demanded in a sharp tone. "Why did he bring you here?"

"He wanted to make a deal."

"What kind of deal?"

"He said he knew who bought Wagner's file. He wanted to barter for the information."

"What did he want you to tell him?"

"He seemed fixated on Mason being back. He asked me multiple times what Mason was up to. I told him I wasn't going to tell him anything."

His knuckles turned white from gripping the steering wheel so tight. "*Did he touch you?*"

"What? No. I made clear no one was to touch me, and for the most part they obeyed."

"Gerard kidnapped you and let you dictate terms?" he asked, shooting a glance at me.

"I told you he wanted to work out a deal."

"Does he know about your visions too?"

"No. I pinned him down on that one, and as far as I could tell, he doesn't have a clue. If anything, he seems confused about your and Dermot's interest in me."

He was quiet for a moment. "The file was just a distraction to throw you off. You were right … he's concerned about Deveraux."

"Why?"

"Because Deveraux had Simmons building a case against Gerard, and last I heard, Simmons is still workin' on it. It was heavy on suspicion and light on evidence. But Gerard must have screwed up somewhere down the line, and now he's worried Deveraux's back to indict him." James looked concerned.

"What's that mean for you?"

"I've done a few deals with him. It could blow back on me."

My stomach seized. "Deals? Gun deals?"

He was silent.

"I already know you sold him those semiautomatic rifles. He said as much. You were in the process of sellin' him more?" I asked in an accusatory tone.

"He's a paranoid prepper, Rose. He's preparing for end of days. He's not out usin' them for drive-by shootings or robbing banks. Easy money."

"He must be doin' something wrong if Joe and Mason were building a case on him."

James remained silent.

"You're not gonna tell me?" I asked, getting pissed.

"You already know too damn much!" he shouted. "You're already at risk."

That stopped me in my tracks. "What does that mean?"

"It means if Gerard gets arrested, he's gonna bring me down with him, and you're a potential witness."

I shook my head. "What?"

"It's gonna be his word against mine, and there's no electronic trail for these deals. We only deal in cash, so it could all hinge on witnesses."

I sank back into the seat as horror made me dizzy. "Mason's not leavin'."

"What?"

I felt nauseous. "He's movin' back to rip the county apart. He's goin' after corruption in the local government. He's goin' after crime." I paused and found his gaze in the mirror. "And he's specifically goin' after you."

He was silent for a moment, his face giving nothing away. "He told you this?"

"He never admitted that he's goin' after you, but it was strongly implied after he confessed the other parts." My voice broke. "He's out for revenge, James. For breakin' us apart."

"He's got nothin'. I'm careful, and I've also got Carter Hale. Don't worry about me."

"But you just said he's goin' after Gerard and they can make me testify what I just heard."

He shook his head. "We're borrowing trouble," he said, then waited a beat before he asked, "I take it you didn't find out who bought the file?"

"No … I refused to tell him what he wanted. He got really pissed, but Brox intervened."

"What do you mean he intervened?"

"He reminded Gerard that he'd pretty much dragged me there—an unwilling participant in brokering a deal. Then he backed off."

"Gerard has a bizarre sense of honor and truthfulness. Brox must have appealed to that. What's surprising is that Brox intervened at all. He's the least likely of all of them to cross his father."

"His father? They all treated him like he was their boss." But it made sense. The ages lined up. "Maybe he felt guilty because he was the one who essentially kidnapped me."

"He doesn't usually bring people to his land. One more reason to believe he's spooked."

And from the look on James' face, he was spooked too.

"When Brox walked me to the car, he told me that Carmichael didn't buy the file. He said it was someone closer to my case."

His gaze lifted to mine in the mirror. "Patsy was found dead this afternoon."

I gasped. "What? When? How?"

"She was strangled. A farmer found her in her car in his field south of town."

"Does Neely Kate know?"

"Jed told her. He's the one who told me." He pushed out a breath. "How did Gerard know about the file? Or you for that matter? He keeps to his land, preparing to fight back when the government marches in to take his property. He stays out of county affairs."

"He knew an awful lot about what was goin' on for someone who remains aloof. Maybe one of his sons convinced him to diversify."

"Maybe."

"We need to find that file. Did Jed talk to Charlene?"

"He found her."

"What does that mean?"

"She was dead. Her trailer burned down around one. They're sayin' her mother's oxygen tank exploded."

My mouth dropped open, but I recovered enough to ask, "Did Jed or you have any part of this explosion?"

"No," he barked. "I told you I wouldn't kill her." Then he added. "And I didn't approve or condone anyone else doin' it either."

"Then who burned down her trailer and murdered her? The person who bought the file? And if so, does that mean they were watching Charlene or watching me and Neely Kate?"

Who would be that desperate for whatever was in that file? Who had enough money and yet was the least threatening potential buyer?

Then it hit me like a lightning bolt. How could I be so stupid? I knew exactly where I needed to go next.

Chapter Twenty-Seven

Take me back to my truck. I think I know who bought the file."

His voice turned into a growl. "If you think I'm dropping you off at your truck to confront a cold-blooded murderer, you're crazy."

"How'd you know Gerard had me snatched?"

"I had you followed by one of my men. He called me straightaway. When he described the red Mustang and its driver, I knew exactly who took you, although I couldn't figure out the why of it."

"If your man was followin' me, then why didn't he intervene? It wasn't a quick snatch and grab. When I refused to get in his car at gunpoint, he up and called his daddy."

"You refused to get in?"

"If he had a mind to use that gun, I figured my chances were better in the parking lot than some abandoned place."

"What convinced you to go?"

"I snatched the phone from him and gave Gerard a piece of my mind. He dangled the information about the file, so I agreed to go with Brox willingly as long as they promised not to hurt me."

"And you trusted him?"

I gave a noncommittal shrug. "For your information, I had it covered. I said no deal and insisted Brox take me back to my truck, which he was in the process of doin' until you showed up."

He was silent for a minute. "Nevertheless, I'm goin' with you to confront your suspected killer. Who is it?"

"Calvin Clydehopper."

WE DECIDED TO stop by Calvin's office first. The plan was for me to leave James waiting in the parking lot behind the building. I'd call him on my phone and then carry it inside so he could keep tabs on what was going on, only we were nearly to Henryetta when I realized my phone was still in my truck down in Pickle Junction.

"It's an office full of people," I said. "How dangerous could it be?"

He gave me a dry look in the mirror. Good thing I hadn't told him that Calvin had held me at gunpoint the day before.

I found June at her desk, her eyes glued on her computer screen while her fingers were flying on the keyboard. "He's not here," she said without looking up.

"Do you know when he left?"

"He hasn't been in all day."

So much for an alibi. He definitely would have had time to murder his wife and Charlene. I decided to play dumb. "Do you know when he'll be back?"

She looked up at me in exasperation. "Have you no shame? The poor man's wife was found murdered." Then her brow wrinkled. "Why are you even here? Patsy was the one who hired you, and now she's dead."

I took a moment to regroup. "True, but I still feel like I owe it to her to clear her name. And if I can find out who did this to her, then all the better."

She shook her head. "I'm sure Mr. Clydehopper's at home … grieving as he should be."

"Do you happen to know why Calvin didn't come in today?"

"You drove him to drink yesterday," she said. "Whatever you said upset him. He probably stayed home to recuperate. Now go away and let him grieve."

"Do you know if anyone has been in to see him over the last few days? Anyone unusual?"

"No."

"Are you sure?"

She glanced up, exasperated. "I take my job seriously, Ms. Gardner. I'm at my desk from before eight until after five, every day. I would know if someone unusual had stopped by."

"You weren't here at lunch today," the woman who'd told Neely Kate the pony story said as she got up from her desk. "You were gone for a couple of hours. And you were gone last Friday too," she called over her shoulder as she headed toward the entrance.

"I was at a dentist appointment last week, and I had a doctor's appointment today," June said, getting ticked. "I was back by one. I *am* allowed some personal time."

"Of course you are," I agreed, trying to find my way back to her good side.

"In fact, I live less than two miles from the factory, so I'm always available when Calvin needs me. I take my responsibility to him very seriously."

She graced me with a scathing look. Obviously I wasn't going to get any help from June, not that I was surprised. She took her gatekeeper job seriously.

I started to head for the door, but the younger assistant was in the hallway, motioning for me to come closer. After I glanced back at June and saw she was engrossed in a phone call, I hurried over to meet her.

She hugged the wall in the hallway and shot a worried glance at the office area. "Do you think Calvin killed his wife?" she asked.

"I don't know," I said, trying to keep a neutral face. "Do *you* think he did?"

She made a face. "Maybe."

"What makes you think that?"

"Because I heard him talkin' to Patsy yesterday afternoon after you left."

"Are you sure?"

"Pretty sure. He was in the hall, probably because June eavesdrops on all his calls. She's like obsessed with him, and some days he just has to get away from her."

"How can you be sure he was talkin' to Patsy and not one of his … girlfriends?"

"Because he called her by name—Patsy. He told her you were onto something and for her to sit tight, that he was gonna take care of everything. He told her to meet him at their special place at noon today."

"Have you told the sheriff's deputies any of this?"

She shook her head with a wild look. "I didn't want to stir up trouble if he was innocent."

"If he turns out to be guilty, do you mind if I give your name to them to help build his case?"

She frowned. "I don't know. He's a VP, and I don't want to lose my job."

"I'm pretty sure he's gonna be the one losin' his job if he's guilty." I collected her name and contact information, then hurried outside and around the building. I got into James' backseat and told him everything.

"I need to get to a phone," I said. "I have to call Deputy Miller."

He shook his head. "No. Not yet."

"Have you lost your ever-lovin' mind? What do you mean not yet?"

"We don't know what's in that file. It might be detrimental if the sheriff's department gets their hands on it."

He had a point, but it felt wrong. "Okay. We need to find Calvin before the sheriff's deputies do, because if we figured this out, you know *they're* going to. It's not like we're dealing with the Henryetta Police Department."

He turned around in his seat to face me. "Any suggestions?"

I pressed my lips together and stared at the building. "I don't know. Maybe his house, but if he's hiding, that would be too obvious. Surely he's not that stupid." I paused. "He's a deacon at the church. He might have gone there for counsel." When he gave me a weird look, I shrugged. "What? I go to Jonah for advice sometimes."

"Jonah Pruitt and Reverend Timothy Baker are two entirely different men."

He had a point. I noticed a back door open and saw June hurry toward a minivan. "Why's Calvin's secretary leaving a half hour early after she missed two hours at lunch for a doctor's appointment? Especially after she made such a big deal about how much time she spends here."

June got into her vehicle and headed for the exit.

"Follow her," I said.

He gave me a look of surprise. "The secretary?" But he put the car in drive and started to tail her.

"Yeah, call it a gut instinct, but I think she knows something. She got on the phone as soon as I walked away. And then she left so quickly."

He simply nodded, accepting my reasoning, and continued to follow her to the south side of town, staying several cars behind her. "Does she live down here?"

"No," I said. "She mentioned she lives two miles from the factory. Said she lives close so she can be there whenever Calvin needs her." My eyes flew wide. "I wonder if that includes aiding and abetting him after he murdered his wife."

"You might be onto something," he said.

Keeping his distance, he followed her to a rural property, stopping the car when she turned off onto a gravel drive that led into the trees.

"Now what?" I asked.

He shot me a look in the mirror. "If you were wearing jeans, I'd suggest we walk through the woods and sneak up on her." He shot me a smirk. "Not that I'm complainin' about the view."

"We have to see what she's up to," I said, ignoring his remark, "but I'm not lettin' you go back there alone."

His grin spread. "I can handle myself."

"I have no doubt of that, but I'll be damned if I'll let you finish this without me."

He laughed. "Then we'll both go."

"How do you propose we handle this?"

"You let me worry about that." He pulled into a turnaround spot about fifty feet down and parked as far off the road as he could get, making sure his car wasn't visible unless someone drove right past it. He got out and opened my back door, reaching a hand in to help me out. When I stood, he wrapped an arm around my back and pulled me flush against him. "I haven't held you since yesterday."

"You've gone longer than that," I whispered, staring up into his dark, hungry eyes.

He lowered his mouth to the sensitive skin on my neck, right below my ear. "But now that I've had several tastes of you, it only makes me want you more."

I shivered.

He lifted his head and gave me a deep kiss.

I gripped his shoulders, my fingers itching to explore across his chest and back, but now was not the time. I leaned back and grinned. "Come on. We've got a file to find."

He spun around, and I thought I'd pissed him off, but he bent his knees. "Hop on."

"You want to carry me on your back?"

"Are you insinuatin' I can't?"

"Far be it from me to threaten your manhood."

He laughed. "Get on."

I jumped onto his back, and he looped his hands over my calves to hold me on as he stood. Then he slipped into the trees, heading toward the makeshift driveway June had turned down. He had to shift my weight a couple of times, especially since the holstered gun kept jabbing into him, but it didn't take him long to follow the gravel road back to a small, dilapidated house. June's minivan was parked out front and so was another car—a shiny white Cadillac. I remembered how Calvin often parked in the back of the church parking lot so it wouldn't get dinged.

"That's Calvin's car," I whispered in his ear. "He loves it almost as much as Patsy loves hers." Then I remembered. "*Loved* her car." The thought that she was gone made me sad, even though she'd been meaner than a hornet most of the time. She'd been alive, and now she was gone.

"This is good," he said, letting me slide down to the ground. He squatted and pulled a handgun from his ankle holster. "Follow me. Stick close."

He moved along the tree line, then darted to the side of the house and motioned me over.

I ran over to him, and he started to inch toward the back of the house. The windows were open, and voices were filtering out—June's and then Calvin's. The closer we got to the back door, the more apparent it was that they were arguing.

"What were you thinkin', June?"

"My job is to take care of you," she said in a pleading voice. "I'm takin' care of you."

"At work! Not in my personal life!" His voice broke. "I loved her. Why did you kill her?"

June killed Patsy Sue? What a tangled mess. I wished I had my phone to record their conversation.

June pressed on, sounding desperate. "She was gonna sell you down the river. She was gonna take the information about you and use it to divorce you and get all the money."

Charlene sold the file to *Patsy*?

"She would never do that!"

"She told me herself this morning! I went to see her to find out what she intended to do with the information in the file."

James shot me a look. Then he pointedly glanced down at my leg before looking back up. I pulled out my gun and followed him as he rounded the corner to the back of the house.

"Have you looked through the file?" Calvin asked. "There's information in there about me?"

"Yes, but I think we can contain it."

James leaned close to me and whispered, "I know you want to be part of this, but I don't want them seeing you. I'm gonna send them running out the front and take the file. Stay hidden out here behind the house until they're gone."

"You're just gonna let them *go*?" I whisper-hissed.

He leaned his face close to mine. "Trust me, they're gonna get caught. The important thing is for us to get that file. You can call Simmons as soon as I get it. Are you with me on this?"

I could see the logic behind his argument, but I'd been burned before. "If you betray me—"

"I won't, Rose. I swear."

"Okay."

He gave me a nod, then opened the back door and walked in bold as he pleased, his gun in hand.

"You're early," June said. "And why are you sneakin' around the back? I told you to come to the front door."

James had set up a meeting? Had he figured this out before me and played me like a fiddle?

"I've heard that before," James said. "Now about that file …"

June began to laugh. "Aren't you forgetting something?"

She sounded entirely too confident for my liking, and she'd just admitted to killing Patsy. I knew James had his own gun, but she seemed crazy enough to shoot him.

I moved underneath a window and reached up on tiptoes to see inside. On the side closest to me, June sat at a small table with a large envelope. She was pointing her handgun at James, who stood in front of the back door. Calvin was on the other side of the room—the actual kitchen—standing in front of the refrigerator. He had a gun too, but he looked just as incompetent holding it as he had yesterday.

When James didn't answer, she said, "You show me the money first, sweetheart—then you can have it. That's the way these things work."

I heard the sound of a car engine approaching from the front of the house, and I scooted to the edge and peered around the corner. It was a truck. One I recognized, and the man getting out of the cab confirmed it.

June had contacted Kip Wagner.

Another man got out of the truck, following behind as Wagner strutted toward the front door.

What was I going to do? I had to let James know, but if I startled June or Calvin, they might shoot him. I was about to call Wagner's name through the screen window when a loud rap landed on the front door.

June looked confused. "I'd presume you brought backup, but why are they knocking on the front door?"

I heard wood crashing at the front of the house. Then Wagner shouted, "I want my damn file."

Clomping footsteps stormed through the house, coming toward the back.

"Where's Patsy?" Wagner asked.

"She's indisposed," June said. "But I have what you're lookin' for."

Patsy had set up the meeting and June had taken over? How had Patsy been involved with Wagner?

Well, I realized, she'd had business dealings with James, so it wasn't a stretch.

"Then hand it over," Wagner snarled, and I realized he was less than six feet from me, inside the kitchen. Where was James, and why hadn't Wagner said anything about him being there?

"Just like I told your associate," June said, her voice more distant than before—she must have moved to the middle of the room—"I need to see the money first."

"*What associate?*" Wagner barked.

"The guy who just showed up expecting me to hand over the file. Why are all y'all here so early?"

"Let me make this clear," Wagner said in a slow, even tone. "That's my file. I'll give you a small finder's fee, but I will not be extorted. Where'd the guy go?"

"Good question," she said in confusion.

"Search the house," Wagner said, and I heard more foot stomping.

He'd sent someone to find James, but where was he? It was a small house. There couldn't be too many places to hide.

"This is your last warning," Wagner said. "Give me the file."

"And for the umpteenth time, show me the money," June sneered.

I heard a gunshot, and Calvin screamed.

"I'm disappointed to see you're part of this, Clydehopper," Wagner said.

"I didn't want to have anything to do with it," Calvin said in a whiny voice. "She dragged me into it."

"Which she? Your dead wife or the dead woman at your feet?"

"June," he wailed. "June killed Patsy after Patsy set up the meetin' with you."

"Was she after the money?" Wagner asked with a bitter laugh. "Or was she after you?"

"Both," Calvin said with a quaver.

"I'm disappointed, Calvin. I really am. I thought we had a deal. I thought you were my man."

"I was," Calvin said. "I am. I swear I didn't know this was happening."

Wagner was quiet for a second, then said, "Too bad I don't believe you."

There was another gunshot, and Calvin screamed again.

"Now I have a new problem, Calvin," Wagner said. "You just saw me kill that woman. What was her name again?"

"June," he said through a sob.

Terror washed over me like a bucket of cold water. Wagner was going to kill Calvin too. I might not have a phone, but I did have a gun, and there was no way I could let him kill another person without intervening.

"Now, if anyone had asked me if I thought you'd squeal on me, I would have said *no way. Calvin's my guy.* But then I never thought you'd extort me, so I guess you never know about a person."

I moved to the open back door and peered around the corner. Wagner's side was to me and Calvin had fallen to the ground, his upper leg already covered in blood. June was lying on the floor, partly under the kitchen table.

"Please," Calvin begged.

"Put the gun down, Wagner," I said as I moved in front of the screen door and pointed my weapon at him. James was going to spit nails when this was over, but so be it. I hadn't managed to save Jeanne—or Patsy, for that matter—but at least I could save Calvin.

Wagner twisted to face me with a startled expression; then he grinned so wide I thought it would split his face. "Lady," he said, still pointing the gun at Calvin. I noticed he was holding the manila envelope in his other hand. "Didn't this take an interesting turn? I was just sayin' the other day that things had gotten dull as dirt, but then you pop up and shake everything up." He turned more to face me. "And here you are, standing in the middle of a bloodbath, only you don't have your shotgun this time."

"And you're not surrounded by your men."

He frowned. "Where is my guy?"

I had been wondering the same thing myself. But even more importantly, where was James? He hadn't slipped out the back, which meant he was still inside.

"So that makes it just the two of us," I said. "Equal playing field."

He laughed. "You think you're my equal? You're *nothin'* compared to me."

"Seems to me Daniel Crocker made that same mistake."

"Crocker was a fool."

"A dead one. Shot by me. Now you're goin' to drop the gun *and* the envelope and walk backward to the front door. Then I'll let you drive away."

"You'll let me drive away?" he said with a short laugh. "You're something else." He shook his head, still pointing his gun at Calvin. "So you want this file after all. Not that I'm surprised. You must have found out what's in it. However, your integrity is now in question. You claim you're neutral, not to mention you claimed you'd return the file to me if you found it. So that also makes you a liar."

"I'm doin' it to …" To make sure there was nothing that could hurt James? Hurt me? Maybe I *was* a liar.

"She wants to destroy it," James said from the entrance to the kitchen, and a wave of relief flooded my head. He was okay. He was still okay.

"So you're the man who tried to buy the file out from under me," Wagner said with a laugh, now spinning to face

James, his gun pointed at his chest. "You worried? You should be."

What did that mean?

"Rose," James said in a deadly calm voice, "take Calvin outside and let me and Wagner settle this dispute."

"I kind of like the idea of Lady stayin'," Wagner said.

"*Rose.*"

Wagner shook his head. "Clydehopper stays, but Lady's welcome to stay outside if she likes. I'll deal with her after I finish you two off."

"Rose," James said. "Go." When I didn't move, he added in a more direct tone, "*Now.*"

"So she *does* take orders from you," Wagner said. "She's your puppet."

"I'm no one's puppet," I said, opening the screen door and walking inside. I knew full well he'd played me, but I'd deal with that later. "Calvin, get up."

"I can't," he said, his face deathly pale. A quick glance at the huge puddle of blood under his thigh was enough to tell me that Calvin was in danger of bleeding to death.

"I'm gettin' a towel, Wagner," I said, backing up to grab a towel from the kitchen counter. "I need to apply pressure to his wound."

"You're wastin' your time," Wagner said. "I'm gonna finish him soon enough."

"I'm getting the towel anyway." Still keeping my gun trained on him, I reached back and grabbed the terrycloth towel before dropping to my knees next to Calvin, splattering blood on my knees and my dress in the process. His pants were covered with so much blood I had trouble finding his wound. Then I saw a hole at the top of his leg and pressed the towel to it, all while still holding my gun on Wagner.

Calvin released a weak cry at the pressure, but I pressed anyway. Even if we called an ambulance now, I wasn't sure it would get here fast enough to save him.

"What happened to my man?" Wagner asked.

"He won't be disturbing us," James said.

Wagner took a step back. "So what's next? I hand you this envelope, and then you let me go?"

"If that's the way you want to play it," James said.

Wagner tilted his head toward me. "So what's the deal with you two? Why are you tryin' to pass her off as neutral?"

"She *is* neutral," James said.

"Then why are you with her now?"

"Because Dermot and I take turns makin' sure she has backup if she needs it."

"I know you must be screwin' her, but why's Dermot involved?"

James' mouth twisted into a smile, but his eyes were deadly cold. "I guess you'll have to ask him."

I couldn't help noticing James didn't deny Wagner's statement about me.

"You know I help settle disputes, Wagner," I said, fighting to keep the gun up and pointed at him. It was tiny compared to my shotgun, but it was still getting heavy. "I helped Dermot locate something that was missing."

"That damn necklace," Wagner said. "But that was for Reynolds. Rumor has it you helped depose Reynolds in favor of Dermot."

"His men made that call, not me."

"You were there when it happened," Wagner said.

"Then you know what I was lookin' for."

"Scooter Malcolm." He motioned his gun toward James. "But I'm smart enough to know that you were really lookin' for *him*."

"I was lookin' out for the good of the county, just like I always have. All this bloodshed only tears it apart. Don't you think Crocker did enough damage? I'm trying to help the county heal."

"Bullshit."

"You can call Dermot and ask him yourself."

"I don't give a shit what Dermot says, because I'll never recognize you as anything other than Malcolm's whore." Then he spun to point his gun at me. "That's why I'm gonna kill you first."

I heard a gunshot. For a moment I wondered if I was in shock and the pain would come later, but then I realized that James had shot him first.

Wagner fell to his knees, then to the floor, his eyes wide open and a bullet hole in his head.

James leaned over and picked up the envelope, then reached out a hand to me. "Come on."

My gaze was still on Wagner, but I lifted it to James. "I can't go. I have to put pressure on Calvin's leg."

"Rose, he's gone."

I dropped my gaze, and Calvin stared up at me with vacant eyes, his chest not moving.

I snatched my hand back, still clutching the towel.

"Come on, Rose. The nearest neighbor's not that far away. They're bound to have heard all the gunshots. We have to get out of here in case they called the sheriff."

That knocked me out of my stupor. "*What?* We can't just leave!"

"We can and we *will*."

"It was self-defense."

"It wasn't. I was protecting you, not myself, and given my history with the sheriff's department, it won't go well. We have to leave."

I shook my head. "If we go, no one will ever know what happened to Patsy. Or June and Calvin for that matter. We can't go."

He held my gaze. "You feel that strongly about it?"

"Yes. I'm not going." I looked up at him. "But you are."

His eyes darkened. "Like hell I'm leavin' you here with this mess. How are you gonna explain who shot Wagner?"

"I'll tell them I did it."

"My fingerprints are all over the gun, Rose!"

"Is it registered in your name?"

He stared at me for a second. "No."

"Then wipe off your prints and I'll hold it."

"That's not enough. You'll have to fire it." He shook his head. "No. I'm staying."

I could see that he would. He would risk his freedom to stay … because of me.

I snatched up his hand. "I'm gonna have a vision."

"Have you had one yet?"

"No, so there's no better time to try." I closed my eyes and concentrated. *What will happen if James stays and admits he killed Wagner?*

My fear nipped at the edge of my hazy eyesight, keeping me from slipping into the vision.

I felt James' arm wrap around my back and pull me close, my body flush with his. He whispered in my ear, "Vision or no vision, I'm here with you, Rose. I won't leave you."

I relaxed into him, resting my cheek on his chest, and the vision burst into life.

I was in James' head, sitting at a table in an interrogation room in the sheriff's office. Mason and Joe were sitting in front of me. Joe was wearing his uniform and had his arms crossed over his chest. His expression was grim. Mason was in a dress shirt and tie. A sly grin spread across his face as he said, "I've got a mountain of charges here. Lucky for you, you've got plenty of time to hear them."

Then the vision changed, and I was sitting in a courtroom. I was standing next to Carter Hale, while Mason stood at the table across the aisle.

Judge McCleary sat at the bench. "How does the jury find the defendant?"

A man in the jury box kept his gaze on a piece of paper in his hand. "In the first charge of second-degree murder, we find the defendant guilty."

There was a gasp in the courtroom.

The jury foreman continued. "In the second charge of second-degree murder, we find the defendant guilty. In the third charge of second-degree murder, we find the defendant guilty."

Then the vision changed again, and I was sitting in front of a tray of food in a large cafeteria filled with men in prison jumpsuits. I felt someone brush against me, and then something sharp stabbed into my back.

"That's from a friend of J.R. Simmons," a man snarled in my ear. "Say hello to him in hell."

My eyes flew open and I stared up at James in horror. "You're gonna get killed in prison."

His face was perfectly blank.

"Aren't you gonna say anything?" I demanded.

"If you stay, I'm stayin'."

"Let me have another one. I want to see what happens if you leave." I didn't have time to give much thought to the fact that the vision had felt different. I'd seen three scenes, whereas before I'd only ever seen one at a time unless I continued to ask questions. "Please. Let me try."

He pulled me tighter. "Okay."

I rested my cheek against him again, his rapid heartbeat in my ear. Closing my eyes, I asked, *What will happen if James leaves me to deal with the sheriff?*

I was at the pool hall, sitting at James' desk in his office. I could feel anxiety rolling off me in waves, and I was tempted to get a drink, but I wanted to be sober if Rose needed me.

The phone rang, and I answered it immediately. "Rose. Where are you?"

"I'm fine," I heard my weary voice say. "They let me go. No charges."

The vision changed, and now I was in Carter Hale's office.

"Why the sudden urge to change your will?" he asked.

"Something … changed. I need to be prepared."

"You already are. We worked it all out years ago. Jed gets most of it, the secret accounts go to Scooter."

"That's why I need it changed. I need to make sure she's taken care of," I growled in frustration.

"Skeeter …"

"Carter, you know what I'm about to do. We both know how it might work out. Why are you fightin' me on this?"

Carter sat back in his seat with a look of resignation. "Okay, I'll make the changes."

The vision shifted again, and I was in James' bedroom, lying next to Vision Rose as he kissed a trail down to her naked stomach. Her left hand rested over her lower abdomen, the stones in her engagement ring glittering in the light. I placed my hand over hers. "It's gonna be okay, Rose," I said in a husky voice.

"You don't know that, James. Let me have a vision."

I shook my head. "No. We both know I have to do this, no matter how it turns out. I'd rather go into it not knowin'."

She nodded, tears in her eyes. "Okay."

I was plunged back into the kitchen, surrounded by three dead bodies, as I said, "I'm not gonna be charged."

He tilted my head back. "What does that mean?"

I was still shaken by the other two visions, but I couldn't think about them right now. "It means if you go and let me deal with it, they'll question me, but they won't charge me." I tried to pull out of his arms and push him way. "You have to go."

"Rose. I can't just leave. We need to come up with a story."

He was right. "Okay."

"We need Jed."

"No. Neely Kate—"

But he'd ignored me and was already pulling up Jed's number.

She was going to kill me. She'd begged me to keep him out of all of this. "James. Stop!"

Taking my hand, he tugged me out the back door as they began to scheme.

Chapter Twenty-Eight

The next morning, I woke up to the song of a bird outside my window, surprised by the bright light streaming in. I leaned over to check the time, alarmed to see it was after eight o'clock. I grabbed a robe to throw on over my pajamas, then headed downstairs.

Neely Kate and Jed were sitting at the table in the kitchen, their heads leaning close together as they talked in low voices. I would have thought they were acting like a new couple in love if Jed didn't reach over to wipe a tear from Neely Kate's cheek.

"I'm sorry," I said. "I'm so sorry I involved Jed last night."

She quickly wiped both cheeks and turned to face me. "What are you talkin' about?"

"James called Jed to help cover everything up. I know you . . ."

A confused look filled Jed's eyes as he looked from her to me. "What am I missin'?"

"Nothing," I said. "I told her I'd stop monopolizing your time."

He gave Neely Kate a surprised look.

"Oh," I said hurriedly. "She never said anything. It's just that I recently realized how much I rely on you, and it's not fair to either one of you."

"Rose," he said as though he were talking to a toddler, "we're friends. Friends help each other."

"Most friends don't ask their friends to help alter crime scenes."

"The only thing I did was suggest you wipe Skeeter's prints off his gun, then have you shoot the wall."

"We altered the story of what happened. You helped with that too."

Within ten minutes, they'd decided on the story I should tell the sheriff's deputies. It went something like this: I suspected June was up to no good, so I listened in on her phone conversation in the office. When I overheard she'd be meeting Calvin, I hid in the back of her minivan, worrying what would happen if she caught me following her. She got out at the cottage, but I stayed to eavesdrop outside. Wagner and his man showed up, but only Wagner came into the kitchen. He and his associate had gotten into an argument, and Wagner had hit him in the head with the butt of his gun in the living room. Everything else remained the same at that point—overhearing his confrontation with June and his attack on Calvin, intervening in the hopes of saving him. The rest was altered. I managed to get ahold of the gun Wagner had gotten off his partner, then used it to shoot him when he tried to kill me. Since I didn't have a cell phone, I had to use the emergency call option on the one I found in June's purse. That's how I'd gotten in touch with Joe.

James had had me open the envelope and find the information about Calvin and Patsy and the list of prostitutes

Wagner had sent to Calvin, ensuring they weren't covered in his prints since we were leaving the papers as evidence. Everything else—including the envelope—went with him. He promised to let me look it over when everything was said and done, but a cursory glance proved Wagner had information on James, Reynolds, Dermot, and quite a few other players in the crime world. We still had to figure out what to do with that, although my first choice was to burn it all.

What I hadn't seen was information on me. Had Charlene been lying about it? Or had she kept it for herself? What I hadn't figured out was who killed Charlene. She'd been murdered shortly after we left her—June had already gotten back to work. But I told Joe we strongly suspected Charlene had killed Carol Ann over Wagner's papers, which was why we'd picked her up from the Big Thief Hollow rec center … and why we'd run from Abbie Lee. We just didn't have proof. I figured I'd let them try to figure out the rest on their own. I felt guilty not telling him about Charlene's confession, but I knew Neely Kate and I would be in big trouble for sitting on it, and the only way we could explain it was by confessing about the file.

Right or wrong, that wasn't happening.

The interrogation had gone on for hours and hours, and my hands were swabbed for gun powder. Close to midnight, Joe had told me I wouldn't be charged and walked me out to the waiting room. Neely Kate was there, and the two exchanged looks.

"Neely Kate," Joe said. "I know this isn't the time or place."

She'd walked toward him and slowly wrapped her arms around his neck.

He held her close for several seconds, then said, "I'm gonna do better. I promise."

She looked up at him with tear-filled eyes and whispered, "I know. I'm sorry I was such a witch."

He shook his head. "You had every right to be upset with me. I'm still learning how to do this brother stuff right. Don't give up on me yet, okay?"

She nodded. "Okay."

He gave her a kiss on her forehead before releasing his hold on her. "Take Rose home, give her a stiff drink, and put her to bed." He paused as he looked at me. "You should make an appointment with Jonah. There's no shame in needing someone to help you work through this."

I didn't understand what he meant at first … and then it hit me. He was talking about me killing Kip Wagner. "Yeah," I said. "That's a good idea." Then I'd gone outside and called James, and the conversation had gone down just like it had in my vision.

Now here I was in my kitchen—a free woman—trying to figure out how to interpret the other two visions.

"I think it's a good thing you're taking the day off," Neely Kate said as she got up from the table and headed for the coffee maker. "You need to take it easy today."

"Actually," I said, "I'm gonna help Bruce Wayne at his job site today. He's got a big job. He could use the help."

"Why don't you stick around here, Rose?" Jed said. "Witt's takin' Marshall back home, so you and Muffy will have the place to yourself."

That sounded like the worst idea ever. I was struggling enough with my guilt over lying to Joe about something so horrific. Stayin' alone would only make it worse.

"Nope," Neely Kate said as she handed me the cup of coffee. "Rose is right. She needs some time in the dirt."

Jed stared at us both like we were crazy but got up and gave Neely Kate a kiss. "Okay," he finally said. "I'm going to make a few phone calls. Still want me to drive you to the office?"

"If you don't mind."

He grinned. "Love to." He headed out the back door, Muffy on his heels.

"How are you really doin'?" she asked.

"Not so great."

She took the coffee, set it on the table, then pulled me into a hug. "I haven't been a good friend lately."

"What are you talkin' about?" I asked, my words muffled by her shoulder. "You've been a great friend."

"No, I'm not. I coerced you into takin' Patsy's case. Then I practically abandoned you to hunt for Becky."

"It was a lead."

She shook her head. "I spent too long on it, and both you and Jed were too nice to tell me to give it up."

"I can't speak for Jed, but I could see you were workin' out some personal demons. Lord knows I have plenty of my own that I struggle with. I love you, Neely Kate. If you need to spend a day lookin' for a lost girl to deal with yours, I'll gladly give it to you." I put my hand on her shoulder and looked her in the eye. "But I wish you'd share your nightmares with me. You know I won't judge you."

She gave me a weak smile. "I'm workin' my way up to it. I'll get there."

"And I'll be here to listen whenever you're ready."

She pushed me toward a kitchen chair. "Drink your coffee before it's cold."

I sat down and took a sip, and she took the seat across from me.

"We need to call Kermit," I said. "He's gonna be ticked he didn't make any money off this one."

She grinned. "I already called him. I'm a little deaf in one ear, but he'll get over it. Even he can hardly blame us that our client was killed."

We sat in silence for a few seconds before Neely Kate leaned over, cradling her coffee cup and looking up at me. "Today's the day you're supposed to give an answer to Skeeter. Have you made up your mind yet?"

I shook my head. But that vision of me in bed with him, wearing an engagement ring … that had kept me up into the small hours of the morning. Had James asked Carter Hale to change his will because of whatever we were discussing in bed? Did it mean I should have done something different last night?

"Rose, do you want my opinion about your answer?"

She shook me out of my musing. "You've already told me your opinion," I said with a sad smile. "Many times."

"I've been thinkin' about it since our last conversation." She paused. "It's obvious you and I see two different men, and Jed swears you make Skeeter a better person. I still think it's a bad idea, but there's no denyin' you have a thing for him, and the heart wants what the heart wants."

"So you're tellin' me I should say yes."

She hesitated. "I'm not going to tell you what to do. Only you can do that, but I know you haven't been happy these past two weeks, Violet aside. You miss him. There's no denyin' that. And we both know he makes you happy." She gave me a soft smile. "But I'm scared for you. Bein' with Skeeter Malcolm is dangerous. So if you say yes, be careful. With your heart and everything else."

"Thanks."

I WENT UPSTAIRS to get ready for the day. After I was dressed and ready to leave, I stopped in Marshall's room before I headed downstairs.

He was sitting up in bed with a somber expression, looking a little older and hopefully wiser than when he'd first shown up in my barn.

"I hear you're goin' home today," I said.

He jumped, looking startled, then settled down. "Yep. Jed said I should be good to go."

"Where will you go?"

"Back home, I guess." He stared down at his lap, makin' it clear he wasn't happy about it.

"I don't think there's any evidence tying you to the robbery, and Kip Wagner's dead. I don't think you'll have to be lookin' over your shoulder."

He nodded. "I heard you were the one to kill him."

I didn't correct him. I was sure he wasn't the last person who would mention it over the next few days.

I moved to the side of his bed. "Marshall, you've been given a gift. You've been given a second chance. Make it a clean slate and stick to the straight and narrow. Find a girl who deserves the risks you'll take for her. Find happiness in the small things, not the moments of excitement. Don't waste all the effort I spent tryin' to keep you safe. Make me proud, and always know you have a place here if you need it. My farm will be your refuge."

He stared up at me, then swallowed. "You saved my life, Lady. Thank you. If you ever need anything from me, ask and I'll give it. Whatever it is."

I gave him a soft smile. "The only thing I ask is that you live a good and full life." I leaned forward and placed a kiss on his forehead. "Goodbye, Marshall."

BRUCE WAYNE'S CREW looked surprised to see me when I showed up an hour later with Muffy in tow. My hair was pulled back into a ponytail, and I was wearing a RBW Landscaping T-shirt, jeans, and work boots, making it obvious I hadn't just shown up for a chat.

As soon as Bruce Wayne saw me, he brought me a shovel and gave me a task, no questions asked. There was no way he didn't know I'd been part of a quadruple murder the night before, and he had to know I'd need to exorcise some demons.

I'd worked with most of the crew before during the spring, so they didn't baby me. They knew I could pull my weight. They left me to myself, as though they recognized I was working things out too. Besides, they didn't need me for entertainment, not when they had Muffy. They spoiled her rotten.

It was a hot day, and I wasn't used to working out in the sun, so Bruce Wayne made me take an extra water break around two, saying he wanted to discuss an install he had in a couple of days.

We sat under a shade tree, and he briefly discussed some minor issues he foresaw before falling silent. We sat like that for nearly a minute before he asked, "Are you still playing your role as the Lady in Black?"

I had a moment of panic that the crew could hear us, but they were too far away, and it didn't really matter. My secret identity was out, more or less.

"If you'd asked me yesterday morning, I would have wholeheartedly said yes."

"And now?"

"Now I'm not so sure. I think Wagner was right. It's naïve to think I can make a difference."

"But you are, Rose."

I turned to look at him. "What?"

"You're makin' a difference. Word's gotten out about that kid."

The blood rushed from my head. "What kid?"

He narrowed his eyes. "The kid that got shot during the Ripper Pawn robbery. They say you took him in and held off Wagner's men to protect him."

I nearly passed out with fear. "How many people know?"

"Don't worry. Joe Simmons won't find out." He paused. "Believe it or not, a lot of guys who follow men like Dermot and Wagner and Skeeter can be loyal to their own, in their own strange way. Now a lot of them will be loyal to you. Their lives are shit, and they need to know they belong somewhere—and when things go south … well, now they think they can come to you for help. You're like their Wendy in *Peter Pan*."

I stared at him wide-eyed. "I think this is too big for me to handle. I almost got myself killed by a guy named Gerard and his mountain men sons, all because I was cocky and thought I could handle myself."

It was his turn to stare at me wide-eyed. "Gerard Collard?"

"I don't know his last name. He lives in the woods with no electricity or running water."

He let out a low whistle. "That's him. He's bad news, Rose. Stay away from him."

"He kind of didn't leave me a choice. His son showed up and invited me at gunpoint. I guess I could have run away or screamed. Brox probably wouldn't have shot me, but I went anyway and got all sassy because I got too big for my britches."

"There's no denyin' you seem to find danger, and I understand if you want to stop, but you've given a lot of guys hope. Just remember that."

I leaned my temple on his shoulder. "Thanks, Bruce Wayne. I needed to hear that."

"That's what partners are for."

WE FINISHED THE JOB around four, and Muffy and I headed home, where I took a long, hot shower and then headed to bed for a nap. It was raining when I woke, and I could see it was getting dark outside. I grabbed my phone to check the time—nearly eight o'clock. Neely Kate had sent a text that she was spending the night with Jed, but she promised to come straight home if I didn't want to be alone.

I texted her back, assuring her I was fine, before I remembered that I still needed to give James an answer. What was I going to tell him?

Should I follow my head or my heart? I decided to follow my instincts. They hadn't failed me yet. I sent James a text.

I HAVE MY ANSWER. CAN I MEET YOU AT YOUR HOUSE? I WANT TO TELL YOU IN PERSON.

He answered about ten seconds later.

9:00?

SEE YOU THEN.

A STORM WAS BREWING to the west when I left home. Muffy hated thunderstorms, so I took her with me, holding her close when I carried her out to my truck. She cuddled on my lap during the drive, hiding her head when the rain began to come down in sheets.

Between the rain and the dark, I nearly missed the turn onto James' gravel driveway a few minutes after nine. I parked in his circular driveway in front of the front door and worried that I'd beat him there. The only lights in the house were the soft glow emanating from the shuttered living room windows.

I rubbed Muffy's head. "Just wait here, girl. This should only take a few minutes."

She gave a soft whine when I set her down on the seat.

James didn't have a roof over his front door, so I dug under the seat and grabbed an umbrella. Cinching my thin raincoat around my body, I left the car, popped the umbrella, and ran up to the porch.

The front door opened before I knocked, and James started to back up so I could come in. His face was an emotionless mask.

"Wait," I said, clutching the umbrella tighter as a gust of wind tried to lift it up. "I have a few things I need to say."

He moved back into the doorway and waited. He looked so tempting in his jeans and the pale gray V-neck T-shirt that showed off the curve of his pecs and his thickly muscled arms. His hair was damp like he'd just taken a shower—or a walk in the rain.

Focus, Rose. I almost chucked my speech, but if I didn't say it now, it might never be said.

"First," I said. "Your world scares me. I know I've jumped in feetfirst to be part of it, but yesterday …" I took a breath. "While I've always known you're involved with criminal activities, I saw some things that really brought it close to home. I struggle to reconcile the man I see standing in front of me with the cold, ruthless man other people see."

"I know," he said softly.

"Second, if we were to do this, we would have to treat it like a dirty little secret. No showing you to my friends and family. No date nights at Jaspers. No walking down the sidewalk hand in hand. We'll have to sneak around like we're havin' an affair. Like I'm ashamed of you. I hate that."

He leaned into the doorframe, his bare feet and the bottom of his jeans getting wet from the rain bouncing off the porch onto him.

"My sister's dyin', James. She's got months to live, but I suspect it's gonna happen sooner than that. She's made some super-secret changes to her will, and I'm pretty sure it has something to do with me bein' able to see her kids after she dies, since my brother-in-law is convinced I'll be a danger to them. And after the last few days—shoot, the last few months—who's to say I'm not? And when she dies, if you and I were together, I'd need you." My voice broke. "I'd need you by my side at her grave, and holding my hand during the visitation, and holding me in bed while I cried myself to sleep. But you couldn't do any of that. If we were together, you couldn't be with me when I need you the most."

"I know, Rose." His voice sounded strangled. "It kills me to know that I can't."

"Mason's back, and he's gonna move heaven and earth to bring you down, and I suspect he's gonna try to use me to do it. Which means I'm dangerous. If we were smart, we'd end this right now."

He didn't respond.

"And last, I want a family. I want kids. I want to be married. I don't want them now, but I know that I will, and you want none of those things. So I go into this knowing it's a short-term commitment until either one of us decides we're bored playing house or the other needs *more*. I've never done a short-term commitment. I'm not sure I can."

He looked heartbroken. "I know."

"And when I look at all those things, there's one thing I *do* know."

He looked down at my feet. "Rose, you don't have to say it."

"I want you."

His gaze lifted in disbelief.

"I want you, James Malcolm, not Skeeter. Not the man the rest of the world sees, the mask you put on for the world. I want the man standing in front of me, the man who knows my faults and sees them as strengths. No other man … shoot, no other person has believed in me even half as much as you do. You see the woman I was meant to be, and you helped set her free."

I stepped toward him and put my hand on his chest, and he covered it with his own. "I want you, James Malcolm. I want as much of you as I can get, and while there will likely come a day when you can no longer give me what I need, until then, I'm yours."

He engulfed me in his arms, his mouth covering mine. I sank into him, the umbrella falling behind me so we were both getting drenched.

He hauled me inside, but I stopped him from shutting the door. "Wait."

"You just told me that you're mine," he growled into my ear. "Don't torture me, Rose."

"Muffy's in the truck. I had to bring her. She's scared of thunderstorms. Neely Kate's not home and—"

He bounded down the steps and opened the passenger door. Seconds later, he had Muffy snugged to his chest with one arm and the small overnight bag I'd left on the passenger seat. He ran up the steps and got inside just as lightning flashed across the sky and thunder boomed after.

Muffy whined louder and buried herself into his chest.

"You brought a bag," he said as he dropped it to the floor.

"I can't keep wearing your clothes home," I teased.

He started to say something when thunder boomed again and Muffy snuggled closer.

I quickly shut the door, staring in amazement as he stroked her head. "It's okay, girl," he said softly. "You're safe here." His gaze lifted to mine. "You both are."

His words and comfort settled her down, and she squirmed, letting him know she wanted down. He set her on the floor and let her wander around as he took a step toward me.

"Maybe I don't want something safe right now," I said in a husky tone. "Maybe I want something dangerous tonight."

A low sound rumbled from his chest. "What about your dog?"

"Unless there's a wild storm, as long as she knows I'm here, she'll be all right." I reached up with one hand and pulled his mouth back to mine while the other snaked around his back and pulled him flush to me.

That was all the encouragement he needed.

He kissed me so thoroughly I felt myself get lost in him. His mouth was on mine again and his hands were everywhere—in my hair, on my hip, sliding up my side to my breast over the raincoat.

I soaked him in, needing this and so much more. I blindly reached for the hem of his shirt and lifted. He broke contact, groaning, for long enough to pull his shirt over his head and then reach for the belt of my rain jacket. When he opened it, his eyes grew wide as he took in my white and black lace panties and bra.

"You drove here in this storm with nothin' over this other than your raincoat?" he asked, his gaze still sweeping over my body.

He slowly pushed the coat over my shoulders until it fell to the floor, and I shivered, not from cold but from anticipation.

"When we've been together before, I never had on sexy underwear …" I grimaced.

His hands lightly skimmed down my waist to my hips, his gaze following. "You're the sexiest goddamned thing I've ever seen. Don't you dare apologize." His eyes lifted to mine. "Don't you get it, Rose? *You're* what makes you sexy. Not what you're wearin'."

His mouth plundered mine as he quickly dispensed with my bra and panties, making them a nonissue. As soon as my panties were gone, his hand slid between my folds.

"You're so wet already," he groaned into my ear, sounding like he was in pain. I felt how hard he was against me. Maybe he *was* in pain.

"I want you, James," I moaned, lifting a leg up and around his waist. "*Now*."

That was all the invitation he needed. He stripped off his jeans in seconds, then lifted me as he plunged in deep, pressing my back against the solid back door. Grabbing my hips, he held me steady as he drove in even deeper.

I clung to his shoulders as I stared up at him, overwhelmed by how much I needed this man. An entanglement with the king of the Fenton County underworld would surely lead me down the path of ruin, but at the moment, I couldn't bring myself to care.

His eyes were dark and possessive as he claimed me. "Tell me you're mine."

"I'm yours," I said in a husky voice I barely recognized. "And you're mine."

His mouth covered mine again, and I lost all sense of time and place as he filled me, taking me higher and higher until I was pleading with him to finish what he'd started.

When I came, I clung to him as wave after wave of pleasure washed over me, vaguely aware of him groaning my name as he gave one last push.

I was still pinned against the door, my legs wrapped around his waist as he leaned into me, his chest heaving as he recovered.

"Is this what it will be like with us?" I asked in wonder.

He lifted his head, a grin spreading across his face. "This is only the beginning, Lady."

I grinned back, truly happy for the first time in months.

Up Shute Creek (Rose Gardner Investigations #4)
November 6, 2018

In High Cotton (Neely Kate Mystery #2)
July 31, 2018

2/23

Made in the USA
Lexington, KY
02 May 2018